'An audacious, profound, and wonderfully intelligent book'
Hermione Lee, author of *Virginia Woolf*

'Enthralling . . . Tóibín displays – in a manner that is masterly –
the wit and metaphorical flair, psychological subtlety and phrases
of pouncing incisiveness with which a great novelist captured the
nuances of consciousness and the duplicities of society'
The Sunday Times

'A marvel of lightly worn research and modulated tone'
John Updike, *The New Yorker*

'*The Master* is a portrait of Henry James that has the depth and
finish of great sculpture . . . a triumph'
Observer

'It is hard to imagine an admirer of Henry James not being
gripped by this novel – a work of literary devotion by a writer
who is himself a master of plush prose and psychological nuance'
The Sunday Telegraph

'In *The Master*, Colm Tóibín takes us almost shockingly close to
the soul of Henry James and, by extension, to the mystery of art
itself. It is a remarkable, utterly original book'
Michael Cunningham, author of *The Hours*

'Ultimately, it is the essence of Henry James . . . which Tóibín
resurrects in this brilliant novel'
The Times

'A must read. Colm Tóibín has not only written a spectacular
novel, he has found a way to pay tribute to Henry James. We
should all be so gifted and so lucky'
Alice Sebold, author of *The Lovely Bones*

'One of the most remarkable novels
Sunday Herald

T0346846

THE MASTER

Colm Tóibín was born in Ireland in 1955. He is the author of eleven novels, including *The Blackwater Lightship, Brooklyn,* and *The Magician,* and two collections of stories. He has been three times shortlisted for the Booker Prize. In 2021, he was awarded the David Cohen Prize for Literature. Tóibín was appointed the Laureate for Irish Fiction 2022–2024.

Also by Colm Tóibín

COLM TÓIBÍN

The Master

First published 2004 by Picador

First published in paperback 2005 by Picador

This edition published 2024 by Picador
an imprint of Pan Macmillan
The Smithson, 6 Briset Street, London EC1M 5NR
EU representative: Macmillan Publishers Ireland Ltd, 1st Floor,
The Liffey Trust Centre, 117–126 Sheriff Street Upper,
Dublin 1, D01 YC43
Associated companies throughout the world
www.panmacmillan.com

ISBN 978-1-0350-2986-0

A CIP catalogue record for this book is available from the British Library.

Printed and bound by CPI Group (UK) Ltd, Croydon, CR0 4YY

Visit **www.picador.com** to read more about all our books
and to buy them. You will also find features, author interviews and
news of any author events, and you can sign up for e-newsletters
so that you're always first to hear about our new releases.

FOR BAIRBRE AND MICHAEL STACK

CHAPTER ONE

January 1895

SOMETIMES IN THE NIGHT he dreamed about the dead – familiar faces and the others, half-forgotten ones, fleetingly summoned up. Now as he woke, it was, he imagined, an hour or more before the dawn; there would be no sound or movement for several hours. He touched the muscles on his neck which had become stiff; to his fingers they seemed unyielding and solid but not painful. As he moved his head, he could hear the muscles creaking. I am like an old door, he said to himself.

It was imperative, he knew, that he go back to sleep. He could not lie awake during these hours. He wanted to sleep, enter a lovely blackness, a dark, but not too dark, resting place, unhaunted, unpeopled, with no flickering presences.

When he woke again, he was agitated and unsure where he was. He often woke like this, disturbed, only half remembering the dream and desperate for the day to begin. Sometimes when he dozed, he would bask in the hazy, soft light of Bellosguardo in the early spring, the distances all misty, feeling the sheer pleasure of sunlight on his face, sitting in a chair, close to the wall of the old house with the smell of wisteria and early roses and jasmine. He would hope when he woke that the day would be like the dream, that traces of the ease and the colour and the light would linger at the edge of things until night fell again.

But this dream was different. It was dark or darkening some-where, it was a city, an old place in Italy like Orvieto or Siena, but nowhere exact, a dream city with narrow streets, and he was hurrying; he was uncertain now whether he was alone or with somebody, but he was hurrying and there were students walking slowly up the hill too, past lighted shops and cafes and restaurants, and he was eager to get by them, finding ways to pass them. No matter how hard he tried to remember, he was still not sure if he had a companion; perhaps he did, or perhaps it was merely someone who walked behind him. He could not recall much about this shadowy, intermittent presence, but for some of the time there seemed to be a person or a voice close to him who under-stood better than he did the urgency, the need to hurry, and who insisted under his breath in mutterings and mumbles, cajoled him to walk faster, edge the students out of his path.

Why did he dream this? At each long and dimly lit entrance to a square, he recalled, he was tempted to leave the bustling street, but he was urged to carry on. Was his ghostly companion telling him to carry on? Finally, he walked slowly into a vast Italian space, with towers and castellated roofs, and a sky the colour of dark blue ink, smooth and consistent. He stood there and watched as though it were framed, taking in the symmetry and texture. This time – and he shivered when he recalled the scene – there were figures in the centre with their backs to him, figures forming a circle, but he could see none of their faces. He was ready to walk towards them when the figures with their backs to him turned. One of them was his mother at the end of her life, his mother when he had last seen her. Near her among the other women stood his Aunt Kate. Both of them had been dead for years; they were smiling at him and moving slowly towards him. Their faces were lit like faces in a painting. The word that came to him, he was sure that he had dreamt the word as much as the scene, was the word 'beseeching'. They were imploring him or somebody, asking, yearning, and then putting their hands out in front of them in supplication, and as they moved towards him he woke in cold fright, and he wished that they could have spoken, or that he could have offered the two people whom he had loved most in his life some consolation. What came over him in the aftertaste of the dream was a wearying, gnawing sadness and, since he knew that he must not go back to sleep, an overwhelming urge to start writing, anything to numb himself, distract himself, from the vision of these two women who were lost to him.

He covered his face for a moment when he remembered one second in the dream which had caused him to wake abruptly. He would have given anything now to forget it, to prevent it from following him into the day: in that square he had locked eyes with his mother, and her gaze was full of panic, her mouth ready to cry out. She fiercely wanted something beyond her reach, which she could not obtain, and he could not help her.

IN THE DAYS coming up to the new year he had refused all invitations. He wrote to Lady Wolseley that he sat all day at rehearsals in the company of several fat women who made the costumes. He was uneasy and anxious, often agitated, but sometimes, too, he was involved in the action on the stage as though it were all new to him, and he was moved by it. He asked Lady Wolseley and her husband to unite in prayers for him on the opening night of his play, not far away now.

In the evening he could do nothing, and his sleep was fitful. He saw nobody except his servants, and they knew not to speak to him or trouble him beyond what was entirely necessary.

His play *Guy Domville*, the story of a rich Catholic heir who must choose whether to carry on the family line or join a monastery, would open on 5 January. All the invitations to the opening night had gone out and he had already received many replies of acceptance and thanks. Alexander, the producer and lead actor, had a following among theatre-goers, and the costumes – the play was set in the eighteenth century – were sumptuous. Yet, despite his new enjoyment of the society of actors and the glitter and the daily small changes and improvements in the production, he was, he said, not made for the theatre. He sighed as he sat at his desk. He wished it were an ordinary day and he could read over yesterday's sentences, spend a slow morning making corrections, and then start out once more, filling the afternoon with ordinary work. And yet he knew that his mood could change as quickly as the light in the room could darken, and he easily could feel only happiness at his life in the theatre and begin again to hate the company of his blank pages. Middle age, he thought, had made him fickle.

His visitor had arrived promptly at eleven o'clock. He could not have refused to see her; her letter had been carefully insistent. Soon she would be leaving Paris for good, she said, and this would be her last visit to London. There was something oddly final and resigned in her tone, a tone so alien to her general spirit that he was quickly alerted to the seriousness of her situation. He had not seen her for many years, but over these years he had received some letters from her and news from others about her. That morning, however, still haunted by his dream, and so full of concern about his play, he saw her as merely a name in his diary, stirring an old memory sharp in its outlines and faded in its detail.

When she came into the room, her old face smiling warmly, her large-boned frame moving slowly and deliberately, her greeting so cheerful, open and affectionate, and her voice so beautiful and soft, almost whispering, it was easy to put aside his worries about his play and the time he was wasting by not being in the theatre. He had forgotten how much he liked her and how easy it was to be taken instantly back to those days when he was in his twenties and lingered as much as he could in the company of French and Russian writers in Paris.

Somehow, in the years that followed, the shadowy presences interested him as much as the famous ones, the figures who had not become known, who had failed, or who had never planned to flourish. His visitor had been married to the Prince Oblisky. The prince had a reputation for being stern and distant; the fate of Russia and his purposeful exile concerned him more than the evening's amusement and the glamorous company who stood around. The princess was Russian too, but she had lived most of her life in France. Around her and her husband there were always hints and rumours and suggestions. It was part of the time and the place, he thought. Everyone he knew carried with them the aura of another life which was half secret and half open, to be known about but not mentioned. In those years, you searched each face for what it might unwittingly disclose and you listened carefully for nuances and clues. New York and Boston had not been like that, and in London, when he finally came to live there, people allowed themselves to believe that you had no hidden and secret self unless you emphatically declared to the contrary.

He remembered the shock when he first came to know Paris, the culture of easy duplicity, the sense he got of these men and women, watched over by the novelists, casually withholding what mattered to them most.

He had never loved the intrigue. Yet he liked knowing secrets, because not to know was to miss almost everything. He himself learned never to disclose anything, and never even to acknowledge the moment when some new information was imparted, to act as though a mere pleasantry had been exchanged. The men and women in the salons of literary Paris moved like players in a game of knowing and not knowing, pretence and disguise. He had learned everything from them.

He found the princess a seat, brought her extra cushions, and then offered her a different chair, or indeed a chaise longue which might be more comfortable.

'At my age,' she smiled at him, 'nothing is comfortable.'

He stopped moving about the room and turned to look at her. He had learned that when he quietly fixed his calm grey eyes on somebody they too became calm; they realized, or so he thought, that what they said next should be serious in some way, that the time for the casual play of half-talk had come to an end.

'I have to go back to Russia,' she said in slow, carefully pronounced French. 'That is what I have to do. When I say go back, I talk as though I have been there before, and yes I have, but not in any way that means anything to me. I have no desire to see Russia again, but he insists that I stay there, that I leave France for good.'

As she spoke she smiled, as she had always done, but now there was anguish and a sort of puzzlement in her face. She had brought the past into the room with her, and for him now, in these years after the death of his parents and his sister, any reminder of a time that was over brought with it a terrible and heavy melancholy. Time would not relent, and when he was young, he had never imagined the pain that loss would bring, pain that only work and sleep could keep at bay now.

Her soft voice and her easy manners made it clear that she had not changed. Her husband was known to treat her badly. He had problems with estates. She began to talk now about some remote estate to which she was going to be banished.

The January light was liquid and silky in the room. He sat and listened. He knew that the Prince Oblisky had left the son by his first marriage in Russia, and had gruffly spent his life in Paris. There was always a whiff of political intrigue about him, a sense that he counted somehow in the future of Russia, and that he was waiting for his moment.

' My husband has said it is time for us all to go back to Russia, the homeland.' He has become a reformer. He says that Russia will collapse if it does not reform. I told him that Russia collapsed a long time ago, but I did not remind him that he had very little interest in reform when he was not in debt. His first wife's family have brought up the child and they want nothing to do with him.'

'Where will you live?' he asked her.

'I will live in a crumbling mansion, and half-crazed peasants will have their noses up against the glass of my windows, if there is glass still in the windows. That is where I will live.'

'And Paris?'

'I have to give up everything, the house, the servants, my friends, my whole life. I will freeze to death or I will die of boredom. It will be a race between the two.'

'But why?' he asked gently.

'He says I have wasted all his money. I have sold the house and I have spent days burning letters and crying and throwing away clothes. And now I am saying goodbye to everyone. I am leaving London tomorrow and I am going to spend one month in Venice. Then I will travel to Russia. He says that others are returning too, but they are going to St Petersburg. That is not what he has chosen for me.'

She spoke with feeling, but as he watched her he sensed that he was listening to one of his actors enjoying her own performance. Sometimes she spoke as though she were telling an amusing anecdote about somebody else.

'I've seen everyone I know who's still alive and I've read over all the letters of those who are dead. With some people I've done both. I burned Paul Joukowsky's letters and then I saw him. I did not expect to see him. He is ageing badly. I did not expect that either.'

She caught his eye for one second and it was as though a flash of clear summer light had come into the room. Paul Joukowsky was almost fifty now, he calculated; they had not met for many years. No one had ever come like this and mentioned his name.

Henry was careful to try to speak immediately, ask a question, change the subject. Perhaps there was something in the letters, a stray sentence, or the account of a conversation or a meeting. But he did not think so. Perhaps his visitor was letting him know for nostalgia's sake what his aura had suggested in those years, his own designed self. His attempt to be earnest, hesitant and polite had not fooled women like her who watched his full mouth and the glance of his eyes and instantly understood it all. They said, of course, nothing, just as she was saying nothing now, merely a name, an old name that rang in his ears. A name that, once, had meant everything to him.

'But surely you will return?'

'That is the promise he has extracted from me. That I will not return, that I will stay in Russia.'

The tone was dramatic, and he suddenly saw her on the stage, moving casually, talking as though she put no thought into it, and then throwing an arrow, a single line intended to hit home. From what she had said, he understood for the first time what had happened. She must have done something very wrong to place herself back in his power. In her circle, there would be knowledge and speculation. Some would know, and those who did not know would be able to guess. Just as she let him guess now.

These thoughts preoccupied him, and he found that he watched the princess, carefully weighing up what she had been saying, while thinking how he could use this. He must write it down as soon as she left. He hoped to hear nothing more, none of the explicit details, but as she continued speaking, it was clear that she was frightened and his sympathy was once more aroused.

'You know, others have gone back and the reports are excellent. There is new life in St Petersburg, but as I told you, that is not where I am going. And Daudet, whom I met at a party, said the most foolish thing to me. Perhaps he thought that it might console me. He told me that I would have my memories. But my memories are of no use to me. I told him that I never had any interest in memories. I love today and tomorrow, and if I am in form I also love the day after tomorrow. Last year is gone, who cares about last year?'

'Daudet does, I imagine.'

'Yes, too much.'

She stood up to go and he accompanied her to the front door. When he saw that she had left a cab waiting, he wondered who was paying for it.

'And Paul? Should I have given you some of the letters? Would you have wanted them?'

Henry put out his hand as though she had not asked the question. He moved his lips, about to say something, and then stopped. He held her hand for a moment. She was almost in tears as she walked towards the cab.

HE HAD BEEN living in these rooms in De Vere Gardens for almost ten years but the name Paul had never once been uttered within the walls. His presence had been buried beneath the daily business of writing and remembering and imagining. Even in dreams, it was years since Paul had appeared.

The bare bones of the princess's story would not need to be set down now. They would stay in his mind. He did not know how he would work it, whether it would be her last days in Paris – burning letters, giving things away, leaving things behind – or her last salon, or her interview with her husband, the moment when she first learned her fate.

He would remember her visit, but there was something else that he wanted to write down now. It was something he had written before and had been careful to destroy. It seemed strange, almost sad, to him that he had produced and published so much, rendered so much that was private, and yet the thing that he most needed to write would never be seen or published, would never be known or understood by anyone.

He took the pen and began. He could have written an indecipherable script, or used a shorthand that only he himself would understand. But he wrote clearly, whispering the words. He did not know why this had to be written, why the stirring of the memory was not enough. But the princess's visit and her talk about banishment and memory, of things that were over and would not come back, and – he stopped writing now and sighed – her saying the name, saying it as though it were still vividly present somewhere within reach, all these things guided his tone as he wrote.

He set down on paper what had happened when he returned to Paris, having received a note from Paul, that summer almost twenty years before. He had stood in the beautiful city on a small street in the dusk, gazing upwards, waiting, watching, for the lighting of a lamp in the window on the third story. As the lamp blazed up he had strained to see Paul Joukowsky's face at the window, his dark hair, the quickness of his eyes, the scowl that could so easily turn into a smile, the thin nose, the broad chin, the pale lips. As night fell, he knew that he himself on the unlit street could not be seen, and he knew also that he could not move, either to return to his own quarters or – he held his breath even at the thought – to attempt to gain access to Paul's rooms.

Paul's note was unambiguous; it had made clear that he would be alone. No one came or went, and Paul's face did not appear at the window. He wondered now if these hours were not the truest he had ever lived. The most accurate comparison he could find was with a smooth, hopeful, hushed sea journey, an interlude suspended between two countries, standing there as though float-ing, knowing that one step would be a step into the impossible, the vast unknown. He waited to catch a moment's further sight of what was there, the unapproachable face. And for hours he stood still, wet with rain, brushed at intervals by those passing by, and never from behind the lamp for one moment more was the face visible.

He wrote down the story of that night and thought then of the rest of the story which could never be written, no matter how secret the paper or how quickly it would be burned or destroyed. The rest of the story was imaginary, and it was something he would never allow himself to put into words. In it, he had crossed the road halfway through his vigil. He had alerted Paul to his presence and Paul had come down and they had walked up the stairs together in silence. And it was very clear now – Paul had made it clear – what would happen.

He found that his hands were shaking. He had never allowed himself to imagine beyond that point. It was the closest he had come, but he had not come close at all. He kept his vigil that night in the rain until the light in the window faded. He waited for a while longer to see if something else would happen, but the windows remained dark, they gave nothing away. Then he walked slowly home. He was on dry land again. His clothes were soaking, his shoes had been destroyed by the rain.

HE LOVED THE dress rehearsals and allowed himself to picture the potential play-goers in each seat in the theatre. The lighting, the extravagant and opulent costumes, the ringing voices filled him with pride and pleasure. He had never, in all the years, seen anyone purchase or read one of his books. And even if he had witnessed such a scene, he would not have known the effects of his sentences. Reading was as silent and solitary and private as writing. Now, he would hear people in the audience hold their breath, cry out, fall silent.

He placed friends, familiar faces, and then, in all the seats near him and in the gallery above, and this was the most risky and exciting prospect, he placed strangers. He imagined bright, intelligent eyes in a man's sensitive face, a thin upper lip, soft, fair skin, a large frame that was carried with ease. Tentatively, he placed this figure in the row behind him, close to the centre, a young woman beside him, her small, delicate hands joined, the tips of her fingers almost touching her mouth. Alone in the theatre – the costume-makers were still backstage – he watched his imaginary, paying theatre-goers as Alexander, playing Guy Domville, appeared. It became clear what the core of the conflict on the stage would be. He kept an eye on the audience he had conjured behind him as the play proceeded, noting how the woman's face lit up at the gorgeousness of Mrs Edward Saker's costume, the elaborate elegance of a hundred years ago, noting then how serious and still the face of his thin-lipped supporter became when Guy Domville, despite his vast wealth and golden future, decided to renounce the world and devote himself to a life of contemplation and prayer in a monastery.

Guy Domville was still too long and he knew that there was disquiet among the actors about the discrepancies between act one and act two. Alexander, his steadfast director, told him to pay no attention to them, they had merely been stirred up by Miss Vetch, who had no role to speak of in act two and barely reappeared in act three. Nonetheless, he knew that in a novel it could not be risked: a character, once established, must remain in the narrative, unless the character were minor, or died before the story closed. What he would never have tried in a novel, he was trying in a play. He prayed that it would work.

He hated making the cuts, but he knew that he could not complain. At the beginning he had grumbled a great deal – indeed expressed a pained amazement – until he had made himself less than welcome in Alexander's offices. He knew that there was no point in claiming that if the play had needed cuts he would have made them before he finished it. Every day now he made excisions, and he thought it strange that after a few hours he remained the only one who noticed the gaps, the missing moments.

During the rehearsals he had little to do. He was both thrilled and disturbed by the idea that only half the work was his, the other half belonged to the director, the actors and the scene-makers. Overseeing the work was the element of time and that was new to him. Over the proscenium arch there was an immense, invisible clock to whose ticking the playwright must attend, its hands moving inexorably on from eight thirty, as precise as the audience's patience. In that busy period of two hours, if the two intervals were taken into account, he must present and solve the problem he had set himself, or be doomed.

As the play came to seem more distant from him, and more real, as he watched the first rehearsals on stage, then the first dress rehearsals, he became sure that he had found his metier, that he had not begun too late to write for the theatre. He was ready now to change his life. He foresaw an end to long, solitary days; the grim satisfaction that fiction gave him would be replaced by a life in which he wrote for voices and movement and an immediacy that through all his life up to now he had believed he would never experience. This new world was now within his grasp. But suddenly, especially in the morning, he would become certain that the opposite was the case, that he would fail, and he would have to return, willingly and unwillingly, to his true medium: the printed page. He had never known such days of strange shifts and excitements.

He felt only affection for the actors. There were times when he would have done anything he could for them. He arranged for hampers of food to be delivered backstage during the long days of rehearsal: cold chicken and beef, fresh salads, potatoes in mayonnaise, fresh bread and butter. He loved watching the actors eat, relishing those moments when they returned from their appointed roles to civilian life. He looked forward to years ahead when he would write new parts and observe them create the parts and play them every night until the run was over and they would fade back into the pale world outside.

He also felt that as a novelist he had fallen upon evil times, any indication of his being hugely wanted by any editor or publisher was declining. A new generation, writers he did not know and did not prize, had taken universal possession. The sense of being almost finished weighed him down; he had been producing little, and publication in periodicals, once so lucrative and useful, was becoming closed to him.

He wondered if the theatre could be not only a source of pleasure and amusement, but a lifeline, a way of beginning again now that the fruitful writing of fiction seemed to be fading. *Guy Domville*, his drama about the conflict between the material life and the life of pure contemplation, the vicissitudes of human love and a life dedicated to a higher happiness, was written to succeed, to match the public mood, and he awaited the opening night with a mixture of pure optimism – an absolute certainty that the play would hit home – and a deep anxiety, a sense that worldly glamour and universal praise would never be offered to him.

Everything depended on the opening night. He had imagined every detail, except what he himself would do. If he stood backstage, he would be in the way; in the auditorium he would be too agitated, too ready to allow every groan or sigh or fall of silence to disturb him or elate him unduly. He thought that he could hide himself in the Cap and Bells, the public house closest to the theatre, and Edmund Gosse, whom he trusted, could slip out at the end of the second act and let him know how it was going. But two days before the opening he decided the plan was absurd.

He would have to do something. There was no one he could have supper with because he had invited everyone he knew to the opening, and most of them had accepted. He could travel to a nearby city, he thought, view the sights and then return on an evening train in time for the applause. But nothing, he knew, could take his mind off his prospects. He wished that he was halfway through a book, with no need to finish until the spring when serialization would begin. He wished he could work quietly in his study with the haunting grey morning light of the London winter filtered through the windows. He wished for solitude and for the comfort of knowing that his life depended not on the multitude but on remaining himself.

He determined, after much indecision and discussion with Gosse and Alexander, that he would go to the Haymarket to see the new play by Oscar Wilde. It was the only way, he felt, in which he would be coerced into quietness between eight thirty and ten forty-five. He could then make his way to St James's Theatre. Gosse and Alexander agreed with him that it was the best plan, the only plan. His mind would be elsewhere at least some of the time, and he could arrive at St James's Theatre at the enraptured moment when his play had ended or was close to ending.

This, he thought, as he prepared himself for the evening, is how the real world conducts itself, the world he had withdrawn from, the world he guessed at. This is how money is made, how reputations are established. It is done with risk and excitement, the stomach hollow, the heart beating too fast, the imagination fired with possibilities. How many days in his life would be like this? If this, the first play of his which he believed could make his fortune, should end triumphantly, the opening nights of the future should be softer and less inflamed. And yet he did not stop wishing, even as he waited for the cab, that he had embarked just now on a new story, that the blank pages were ripe and waiting for him, that the evening was empty and he had nothing to do but write. The will to withdraw was strong in him as he set out for the Haymarket. He would have given anything now to be three and a half hours into the future, to know the result, to bathe in the praise and the adulation, or to know the worst.

As the cab made its way to the theatre he felt a sudden, strange, new, fierce desolation. It was too much, he thought, he was asking too much. He forced himself to think about the scenery, the golden lighting, the costumes, and the drama itself, and those who had accepted the invitations, and he felt only hope and excitement. He had chosen this and now he had it, he must not complain. He had shown Gosse the list of those who would fill the stalls and dress circle and Gosse had said that such a galaxy of aristocratic, literary and scientific celebrity would gather in St James's Theatre as had never before been seen in a London playhouse.

Above them would be – he hesitated and smiled, knowing that if he were writing now he would stop and see if he could find the right tone – above them would be – how should he say it? – the people who had paid money, the real audience whose support and applause would mean more than the support and applause of his friends. They were, he almost said it aloud, the people who do not read my books, that is how we will know them. The world, he smiled as the next phrase went through his mind, is full of them. They are never at a loss for kindred company. Tonight, he hoped, these people would be on his side.

Instantly, as soon as he set foot on the pavement outside the Haymarket, he became jealous of Oscar Wilde. There was a levity about those who were entering the theatre, they looked like people ready to enjoy themselves thoroughly. He had never in his life, he felt, looked like that himself, and he did not know how he was going to manage these hours among people who seemed so jolly, so giddy, so jaunty, so generally cheerful. No one he saw, not one single face, no couple nor group, looked to him like people who would enjoy *Guy Domville*. These people were out for a happy conclusion. He winced now at the arguments with Alexander over the less than happy ending of *Guy Domville*.

He wished he had demanded a seat at the end of a row. In his allotted place he was enclosed, and, as the curtain rose, and the audience began to laugh at lines which he thought crude and clumsy, he felt under siege. He did not laugh once; he thought not a moment was funny, but more importantly, he thought not a moment was true. Every line, every scene was acted out as though silliness were a higher manifestation of truth. No opportunity was missed in portraying witlessness as wit; the obvious and shallow and glib provoked the audience into hearty and hilarious laughter.

If *An Ideal Husband* were feeble and vulgar, then he was clearly the only one who thought so, and when the first interval came, his longing to leave was profound. But the truth was that he had nowhere to go. His sole consolation was that this was not an opening night, there was no fashionable crowd, no one whom he recognized and no one who recognized him. Most consoling of all, there was no sign of Wilde himself, loud and large and Irish as he was, or of his entourage.

He wondered what he could have done with such a story. The writing, line by line, was a mockery of writing, an appeal for cheap laughs, cheap responses. The sense of a corrupt ruling class was shallow; the movement of the plot was wooden; the play was badly made. Once it was over, he thought, no one would remember it, and he would remember it only for the agony he felt, the pure, sheer tension about his own play going on just a short walk away. His drama was about renunciation, he thought, and these people had renounced nothing. At the end, as they called the actors back for further bows, he saw from their flushed and happy faces that they did not appear to have any immediate plans to amend their ways.

As he walked across St James's Square to learn his own fate, the complete success of what he had seen seemed to him to constitute a dreadful premonition of the shipwreck of *Guy Domville*, and he stopped in the middle of the square, paralysed by the terror of this probability, afraid to go and learn more.

Later, over years, he would hear hints and snatches of what had occurred. He never discovered everything, but he knew this much: that the clash between the invited audience and those above them who had paid was as unbridgeable as the gap between himself and the audience at the Oscar Wilde play. The paying public, it seemed, had begun to shift and shuffle, cough and whisper, even before the first act was over. In the second act they laughed when Mrs Edward Saker appeared in her large and expansive period costume. And once they began to laugh, they began to enjoy being offensive. It was not long before the laughter turned to jeers.

He learned later, much later also, what happened when Alexander uttered his last lines: 'I'm the last, my lord, of the Domvilles.' Someone from the gallery had shouted, 'It's a damned good thing you are!' They hooted and roared and when the curtain came down they catcalled and yelled abuse as those in the stalls and dress circle applauded enthusiastically.

That night he entered the theatre by the stage door, meeting on arrival the stage manager, who assured him that all had gone well, his play was a success. Something about the way it was said made Henry want to enquire further, find out the scale and quality of the success, but just then the first applause came, and he listened, mistaking the catcalls for roars of approval. He glimpsed Alexander, noted how stiff and serious he was as he came off the stage and waited for a moment before returning to take his bow. He moved closer to the side of the stage, certain that Alexander and the other actors were triumphant. The whistles and roars, he still believed, indicated special approval of one or two of the performers, Alexander surely among them.

He stood and listened, close enough to the wings for Alexander to see him as he walked off from taking his bow. Later, he was told that there were wild shouts of 'Author! Author!' from his friends in the audience, but they were not wild enough for him to hear. Alexander heard them, however, or so he later said, because on catching the author's eye he approached him, his face solemn, his expression fixed, and led him slowly and firmly by the hand onto the stage.

This was the crowd he had imagined over those long days of rehearsal. He had imagined them attentive and ready to be moved, he had imagined them still and sombre. He had not prepared himself for the chaos of noise and busy fluttering. He took it in for a moment, confused, and then he bowed. And when he lifted his head he realized what he was facing. In the stalls and in the gallery the members of the paying public were hissing and booing. He looked around and saw mockery and contempt. The invited audience remained seated, still applauding, but the applause was drowned out by the crescendo of loud, rude disapproval which came from the people who had never read his books.

The worst part was now – when he did not know what to do, when he could not control the expression on his own face, the look of panic he could not prevent. And now he could make out the faces of friends – Sargent, Gosse, Philip Burne-Jones – still gallantly applauding, futile against the yells of the mob. Nothing had prepared him for this. Slowly, he moved off the stage. He did not attend to Alexander's speech to calm the audience. He blamed Alexander for leading him onto the stage, he blamed the crowd for booing, but more than anyone he blamed himself for being here. There was no alternative now, he would have to leave by the stage door. He had dreamed so much of moments of triumph, mingling with the invited guests, pleased that so many old friends had come to witness his theatrical success. Now he would walk home and keep his head down like a man who has committed a crime and is in imminent danger of apprehension.

He waited in the shadows backstage so that he would not have to see the actors. Nor did he wish to leave just yet as he did not know whom he might see in the streets around the theatre. Neither he nor they would know what to say, so great and so public was his defeat. For his friends, this night would be entered into the annals of the unmentionable, pages in which he had so studiously avoided having his name appear. As time passed, however, he realized that he could not betray the performers now. He could not give into his own horrible urge to be alone in the darkness, to escape into the night and walk as though he had written nothing and was nobody. He would have to go to them and thank them; he would have to insist that the repast planned after the triumph of his play should go ahead. In the half light he stood preparing himself, steeling himself, ready to suppress whatever his own urges and needs might be. He made his hands into fists as he set out to smile and bow and imagine that the evening in all its glory had been due entirely to the talents of the actors in the great tradition of the London stage.

CHAPTER TWO

February 1895

AFTER THE FAILURE OF *Guy Domville*, his determination to work did battle with the feeling that he had been defeated and exposed. He had failed, he realized, to take the measure of the great flat foot of the public, and he now had to face the melancholy fact that nothing he did would ever be popular or generally appreciated. Most of the time he could, if he tried, control his thoughts. What he could not control was the terrible ache of the morning, an ache that stretched now towards noon and often did not lift. There was a line in Oscar Wilde's play that he had liked in which the question was put – did the sadness of Londoners cause the fog or did the fog cause the sadness? His sadness, he thought, as the spare light of the winter morning peered in his window, was like the London fog. Except that it did not seem to lift, and it was accompanied by a weariness that was new to him, and a lethargy that shocked and depressed him.

He wondered if at some point in the future he would go out of fashion even more than now, and if the dividends from his father's estate were to dry up, whether his reduced circumstances would represent a public humiliation. It came down to money, the sweetness it added to the soul. Money was a kind of grace. Everywhere he had been, the having of it and the holding of it had set people apart. It gave men a beautiful distant control over the world, and it gave women a poised sense of themselves, an inner light which even old age could not obliterate.

It was easy to feel that he was destined to write for the few, perhaps for the future, yet never to reap the rewards that he would relish now, such as his own house and a beautiful garden and no anxiety about what was to come. He retained his pride in decisions taken, the fact that he had never compromised, that his back ached and his eyes hurt solely because he continued to labour all day at an art that was pure and unconstrained by mere mercenary ambitions.

For his father and his brother, and for many in London too, a failure in the market was a kind of success, and a success in the market a matter not to be discussed. He did not ever in his life actively seek the hard doom of general popularity. Nonetheless, he wanted his books to sell, he wanted to shine in the marketplace and pocket the proceeds without compromising his sacred art in any way.

It mattered to him how he was seen; and being seen not to lift a finger to make his works popular pleased him; being seen to devote himself in solitude and selfless application to a noble art gave him satisfaction. He recognized, however, that lack of success was one thing, but abject failure was another. Thus his failure in the theatre, so public, so notorious and so transparent, managed to make him uneasy in company and unwilling to venture much into the wider world of London society. He felt like a general who had come back from a battlefield complete with a scent of defeat, and whose presence in the warm bright rooms of London would seem incongruous and unhappy.

He knew military men in London. He had moved carefully and easily among the powerful, and he had listened with close attention to the English talk about political intrigue and military valour. As he sat amid the usual collection of rich accessories and old warriors at Lord Wolseley's house in Portman Square, he often thought of what his sister Alice or his brother William would say if they heard the densest of imperial war talk after dinner, the deep and hearty discussions about troops and attacks and slaughter. Alice had been the most anti-imperialist of the family; she had even loved Parnell and longed for Home Rule for Ireland. William had his Irish sentiments too and indeed his anti-English attitudes.

Lord Wolseley was cultivated, as all of them were, and he was well-mannered and fascinating with rosy dimples and piercing eyes. Henry was in the company of these men because their wives wished him to be. The women liked his manners and his grey eyes and his American origin, but more than anything they enjoyed his way of listening, of drinking in every word, asking only pertinent questions, acknowledging by his gestures and replies the intelligence of his interlocutor.

It was easier for him if there were no other writers present, no one who knew his work. The men who gathered after dinner for anecdotes and political gossip never interested him as much as what they said interested him; the women, on the other hand, always interested him, no matter what they said. Lady Wolseley interested him a great deal because she was all cleverness and sympathy and charm and had the air and manners and taste of an American. She had the habit of surveying the room in wonder and open admiration for her guests, and then turning her smile on her closest companion and speaking quietly as though imparting a secret.

He needed to leave London, but he did not think that he could bear to be alone anywhere. He did not want to discuss his play and he did not think he could work. He determined that if he travelled things would be different on his return. His mind was full of visions and ideas. He prayed and hoped that his imagination might be equal to pages written. That was all he wanted, he now believed.

He went to Ireland since it was easy to travel there and because he did not believe it would strain his nerves. Neither Lord Houghton, the new Lord Lieutenant, whose father he had also known, nor Lord Wolseley, who had become Commander-in-Chief of Her Majesty's forces in Ireland, had seen his play; he agreed to spend a week with each. He had been surprised by the vehemence of the invitations and the tussle between the two as to how much time he would spend with one and how much with the other. It was only when he was installed in Dublin Castle that he understood the problem.

Ireland was in a state of unrest and Her Majesty's government had not merely failed to put down the unrest but given in to it by making concessions. These had been relatively easy to explain to Parliament but impossible to explain to the Irish landlords and local garrisons, who were boycotting all the social events of the season at Dublin Castle. Lord Houghton was depending on imported guests and this explained the enthusiasm of his invitation.

While old Lord Houghton had been informal in both his manners and his personal habits, and given especially in his later years to delighting himself and amusing others, his son was stern and self-important. In his position as Lord Lieutenant, the new Lord Houghton had found true happiness. He strutted about the place, being the only one it seemed not to realize that while he meant well, he did not matter. He represented the queen in Ireland, and he did so with all the ceremony and attention to detail he could muster, filling his day with inspections and receptions and salutes and his evening with balls and banquets. He oversaw his household as though the queen were in residence and likely to appear at this very moment in all her imperial grandeur.

The little viceregal court in all its pomposity was, for Henry, a weariness to flesh and spirit alike. There were four balls in six days and a banquet every night. The bare official and military class peopled them, with the aid of a very dull and second-rate, though large, house party from England. Fortunately, most of the guests had never heard of him; he made no effort to alter that.

'Now my advice to you,' one of the English ladies said to him, 'is to hold your nose and close your eyes and if you can find a way to stuff your ears do so as well. Begin the moment you arrive in

Ireland and don't stop until you enter the castle or the viceregal lodge or wherever you are staying.'

The lady glowed with satisfaction. He wished his sister Alice, now three years dead, were here to rout her. Alice, he knew, would prepare a speech for later and write many letters about the lady's facial hair and her teeth and the crack which came in her voice when she reached the higher notes of admonition. The lady smiled at him.

'I hope I have not alarmed you. You seem alarmed.'

He was indeed alarmed because he had found a small room with a writing table and paper and ink and some books, and he was busy writing a letter. It suddenly occurred to him that the best way of clearing this woman out of the room was by waving his two hands at her and making a noise as though she were a flock of hens or a gaggle of geese.

'But it is lovely here,' she continued, 'and last year the balls were the most glittering events, much better than anything in London, you know.'

He stared at her grimly and, he hoped, blankly and said nothing.

'And there are other people here,' she began again, 'who could learn a great deal from his lordship. You know in London we are invited regularly to several of the great houses. But we don't know Lord Wolseley nor indeed do we know his wife. Lord Houghton was kind enough to introduce us at the intimate evening he held when we first arrived and I was placed beside him, and my husband, who is a very kind and sweet man and also very rich, if you don't mind me saying so, and honest, of course, had the misfortune to be placed beside Lady Wolseley.'

She stopped to catch her breath and to move her indignant tone up one notch.

'And Lord Wolseley must have learned a signalling system in one of his wars and he must have secretly instructed her to ignore my husband as he ignored me. The rudeness of him! And the rudeness of her! Lord Houghton was mortified. They are, I believe, the Wolseleys, a very, very rude pair.'

Henry took the view that it was time to terminate the conversation, but saw that she was sharply on the lookout for rudeness. Nonetheless, he felt that rudeness now would be a small matter compared with further minutes listening to her conversation.

'I'm afraid that I have to return to my chambers urgently,' he said.

'Oh my,' she replied. She was blocking the door.

When he moved towards her, she did not budge. Her face was locked in a resentful smile.

'And of course we won't be invited to the Royal Hospital now. My husband says that we would not go if we were, but I myself would love to see it, and the evenings there are splendid, I'm told, despite the rudeness of the hosts. And young Mr Webster, the MP, who my husband says is the coming thing and will be prime minister some day, is going to be there.'

She stopped and considered the top of his head for a moment and pinched her cheek. And then she continued.

'But we're not good enough, that's what I said to my husband. But you have a great advantage. You are an American and nobody knows who your father was or who your grandfather was. You could be anybody.'

He stood coldly watching her across the carpet.

'I don't mean any offence,' she said.

He still did not speak.

'I meant that America seems to be a very fine democracy.'

'You would be very welcome there,' he said and bowed.

Two days later he made the journey from Dublin Castle to the Royal Hospital at Kilmainham across the city. He had seen Ireland before, having travelled once from Queenstown in Cork to Dublin, and he had stayed also in Kingstown briefly. He had liked

Kingstown, the sea light and the sense of calm and order. But this journey now reminded him of travelling across the country, witnessing a squalor both abject and omnipresent. There were times during that journey when he was not sure whether a cabin had been partly razed to the ground or was fully inhabited. Everything seemed ruined or partly ruined. Smoke appeared from half-rotten chimneys, and no one, emerging from these cabins, could refrain from shouting after a carriage as it passed or moving malevolently towards one if it slowed down. There was no moment when he felt free of their hostile stares and dark accusing eyes.

Dublin, in some respects, was different. There was greater mingling between the mendicant class and those who possessed money and manners. But still the squalor of Ireland came right up to the castle gates and left him depressed and haunted. Now, as the official carriage took him from the castle to the Royal Hospital, he noted more than anything the sullenness of the Irish. He tried to keep his eyes averted but he could not. The last few streets were too narrow for him to avoid noticing the poverty in the faces and the buildings and the feeling that at any moment the way could be blocked by importuning women and children. Had William been with him, his brother would have had strong words for this neglected and impoverished backyard.

He was relieved as the carriage made its way up the avenue of the Royal Hospital, and surprised at the stateliness of the building, the sense of grace and symmetry and decorum in the grounds. It was, he smiled to himself at the thought, like entering the kingdom of heaven after a rough ride through the lower depths. Even the staff who came to greet him and take his luggage appeared different, of a heavenly disposition. He felt that he should demand that they shut the gates and save him from having to face the poverty of the city again until it was absolutely necessary.

He knew that the hospital had been built in the seventeenth century for old soldiers, and on his first tour of inspection, he learned that a hundred and fifty of them lodged off the long corridors which gave on to a central square, happily growing older in splendid surroundings. When Lady Wolseley apologized for their proximity, he told her that he too in his own way was an old soldier, or at least an ageing one, and that he would surely be at home here if any sort of bed could be found for him.

His room looked away from the hospital towards the river and the park. In the morning, when he woke early, there was a white mist over the lawns. He slept again, this time deeply and peacefully, and was woken by a tip-toeing presence in the room, moving in the shadows.

'I have left some hot water here for washing, sir, and will draw a bath at your convenience.'

It was a man's voice, an English accent, soft and reassuring.

'Her ladyship says that you can, if you wish, be served breakfast in your room.'

Henry asked for his bath now and breakfast in his room. He wondered how her ladyship would take to his not appearing at all until lunchtime and presumed he could claim his art as a licence for solitude. The prospect of a morning alone with the view from the windows and the lovely proportions of the room for company filled him with happiness.

When he asked the manservant his name, he discovered that he was not a manservant at all, but an army corporal, and he realized that the Wolseleys had vast numbers of these at their disposal. He was called Hammond and had a quiet voice and an air of smooth discretion. Henry felt immediately that Hammond would be in great demand as a manservant should the army ever run out of use for him.

At lunch the conversation turned, as he knew it would, to events at Dublin Castle.

'The Irish were awful anyway,' Lady Wolseley said, 'and their not attending the season should be greeted with relief. The dreary matrons dragging their dreary daughters about the place and dinnering up every possible partner for them. The truth is that no one wants to marry their daughters, no one at all.'

There were five guests from England, two of whom he knew slightly. He noticed their quietness, their smiling faces and sudden bursts of laughter as their host and hostess competed with each other to be amusing.

'So Lord Houghton,' Lady Wolseley continued, 'thinks he is the royal family in Ireland and the first thing the royal family has to have is subjects, but since the Irish refuse to be his subjects, he has imported a whole cargo of subjects from England, as I'm sure Mr James knows only too well.'

He did not speak and was careful to make no gesture which might signify assent.

'He has invited anyone who would come. We had to rescue Mr James,' her husband added.

He thought to say that Lord Houghton was a very good host, but he realized that it was better he should not take part in this conversation.

'And to make it all seem jolly and normal,' Lady Wolseley continued, 'he has had balls and banquets. Poor Mr James was so exhausted when he arrived here. And Lord Houghton last week invited us to an evening in his own apartments. It was indeed gruesomely intimate. I was placed beside a very rough man and Lord Wolseley placed beside his very rough wife. The husband at least knew not to speak but the wife was not so trained. We didn't mind them, of course, we didn't mind them at all.'

That evening as he was retiring, Lady Wolseley walked down one of the long corridors with him. Her tone suggested that she was ready to offer him confidences about the other guests.

'Is Hammond satisfactory?' she asked. 'I'm sorry he was not here to meet you when you arrived.'

'He is perfect, he could not be better.'

'Yes, that is why I chose him,' she said. 'He has great charm, does he not, and discretion, I think?'

She studied him. He said nothing.

'Yes, I thought you would agree. He's looking after you and nobody else, and, of course, available all the time. I think he feels honoured to be looking after you. I told him that when we were all dead and forgotten, only you would be remembered and your books read. And he said something very lovely, in that lovely quiet voice of his. He said, "I will do everything to make him happy during his stay." So simple! And I think he meant it.'

They had arrived at the foot of the staircase; her face seemed to glow with insinuation. He smiled at her mildly and said good-night. As he turned to go up the second flight he could see that she was still watching him, smiling strangely.

The curtains had been drawn and a fire was burning in his sitting room. Soon, Hammond came in with a jug of water.

'Will you be up late, sir?'

'No, I will retire very soon.'

Hammond was tall and his face in the firelight seemed thinner now and softer. He moved towards the window and straightened the curtains, and then approached the fireplace to rake the fire in the grate.

'I hope I am not disturbing you, sir, but this coal is most inferior,' he said, almost whispering.

Henry was sitting in an armchair beside the fire.

'No, please, go ahead,' he said.

'Would you like your book, sir?'

'My book?'

'The book you were reading earlier. I can fetch it for you, sir, it's in the other room.'

Hammond's brown eyes rested on him, the expression friendly, almost humorous. He wore no beard or moustache. He stood still in the yellowish gaslight, at his ease, as though Henry's failure to reply were something he had anticipated.

'I don't think I will read now,' Henry said slowly. He smiled as he began to rise.

'I feel I have disturbed you, sir.'

'No, please, do not worry. It is time for bed.'

He handed Hammond a half-crown.

'Oh thank you, sir, but it is not necessary.'

'Please, I'd like you to take it,' he said.

'I'm grateful, sir.'

By LUNCHEON the next day more guests had arrived to people the empty rooms and corridors of Lord and Lady Wolseley's apartments. Soon, jolly noises and much laughter filled their quarters. The Wolseleys announced that they were to have their own ball, Lady Wolseley adding that those at the castle might benefit from a lesson in how a proper ball might be held so far away from home.

When fancy dress was mentioned, however, Henry demurred, stating that he was too old-fashioned to dress up. As he spoke to Lady Wolseley towards the end of the evening, she insisting that he dress in military costume, and he insisting that he would not, a young man, clearly one of the new arrivals, interrupted them. He was eager and confident and obviously a great favourite of Lady Wolseley.

'Mr James,' he said, 'my wife wishes to go as Daisy Miller, perhaps you can help us design her costume.'

'No one can be Daisy Miller,' Lady Wolseley said, 'the rule for the ladies is that we must be a Gainsborough, a Romney or a Sir Joshua. And I can tell you, Mr Webster, that I intend to outshine all.'

'How strange,' the man replied, 'that is precisely what my wife said this morning. What an extraordinary coincidence!'

'No one can be Daisy Miller, Mr Webster,' Lady Wolseley said sternly, as though she were angry, 'and please remember that my husband commands an army and bear in mind also that some of the old pensioners when roused can be very fierce.'

Later, Henry took Lady Wolseley aside.

'And who, pray, is Mr Webster?' he asked.

'Oh he's an MP. And Lord Wolseley says that he will go places if he can stop being so clever. He speaks a great deal in the House and Lord Wolseley says he must stop doing that too. His wife is very rich. Grain or flour, I think, or oats. Anyway, money. She has the money, and he has everything else you could want, except tact. And that is why I am so glad you are here. Perhaps you could teach him some of that.'

HAMMOND WAS Irish, although he spoke with a London accent, having been taken to England when he was a child. He seemed to like lingering over his tasks and talking as he cleaned. He apologized as he came and went. Henry made clear that he did not mind the interruptions.

'I like the hospital, sir, and the old soldiers,' he said. His voice was soft. 'They've mostly been in the wars and some of them fight their wars all day, sir. They think the windows and doors are Turks and Zulus or whatever and want to charge at them. It's funny here, sir. It's half Ireland and half England, like myself. Maybe that's why I feel at home.'

His presence remained easy and welcome. He was agile and light on his feet, despite his height. His eyes were never cast down, they looked ahead in a way which made their owner equal to what he saw, instantly taking everything in, understanding everything. He seemed to make calm judgements as he moved about.

'Her ladyship told me I should read one of your books, sir. She said they were very good. I would like to read one of them, sir.'

Henry told Hammond that he would send him a book when he returned to London. He would send it to the Royal Hospital.

'To Tom Hammond, sir, Corporal Tom Hammond.'

Each time Henry returned to his chambers from a meal or a walk in the grounds, Hammond would find a reason to visit. The reasons were always good. He never idled or made unnecessary noise, but slowly, as the days went on, he became more relaxed, spent time standing by the window talking and asking questions and listening carefully.

'And you came from America to England, sir. Most people do it the other way. Do you like London, sir? You must like it.'

Henry nodded and said that he did like London, but tried to explain that sometimes it was difficult to work there, too many invitations and distractions.

At meals, amid all the talk and laughter and effort to amuse, Henry longed for the moment when Hammond first came into the room. That was the moment he waited for, the moment which filled his thoughts as he sat through dinner, Lady Wolseley and Mr Webster competing with each other in conversation. He thought of Hammond standing against the window of the sitting room listening. Once back in his chambers, however, after a few questions from Hammond, or after he had tried to explain something to him, he longed for silence again, for Hammond to leave him now.

He knew that everything he had done in his life, indeed everything he had written, his family background and his years in London, would seem impossibly strange to Hammond. Yet despite this, there were times when Hammond was in his chambers when he felt close to him, felt uplifted somehow by the talk between them. But then Hammond would begin to speak about his own life, or his hopes, or his views on the world, and a vast distance would appear between them, made all the greater because Hammond did not recognize it as he chattered on, honest and unselfconscious, and – Henry had to admit this – quietly tedious.

'IF THERE WERE a war between Great Britain and the United States, Mr James, where would your loyalty lie?' Webster asked him during a lull in the conversation after dinner.

'My loyalty would lie in making peace between them.'

'And what if that should fail?' Webster asked.

'I happen to know the answer,' Lady Wolseley interrupted. 'Mr James would find out which side France was on and he would join that side.'

'But in Mr James's story about Agatha Grice, his American loathes England and he has the most horrible things to say about us.' Webster spoke loudly so that the entire table now paid attention. 'I think he has a case to answer,' Webster continued.

Henry looked across the table at Webster whose cheeks were reddened by the heat of the room, and whose eyes were bright with excitement at holding the table like this, managing the conversation.

'Mr Webster,' Henry said quietly when he was sure that the young man had finally finished, 'I witnessed a war and I saw the injuries and the damage done. My own brother came close to death in the American Civil War. His injuries were unspeakable. I do not, Mr Webster, speak lightly of war.'

'Hear, hear,' Lord Wolseley said. 'Well spoken!'

'I merely asked Mr James a simple question,' Webster said.

'And he provided you with a very simple answer which you seem to have trouble comprehending,' Lord Wolseley said.

As Lord and Lady Wolseley made preparations for their ball, consulting their guests about arrangements and details, and spending a good deal of time supervising decorations in the Great Hall, more friends began to arrive, including a woman whom Henry had met several times at Lady Wolseley's. Her name was Gaynor, and her late husband had held some important rank in the army. She appeared with her daughter Mona, aged ten or eleven, and Mona, as the only child among them, became much admired and discussed because of her shy beauty and natural manners. She moved with poise and managed to seem happy not to speak much or make any demands, merely to be charmingly present.

On the day before the ball a great cold descended on Dublin and Henry was forced to return early from his walk in the grounds. He found himself passing by one of the small rooms downstairs in the Wolseleys' apartments. Lady Wolseley was busy gathering wigs together so that the ladies could try them on before dinner. Mr Webster was with her, and Henry stopped in the doorway, preparing himself to speak to them. They were involved in the game of choosing the wigs, examining them and laughing and handing them one to the other, like conspirators in some happy dream as Lady Wolseley forced Webster to try on a wig and then threw her head back with laughter as he tried it on her. They were too deep in conspiracy to be decently interrupted. Suddenly, he noticed that the child Mona was seated in one of the armchairs. She was doing nothing, neither assisting them at the round table, nor joining in whatever joke had caused them to turn towards each other once more, Lady Wolseley covering her mouth with her hand.

Mona was a picture of girlish perfection, but as Henry watched her he noticed how hard she seemed to be concentrating on the scene in front of her. Her gaze was neither puzzled nor hurt, but there was a sense that she was putting energy into a look of mild contentment and sweetness.

He pulled himself back from the doorway just as Lady Wolseley let out another shrill laugh at some remark of Mr Webster's. In his last glimpse of Mona she was smiling as though the joke had been a pleasantry to amuse her, everything about her an effort to disguise the fact that she was clearly in a place where she should not be, listening to words or insinuations she should not have to hear. He went back to his rooms.

He thought about the scene he had witnessed, how vivid it was for him, like an event he had observed before and knew well. He sat in his own armchair and allowed his mind to picture other rooms and doorways, other silent lockings of eyes and his own distant presence, as he read into the moment a deeply ambiguous meaning. He realized now that this was something he had described in his books over and over, figures seen from a window or a doorway, a small gesture standing for a much larger relationship, something hidden suddenly revealed. He had written it, but just now he had seen it come alive, and yet he was not sure what it meant. He pictured it again, the girl so innocent, and her innocence so crucial to the scene. There was nothing, no nuance or implication, which she did not seem capable of taking in.

When he looked up, Hammond was calmly watching him.

'I hope I didn't disturb you, sir. The fire needs constant attention in this weather. I will try not to make any noise.'

Henry was aware that at the moment he had lifted his head from his reveries, Hammond had been studying him unguardedly. And now he was making up for it by moving quickly, as though he were going to remove the coal scuttle without speaking again.

'Have you seen the little girl, Mona?' Henry asked him.

'Recently, sir?'

'No, I mean since she arrived.'

'Yes, I meet her in the corridors all the time, sir.'

'It's strange for her to be alone here with no one else her own age. Does she have a nurse with her?'

'Yes, sir, and her mother.'

'What does she do all day, then?'

'God knows, sir.'

Hammond was studying him again, examining him with an intensity which was almost unmannerly. Henry returned his gaze as calmly as he could. There was silence between them. When Hammond finally averted his eyes, he seemed pensive and depressed.

'I have a sister who is the age of Mona, sir. She is pretty.'

'In London?'

'Yes, sir, she is the youngest by far. She is the light of all our lives, sir.'

'Does Mona put her in your mind when you see her?'

'My sister does not roam freely sir, she is a real treasure.'

'Surely Mona is protected by her nanny and, indeed, her mother?'

'I'm sure she is, sir.'

Hammond cast his eyes down, looking troubled as though he wished to say something and was being prevented. He turned his head towards the window and remained still. The light caught half his face while half stayed in shadow; the room was quiet enough for Henry to hear his breathing. Neither of them moved or spoke.

35

Henry appreciated that if anyone could see them now, if others were to stand in the doorway as he had done earlier, or manage to see in through the window, they would presume that something momentous had occurred between them, that their silence had merely arisen because so much had been said. Suddenly, Hammond let out a quick breath and smiled at him softly and benignly before taking a tray from the table and leaving the room.

HENRY FOUND himself that evening close to Lord Wolseley at supper and thus free, he thought, from Webster. One of the ladies beside him had read several of his books and was much exercised by their endings and by the idea of an American writing about English life.

'You must find us quite blank compared to the Americans,' she said. 'Lord Warburton's sisters in your novel, now they were quite blank. Now Isabel isn't blank or Daisy Miller. If George Eliot had written Americans, she would have made them quite blank too.' She clearly enjoyed the phrase 'quite blank' and placed it in several more of her comments.

Webster, in the meantime, could not stop attempting to control the table. When he had teased all the women about what they could not, or would not, or might not wear at the ball, he turned his attention to the novelist.

'Mr James, are you going to visit any of your Irish kinsmen while you are here?'

'No, Mr Webster, I have no plans of any sort.' He spoke coldly and firmly.

'Why, Mr James, the roads, thanks to his lordship's steady command of the forces, are safe from marauders. I'm sure her ladyship would put a carriage at your disposal.'

'Mr Webster, I have no plans.'

'What was the name of that place, Lady Wolseley? Bailieborough, that's right, Bailieborough in County Cavan. It is where you will find the seat of the James family.'

Henry noticed Lady Wolseley blushing and keeping her eyes from him. He looked at her and at no one else before turning to Lord Wolseley and speaking softly.

'Mr Webster will not desist,' he said.

'Yes, a stretch in barracks might improve his general deportment,' Lord Wolseley said.

Webster did not hear this exchange but he saw it, and it seemed to irritate him that both men had smiled knowingly at each other.

'Mr James and I,' Lord Wolseley boomed down the table, 'were agreeing that you have a considerable talent for making yourself heard, Mr Webster. You should consider putting it to some useful purpose.'

Lord Wolseley looked at his wife.

'Mr Webster will one day be a great orator, a great Parliamentarian,' Lady Wolseley said.

'When he learns the art of silence he will be a very great orator indeed, even greater than he is now,' Lord Wolseley said.

Lord Wolseley turned back to Henry. They studiously ignored the other end of the table. Henry felt as though he had been struck with something and the blow had stunned him into pretending that he was following Lord Wolseley, while with all his secret energy he concentrated on what had just been said.

He did not mind Webster's clear malice; he would never, he hoped, have to see him again, and Lord Wolseley's words had meant that Webster would never be able to raise his voice at the table again. Rather it was the sneer on Lady Wolseley's face when Webster had mentioned Bailieborough that Henry remembered. It had disappeared quickly, but nonetheless he had seen it and she knew he had seen it. He was still too shocked to know whether it was careless or deliberate. He simply knew that he had done nothing to provoke it. He also knew that Webster and Lady Wolseley had discussed him and his family's origins in County Cavan. He did not know, however, where they had got their information.

He wished that he could leave the house now. When he looked down the table, he caught a glimpse of Lady Wolseley in discussion with her neighbour. She seemed chastened, but he wondered if he merely imagined this because he wished her to be so. He nodded carefully as Lord Wolseley came to the end of the story of one of his campaigns; he smiled as best he could.

When Webster stood up Henry saw from his face that he was flustered, that he had taken Lord Wolseley's remark about silence to heart. Henry knew, and Webster must have known too, that Lord Wolseley had spoken as fiercely as he was capable of doing outside a military tribunal. Also, Lady Wolseley's quick defence of Webster had come too fast. It would have been better if she had not spoken. Henry knew now that it was important to get to his rooms without crossing the paths of either Webster or Lady Wolseley, who were both still in the dining room, keeping away from each other, not becoming directly involved in any conversation.

THE GAS LAMPS were lit in his apartment and the fire was blazing. It was as though Hammond had known he would be returning early. The sitting room was beautiful like this, old wood and flickering shadows and long dark velvet curtains. It was strange, he thought, how familiar these rooms had become to him, and how much he needed the peace they provided.

Soon after he had placed himself in the armchair beside the fire, Hammond arrived with tea on a tray.

'I saw you in the corridor, sir, you looked poorly.'

He had not seen Hammond, and he felt unhappy that he had been watched as he made his way from the dining room.

'You look as though you've seen a ghost, sir.'

'It's the living I've been looking at,' he said.

'I brought you tea, and I will make sure that the fire is going properly in your bedroom. You need a long night's rest, sir.'

Henry did not reply. Hammond carried over a small table and put the tray down and began to pour the tea.

'Would you like your book, sir?'

'No, thank you, I think I'll sit here and have my tea and go to bed as you suggested.'

'You look shaken, sir. Are you sure you will be all right?'

'Yes, thank you very much.'

'I can look in during the night if you like, sir.'

Hammond was moving towards the bedroom. His glance back as he spoke was casual as though he had said nothing unusual. Henry was not sure if he quite understood, if the offer had been made innocently or not. All he knew for certain was his own susceptibility; he could feel himself holding his breath.

Because he did not reply, Hammond stopped and turned and they locked eyes. The expression on Hammond's face was one of mild concern, but Henry could not tell what it concealed.

'No, thank you, I'm tired and I think I will sleep well.'

'That's fine, sir. I'll check the bedroom and then I will leave you in peace.'

Henry lay in bed and thought of the house they were in, a house full of doors and corridors, strange creakings and odd night sounds. He thought of his hostess and Mr Webster and his mocking tone. He wished he could leave now, have his bags packed and move into a city hotel. But he knew that he could not go, the ball was the following night and to leave before the ball would be to offend. He would leave on the morning after the ball.

He felt hurt and wounded, knowing that his hostess had conspired against him. He thought about what Webster had said. He had never spoken to anyone in Lady Wolseley's circle about County Cavan. It was not a secret or a matter of shame, although by his sneering tone Webster had made it seem so. It was simply the place where his grandfather had been born and his father had visited almost sixty years earlier. What could it mean to him? His grandfather had come to America in search of freedom, and in America he had found more than freedom. He had found great wealth, and that had changed everything. County Cavan did not cost Henry a thought.

He put his hands behind his head in the darkness of the bedroom, the firelight having fully dimmed. He was disturbed by the idea that he longed, now more than ever before, in this strange house in this strange country, for someone to hold him, not speak or move even, but to embrace him, stay with him. He needed that now, and making himself say it brought the need closer, made it more urgent and more impossible.

LATE THE FOLLOWING morning he sat by the window, watching the sheer blue sky over the Liffey. It was another freezing day and thus he was surprised to see the child Mona on the lawn, unaccompanied and bare-headed. He himself had been for an early walk and had been glad to get back inside the house. The girl, he noticed, had her arms outstretched and she was moving in circles; the lawn was wide and he searched with his eyes for her nurse or her mother, but there was no one.

If anyone, he thought, saw her they would feel as he did. She must be rescued, there was too much lawn, too much broad, unwatched territory around her. It was appalling that she was there in the cold March morning unprotected. She was still moving about the centre of the lawn, half-running and then stopping, following a route of her own devising. Her coat, he saw, was open. As time passed and no protector arrived to take her indoors, he imagined a figure in the shadows watching her, or a figure emerging from the shadows. Suddenly, she stopped her movements and stood still, facing him. He could see that she was shivering with cold. She made a gesture and shook her head. He realized that she must be in silent contact with someone at another window, presumably her mother or her nurse. She did not move again, but stood there on the lawn alone.

It was the dead, inert silence of her long gaze which held his attention. In her stillness, she seemed both frightened and acquiescent, and he could not begin to imagine what her watcher at the window was indicating.

He fetched his coat from the stand near the door. He could not resist inspecting the scene at first hand, and he planned to turn the corner casually and glance up at the window, without losing a moment, as soon as he came into view. He believed that the person at the window, whoever she was, would pull back once he appeared. Anyone, he thought, would be ashamed to conduct the minding of a young girl, who should, in any case, be indoors, from an upstairs window. He found his way to the side door without meeting anyone.

The day had become colder and he shivered as he walked around the house to the lawn. He waited at the corner for a second and then turned sharply, staring immediately up at the windows along his floor even before checking that Mona was there. He saw no one at the windows, no one withdrew into the shadows as he had expected. Instead, directly in front of him, wearing a blue hat and with her coat fastened, stood Mona with her nurse. The child was being led by the hand towards him. He greeted her and the nurse and then passed on quickly. When he turned to watch them, he noticed the nurse speaking gently to the child, and Mona smiling up at her, contented and not in need of anything. He checked all the upper windows once more but there was no one watching.

As he passed the Great Hall he saw that the servants were already working, laying the tables, putting the candles in place and decorating the room. Hammond was not among them.

He had told Lady Wolseley a second time that morning that he would not wear any form of fancy dress, that he was neither a lord nor a fop, but a poor scribbler. She had told him that he would be alone at the ball, that the ladies one and all were prepared and no gentleman was coming as himself.

'You are among friends, Mr James,' she said.

When she spoke, she stopped for a moment and hesitated, clearly deciding not to make the next statement that had come into her mind. He studied her carefully and directly until she looked almost embarrassed and then he told her that he would be leaving early in the morning.

'And Hammond? Will you not miss him?' she asked, attempting to restore a playful tone to their conversation.

'Hammond?' He looked confused. 'Oh, the manservant. Yes, thank you, he has been splendid.'

'He's normally so serious, but all week he has been smiling.'

'You know,' Henry said, 'I will miss your hospitality enormously.'

He determined that he would not speak to Webster that evening, rather he would avoid him at all times. As soon as he reached the stairway on his way to the ball, however, Webster was upon him. He was dressed in a hunting outfit Henry considered absurd and brandishing an envelope with an air of hideous glee.

'I did not know we had friends in common,' he said.

Henry bowed.

'I searched for you this morning,' Webster said, 'to tell you that I have a missive here from Mr Wilde, Mr Oscar Wilde, who sends his fond regards to you. At least he says he does, one can never tell with him. He says that he wishes he were here, and of course he would be a great addition to things and he is a great favourite of her ladyship. His lordship, I understand, draws the line before him. I don't think he would have wanted Mr Wilde in his regiment.'

Webster stopped and moved to go down the stairs with Henry in front of him. Henry remained motionless.

'Of course, Mr Wilde is very busy with the theatre. He tells me that a play of yours was taken off to make way for his second success of the season and he seems rather pleased with the association. Yours was about a monk, he says. All the Irish are natural writers, my wife says, it comes naturally to them. She adores Mr Wilde.'

Henry remained silent. When Webster stopped as though to let him speak, he bowed again and motioned Webster to go down the stairs, but Webster did not move.

'Mr Wilde says that he longs to see you in London. He has many friends. Do you know his friends?'

'No, Mr Webster, I do not think that I have had the good fortune to meet his friends.'

'Well, perhaps you know them and are not aware that they are his friends. Lady Wolseley came with us to the play about Ernest. You must join us for the next play. I shall inform Lady Wolseley that you must.'

Webster was making a greater effort than usual to be amusing. He also managed somehow to make sure that there was no gap in the conversation so that Henry could take his leave. Clearly, he had more to say.

'Of course I think artists and politicians have one thing in common. We all pay the price, I think, unless we are lucky and struggle hard. Mr Wilde is having trouble with his wife. It's a difficult time for him, as I'm sure you understand. Lady Wolseley tells me that you have no wife. That might be one solution. As long as it doesn't catch on, I suppose.'

He turned and indicated to Henry that they could now walk down the stairs together.

'But being a bachelor must leave you open to all sorts of . . . How shall I put it? All sorts of sympathy.'

THE GREAT HALL of the Royal Hospital basked in the glow of a thousand candles. There was music from a small orchestra, and waiters moved among the guests offering champagne. The tables were set, as Lady Wolseley had told him, with silver which Lord Wolseley had recently inherited, shipped from London specially for the occasion. So far only the men were present. He was informed that none of the ladies wanted to be the first to arrive, all of them were in their chambers waiting for news from their maids, who regularly spied down into the hall from the stairwell. Lord Houghton was in his full regalia as the queen's representative in Ireland and he took the view that Lord Wolseley would have to organize a cavalry charge to force the ladies to appear. Lady Wolseley, it seemed, was the most recalcitrant of all and had sworn that she would be the last to arrive in the room.

Henry watched Webster; not for one moment was he unaware of Webster's movements. He had had enough of him. Should Webster dart in his direction, he was ready to turn away abruptly. This meant that he could not, under any circumstances, become involved in an engrossing conversation.

As Webster, indulging in constant laughter, moved across the hall, Henry followed him with his eyes and thus he noticed Hammond for the first time. Hammond was wearing a black suit and a white shirt and a black bow tie. His dark hair seemed shinier and longer than before. He was freshly shaved and this gave his face a thin, pure beauty. As soon as Henry caught his eye, he knew that he had been examining him too closely, that he had, in one flash, given more away than he had done all week. Hammond seemed unembarrassed and did not avert his eyes. He held a tray but did not move from where he stood and managed, without any trace of emotion, to outstare Henry, who was standing in a group, half-listening to an anecdote. Henry returned his attention to the company. Once he withdrew his gaze, he was careful not to look again.

Lord Wolseley had spoken to the orchestra and arranged a small fanfare, and negotiated with the maidservants that at the sound of the music each lady, including his own wife, would venture from her chamber and present herself in the hall for much fussing and admiration. No one was allowed to stay behind. When the fanfare sounded, the gentlemen stood back and the doors were ceremoniously opened. Two dozen ladies descended on the room, all of them wearing elaborate wigs and cakes of make-up and dresses fresh from the greatest paintings of Gainsborough, Reynolds and

Romney. The gentlemen applauded as the orchestra played the opening of a waltz.

Lady Wolseley had been right when she told them that her costume would triumph. A mixture of peacock blue and a deep red, her silk dress had an enormous sash, and was full of tucks and flourishes and bulges. It was low-cut to a degree that none of the other ladies had risked. Lady Wolseley was not wearing a wig, merely her natural hair with ringlets added, the connection between the real and the false hair seamless. Her face and eyes had been painted so expertly that it appeared as though she were wearing no make-up at all. Having asked the orchestra to stop playing, she motioned her guests to stand back. Her husband did not seem to know who or what was on the other side. The doors closed and then began slowly to open again.

What they revealed was the child Mona as the Infanta from Velázquez, wearing a dress five times larger than she was. She came as far as the doorway and stood still, keeping her eyes on the far distance, playing perfectly the part of the princess too noble to survey her subjects, abstracted by her great role and destiny, smiling softly as the guests applauded her and declared her to be the success and surprise of the evening.

Immediately, Henry was disturbed by her, the flaunting of her female self, and her own poised alertness to her allure. He searched the faces of the other guests to see if anyone judged as he did on the strange precocity of the child, the unsuitable nature of the attention. But they took their seats in a spirit of innocence and hilarity.

When Henry turned to speak to the lady on his left, he did not recognize her. She was wearing an outlandishly large red wig and a great deal of face paint, but perhaps more importantly, she had not spoken. Once she did speak, he recognized her immediately as the lady who was staying at Dublin Castle, who had been ignored by the Wolseleys.

'Mr James,' she whispered, 'do not ask me if I was invited because I will have to tell you that I was not. My husband is refusing to speak to me and he is sulking back in the castle. But Lord Houghton, who dislikes rudeness, insisted that I come and he asked the other ladies to supervise my costume and render me unrecognizable.'

She glanced around her to see if anyone was listening.

'My husband says you go where you are asked, but the entire purpose of fancy dress is that these rules don't exist.'

He was concerned lest her neighbours should hear her and with his hand he cautioned her that she should lower her voice.

Mona was the focus of attention, the most honoured guest. Mr Webster, who was close to her, continually roared flattering remarks and ambiguous compliments at her; Lady Wolseley, sitting close to her husband, was high with excitement.

Hammond moved with a bottle in his hand pouring drinks. He remained calm and unflustered no matter how busy he was. He had, Henry felt, the most beautiful temper in the hall that night.

Henry did not dance, but had he done so he would surely have had to dance with Mona, because all the gentlemen did. As each dance ended, a new partner awaited her. In flirting with her and treating her as an adult, they succeeded, Henry thought, in mocking her. They paid no attention to the fact that she was a little girl who had dressed up and should be going to bed. Henry watched Hammond watching her, understanding that he might be the only other person in the room who viewed Mona's frolics with something less than complacency.

Most of the time Henry stood alone, or with another gentleman or pair of gentlemen, observing the dancing, the candles slowly burning down, the gowns and wigs increasingly tawdry in their appearance, the cheeks of the dancers burning red and the orchestra clearly tired. It suddenly struck him that what he longed for now was an American, preferably someone from Boston, a compatriot who would understand or at least appreciate, as nobody present seemed to, the strangeness here.

These were the English in Ireland. This building was an oasis with chaos and squalor all around. The Wolseleys had imported their silver as they had their guests and their manners. He liked Lord Wolseley and did not wish to judge him harshly. Nonetheless, he wished for the view of an American brought up on ideals of freedom and equality and democracy. For the first time in years, he felt the deep sadness of exile, knowing that he was alone here, an outsider, and too alert to the ironies, the niceties, the manners and, indeed, the morals to be able to participate.

As he woke from his reverie, he saw Hammond in front of him carrying still the deportment of high sympathy that he had exuded all evening. He seemed extraordinarily handsome. Henry took a glass of water from the tray and smiled at him, but neither of them spoke. In all likelihood, Henry realized, they would not meet again.

Across the hall, Mona was sitting on Webster's knee. He was holding her hands, rocking her up and down. Henry smiled at the thought of his imaginary American friend coming into the room now and witnessing this less than edifying scene. As he watched them, Webster caught his eye and shrugged carelessly.

It was late now and Hammond had joined the servants taking away glasses and cleaning the wax which had fallen from the candles onto the tables and the floor. Already he missed the glow of pleasure which Hammond's calm face had given him. Soon, it would be lost to him, and this made him feel that he was a great stranger, with nothing to match his own longings, a man away from his own country, observing the world as a mere watcher from a window. Abruptly, he left the Hall and walked briskly back to his own quarters.

CHAPTER THREE

March 1895

OVER THE YEARS HE HAD learned something about the English which he had quietly and firmly adapted to his own uses. He had watched how men in England generally respected their own habits until those around them learned to follow suit. He knew men who did not rise until noon, or who slept in a chair each afternoon, or who ate beef for breakfast, and he noticed how these customs became part of the household routine and were scarcely commented on. His habits, of course, were sociable and, in the main, easy; his inclinations were civil and his idiosyncrasies mild. Thus it had become convenient to himself, and simple to explain to others, that he should turn down invitations, confess himself busy, overworked, engaged both day and night in his art. His time as an inveterate dinner guest in the great London houses had, he hoped, come to an end.

He loved the glorious silence a morning brought, knowing that he had no appointments that afternoon and no engagements that evening. He had grown fat on solitude, he thought, and had learned to expect nothing from the day but at best a dull contentment. Sometimes the dullness came to the fore with a strange and insistent ache which he would entertain briefly, but learn to keep at bay. Mostly, however, it was the contentment he entertained; the slow ease and the silence could, once night had fallen, fill him with a happiness that nothing, no society nor the company of any individual, no glamour or glitter, could equal.

In these days after his opening night and his return from Ireland he discovered that he could control the sadness which certain memories brought with them. When sorrows and fears and terrors came to him in the time after he woke, or in the night, they were like servants come to light a lamp or take away a tray. Carefully trained over years, they would soon disappear of their own accord, knowing not to linger.

Nonetheless, he remembered the shock and the shame of the opening night of *Guy Domville*. He told himself that the memory would fade, and with that admonition he tried to put all thoughts of his failure out of his mind.

Instead, he thought about money, going over amounts he had received and amounts due; he thought of travel, where he would go and when. He thought of work, ideas and characters, moments of clarity. He controlled these thoughts, he knew that they were like candles leading him through the dark. They could easily, if he did not concentrate, be snuffed out and he would again be pondering defeats and disappointments, which if not managed could lead to thoughts that left him desperate and afraid.

He woke early sometimes and when such thoughts took over he knew that he had no choice but to rise. By operating decisively, as though he were rushing somewhere, as though the train were on time and he was late, he believed that he could banish them.

Nonetheless, he knew that he had to allow his mind its freedoms. He lived on the randomness of the mind's workings, and, now, as the day began, he found himself involved in a new set of musings and imaginings. He wondered how an idea could so easily change shape and appear fresh in a new guise; he did not know how close to the surface this story had been lurking. It was a simple tale, made simpler still by his friend Benson's father, the Archbishop of Canterbury, who had tried to entertain him one evening after the failure of his play. He had hesitated too much and stopped too often as he attempted to tell a ghost story, knowing neither the middle nor the end and unsure even of the contours of the beginning.

Henry had set it down as soon as he arrived home. He wrote in his notebook:

> Note here the ghost story told me at Addington (evening of Thursday 10th), by the Archbishop of Canterbury: the mere vague, undetailed, faint sketch of it: the story of the young children (indefinite number and age), left to the care of servants in an old country house, through the death, presumably, of parents. The servants, wicked and depraved, corrupt and deprave the children: the children are bad, full of evil to a sinister degree. The servants die (the story vague about the way of it) and their apparitions return to haunt the house and children.

He did not need to look back at his notebook to be reminded of the story; the events remained with him. He thought of setting it in Newport, in a remote house by the rocks, or in one of the newer mansions in New York, but none of these settings captured him, and gradually he abandoned the idea of an American family. It became an English story set in the past; and in the early and slow elaboration of the story he reduced the children to merely two – a boy and his younger sister.

He thought often of the death of his sister Alice, who had died three years earlier. He had read her diaries, so full of indiscretions, for the first time. Now he felt alone, much as she had throughout her life, and he felt close to her, although he never suffered her symptoms or maladies and lacked her stoicism and her acceptance.

In his darkest hours, he felt that both of them had somehow been abandoned as their family toured Europe and returned, often for no reason, to America. They had never been fully included in the passion of events and places, becoming watchers and non-participants. Their brother William, the eldest, and then Wilky and Bob, who came between Henry and Alice, had been ready for the world, expertly moulded, while Henry and Alice had been left unprotected and unready. He had become a writer and she had taken to her bed.

He could clearly remember the first time he sensed Alice's panic. They had been caught in the rain in Newport, having become too distracted by their own talk and laughter to pay attention to the darkening of the sky. She could have been fourteen or fifteen, but she had developed none of the strange, shy assurance of her cousins when they came to that age; their poised and careful way of coming into a room, or talking to a stranger, their easy and spontaneous way of being with friends and family, all this confidence Alice lacked.

It began to rain hard that hot summer's day and the sky over the sea was a purple-grey mass of cloud. He was wearing a light jacket, but Alice was wearing only a summer dress and a flimsy straw hat. There was no shelter at hand. A few times they tried to shelter under bushes but the rain, driven by the wind, was insistent. He took off his jacket and held it over both of them and they moved slowly and silently, huddled close together, towards home. He sensed her happiness as intense, almost shrill. He had never before understood the extent of her need for the full attention, the full pity and protection, of him or William or their parents. In these minutes, as they walked the wet sandy soil of the lane from the sea walk back to the village, he felt his sister on fire with satisfaction at being close to him. Watching her radiance and delight as they neared home, he had his first sense of how difficult things were going to be for her.

He began to watch her. Until now, he had considered the joke that William was going to marry her as a light tease, a way to make her smile and William laugh and all the family join in. It was also a show put on for visitors. William, the eldest, was six years older than Alice. As soon as Alice began to present herself to visitors, wear colourful dresses and become alert to the effect she could have on a roomful of adults, the joke that she was going to marry William became a kind of ritual.

'Oh, she's going to marry William,' Aunt Kate would say, and if William were there, he would come over to her, take her arm, kiss her on the cheek. And she would say nothing, merely watch everybody, her eyes almost hostile before their smiles and laughter. Her father would lift her and hug her.

'Oh, it won't be long now,' he would say.

Alice, Henry thought, never believed that she was going to marry William. She was rational and even when she was in her teens her intelligence had at its core a brittle anger. Yet because the idea that she would marry William had been spoken so many times, and because no outsider had presented himself as even vaguely plausible, the notion had entered surreptitiously but firmly into the silent places of her soul.

As he pondered and tried to shape the story of the two abandoned children told to him by the Archbishop, he found himself thinking about his sister's puzzling presence in the world. He went over the scenes where she had made clear to them her considerable intelligence and her raw vulnerability. She was the only little girl he had ever known, and now, as he began to imagine a little girl, it was his sister's unquiet ghost which came to him.

He remembered a scene when Alice must have been sixteen. It was one of those long dinners with one or two guests, he remembered, and someone was talking about life after death, and meeting members of their family after death, or hoping to, or believing they might. Then one of the guests, or Aunt Kate, had suggested praying to meet the loved ones in the next life when suddenly Alice's voice rose above all others and everyone stopped and looked at her.

'One need pray for nothing,' she said. 'Reference to those whom we should meet again makes me shiver. It is an invasion of their sanctity. It is the sort of personal claim to which I am deeply opposed.'

She had sounded like Emerson's aunt, someone steeped in the philosophy of life and death, someone who prided herself on the independence of her thought. It was clear to her family that she had a sharp mind and a great wit but that she knew that she would have to conceal them if she wanted to be like the other young women of her age.

Alice had friends and visitors and went on outings. She learned to be acceptable to the sisters of her brothers' associates. But Henry observed her when a young man came into the room and he noticed the change in her behaviour. She could not relax and her silences were full of force. She would become garrulous, talking a mixture of nonsense and paradox. There was a terrible shrillness and uneasiness about her. He saw how these social occasions must exhaust her.

Even family meals could be a trial for her, as Bob and Wilky learned to delight in teasing her and leaving her defenceless. These were the years of their father's great restlessness, when they crossed the Atlantic in search of something that none of them understood, a distraction from his father's passionate and eager bewilderment. They were dragged from city to city, hotel to apartment, tutor to school. They spoke French fluently and they knew themselves to be strange. It made all five of them stand apart from their generation; they knew both more and less than others. More about opulence and history and European cities, more about solitude and uncertainty, more about standing alone and being independent. Less about America, and the web of connections and affections being woven by their contemporaries. In these years, they learned to lean on each other, offer each other a private language, a containment, a coherence. They were like an old walled city. No one, no matter how strong the siege, could break down their defences. And Alice, as she grew older, was trapped inside.

Henry had no real memory of Thackeray's visit to the family table in Paris, although he remembered other sightings of him. The story was told and retold, and everyone in the family, including their mother, who was normally careful and reticent, believed that it merited recounting to every visitor.

Alice must have been eight or nine at the time. She had been placed beside the novelist and Henry knew that this could not have been easy for her. She would have been nervous about every gesture that she made, every morsel of food touched by her knife and fork. She would have spent the meal wondering what the great man thought about her. Henry knew that on these occasions her pulse would have been faster, her efforts to impress would have been complex and self-conscious and laborious.

He never remembered her wearing crinoline in those years, but the story centred on this. Thackeray turned to her and studied her attire.

'Crinoline!' he said. 'I never would have guessed. So young and so depraved!'

The remark, which might have been meant kindly, would have come as a sudden blow to his sister. In the moments that followed she would have felt only shame, as though a secret, dark part of her had been exposed. He imagined the suddenness of the remark, saw his sister's incomprehension, her attempt to smile. Henry alone understood the full cruelty of it, but he did nothing to silence the rest of them as they paraded the story in front of everyone who would listen, happiest if Alice were in the room to hear the story of her own humiliation at the hands of one of the most distinguished novelists of the age.

William was the eldest and the least vulnerable. No amount of travelling or disruption seemed to make any difference to him. He was strong and popular among his schoolmates. He was certain of his entitlement to be part of the next game. He loved shouting and noise; he loved loud companions. He loved banging doors and playing sport. No one noticed the bookish part of him, and he may not even have noticed it himself until he began to argue fearlessly with his father. He did so with such relish and exuberance that by his early teens he was doing to words and phrases and opinions what he had done previously to fences and well-tended lawns.

Alice tried to be sophisticated for William, a woman of the world, a French diarist of the eighteenth century. Their mother one day spoke of how deeply affected Ned Lowell had been by the Boston portrayed in Howells's new novel. Alice clearly wanted to say something, and they all turned to her. She could not begin. Her face was flushed.

'Oh, the poor dear!' she stammered out. 'If he is so affected by a novel, one wonders how he feels about the Sack of Rome, or indeed his own wife's flirtations.'

Once more, the table stopped. Their mother made as though to stand up, and moved her chair back. The others looked at Alice in surprise. William did not smile at her. She kept her eyes down. She had misjudged the moment, and they had learned how strange an impression she might make if she were to be let loose on the world.

That image of her stayed with him; the gap between her inner life in all its confused privacy and the life which had been mapped out for her intrigued him. As the long winter in London began to soften and the days lengthen, he worked on no novels, instead taking notes for stories and making some tentative beginnings. His sister's premature death haunted him, and the details of her strange life came to him when he least expected them, adding to his sense of unrecoverable past.

He remembered one night also when his sister must have been eighteen or nineteen. He had come back to the house with news of some sort, a lecture he had heard which would interest his father, or something he had published. He had walked in the door full of bright expectation to be met by his Aunt Kate who immediately alerted him to the fact that his sister was not well.

As he sat downstairs, he could hear Alice calling out. Both parents ministered to her, and Aunt Kate regularly ascended the stairs to hover near her room or join them briefly and then come back down to report to Henry in hushed tones. He could not remember precisely what term his aunt had used to describe Alice's trouble. Alice was having an attack, perhaps, or Alice was suffering from her nerves, but he knew that during the night both of his parents in turn had come to speak with him, and he had noticed their excitement at the new dilemma presented to them. Their nervous daughter and her strange illness deserved all their sympathy and attention.

That night, when her sobs did not die down in the room above, and he knew she was being held and comforted, Henry had noticed also that his mother, so often dismissed by Alice for her banal concern with the merely domestic, now was needed desperately by her daughter, and she seemed, in the dim light of the old parlour as she came down and sat with Henry, to derive a certain satisfaction in being so needed.

Nothing was as it seemed. He had an image for his story of a governess, a person full of sweetness and intelligence and competence, excited by the challenge of her new duties, her charges the boy and girl whom the archbishop had told him about. And he had an image also of his mother and his Aunt Kate, one of them carrying a lamp, entering the parlour where he sat, both appearing worried and exhausted, his mother's lips pursed but her eyes all bright and her cheeks flushed, both of them sitting with him as Alice's muffled cries came from upstairs, both women grim and dutiful in their chairs, more alive, more intensely involved than he had seen them for many years.

He had an image too of being in Geneva with Alice and Aunt Kate some years later, a time in which none of them dared say to Alice or to each other that her suffering seemed almost willed. They tried to name her malady, and the nearest her mother could come to describing it was to say that Alice was suffering from genuine hysteria. Her illness was incurable, Henry realized, because she looked after it and clung to it as though it were a visitor with whom she had fallen helplessly in love. In Geneva, during their tour of Europe, they must have seemed to onlookers, and at times even to each other, a picture of rare and dutiful New Englanders taking in the sights, observing the Old World with an intelligent and sensuous eye, the brother and sister travelling with their aunt in the time before they would settle. His sister had seemed to him at her happiest, her wittiest and her most hopeful.

He remembered how each afternoon the three of them would walk by the lake, Aunt Kate having ensured that Alice had rested enough in the morning.

'The geography book never mentioned,' Alice said on one of these walks, 'that lakes have waves. The whole of poetry will have to be rewritten.'

'Where shall we start?' Henry asked.

'I shall write to William,' Alice replied. 'He will know.'

'You must rest every day, my dear, and not write too many letters,' Aunt Kate said.

'How else shall I let him know?' Alice asked. 'Walking is more tiring than writing letters and all this fresh air shall, I fear, be the death of me.'

She smiled condescendingly at her aunt, who did not seem amused, Henry noticed, at the mention of death.

'Lungs love hotels,' Alice said. 'They long for them, especially the lobby and the stairs, but also the dining room and the bedroom, if it has a nice view and a shut window.'

'Walk slowly, my dear,' Aunt Kate said.

Henry watched Alice as she tried to think of a further remark which would amuse him and annoy Aunt Kate, and then, as they continued walking, she became briefly contented in her silence and in their company.

'The heart,' she then continued, 'prefers a nice, warm train and the brain, of course, cries out for an ocean liner. I shall convey all of this to William as soon as I return to the hotel, and we must walk fast, aunt, dear, slow walking is anathema to the memory.'

'If Dorothy Wordsworth,' Henry said, 'had let her brother know such things, then his poetry would, I think, have been much improved.'

'Was Dorothy Wordsworth not the poet's wife?' Aunt Kate asked.

'No, that was Fanny Brawne,' Alice said and smiled mischievously at Henry.

'Walk slowly, my dear,' Aunt Kate repeated.

That evening, as she came down to dinner, Henry noticed how carefully Alice had dressed and done her hair, and he knew that things might have been different for her if she had been a great beauty, or not an only girl, or if her intelligence had been less sharp, or her childhood more conventional.

'Could we move around the world staying in nice hotels, just we three, and writing letters home when some very witty remark is made by one of us?' Alice asked. 'Could we do this for ever?'

'No, we could not,' Aunt Kate said.

Aunt Kate took on the role, Henry remembered, of a stern but benevolent governess caring for two orphaned children, Henry obedient and considerate and reliable, and Alice flighty but also ready to do what she was told. And all three of them were happy in those months as long as they put no thought into what would happen to Alice when she returned home.

No one watching them could have guessed that Alice was already a strange and witty invalid. Alice came close in their company to recovery, but Henry knew even then that they could not travel from city to city with her for ever. Behind the smiling face and the figure who came so happily down the stairs of the hotel to meet them in the lobby each morning, there was a darkness ready to emerge when the time came. By then Alice's doom was somehow written into every aspect of her being, and, despite those days of equilibrium and happiness in Geneva, what was ahead for her had the shape of a story which now puzzled him and fascinated him, of a young woman who appeared to be light and ambitious and dutiful, but who would soon hear shrill sounds in the night and see frightening faces at the window and allow her daydreams to become nightmares.

The worst time for her was the period before and just after William's marriage, when she had her most severe nervous breakdown, an aggravated recurrence of her old troubles. In England, years later, she told him that most of her had died then, that in the hideous summer of William's marriage to a woman, pretty and practical and immensely healthy, whose name, most cruelly, was also Alice, Alice James went down to the deep sea, and the dark waters clouded over her.

Yet, despite her fearful and debilitating maladies, she maintained a strange mental energy; nothing she did was predictable, or without deliberate ironies and contradictions. When her mother died the family watched her closely, believing this would surely cause her final and complete disintegration. Henry stayed on in Boston, imagining ways he could help her and help his father. But Alice had no more attacks; she became, as plausibly as she could, the competent, dutiful and loving daughter, organizing the domestic life of the house with a light spirit and communicating with the rest of the family as though it were she who held things together. Before he left for London, he saw her one day standing in the hallway of the house as a visitor took leave, her arms folded and her eyes bright as she told the guest to come again soon. He watched her smiling warmly and then almost sadly as she closed the door. Everything about her in those moments, from her stance, to the expressions on her face, to her gestures as she turned back to the hallway, was borrowed from their mother. She was making an effort, Henry saw, to become the woman of the house.

Their father died within a year and once he was buried her act fell apart. She had developed a close friendship with Katherine Loring, whose intelligence matched hers and whose strength equalled her weakness in its intensity. Miss Loring accompanied her when Alice decided to come to England to avoid being cared for by her Aunt Kate, an act of defiance and independence and also, of course, a cry to Henry for help. She would live for eight more years, but they were spent mainly in bed. It was, as she often said, only the shrivelling of the empty pea pod which awaited completion.

HE REMEMBERED this as he waited for her at Liverpool, on her arrival in England, and he knew that her stubborn sense of purpose and preference, and her considerable inheritance from her father's estate, would, with the aid of Miss Loring, delay this completion for some time. He resolved not to entertain the idea that she would disturb his solitude and the fruitfulness of his exile. Nevertheless, he was frightened when he saw her, carried from the ship helpless and ill. She could not speak to him as he approached; she closed her eyes and turned her face away in distress when she thought he was going to touch her. It was clear that she should not have travelled. Miss Loring supervised the moving of Alice to suitable quarters and the finding of a nurse. She rather depended on the invalid state of his sister, Henry came to feel, as much as Alice depended on her.

She did not wish Miss Loring to leave her sight. She had lost her family and she had lost her health, but her will joined now with her intense need to have Katherine Loring to herself. Henry noticed Alice's deterioration verging on hysteria when Miss Loring was absent, and her taking quietly, almost happily, to her bed once Miss Loring promised to stay with her and minister to her. He wrote to his Aunt Kate and to William about this strange pair. He tried to make clear his gratitude to Miss Loring for her devotion, so generous and so perfect, but he knew that this devotion depended on Alice remaining an invalid. He was unhappy at the connection between them, the way it revelled in the unhealthy. He disliked Alice's abject dependence on her steadfast friend. Sometimes, he even believed that Miss Loring did his sister harm, but he could not see who, instead, would do her good and eventually he became resigned to Miss Loring.

Miss Loring stayed with Alice most of the time, caring for her, tolerating her, admiring her as no one ever had. Alice specialized in strong opinions and morbid talk, and Miss Loring seemed to enjoy listening to her as she expressed her views on death and its attendant pleasures, on the Irish question and the iniquity of the government, and on the nastiness of English life. When Miss Loring was away, however briefly, Alice became sad and indignant that she, who had sat at the table of her brothers and her father, the greatest minds of the age, was now left to the shallow mercies of an English nurse whom Miss Loring had employed.

Henry visited her as often as he could, even when she and Miss Loring took lodgings outside London. Sometimes he listened to her with wonder and fascination. She loved elaborate jokes, taking something small and odd and making it seem, by force of her personality, enormously funny. Mrs Charles Kingsley's devotion to her late husband was a topic she relished and she was apt to tell the story over and over with indignant mockery, demanding her visitors' agreement that it was worth the retelling quite before she had finished.

'Did you know,' she would say, 'that Mrs Charles Kingsley was devoted to her husband's memory?'

She would stop as though that were enough, there was no more to be said. And then, by a toss of her head, she would make clear she was ready to continue.

'Did you know that she sat with his bust beside her? When you visited Mrs Charles Kingsley, you had to visit her husband too. Both of them glowered at you.'

Alice glowered herself as though pure evil were being described.

'And what's more,' she went on, 'Mrs Charles Kingsley has her dead husband's photograph pinned to the adjoining pillow on her bed!'

She would close her eyes and laugh drily and at length.

'Oh a good night's sleep for Mrs Charles Kingsley! Can you think of anything more grotesquely loathsome?'

And then the doctors. Their visits and prognostications filled her with both contempt and glee, even when she was told she had cancer. One tiny foolish remark from a doctor provided conversation for days. She declared one day that she had been visited by Sir Andrew Clarke and his ghastly grin, as though the latter were a well-known appendage of his. And then, gasping, she would tell her story of how a friend, years before, had been kept waiting by Sir Andrew who announced himself upon arrival as 'the late Sir Andrew Clarke'.

'So I said to Miss Loring as we waited for Sir Andrew that I would bet money he would make precisely the same exclamation all these years later on coming into the room. "Hark," I said, the door opened and a florid gentleman came in, complete with his ghastly grin, and the phrase "the late Sir Andrew Clarke" fell from his lips, as though he were saying it for the first time, followed by a very ripe burst of hilarity from the same Sir Andrew, rather too ripe indeed.'

She watched herself expectantly for signs of dying, appearing as fearless in the face of mortality as she was fearful in the face of all else. She disliked the clergyman who lived in the apartment below and discussed her dread that he might, should she take ill in the night, minister to her at the end before he could be stopped.

'Imagine,' she said, 'opening your eyes for the last time and seeing this bat-like clergyman.'

She stared proudly into the distance as she spoke.

'It would spoil my post-mortem expression which I have been practising for years.'

She laughed bitterly.

'It is terrible to be an unprotected being.'

AS TIME WENT ON, he understood that his sister would not ever leave her bed and he discovered that Miss Loring took the same view. She vowed to remain with Alice to the end. This constant talk of 'the end' disturbed him, and sometimes when he watched the two of them together, the permanent patient and her companion, so cheerful and bustling and brisk, he felt an urgent need to be away from them, to cut short his stay, to return to his own hard-won solitude.

He wrote two novels during Alice's stay in England, which were saturated with the peculiar atmosphere of his sister's world. He understood the dilemma of a woman in an age of reform pulled between the rules of her upbringing and the need to change those rules, but also, and, he thought, more crucially, the dilemma of a woman brought up in a free-thinking family which confined its free thought to conversation and remained respectable and conformist in every other way. When he came to write *The Bostonians* he had no difficulty imagining the conflict between two people who seek power over a third. Such a struggle had occurred briefly between him and Miss Loring until he had abandoned it and left the field to her. In the other novel, *The Princess Casamassima*, also written after Alice's arrival in England, he wrote, at first without realizing, a double portrait of her. In one half she was the princess herself, subtle, brilliant and darkly powerful, recently arrived in London. The other half she must have recognized: she was Rosy Munniment, confined to her bed, 'a strange bedizened little invalid', a 'small, old, sharp, crippled, chattering sister', a 'hard, bright creature, polished, as it were, by pain'.

She read all his work, and expressed her great admiration for this new novel without mentioning the bedridden sister who is much disliked by the two main characters. In her diary she wrote of Henry's industry and William's success. It was not, she wrote, a bad show for one family, especially, she added, if I get myself dead, the hardest job of all.

Thus, having moved to London, she began to die in earnest, she who had played at dying for so great a duration. She longed, she told Henry, for some palpable disease, and the arrival of her cancer she viewed with enormous relief. She was only forty-three. She dreamed she saw a boat being tossed on the sea, and passing under a great black cloud she saw her dead friend Annie Dixwell who had looked back at her. She was ready to go to her.

Henry and Miss Loring watched over her as she weakened, her pain kept at bay by morphine. She seemed not to change at all and he wondered if she might slip away like this; die, as it were, without noticing. But her dying was not easy.

One day he came into her room and was startled by the change in her. She was in distress, breathing with difficulty, and her pulse, Miss Loring said, was weak and erratic. A fever had made her quiet, but at intervals a hard cough began until she retched and retched and then lay back exhausted. When she tried to speak, the cough returned and shook her to pieces, and then she became silent. The doctor said that there was no reason why she could not go on like this for days.

He watched her, desperate to offer any comfort. He was frightened for her, and believed that, despite everything she had said, she was frightened too. At every moment he expected she would go, and he waited knowing that she would need to say one last thing before sinking into death.

And then another change came. In a few hours all the pain and discomfort seemed to cease, and all the coughing and even the fever abated, and the deathly look on her face took on a new intensity. She did not sleep. As he sat close to her, he wished his mother were here to talk to her now with words which would help her to let go, to ease herself out of the world. He tried to picture his mother in the room, he almost whispered to her to come now into the room, hover here, mother, help Alice with your tenderness. He wanted to ask his sister if she could feel their mother's spirit in the room.

It was clear that she would not last, yet Katherine Loring insisted that he not stay into the small hours and he agreed that there was nothing he could do. He prepared to leave. But before he did he saw her becoming restless again, unable to turn in the bed and struggling to breathe. And then she whispered and both he and Miss Loring looked at each other sharply. Slowly, with effort, Alice raised her voice so that they could now hear her clearly.

'I cannot bear to live another day,' she said. 'I beg that it might not be asked of me.'

The words helped him as he walked slowly back through Kensington to his own chambers. He had always feared that when the end came for her it might be what she had dreaded most, that all her talk of wanting to die might turn out, in her last days, to have been mere bravado. He felt relieved that his sister had meant what she had said. He had watched her, knowing that in her place he would be terrified, but she was different. She did not flinch.

In the reaches of the night, Katherine Loring told him, she sank into a gentle sleep. As he began another day's vigil by her bed, he wondered about her dreams and hoped that the morphine made them golden and took away all the darkness and fear that had clouded her life. He willed her to be happy now. But he could not stop himself wanting her to go on breathing, despite everything, not to let go. He could not imagine her dead, having watched her dying for so long. The doctor, when he arrived, asked leave not to treat her, as she was in need of no further medical assistance.

For Henry, now almost fifty, this was his first death. He had not been present when his mother died nor his father. He had sat by his mother's dead body, but he had not witnessed her last breath. He had described dying in his books, but he had not known about this, the long day waiting as his sister's breath grew shallow, then seemed to fade, then rose again. He tried to imagine what was happening to her consciousness, her great barbed wit, and he came to feel that all that was left of her was her fitful breath and her weakened pulse. There was no will and no knowledge, merely the body moving slowly towards its end. And this to him made her even more pitiful.

Always, he had the image of the house of death as a silent place, still and watchful, but now he knew that there was no silence in this house because the sound of his sister's breathing, the changes in its levels of intensity, filled the air. Her pulse flickered and briefly stopped but still she did not die. He wondered if his mother's death had been like this. Alice was the only one who would know, the only one he could have asked.

He stood up and touched her as her breathing became easy and regular, her sleep peaceful. And this lasted an hour. She was still not ready to go, and he wondered who she was now, what part of her existed in these last hours? As her breathing stopped, he watched in alarm. He was unprepared, despite those days and nights of vigil. She took another breath, laboured and shallow. He wished once more that his mother was here to sit by him, hold his hand as Alice finally slipped away. Miss Loring now began to time her breathing, just one breath every minute, she said. As the end came, Alice's face seemed clearer in a way that was strange and oddly touching. He stood up and went to the window to let in some light and when he came back to the bed she had drawn her last breath. The room was finally still.

He stayed by her body, knowing that lying peacefully in death was what she had craved to do. She looked beautiful and noble, and he believed, after all his earlier doubts, that if she could see herself as her body awaited cremation, she would feel a grim delight at what she had become. It meant a great deal to him that her ashes would be returned to America to rest beside her parents in the cemetery in Cambridge. It consoled him that they would not bury her in England, would not leave her far from home in the wintry earth.

Her dead face changed as the light changed. She seemed young and old, exhausted and quite utterly beautiful. He smiled at her as she lay still, her face pale and drawn, yet exquisite and fine. He remembered her anger at being left a life interest in a shawl and other worldly goods by her Aunt Kate. Both he and his sister would die childless; what they owned was theirs only while they lived. There would be no direct heirs. They had both recoiled from engagements, deep companionship, the warmth of love. They had never wanted it. He felt they had both been banished, sent into exile, left alone, while their siblings had married and their parents had followed one another into death. Sadly and tenderly, he touched her cold, composed hands.

CHAPTER FOUR

April 1895

ONE EVENING AS HE RODE along in a rattling four-wheeler to go to dinner, an idea came to him for a story whose drama would reside in the peculiar and intense affection between an orphaned brother and sister. He did not immediately have a picture of the pair nor imagine anything about their direct circumstances. What came to him was vague and scarcely distinct enough to write in his notebook. The brother and sister were involved in a union of sympathy and tenderness which meant that they could read each other's feelings and impulses. They did not control each other, however; rather, they understood each other too well. Fatally well, he thought, and wrote that in his notebook without any idea of a plot or an incident which could illustrate it. Maybe it was too much, but the idea of a fused self stayed with him. Two beings with one sensibility, one imagination, vibrating with the same nerves, the same suffering. Two lives, but close to one experience. Both of them, for example, acutely aware of their parents' passing, the irrevocable loss involved haunting both of them with an almost paralysing pathos.

Often, ideas came like this, casually, without warning; often, they occurred to him at moments when he was busy with other things. This new idea for a story about a brother and sister developed with a sort of urgency, as something that he barely needed to write down. He would not forget it. It stayed fresh and clear in his imagination. Slowly and mysteriously, it began to fuse with the ghost story told to him by the Archbishop of Canterbury, and slowly he began to see something fixed and exact as though the processes of imagination themselves were as a ghost, becoming more and more corporeal. He saw the brother and sister, lonely and abandoned somewhere, banished siblings in a loveless old house, both of them operating with one mind, one soul, equal in their suffering and unpreparedness for the great ordeal which was to come their way.

Once it became more solid, the emerging story and all its ramifications and possibilities lifted him out of the gloom of his failure. He grew determined that he would become more hard-working now. He took up his pen again – the pen of all his unfor-gettable efforts and sacred struggles. It was now, he believed, that he would do the work of his life. He was ready to begin again, to return to the old high art of fiction with ambitions now too deep and pure for any utterance.

In the idleness of the afternoon sometimes he let his gaze wander through his notebooks again. One day he almost smiled to himself when he saw a few lines, which had seemed so promising less than three years earlier that he had allowed them to fill his workday and his dreams alike, the very lines which were the cause of the months of lethargy and pain and disappointment through which he now was emerging. He forced himself to read them to the end:

Situation of that once-upon-a-time member of an old Venetian family (I forget which), who had become a monk, and who was taken almost forcibly out of the monastry and brought back into the world to keep his family from becoming extinct. He was the *last* – it was absolutely necessary for him to marry. Adapt this somehow or other to today.

His eye moved quickly to the list of names, ghost names taken from obituaries and death notices, names for characters and places, names which could lie inert in his notebooks or could still be used; he could spend day after day giving life to them. *Beague – Vena (Xtian name) – Doreen (ditto) – Passmore – Trafford – Norval – Lancelot – Vyner – Bygrave – Husson – Domville.* Those last eight letters had been placed on the page in all innocence. He had no memory now of where the name had come from, nor indeed the exact provenance of any of the names which came before it. Nor had he any real idea why that name had been used, and the others, left there, had not. The note and the name seemed distant now, and it appeared extraordinary to him that his play had arisen from such unpromising beginnings and, once it was replaced by a new play by Oscar Wilde, had suffered an equally unpromising end.

HIS PARENTS dying, he thought, had brought with it a strange relief. It was the sense that it could not happen again, his mother's body could lie in repose only once, she could be consigned to the earth on only one occasion. And that occasion, in all its black brutal sorrow, had passed. With his parents dead and Alice gone, he had believed that nothing could touch him. Thus his failure in the theatre remained a shock, something whose intensity and sharpness he had never thought he would have to deal with again. It was, he had to admit, close to grief, even though he knew that such an admission was a kind of blasphemy.

He knew that he would suffer no further indignity at the hands of theatre audiences; he would devote himself, as he had pledged, to the silent art of fiction. If only he could work now, his days could be perfect, full of the delight of solitude and the pleasure wrought from finished pages.

Not long after his return from Ireland, as he settled himself into a routine of reading and letter writing and the creation of domestic order, his young friend Jonathan Sturges came with news, and he was soon followed by Edmund Gosse with the same news. It concerned Oscar Wilde.

Wilde had been much on Henry's mind over the previous months. His two plays were still running at the Haymarket and the St James's. Henry had no difficulty adding up the money Wilde had been making. He wrote to William about it, noting one of the new phenomena of London life, the inescapable Oscar Wilde, suddenly successful rather than preposterous, suddenly industrious and serious rather than someone busy wasting his time and that of others.

Both Sturges and Gosse offered information, however, which Henry did not pass on to William nor indeed to anyone else. Both his friends enjoyed knowing and telling fresh news and he allowed each to feel that he was the first, partly because he was not sure that he wanted either of them to know that the antics of Oscar Wilde were matters much discussed under his roof.

Even before he went to Ireland, Henry had heard that Wilde had abandoned all due discretion. He was doing as he pleased in London and telling whomsoever he pleased about it. He was everywhere, flaunting his money, his new success and fame, and flaunting also the son of the Marquess of Queensberry, a boy as deeply unpleasant as his father, in Gosse's opinion, but rather better-looking, Sturges allowed himself to admit.

Henry presumed that what was relayed to him by his two visitors was known to all. He knew that Wilde's relationship with Queensberry's son was common knowledge, but both Sturges and Gosse appeared to feel that they and a mere few others knew the details, and the details, they insisted, were so appalling they could scarcely be whispered. Henry watched them calmly and ordered tea for them and listened carefully to their delicate phrasing of matters which were not, to say the least, very delicate. Boys from the street, Gosse called them, but Sturges amused him more by mentioning, sotto voce, young men whose abode was not very fixed.

'He orders them as you would a cab,' Gosse finally made himself clear.

'For payment?' Henry asked innocently.

As Gosse nodded gravely, Henry was tempted to smile, but he too remained grave.

It did not strike him as odd or shocking; everything about Wilde, from the moment Henry had first seen him, even when he had met him in Washington in the house of Clover Adams, suggested deep levels and layers of hiddenness. Had Gosse or Sturges told him that Wilde went out every night dressed as a clergyman's wife to give alms to the poor, it would not have surprised him. He remembered something vague being told to him about Wilde's parents, his mother's madness or her revolutionary spirit, or both, and his father's philandering or perhaps, indeed, *his* revolutionary spirit. Ireland, he supposed, was too small for someone like Wilde, yet he had always carried a threat of Ireland with him. Even London could not contain him with two plays and many rumours all running at the same time.

'Where is Wilde's wife?' he asked Gosse.

'At home waiting for him, with unpaid bills everywhere and two young sons.'

Henry could not picture Mrs Wilde and did not think he had ever met her. He did not even know, nor did Gosse, whether she was Irish or not. But the idea of the two boys, who looked like angels, Gosse had assured him, struck him forcibly. He imagined the two sons waiting for their monstrous father to return and was glad he did not know their names. He thought of them, both unaware of their father's reputation, yet slowly gathering an impression of him and longing for him now that he was away.

Despite the fact that he believed, as the gossip came his way, that he had the measure of Wilde, he held his breath and moved about the room in silence when Gosse told him that Wilde was suing the Marquess of Queensberry in open court for calling him a sodomite.

'It seems that he could not even spell the word,' Gosse said.

'Spelling, I imagine, was not ever his strong point.' Henry stood at the window glancing out as though expecting Wilde or the marquess himself to appear on the street below.

Gosse managed to imply at all times that his information came from the highest and most reliable source. He suggested somehow that he was in touch with members of the cabinet, or the prime minister's office, or on certain occasions an informant close to the Prince of Wales. Sturges, on the other hand, made it clear that all he knew came from club gossip, or chance meetings with informants who might not be entirely reliable. The visits of Gosse and Sturges never coincided during these frenzied weeks, which was fortunate, Henry thought, as each of them came bearing precisely the same information.

Gosse began to call every day, Sturges merely when there was news, although once the trial opened Sturges came daily too. There was always some embellishment and some new piece of intrigue. Gosse had met George Bernard Shaw who had told him of his meeting with Wilde, of his warning him not to bring the case against the Marquess of Queensberry. Wilde had agreed, Shaw said, that it would not be wise, and everything was settled until Lord Alfred Douglas arrived, brazen and petulant, as Shaw had described him, demanding that Wilde sue his father and attacking those who advised caution, insisting that Wilde leave with him there and then. Douglas was red-faced with anger, Shaw said, a spoiled boy. The strange thing though was that Wilde seemed totally under his power, followed him and appeared to give in to him. He melted under the heat of the young man's anger.

Sturges was the first to arrive with the news of what the Marquess of Queensberry intended to tell the court.

'He has, I've been told, witnesses. Witnesses who will not spare us any detail.'

Henry looked at Sturges's young face and his wide-eyed expression. He wanted to pat him on the shoulder and tell him that he was eager to hear the detail, all of it, as soon as it was known, he wanted to be spared nothing.

The story of Wilde filled Henry's days now. He read whatever came into print about the case and waited for news. He wrote to William about the trial, making clear that he had no respect for

Wilde, he disliked both his work and his activities on the stage of London society. Wilde, he insisted, had never been interesting to him, but now, as Wilde threw caution away and seemed ready to make himself into a public martyr, the Irish playwright began to interest him enormously.

'I HAVE HEARD news of the greatest import.' Gosse did not wait to sit down before he spoke, and moved as though he were standing on the deck of a ship.

'I believe that Douglas's father will produce a number of scallywags. Young unwashed boys will give evidence against Wilde and, I have been told, their evidence will be irrefutable.'

Henry knew that there was no need to ask questions. He did not, in any case, quite know how to frame the question that needed to be asked.

'I have seen the names of the witnesses,' Gosse said dramatically, 'and they include a number of worms. Wilde, it seems, has been consorting with worms, with thieves and blackmailers. The price must have seemed cheap at the time, but it seems now it will cost him dear.'

'And Douglas?' Henry asked.

'I am told that he is up to his neck in this. But Wilde wants him kept out of it. It seems when Wilde was finished with his filthy young purchases he passed them on to Douglas, and God knows who else. It appears there is a list of those who rented these boys.'

Henry noticed that Gosse was watching him, waiting for his response.

'It is a dreadful business,' he said.

'Yes, a list,' Gosse said, as though Henry had not spoken.

NEITHER STURGES nor Gosse went to the trial, yet they both seemed to know the exchanges by heart. Wilde, they said, was confident and arrogant. He spoke, Sturges said, like someone who could burn his boats because he was about to go to France. He was witty and lofty, careless and contemptuous. Gosse heard from his usual sources one evening that Wilde had already taken off, but the following day when it was clear that this had not happened, Gosse did not mention it. Nonetheless, both of Henry's informants were sure that he would go to France and both also had names for the boys who would give evidence and spoke of them as personages, each with his own different character and profile.

On the third day of the trial, Henry noticed a new intensity in the tone of both Gosse and Sturges. They had separately been up late the night before and discussing the case; had waited until they knew that Wilde had turned up in court that day so that they could come with fresh news. Gosse had spent part of the previous evening with the poet Yeats, who, Gosse said, was alone among those to whom he had spoken in his admiration for Wilde and had nothing but praise for his courage. The poet had attacked the public for its hypocrisy, Gosse said.

'I was not aware,' he added, 'that the public had been trawling in the sewers and I told Yeats so.'

'Does he know Wilde?' Henry asked.

'They're all Irish together,' Gosse said.

'Does he know him well?' Henry persisted.

'He told me an extraordinary story,' Gosse said. 'He told me of a Christmas Day he spent with the Wildes. The house, he said, was more beautiful than anyone has mentioned, everything white and full of strange and beautiful objects. Chief among them, he said, was Mrs Wilde herself, who is clever and quite beautiful, according to Yeats. And the two boys, he said, were curly-headed pictures of innocence and sweetness, perfect creatures. It was all perfect, he said, a household of infinite perfection, not only great taste, but great warmth, he said, and great beauty and great love.'

'Obviously not enough,' Henry said drily, 'or perhaps too much.'

'Yeats intends to call on him,' Gosse said. 'I wished him luck.'

Sturges listened carefully as Henry, for once, passed on what Gosse had told him.

'It is all clear,' Sturges said. 'Bosie is the love of his life. He would give up anything for him. Wilde has found the love of his life.'

'Then why can he not take him to France?' Henry asked. 'That is where such people are normally taken.'

'He may still go to France,' Sturges said.

'The fact that he has not yet gone is inexplicable,' Henry said.

'I think I know why he has not gone,' Sturges said. 'I have spent much time discussing it with those who know him, or at least think they do, and I think I might know.'

'Do pray tell,' Henry said, placing himself in a chair by the window.

'In one short month,' Sturges said, speaking slowly as though thinking ahead to the next phrase, 'he has sat in an audience for two of his plays and witnessed triumph, universal praise and his name in large letters. For any man it would be unsettling. No man should make a judgement who has recently published a book or put on a play.'

Henry did not say anything.

'In this time,' Sturges went on, 'he has also been to Algeria, if you can imagine, and news of some of his activities there has filtered back. It seems that neither he nor Douglas was shy in making himself known to the local tribes, and the excitement must have been unsettling for Wilde and, indeed, for the tribes, if for no one else.'

'I can imagine,' Henry said.

'And when he returned, he was homeless, he has lived in hotels. And also, he has no money.'

'That is not the case,' Henry said. 'I have calculated his income from the theatre. It is very high.'

'Bosie has spent it for him,' Sturges replied, 'and he had debts to match. I believe that he has not enough money to pay his hotel bill and the manager has captured his belongings, such as they are.'

'That does not prevent him from going to France,' Henry said. 'He can acquire some belongings there, perhaps even make significant improvements to them.'

'He has lost his moorings, lost his judgement,' Sturges said. 'He is incapable of making a decision. The success and the love and the hotel rooms have been too much for him. Also, he believes that it will be a blow for Ireland but I can make nothing of that.'

ONCE THE TRIAL was over, it was clear to Gosse that Wilde, if he did not flee, would be arrested. As each hour went by, since the police knew where he was, his being charged with indecency and worse was more and more likely, with witnesses appearing from the sewers of London, Gosse said.

'There is a list, as I told you, and there is great fear in the city and a great determination on the government's side, I am told with some authority, that rampant indecency will be stamped out. I fear there will be other arrests. I have heard names. It is rather shocking.'

Henry studied Gosse and paid attention to his tone. Suddenly, his old friend had become a rabid supporter of the stamping out of indecency. He wished there were someone French in the room to calm Gosse down, his friend having joined forces, apparently, with the English public in one of their moments of self-righteousness. He wanted to warn him that this would not help his prose style.

'Perhaps a period of solitary confinement will help Wilde,' Henry said. 'But not the martyrdom. One would wish that on no one.'

'Apparently, the Cabinet has discussed the list,' Gosse went on. 'The police, it seems, have already questioned people and many have been advised to cross the channel. And I believe that many are crossing as we speak.'

'Yes,' Henry said, 'and besides the moral climate I think they will find the diet rather better over there too.'

'It is unclear who is under suspicion, but there are many rumours and suggestions,' Gosse continued.

Henry noticed Gosse watching him.

'It is advised, I think, that anyone who has been, as it were, compromised should arrange to travel as soon as possible. London is a large city and much can go on here quietly and secretly, but now the secrecy has been shattered.'

Henry stood up and went to the bookcase between the windows and studied the books.

'I wondered if you, if perhaps . . .' Gosse began.

'No.' Henry turned sharply. 'You do not wonder. There is nothing to wonder about.'

'Well that is a relief, if I may say so,' Gosse said quietly, standing up.

'Is that what you came here to ask?' Henry kept his eyes fixed on Gosse, his gaze direct and hostile enough to prevent any reply.

STURGES CONTINUED to visit in the period leading up to Wilde's trial, when Wilde was in custody and all possibility of going to France had faded.

'His mother, I am told, is jubilant,' Sturges said. 'She believes he has delivered a great blow against the Empire.'

'It is difficult to imagine him having a mother,' Henry said.

Henry asked his two visitors and anybody else whom he saw in these weeks if they knew anything about Wilde's two golden children whose very name was disgraced for ever. It was Gosse who came with the news.

'Although he is bankrupt, his wife is not. She has her own money and has moved to Switzerland, as far as I know. And she has changed her name and that of her sons. They no longer bear their father's name.'

'Did she know about her husband before the trial?' Henry asked.

'No, I understand that she did not. It has been an enormous shock to her.'

'And what do the boys know?'

'I cannot tell you that. I have not heard,' Gosse said.

For days he thought about them, watchful, beautiful creatures in a country where they could not understand a word of the language, their very names obliterated, their father responsible for some dark, nameless crime. He thought of them in some turreted Swiss apartment house in high rooms with a view of the lake, their nurse refusing to explain why they had come all this way, why there was so much silence, why their mother kept apart from them and then suddenly came close to them as though they were in danger. He thought of how little they would need to say to each other about the demons that were around them, their new name, their great isolation, the upheaval which had resulted in their spending days alone together in those cold rooms, as though waiting for a catastrophe to unfold, their father a ghostly memory, standing smiling at them on the bare half-lit landing as they climbed the staircase, beckoning in the shadows.

WHEN WILDE had been sentenced and the scandal surrounding London's dark underworld had died down, Henry's relationship with Edmund Gosse returned to what it had been, as Gosse himself underwent a restoration of his old self. Immediately after Wilde was imprisoned, Gosse ceased to sound like a member of the House of Lords.

One afternoon, as they sat in Henry's study drinking tea, an old subject of theirs, which had been much on Henry's mind, arose. The subject was John Addington Symonds, a friend and correspondent of Gosse, who had died two years earlier. Of all the people, Henry said, who would have been fascinated by every moment of the Wilde case, surely JAS, as he called him, would have been the most intrigued. It would almost have made him come back to England.

'He would have loathed Wilde, of course,' Gosse said, 'the vulgarity and the filth.'

'Yes,' Henry said patiently, 'but he would have been captured by what came into the open.'

Symonds had lived mainly in Italy and had written with great, perhaps too great sensuousness about the landscape and the art and the architecture. He became a connoisseur of Italian light and colour, but he also became an expert on another more dangerous matter, what he called a problem in Greek ethics, the love between two men.

Ten years earlier, Henry and Gosse had discussed Symonds as avidly as they discussed Wilde during the trial. This was when Gosse moved less freely among the powerful, and there had been a tacit understanding between them that these preoccupations of Symonds mattered to both of them personally, an understanding which had lessened as the years passed.

Throughout the 1880s Symonds, writing from Italy, made no secret of his own leanings. He wrote explicit letters to all his friends and many who were not his friends. He sent his book on the matter to those in England whom he thought might initiate a debate. Many who received the book were infuriated and embarrassed. Symonds wanted it brought into the light, discussed openly, and this, Henry remarked to Gosse at the time, was a sign of how long he had been out of England, how many years he had been basking in Italian sunshine. Gosse was interested in public life and wished to discuss the implications of what Symonds was saying for legislation or public attitudes. Henry, on the other hand, became fascinated by Symonds. By this time Henry had received several letters from Symonds about Italy, and had by chance, several years before, sat beside Symonds's wife at dinner. He remembered her as mostly silent, quite dull, and he failed to recollect, when he became interested in her case, a single word she had said.

Yet he brought away a sense of her, as someone with fixed opinions, hardened attitudes, and as Gosse continued to tell him more about Symonds, Henry began to work his imagination on

Mrs Symonds, as though he were a portrait painter. She was, Gosse said, in no sort of sympathy with what her husband wrote, she disapproved of his tone when he wrote about Italy, the hyper-aesthetic manner he had developed appalled her, and then she loathed his entire concern with love between men. She was, to start with, Gosse said, of a narrow, cold, Calvinistic disposition, as morbid in her search for moral purpose as her husband was in search of ultimate beauty. One of them, Gosse said, seemed to aggravate the other so that as time went by Mrs Symonds increasingly craved the sackcloth while her husband longed for Greek love.

Gosse spoke idly of the Symondses and did not realize how Henry was taking this in. The story came to Henry, in any case, so quickly and easily that he did not have time to tell Gosse. He set to work.

What if such a couple had a child, a boy, impressionable, intelligent, alert to the world around him and deeply loved by both his parents? How would the child be educated? How would the child be taught to look at life? He listened to Gosse and asked questions and from the answers began to construct his story. His first ideas emerged later as too stark and so he abandoned the ambitions of the parents for their son − one wanting the child to serve the Church, the other, the father, wanting the child to become an artist. Instead he dramatized the idea that the mother merely wanted to save her son's soul, and in order to do so she needed to protect him from his father's writings.

He wondered at first if he should allow the child to grow up a lout and an ignoramus, as far away as possible from his mother's hopes and his father's ambitions. But as he worked, alone, away from Gosse's conversation, he decided to deal only with the boy, and to make the time frame of the story short and dramatic. And he would bring in an outsider, an American, an admirer of the father's work, one of the few who understood the father's true genius. The father, he thought, could be a poet or a novelist or both. The American is very kindly received, he remains near the family for some weeks, weeks which coincide with the child's illness and death. The American understands something which the father does not know – that during the night, as the child lay ill, his mother made up her mind secretly that it were better he should die, and she watched him sink, holding his hand, but doing nothing, allowing him for very tenderness to fade away. The American never imparts this information to the author he so much admires.

Henry wrote down the bones of the story one night after Gosse had departed and then worked steadily, daily. He knew that it would take prodigious delicacy of touch, and even then would probably be too gruesome and unnatural. Nonetheless, the story intrigued him, and he thought he would try it, for the general idea, corruption and Puritanism and innocence, was also full of interest and typical of certain modern situations.

Gosse, he remembered, had been frightened by the appearance of the story in the pages of the *English Illustrated* magazine. Most people would recognize the Symondses, he said, and those who did not would imagine that the subject was Robert Louis Stevenson. Henry told him that the story was now written and published; it did not cost him a thought who recognized themselves or others. Gosse remained nervous, knowing how much he had contributed. He insisted that writing a story using factual material and real people was dishonest and strange and somehow underhand. Henry refused to listen to him. In retaliation, Gosse began to refrain from providing him with his usual store of gossip. Soon, however, his friend forgot his objections to the art of fiction as a cheap raid on the real and the true, and began once more to tell Henry all the news he had picked up since their last meeting.

As Sturges told Henry that Wilde's wife had travelled from Switzerland to tell her prisoner husband personally of his mother's death, he mused once more on the fate of the children of a union between two opposing forces. He pictured himself and William at the window of the Hôtel de l'Ecu in Geneva when he was twelve and William thirteen and their time in Switzerland seemed to him an eternity of woe: infinite hours of dullness, the dingy streets, the courtyards and alleys black with age. He imagined Oscar Wilde's two sons, their names changed and their fate uncertain, watching from a window as their mother departed. He wondered what they feared most now when night came down, two frightened children in the unforgiving city, its shadows steep and sombre, half knowing why their mother had left them in the care of servants and haunted by unnamed fears and barely grasped knowledge and the memory of their evil father who had been shut away.

CHAPTER FIVE

May 1896

HIS HAND HURT HIM. If he wrote with it, moving the pen calmly with no flourishes, then he did not feel even a mild discomfort, but when he stopped writing, when he moved his hand about, he could, on turning a door handle, for example, or shaving, feel an excruciating pain in his wrist and the bones which ran towards his little finger. Lifting a sheet of paper was a form of mild torture now. He wondered if this were a message from the gods to keep writing, to wield his pen at all times.

Every year as the summer approached he felt the same persistent dull worry which led eventually to panic. As transatlantic travel became easier, and more comfortable, it also became more popular. As time went by, his many cousins in America seemed to develop many more cousins of their own, and his friends many more friends. In London all of them wished to visit the Tower and Westminster Abbey and the National Gallery, and over the years his name had been added to the list of the great local monuments, essential to see. As soon as the evenings lengthened and the swallows returned from the south, the letters began to arrive, letters of introduction and what he called letters of determination from the very tourists themselves, certain that their visit to the capital would lack all due shine were they to miss the famous writer and not receive the benefit of his company and counsel. Should his gates be locked to them, their letters implied – indeed, they often insisted and implored – then they would not get full value for their money, and this he discovered meant more and more to his compatriots as the century came to an end.

He remembered what he had written in his notebook the previous year; it was a scene which had been on his mind since then. Jonathan Sturges had told him of a meeting in Paris with William Dean Howells, now almost sixty. Howells had told Sturges that he did not know the city, all of it was new to him, and every sensation came to him freshly. Howells seemed sad and brooding, as if to suggest that it was too late for him in the evening of his life when he could do nothing except take in the sensations and regret that they had not come to him when he was young. Then, in response to something Sturges had said, Howells laid his hand on his shoulders and exclaimed: 'Oh you are young, be glad of it and live, live all you can, it's a mistake not to. It doesn't so much matter what you do – but live.' Sturges had acted out the lines, making them into a strange and plaintive appeal, a sudden burst of drama, as though Howells were speaking the truth for the first time.

Henry had known Howells for thirty years and corresponded with him regularly. Whenever Howells came to London, he behaved as though he were at home there, as though he were a well-travelled cosmopolitan gentleman. Henry was amazed then by his response to Paris, the sense Sturges got from him that he had not lived at all and that it was too late for him now to begin to do so.

Henry wished that London made his American guests express themselves as Howells did. He wished that the visits instilled awe or regret, or caused them to understand the world and their place in it as never before. Instead, he listened as they told him and each other that there were towers in the United States too, and that some of their own correctional institutions compared rather favourably in size, if nothing else, with the Tower of London. And, in addition, their own Charles River seemed to serve its purpose more efficiently than the Thames.

Nonetheless, as each summer came around, watching London through his visitors' eyes interested him; he imagined himself as them, seeing London for the first time, just as he imagined the lives he could have lived when he went to Italy or on his return visits to the United States. A new streetscape, even a single building, could fill him with thoughts about who he might have become, who he might be now had he stayed in Boston or spent his days in Rome or Florence.

For him as a boy and for William, and perhaps even for Wilky and Bob and maybe even Alice, the reasons given for moving from Paris to Boulogne or from Boulogne back to London, or from Europe in general back to the United States, never seemed as solid as their father's own restlessness, his great agitation, which they knew but never managed to understand. The finding of a haven only to be uprooted after a time, or the arriving, as his family did throughout his boyhood, at an unfortunate lodging, not knowing how long it would take his father to announce that they would soon have to depart, made him long for security and settlement. He could not think why his family had translated themselves from Paris to Boulogne. He must have been twelve or thirteen then, and there may have been a crisis on the stock exchange or a failure of some leaseholder to pay rent or an alarming letter about dividends.

In the time they lived in Boulogne, Henry walked with his father on the beach. On one of those occasions, it was a windless and calm day, the beginning of summer, with a long sandy expanse and a wide sweep of sea. They had been to a cafe with large clear windows and a floor sprinkled with bran in a manner that for Henry gave it something of the charm of a circus. It was empty save for an old gentleman who picked his teeth with great facial contortions and another gentleman who soaked his buttered rolls in his coffee, to Henry's fascinated pleasure, and then disposed of them in the little interval between his nose and chin. Henry did not wish to leave, but his father wanted his daily walk on the beach and thus he had to abandon his delight in observing the eating habits of the French.

His father must have talked as they went along. The image in his mind now, in any case, was of him gesticulating, discussing a lecture or a book or a new set of ideas. He liked his father talking, especially when William was elsewhere.

They did not paddle or walk too near the waves. His memory was that they walked briskly. His father may even have carried a stick. It was a picture of happiness. And for a stranger watching, it might have remained like that, an idyllic scene of a father and son at ease together in the late morning on the beach in Boulogne. There was a woman bathing, a young woman being watched by an older woman on the beach. The bather was large, perhaps even overweight, and well protected from the elements by an elaborate bathing costume. She swam out expertly, allowing herself to float back with the waves. Then she stood facing out to sea letting her hands play with the water. Henry barely noticed her at first as his father stopped and made as though to examine something on the far horizon. Then his father walked forward for a while, silently, distracted, and turned back to study the horizon once more. This time Henry realized that he was watching the bather, examining her fiercely and hungrily and then turning away, observing the low dunes behind him, pretending that they also interested him to the same intense degree.

As his father turned away once more and began walking towards home, he sounded out of breath and did not speak. Henry wanted to find an excuse to run ahead and get away from him, but then his father turned again, the expression on his face vivid, the skin blotched and the eyes sharp as though he were angry. His father was now standing on the shore, trembling, watching the swimmer who had her back to him, her costume clinging to her. His father made no further effort to seem casual. His stare was deliberate and pointed, but no one else noticed it. The woman did not look behind, and her companion had moved away. It was important, Henry knew, for him to pretend that this was nothing; there was no question that this could be mentioned or commented on. His father did not move, and seemed unaware of his presence, but he must have known he was there, Henry thought, and whatever this was, this keen-eyed drinking in of the woman bather, it was enough to make his father not care about Henry's presence. Finally, as he turned and set out on the journey home, his father stared back regularly with the look of someone who had been hunted down and defeated. The woman, once more, swam out to sea.

HENRY LOVED the softness of the colours on the beach near Rye, the changing light, the creamy clouds moving across the sky as though with a purpose. He had spent the last few summers here, and this summer in particular, as he walked briskly, trying for once to enjoy the day without making plans, he could not stop asking himself what he wished for now, and answering that he wanted only more of this – calm work, calm days, a beautiful small house and this soft summer light. Before he left London, he had purchased the bicycle which now lay waiting for him in the lane that led to the beach. He realized that he did not even want the past back, that he had learned not to ask for that. His dead would not return. Being freed of the fear of their going gave him this strange contentment, the feeling that he wanted nothing more now but for time to move slowly.

He wished every morning when he stood on his terrace that he could find some way to catch this picture of beauty and keep it close to him. The terrace was paved and curved like the prow of a ship and it overhung a view both as pure and as full of change as an expanse of sea. And below was Rye, the most un-English of English places, red-roofed with meandering streets and clustered buildings, an Italian hill town with cobbled streets, its atmosphere sensuous, but reticent also and austere. He walked the streets of Rye almost every day now, studying the houses, the old shops with small-paned windows, the square church tower, the weathered beauty of the brick. Back home, his terrace was his opera box, from where he could survey all the kingdoms of the earth. His terrace, he thought, was as amiable as a person, perhaps even more so. He wished he could buy this house; he knew that he had already begun to resent the owner's plans to retake the cottage at the end of July.

In June there was hardly any night at all. He lingered on the terrace as a slow mist came over the valley and a mild, gauzed darkness fell. Within a few hours there would be hints of the beginning of dawn. His only visitor in these days of industry and indolence wrote once again to confirm his arrival and departure. Oliver Wendell Holmes junior was an old friend, become now a distant one, part of a group of associates, young men he had known in Newport and Boston, who had become eminent in their thirties and were now leading influences on the age. When they came to England, they appeared mysterious to him, so confident, so adept at finishing their sentences, so used to being listened to, and yet they seemed to him, compared with men of their kind in England and France, oddly raw and boyish, their brashness a kind of innocence. His brother William had all of that too, but it was only one half of him; the other half was made up of a deep self-consciousness where all his rawness and freshness had been buried in irony. William knew the effect which his own deliberate and complex personality could have, but this was something that their contemporaries, who held power in the literary world in the United States, or in the law, knew nothing about. They remained natural, and this, for Henry, was a matter of enormous interest.

Thus William Dean Howells could fall for Paris, having built no defences against the sensuous world, defences that any European man of his age would assiduously and carefully have developed. Howells was ready to be seduced by beauty and pre-pared to feel deep regret that beauty had passed him by in Boston. Henry loved the yearning openness of Americans, their readiness for experience, their eyes bright with expectation and promise. As he worked on his novels of English morals and manners, he felt the dry nature of the English experience – sure of its own place and unready for change, steeped in the solid and the social, a system of manners developed without much interruption for a thousand years. On the other hand, these educated and powerful American visitors seemed so shiny, so ready to be new, so sure that their moment had come that now, as he sat on his terrace in the twilight, he felt their force, how much could still be done with them, how little attention he had paid them in recent years. He was glad then that he had invited Oliver Wendell Holmes to stay at Point Hill and he vowed that he would see him in London also if he could. He who had come to dread these interruptions found himself rather interested in this one.

When he began to picture Holmes, to place him against the background of when he had first known him, he remembered the aura of certainty and dependability which lay about his friend. Even at twenty-two Holmes had believed that the world he inhabited was a world in which he would thrive. He was formed like a planing machine to gorge a deep self-beneficial groove through life. He made sure that when fresh experience came his way it was rich and rewarding and gave him pleasure. As he learned to think, however, his mind became like a stiff spring. He was caught thus between the venal and the exacting and it made his presence nervous and exciting. He had found a public voice, a way of holding himself and forming sentences and formulating policy and judgement, to ensure that the personal and the carnal would be held in check and not have to be on parade. He could be pompous and intimidating when he pleased. Henry had known him too well to be affected by this, yet, at William's instigation, he had paid enough attention to Holmes's role as a judge to be deeply impressed by him at the same time.

From William, too, he learned about aspects of Holmes which Holmes was careful never to display to him. Holmes loved, it seemed, to talk lightly of women to his old friends. This was something which offered William considerable amusement, especially when he learned that Holmes never alluded to such matters when Henry was present. In company, William insisted, Holmes also loved to refight the battles of the Civil War and explain his wounds to the assembled listeners.

'When it gets late,' William said, 'Holmes becomes like his father, the old doctor and autocrat. He enjoys his own often-told anecdotes and loves a listener.'

William expressed incredulity that Holmes, in his meetings with Henry over the previous thirty years, had never mentioned the Civil War.

'It's all day long and then through the night, William went on, bullets whizzing and rifles and men charging and the dead lying everywhere and the wounded beyond description. And, indeed, his own wounds, even when there are ladies present he discusses his wounds. The only wonder is that he did not die of them. Surely he has shown you his wounds?'

Henry remembered that this conversation had taken place in William's study. He could see William enjoying his own tone, allowing himself freedoms with his brother that he normally reserved for his wife.

Henry remembered with satisfaction how the conversation had ended.

'What then do the two of you talk about?' William asked. He seemed to want real information, a factual response.

Henry hesitated and looked into the distance, then focussed his eyes carefully on a number of leather-bound volumes on a far shelf, and quietly responded, 'Wendell is formed, I fear, to testify simply and solely about himself.'

HE WAITED on his terrace after supper as night came down. Holmes, he remembered now, generally spoke to him about his career, his colleagues, new cases, new developments in law and politics and then new conquests he had made among the British aristocracy. He gossiped about old friends and boasted about new ones, speaking freely and solemnly. Henry loved his worldliness, his practised, clipped sentences and then a sudden burst of something else when he allowed himself to use words and phrases which hardly belonged to the law or the war, but more to the pulpit or the essay. Holmes loved to speculate, argue with himself, explain his own logic as though it were a side in a battle with opposing forces and much interior drama.

Henry did not mind what Holmes said. He saw him seldom and knew that what connected them was simple. They were part of an old world, fully respectable and oddly Puritan, led by the enquiring, protean minds of their fathers and the deeply cautious, watchful eyes of their mothers. They both had a sense of their destiny. More precisely, they belonged to the group of young men who had been to Harvard and who had known and loved Minny Temple, had sat at her feet and sought her approval and whom she haunted as they grew into middle age. In her company, they remembered, their experience had meant nothing, nor their innocence either, as she demanded something else from them. She elated them, and they felt a strange and insistent nostalgia when they recalled the time when they knew her.

She was Henry's cousin, one of six Temple children, left as orphans when their parents died. For Henry and for William, the idea of the Temples not having parents made their cousins interesting and romantic. Their position seemed enviable, as all authority over them was vague and provisional. It made them appear free and loose, and it was only later, as each of them struggled in various ways, and indeed suffered, that he understood the unrecoverable nature and the deep sadness of their loss.

There was, between the time when he envied them and the time when he pitied them, a long gap. When he first reencountered Minny Temple aged seventeen, not having seen her for some years, the sentiment was still very much one of admiration, even awe. He instantly knew that she, among her sisters, would be special for him and that she would remain so. There were many words to describe her: she was light and curious and spontaneous and she was natural – that was important – and, perhaps, he felt, her lack of parenting gave her a sort of ease and freshness; she had never had to reflect anyone, or seek to become like anyone, or fight against such influences. Maybe, he later thought, in the shadow of so much death, she had developed what was her most remarkable feature – a taste for life. Her mind was restless; there was nothing she did not want to know, no matter on which she did not wish to speculate. She managed, he thought, to combine a questioning inner life with a quick sense of the social. She loved coming into a room to find people there. More than anything else, he remembered her laugh, its suddenness and its richness, but also its lightness, the strange, touching, ringing sound of it.

She had not, when she struck him first with all her moral force, appeared so ethereal. She came to Newport with one of her sisters and they seemed to him beautiful and clear-eyed and free, being looked after lightly at the time by their aunt and uncle. On that first visit Minny had argued with Henry's father. Henry had never known a time when people did not argue with his father. As soon as he could listen, he had witnessed William and his father in deep discussion which involved raised voices and heated divergence of views. Most male visitors and some female ones too seemed to come to the house specifically to argue. Freedom of all sorts, and especially religious freedom, was his father's great subject, but he also had many others; he did not believe in confining himself, it was one of his principles.

Minny Temple sat in the garden and at first listened silently to Henry's father, who was addressing most of his remarks to William, nodding at times in the direction of Henry and the Temple sisters. There was a jug of lemonade and some glasses on the low garden table, and it might have been an ordinary, easy summer gathering of cousins amusing themselves at the feet of the older generation. Everything his father said had been uttered many times before, but despite this William grinned in encouragement as his father began now to discuss women and their deep inferiority and the need for them to remain not only subservient but patient.

'By nature,' he spoke quickly and emphatically, 'woman is inferior to man. She is man's inferior in passion, his inferior in intellect and his inferior in physical strength.'

'My father has many convictions,' William said amiably. He smiled at Minny, but she did not return his smile. Her gaze was still and serious. She sat up straight, seeming unrelaxed as if poised to speak. His father noticed her discomfort, and looked at her impatiently. For a few moments, the group was silent, waiting to see if she would say something. Her voice was low when she eventually began so that the old man had to strain to hear her.

'Perhaps it is my very inferiority,' she said, 'which causes me to wonder.'

'Wonder what?' William asked.

'Do you really wish to know?' she asked. She almost laughed.

'Say it out,' the father said.

'Very simply, sir, I wonder if what you are saying is true.' Suddenly, her tone was direct and clear.

'Do you mean you don't agree with it?' William asked.

'No, I don't mean that,' Minny said. 'If I had meant that I would have said it. I meant what I said. I wonder if it is true.' A sharpness had entered her tone.

'Of course it's true.' The old man's eyes displayed his anger now. 'A man is physically stronger than a woman. That much is clear, that much is true, if true is the word you want. And in passion a man is stronger, as I have said. And in intellect. Plato was not a woman, nor Sophocles, nor Shakespeare.'

'How do we know Shakespeare was not a woman?' William interjected.

'Does what I have said satisfy you, Miss Temple?' the father asked.

Minny did not answer him.

'It is a woman's job,' he went on, 'to be submissive. To see to her needlework and her cooking and her preparation to become the sleepless guardian of her husband's children. We judge a woman by her obedience and her attention to duty.'

His voice had become rancorous and he was obviously annoyed.

'Thus spake our father,' William said.

'Is that settled then?' the old man asked Minny.

'Not at all, sir. Nothing is settled.' She smiled at him. Her expression was almost condescending as she continued. 'Very simply, I do not know if being physically weaker than man means we understand less, or live less intelligently in the world. You see, I have the evidence close at hand which is my own weak mind, but I do not think it is weaker than anyone else's.'

'Women must live in Christian humility,' Henry senior said.

'Is that in the Bible, sir, or is it one of the Commandments, or did you learn it at school?' Minny asked.

By suppertime the news had spread. Mrs James, Aunt Kate and Alice had been alerted to the outrage which had occurred.

'She will not mind women cooking for her and keeping house for her,' Henry's mother said to him as they met in the hallway. 'She has not been disciplined and she has not been cultivated, and we must pity her because her future will be grim.'

IN THE SUMMER of 1865, the Civil War over and his first two stories published, Henry prepared to spend the month of August with the Temples in New Hampshire. Oliver Wendell Holmes, who had refused an invitation to Newport, agreed to go to North Conway, where the Temples were staying, once he discovered that there would be abundant female company. He was to travel with Henry, and John Gray, also fresh from the Civil War, was to follow. Henry wrote to Holmes to tell him that Minny Temple, after superhuman efforts, had ferreted out a single room, the only one in the area, and that the wretch who owned the room had, despite Minny's protests and her charm, refused to furnish the room with two beds.

They would, Henry told him, pull the fellow's own bed out from under him. In the meantime, Minny had her eye peeled for another bed, or indeed another room. Holmes seemed thrilled at the idea of an enemy who could be made to hand over his bed to his visitors. As they travelled to North Conway, he listed the tactics they could use, mentioning several technical terms and placing himself in the foreground as leader and hero and placing Henry, two years younger than he and not a veteran of any war, merely as a decoy. He did not seem to mind when Henry fell asleep.

They were to go for supper, as invited, at the house where the Temple girls were being chaperoned by their great-aunt, who looked, in Henry's opinion, like George Washington. But first, on arrival at North Conway, they set out to find directions to their lodgings, and, after several wrong turns, they discovered a large and surly landlord who managed instantly to express his dislike for people who were not born and bred in North Conway and its immediate surroundings. Neither Holmes's uniform, which he was wearing, nor his moustache, seemed to impress him. The landlord did not look at Henry. One bed, he said, that's what he had told the lady, and one bed it was, but the room had a nice clean floor and you could sleep a whole regiment there, he added insolently as he gave them the key.

The room was bare, except for a washstand, a jug and basin, a closet and a small iron-framed bed covered by a strangely beautiful coloured quilt out of keeping with the spartan decor. They left their luggage at the door, as if unsure that they were going to stay.

'I believe we should call for reinforcements and attack him forthwith,' Holmes said.

Henry tested the bed, which sagged in the middle.

'Perhaps it is the sort of room which benefits from its inhabitants remaining outdoors,' Henry said.

He picked up a small lamp from the floor.

'I fear,' he said, 'that every moth in New Hampshire has visited this shrine. It looks as though it came with the founding fathers.'

'Is your cousin Minny wise?' Holmes asked.

'Yes, she is,' Henry said.

'In that case, I am sure she has found us another room.'

Henry went to the small window and looked out. The day was still bright and the smell of pine filled the air.

'In the meantime,' he turned to Holmes laughing, 'I don't mind if you don't, as the lady said when the puppy dog licked her face.'

'It is, I fear, going to be a long month,' Holmes said.

MINNY AND TWO of her sisters were sitting on chairs on the back lawn when their cousin and his friend arrived. Henry was deeply conscious now of what Minny must look like to Holmes. She was not beautiful, he thought, until she spoke, or until she smiled. And then she managed a sympathy for her company and exuded a deep seriousness and a high good humour at the same time. Henry instantly thought that Holmes preferred her two sisters, Kitty and Elly, who were more conventionally pretty, more polite and shy than their sister.

As soon as they sat down, Henry noticed that Holmes became a military man, a Civil War veteran who had seen many battles and come close to death. Suddenly, military tactics were no longer a joke. The three Temple girls, whose brother William had been killed in the war, and their great-aunt stared at the soldier sadly and admiringly. Henry watched Minny carefully to see if all Holmes's talk impressed her as much as it seemed to, but she gave nothing away.

After supper the two young men walked back to their room, happy with the news that Minny had found them other quarters to which they could move when John Gray arrived. Holmes was in good spirits; he had enjoyed the girls' company and knew that he had a receptive audience, young and graceful and cheerful, for the duration of his stay. He made jokes and laughed, working out further methods of unsettling the landlord and winning the battle for the extra bed.

Neither of them had discussed how they would actually sleep, whether one of them would try the floor, or whether they would sleep head to toe, or alongside each other. Henry knew that Holmes would decide, and he lingered at the window while he waited for him to do so. Holmes, in the meantime, made brave efforts to light the lamp.

When it was lit, the room, in all its spareness and its shadows, seemed larger, more inviting; the quilt took on a new radiance. Holmes became serious, as though he were concentrating hard on a difficult subject. He moved to the basin with a bar of soap and a towel he had taken from his bag. He poured water from the jug into the basin and then quickly undressed until he was naked. Henry was surprised at how large-boned and strong Holmes seemed, almost fleshy in the quivering, shadowy light. For a second, as his friend remained still, he could have been a statue of a young man, tall and muscular. As Henry watched him, he forgot his moustache and his craggy features. He had never imagined he would see him like this. He supposed undressing as Holmes had done meant nothing to someone who had been a soldier for so long. Yet surely he knew that it was different, in the silence of the night in this strange, bare room, to undress completely in front of his friend? Henry studied his strong legs and buttocks, the line of his spine, his delicate bronzed neck. He wondered if Holmes would put his underwear back on before he went to bed. He too began to undress, and he was almost naked when Holmes opened the window and flung out the dirty, soapy water. Holmes replaced the basin and walked naked to the bed, moving the lamp close to him.

Henry did not know if Holmes was watching him as he stood, naked now, at the basin. He was acutely conscious of himself, lacking the ease and confidence which Holmes had just displayed. He washed himself slowly, and when Holmes spoke to him he half turned to find his friend lying in the bed with his hand behind his head.

'I hope you don't snore. We had a way of dealing with people who snored.'

Henry tried to smile and turned away. When he had dried himself and thrown the water out of the window, he knew that he would have to turn and that Holmes was now nonchalantly and casually watching him. He was embarrassed and still did not know if Holmes expected him to lie naked in the bed beside him. He was unsure if he should ask if this was the plan.

'Can you put out the lamp?' Henry asked.

'Are you shy?' Holmes asked, but he did not put the lamp out.

Henry turned and moved slowly towards the bed with his towel hanging loosely over his shoulder, half covering his torso. Holmes's eyes were amused and involved. As Henry dropped the towel, Holmes leaned over and turned off the lamp.

They lay side by side without speaking. Henry could feel the bone of his pelvis hitting against Holmes. He wondered if he could suggest moving to the bottom of the bed but somehow, he understood, Holmes had taken control and silently withheld permission for him to make any suggestions. He could hear his own breathing and sense his own heart beating as he closed his eyes and turned his back on Holmes.

'Goodnight,' he said.

'Goodnight,' Holmes replied. Holmes did not turn but lay flat on his back. To make sure that he did not fall out of the bed, Henry had to move closer to him, but then moved away, keeping near the edge, yet still touching Holmes, who lay impassive.

He wondered if he would ever again be so intensely alive. Every breath, every hint that Holmes might move, or even the idea that Holmes too was awake, burned in his mind. There was no possibility of sleeping. Holmes, he thought, must have his arms folded on his chest, and there was no sound from him. His very immobility suggested that he was lying awake and alert. Henry longed to know if Holmes were as conscious as he was of their bodies touching, or if he lay there casually, unaware of the mass of coiled heat which lay up against him. The following day they would move to other rooms, so it would not be like this again for them. It had not been planned, and Henry had put no thought into it until he had seen Holmes by lamplight moving naked at the washstand. Even now if there was a choice, if another bed became available, he would go there instantly, creep out of here through the darkness. Nonetheless, he felt his powerlessness as a kind of ease. He was content not to move or speak, and he would feign sleep if he needed to do so. He knew that his remaining still and his silence left Holmes free, and he waited to see what Holmes would do, but Holmes did not move.

Since leaving Boston with Holmes he had felt a strange lack of tension and this had remained with him all evening. He knew what it was. William was not with them, having gone on a scientific expedition to Brazil. His older brother's absence had, he knew, lightened things for him, removed a source of pressure which often became oppression, however mild. Holmes was William's friend, a year older than William, yet Holmes had none of William's ability to undermine him, or allow him to feel that every word he said, or every gesture, would be open to censure, or correction, or mockery.

Now suddenly Holmes moved towards the centre of the bed. His movement seemed to Henry like an act of will and not the unconscious movement of a man in his sleep. Quickly, without leaving himself time to think, Henry edged his way closer to Holmes, and they lay thus without stirring for some time. He could feel Holmes's breathing presence, his large bony frame, close to him now, but he was careful to keep his breathing as shallow and quiet as he could.

When Holmes turned away from him, as he did now as suddenly as he had turned before, Henry realized that it would be his fate to lie here through the night, his mind racing, with this figure beside him, who was perhaps unaware of him, used to the company of men at close quarters. Holmes had, he now believed, fallen asleep. Henry did not know whether he was disappointed or relieved, but he wished he too could fall unconscious so that he would not have to think again until morning.

After a time, however, he became sure that Holmes was not sleeping. As they lay back to back he could feel the carefully tensed presence against him. He waited, knowing it was inevitable that Holmes would turn, inevitable that something would occur to break this silent, slow, deadlocked game they were playing. Holmes, he felt, was as consciously involved as he was in what might happen.

He was not surprised then when Holmes turned and cupped him with his body and placed one hand against his back and the other on his shoulder. He knew not to turn or move, but he sought to make clear at the same time that this did not imply resistance. He remained still as he had done all along, but subtly he eased himself more comfortably into the shape of Holmes, closing his eyes and allowing his breath to come as freely as it would.

He dozed and woke briefly and dozed again. When he woke finally, the room was bright with sunshine, and what surprised him now, with Holmes already awake, was how unafraid his friend was to catch his eye or come close to him again. He imagined that what had happened between them belonged to the secret night, the privacy that darkness brought. He knew that this would never be mentioned between them, nor mentioned by either of them to anybody else, and so he presumed that daylight would make all the difference to them. Also, he knew enough about what Holmes had been through in the war to know that he had stared evenly at death, had suffered painful injuries, and, more importantly, at the ages of twenty-one and twenty-two had learned a steely fearlessness. Henry had not supposed that this fearlessness could make its way so completely into the private realm, but it did so now in this rented room in New Hampshire in the bright morning.

By eleven the two men were washed and dressed, their luggage repacked, their landlord paid, and they were ready to present themselves at the court of the Temple sisters. They sat once more on the chairs on the back lawn and made plans for walks and outings. As the tea was served and the conversation began, Henry felt as though he had been dipped in something; what had happened lingered as an obsession importunate to all his senses; it lived now in every moment and in every object; it made everything but itself irrelevant and tasteless. It came to him so powerfully as he drank his tea and listened to his cousins that he had to remind himself that it was not still in progress, and a new day had begun with a new day's duties.

As time went by, he noticed that Minny was remaining apart from the plans and seemed unusually quiet and reserved. He spoke to her alone when the others were busy with further talk and laughter.

'I did not sleep,' she said. 'I don't know why I did not sleep.'

He smiled at her, relieved that her distance from them was something which could be rectified.

'And did you sleep?' she asked.

'It was not easy,' he said. 'The bed was not comfortable, but we managed. Despite the bed perhaps, rather than because of it.'

'The famous bed!' She laughed.

WHEN JOHN GRAY arrived that afternoon, Henry noticed that Holmes, who, even in the short time away from other soldiers, had lost some of his military glow, now continued his role as the veteran of a war, and Gray did everything possible to complement that role and take it on, indeed, himself. They were led to an old farmhouse a few miles from the Temples' quarters where each of them was given an attic room by a friendly young farmer's wife. The floorboards creaked and the beds were old and the ceilings were low but the fare was reasonable and the husband, when he appeared, offered to ferry the young gentlemen through the neighbourhood should they require transport. Indeed, he added in a friendly, earnest tone, should they require anything at all, he would provide it if he could at the most reasonable rates in all of North Conway.

Thus began their holidays, the two men of action settling into the world of easy civilian life. It was a little realm of relaxed and happy interchange, of unrestricted conversation, with liberties taken while delicacies were observed, allowing the discussion of a hundred human and personal things as the American summer drew out to its last generosity.

Henry basked in the afterglow of his introduction to North Conway. It played for him the part of a treasure kept at home in safety and sanctity, something he was sure of finding in its place each time he returned to it. He watched his friends, waiting for a pattern to emerge, conscious that he wanted his two fellow guests to appreciate Minny Temple as he did, to differentiate her from her two sisters, sweet and charming as they were, knowing that Minny was the glittering spirit among them. He found himself silently promoting her, attempting also in various small ways to quicken their appreciation of her. When he saw Holmes engaging with her, he felt deeply implicated in what passed between them, and wanted nothing more than to witness their growing interest in one another.

Gray's tone was dry; in his regiment and in his own domestic setting he had obviously been listened to a good deal, and his study of the law now added to his language a Latinate vocabulary of which he grew fonder as the days went on. He had much to say about books, and each day would cross his legs and clear his throat and talk to the ladies about Trollope, how droll and excellently drawn his characters were, how fascinating his situations, how strong his grasp of the rich public life of his country, what a pity no American novelist had emerged who could compete with him.

'But does he,' Minny interjected, 'does he understand the real intricacies of the human heart? Does he understand the great mystery of our existence?'

'You have asked two questions, and I will answer them separately,' Gray said. 'Trollope writes with precision and feeling about love and marriage. Yes, I can assure you of that. Now, the second question is rather different. Trollope, I believe, would take the view that it is the function of the preacher and the theologian, the philosopher and perhaps the poet, but emphatically not that of the novelist, to deal with what you call "the great mystery of our existence". I would tend to agree with him.'

'Oh, I don't agree with either of you then,' Minny said, her face bright with excitement. 'When you close *The Mill on the Floss*, for example, you know much more about how strange and beautiful it is to be alive than when you read a thousand sermons.'

Gray had not read George Eliot and when presented with a copy of *The Mill on the Floss* by an enthusiastic Minny he flicked through the pages judiciously.

'She is,' Minny said, 'the person in the world I most adore, the person I would most like to meet.'

Gray looked up quizzically, suspiciously.

'She understands,' Minny went on, 'the character of a generous woman, that is, of a woman who believes in generosity and who feels keenly how hard it is, practically, to,' she stopped for a moment to think, 'why, to live it, to follow it out.'

'Follow "it" out?' Gray asked. 'What's the "it"?'

'Generosity, as I said,' Minny replied.

Minny also handed Gray a copy of the March issue of the *North American Review* which had a story by Henry called *The Story of a Year*. She told him that while she and her sisters had been forbidden to read Henry's previous story, full, they were told, of highly French immorality, they had been permitted to read his new one. Over the previous days, Henry, a novice in the matter of publication, had waited for Holmes to say something about the story. He knew Holmes had told William that he believed the mother in the story was based on his mother and the soldier was based on him. Suddenly then, William had a new and interesting way to tease Henry. The Holmes family, he told him, was in a rage and old father Holmes was going to complain to Henry's father. Later, William had confessed that he had invented most of this, except for Holmes's original comments.

Holmes had said nothing. Now Henry watched Gray crossing the garden with a chair in one hand and the *North American Review* in the other to find a shady place in which he could sit and read the story. Henry was nervous about Gray's response, but pleased also that the story could now be mentioned. He imagined Gray reading it with the sharp eye of a war veteran, finding not enough about the action of the war and finding too much about women. Watching him begin the story, and being able from the vantage point of another chair in the garden some distance away from him to see him proceed, was difficult, almost unnerving. After a while he could manage it no more, he had had enough, and he took a long walk that afternoon and did not come back until suppertime.

As soon as they were sitting down, Minny spoke.

'So, Mr Gray, what did you think of the story? For me, it is so exciting having a cousin who is a writer, it is exciting beyond imagining.'

Henry realized, and he wondered if Minny did too, the effect her words would have on the two young men who had offered their lives for their country. For them, the war remained raw and fresh, and their very presence was a reminder to all of the great losses and heroism of their side. In her enthusiasm for Henry's story, Minny now seemed to be lessening the importance, indeed the excitement, of having two soldiers at her table.

'Interesting,' he said, and seemed ready to leave it at that.

'We all loved it and are so proud of it,' Elly, Minny's sister, said.

'If it had not had his name on it,' Gray said, 'I would have guessed that the author was a woman, but perhaps that was part of your plan.'

He turned to Henry, who looked at him but did not speak.

'He wrote a story, not a plan,' Minny said.

'Yes, but if you think about the war, or speak to those involved, or even read about it, I'm sure there are more interesting stories, ones that are more true to life.'

'But this wasn't about the war,' Minny said. 'It was about a girl's heart.'

'Are there not plenty of girls who can write such stories?' Gray asked.

Holmes put his hands behind his head and began to laugh.

'We cannot all be soldiers,' he said.

The talk between the three visitors and the Temple sisters returned again and again to the war. Since the girls' brother and their cousin Gus Barker had been killed, the two soldiers had to be careful not to gloat too much about their survival, or their bravery. Nonetheless, it was difficult to avoid discussing specific exploits and the extraordinary phenomenon of injured soldiers such as Henry's brother Wilky and Holmes himself and Gus Barker who insisted, once recovered, on returning to the fray. Holmes and Wilky had lived to receive more injuries and survived them too. Gus Barker, however, had been killed by a sniper two years earlier, when he was barely twenty, at the Rappahannock River in Virginia. All of them grew silent now as his name and the place where he died were mentioned.

Henry had seen him on return trips to America during his childhood at his grandmother's house in Albany, where he had also met the Temples, and later at Newport. As the others started again to talk about him, Henry's mind wandered back to five years earlier when the Civil War seemed an impossible nightmare and the James family had returned to Newport from Europe so that William could study art.

One day in the fall of 1860 Henry had come into the studio to find his cousin Gus Barker standing naked on a pedestal while the advanced students sketched him. Gus was strong and wiry, red-haired and white-skinned. He stood immobile and unembarrassed as the five or six students, including William, worked on their drawings as though they did not know the model. Gus Barker, like the Temples, had lost his mother, and his orphanhood gave him the same mystery and independence. No mother could arrive to tell him to cease this display and put on his clothes forthwith. His form was beautiful and manly, and Henry was surprised by his own need to watch him, while pretending that his interest in Gus Barker, like that of the other students, was distant and academic. He studied William's drawing closely so that he could then raise his eyes and study at some length his naked cousin's perfect gymnastic figure, his strength, and his calm sensual aura.

It struck him all these years later that he had been thinking something which he could not tell Gray or Holmes or even Minny, that his mind during these few minutes had wandered over a scene whose meaning would have to remain secret to him. He simply did not suppose that Gray's mind worked like that, or the mind and imagination of Holmes, or the Temple sisters. He did not even know if his brother William's mind moved into areas that would always have to remain obscure to those around him. He thought about the result if he spoke his mind, told his companions as truthfully as he could what the name Gus Barker had provoked in his memory. He wondered at how, every day, as they moved around each other, each of them had stored away an entirely private world to which they could return at the sound of a name, or for no reason at all. For a second as he thought about this, he caught Holmes's eye, and he found that he had not been able to disguise himself fully, that Holmes had seen through his social mask to the mind which had strayed into realms which could not be shared. Both of them shared something now, tacitly, momentarily, which the others did not even notice.

Gradually, then, over the days, Minny Temple made a choice. She chose subtly and carefully so that no one saw at first that she had done so, but what was not apparent to Gray or Holmes or her sisters became clear to Henry because she wished it to be clear to him. She chose Henry as her friend and confidant, the one she trusted most, could speak to most easily. And she may have chosen Holmes for something too because she never ignored him, or shone her light on the others more than on him. But she chose Gray as the one on whom she could have most effect, who most needed her. She paid no attention to his military talk and his gruff, practical comments and his clipped witticisms. She wished to change him, and Henry watched her gently cajoling him, without allowing herself to become offensive.

One day when she handed Gray lines of Browning to read, he held back and asked her to read them aloud.

'No, I want you to read them to yourself,' she said.

'I can't read poetry,' he said.

Henry and Holmes and her two sisters did not speak; this, Henry knew, was a decisive moment in Minny's fight to mould John Gray into a shape acceptable to her.

'Of course you can read poetry,' she said, 'but you must first forget the "read" part and the "poetry" part and concentrate on the "I" part and find new credentials for it, and soon you will be a changed man and your youth will return. But if you really want me to, then I will read the verse aloud.'

'Minny,' her sister said, 'you must not be abrupt to Mr Gray.'

'Mr Gray is going to be a great lawyer,' Holmes said. 'He is learning to defend himself, I feel, so that he will in time learn to defend others more worthy of defence, perhaps.'

'I long for you to read it aloud,' Gray said.

'And I long for the day when you will read it too, quietly and with emotion,' Minny said taking the book.

HENRY BEGAN to imagine an heiress, recently orphaned, who had three suitors, a young woman whose patient intelligence had never been fully appreciated by those around her. He did not want to make her as beautiful as Minny was that August; instead, he made his heroine positively plain but for the frequent recurrence of a magnificent smile. He made two of the suitors military men; the third, who gave his name to the story, Poor Richard, whose manner was that of a nervous headstrong man, brought close to desperation by unrequited love, was a civilian. Richard adored Gertrude Whittaker, but she did not take him as seriously as she took the two Civil War soldiers. One of them, Captain Severn, was himself a serious and conscientious man, who was discreet, deliberate and unused to acting without a definite purpose. And Major Lutrell, on the other hand, who could play the part of Gray, was both agreeable and insufferable. All three began a siege to win Miss Whittaker's love and marry her. In the end, she accepted none of them.

The story began for him in a small single moment in which Richard watches Captain Severn sinking into a silence very nearly as helpless as his own as they observe the progress of a lively dialogue between Miss Whittaker and Major Lutrell. So too at North Conway had this become for Henry and for Holmes a daily routine, as Minny continued her battle to soften Gray, to make him more conscious of his soul than his uniform, of his deepest fears and longings rather than of his self-protective army talk, suitably censored for ladies. Holmes began by believing that Minny did not like Gray, which pleased him, and then became aware with flashes of alarm that Gray was winning. Holmes's alarm made a sound that Minny and her sisters and Gray were too distracted to hear, but which Henry picked up easily and stored and thought about when he was alone.

He did not realize then and did not, in fact, grasp for many years how these few weeks in North Conway – the endlessly conversing group of them gathered under the rustling pines – would be enough for him, would be, in effect, all he needed to know in his life. In all his years as a writer he was to draw on the scenes he lived and witnessed at that time: the two ambitious, patrician New Englanders, already alert to the eminence which awaited them, and the American girls, led by Minny, fresh and open to life, so inquisitive, so imbued with a boundless curiosity and charm and intelligence. And between them much that would have to be left unsaid and a great deal that would never be known. Already, on that lawn beside the house where the Temple sisters stayed that summer, there were secrets and unstated alliances, and already a sense that Minny Temple would escape them and soar above them, although none of them had an idea how soon this would happen and how sad it would be.

He had no memory of when he first knew she was dying. Certainly, that summer there was no intimation of any illness.

He remembered that some time later his mother had mentioned Minny's being poorly, her tone disapproving, as though believing at first that Minny's illness was a way of drawing attention to herself.

Their group met once more in his parents' parlour in Quincy Street near the end of the following year; he recalled how surprising it was to find that Minny had been corresponding with both Gray and Holmes. His mother, he remembered, liked Gray and thought he was as nice as ever, nicer than Holmes, and reported later that Minny had told her she was quite disenchanted with Holmes and had talked to her of Holmes's egotism, but also his beautiful eyes. Henry was surprised that Minny now seemed to be confiding in his mother.

He sat on his terrace now thousands of miles away and many years later. As the crescent moon appeared, he studied its strange, thin, implacable beauty, and sighed as he remembered William coming into his room with the news that Minny had a deposit on her lung. Henry was not sure that this was his first hearing of the news, but he was certain that it was the first time it was not whispered. Henry recalled his own depression in the months that followed, his own immobility, and he knew that he had not seen her, but was kept abreast of the news by his mother, who was keenly interested in the illness of everyone, but especially young women of marriageable age, and was now taking Minny's illness seriously.

He tried to think when John Gray had told him first of Minny's long letters to him. Gray had found them difficult, somewhat embarrassing, he said, confidential and feverish, but he had replied, and so she wrote to Gray over and over in the last year of her life. And in one of those letters she had written the words which Gray had repeated to him and which Henry thought now maybe meant more to him than any others, including all the words he had written himself, or anyone else had written. Her words haunted him so that saying them now, whispering them in the silence of the night, brought her exacting presence close to him. The words constituted one sentence. Minny had written: 'You must tell me something that you are sure is true.' That, he thought, was what she wanted when she was alive and happy, as much as when she was dying, but it was her illness, her knowledge that time was short, that made her desperate to formulate the phrase that summed up her great and generous quest. 'You must tell me something that you are sure is true.' The words came to him in her sweet voice, and as he sat on his terrace in the darkness he wondered how he would have answered her if she had written the sentence to him.

He asked himself if the intensity of her personality, and the sheer originality of her ambitions, placed against the dullness and banality and penury which surrounded her, might have unsettled her will to live. He felt this especially when her sisters married for security rather than love, and when Minny was forced to depend on their husbands for her upkeep as her lungs began to haemorrhage and her health began to fail. He remembered seeing her in New York for the last time two days before he sailed for Europe alone for the first time, and he made an effort then to disguise, as much as he could, his pure excitement, his boundless appetite for what was to come. They had agreed that the same journey would be the right thing for her and it was detestable that he was sailing off without her. Despite her illness and her envy, the hour they spent that day was bright, their talk all gaiety. They spoke of meeting in Rome the following winter, and of his plans in London, whom he would see, where he would visit. Her envy became extravagant only when he spoke of a possible visit to Mrs Lewes, her beloved George Eliot. She tossed her head and laughed at the enormity of her own jealousy.

It was clear that she was ill, and so apparent to them both that she would not recover that they did not mention it. Nonetheless, as he was leaving her, he asked her how she was sleeping.

'Sleep,' she said. 'Oh, I don't sleep. I've given it up.'

But then she laughed bravely and freely and her smile to him was carefully arranged so that there was nothing hollow or false about it. And then she left him.

In England when he came to visit Mrs Lewes on a Sunday afternoon at North Bank, having secured admission through the intervention of a family friend, he imagined Minny with him, asking George Eliot the questions that no one in Minny's own circle wished to ask, or wished indeed to answer. He imagined her voice, awed now but slowly building in richness in the room. At the moment of departure he pictured his cousin standing up and being noticed by the novelist, having made an impression, and reaching out warmly to shake her hand, and being invited to return. In a letter, he tried to describe Mrs Lewes to Minny, her accent, the calm severity of her gaze, her strange ugliness, her mingled sagacity and sweetness, her dignity and character, her graciousness and remote indifference. It was easier, however, to write to his father about her; writing to Minny had now become like writing to a ghost.

MINNY DIED in March, a year after he had last seen her. He was still in England. He felt it as the end of his youth, knowing that death, at the last, was dreadful to her. She would have given anything to live. In the years that followed, he longed to know what she would have thought of his books and stories, and of the decisions he made about his life. This sense of missing her deep and demanding response made itself felt to Gray and Holmes as well, and also to William. All of them wondered in their nervous ambition and great, agitated egotism what Minny would have thought about them or said about them. Henry wondered too what life would have had for her and how her exquisite faculty of challenge could have dealt with a world which would inevitably attempt to confine her. His consolation was that at least he had known her as the world had not, and the pain of living without her was no more than a penalty he paid for the privilege of having been young with her. What once was life, he thought, is always life and he knew that her image would preside in his intellect as a sort of measure and standard of brightness and repose.

It was not true to say that Minny Temple haunted him in the years that followed; rather, he haunted her. He conjured up her presence everywhere, when he returned to his parents' house, and later when he travelled in France and Italy. In the shadows of the great cathedrals, he saw her emerge, delicate and elegant and richly curious, ready to be stunned into silence by each work of art that she saw, and then trying to find the words which might fit the moment, allow her new sensuous life to settle and deepen.

Soon after she died he wrote a story, 'Travelling Companions', in which William, travelling in Italy from Germany, met her by chance in Milan Cathedral, having seen her first in front of Leonardo's *The Last Supper*. He loved describing her white umbrella with a violet lining and the sense of intelligent pleasure in her movements, her glance and her voice. He could control her destiny now that she was dead, offer her the experiences she would have wanted, and provide drama for a life which had been so cruelly shortened. He wondered if this had happened to other writers who came before him, if Hawthorne or George Eliot had written to make the dead come back to life, had worked all day and all night, like a magician or an alchemist, defying fate and time and all the implacable elements to re-create a sacred life.

He could not stop wondering how she would have lived, what she would have done. With Alice, the question of Minny was not to be raised, as his sister envied everything that Minny had possessed: her strange beauty and allure, her confidence, her deep seriousness, her effect on men. And later, Alice envied Minny her being dead.

Speculation about Minny did, however, interest William, and both he and Henry were certain in their discussion on the subject that she would not have known whom to marry, that her choice, had she lived, would have been too idealistic, or too impetuous, or too unnatural. Her marriage, both agreed, would have been mistaken, and this seemed to suggest that something in her complex organism had understood this, had known that her future as a penniless, clever woman was a sadly insoluble problem.

Both brothers had felt that, at some level, at most levels, narrow life contained no place for her. All her conduct and character, Henry thought, seemed to have pointed to this conclusion – how profoundly inconsequential, in her history, continued life might have been.

He often imagined her married to Gray or Holmes or William, how diminished she would seem, how marriage for her would be a battle that she would have to lose. In *Poor Richard*, he had sent her to Europe where she did not marry. In *Daisy Miller*, in which he had emphasized her brashness and bravery and careless attitude to conventions, she had died in Rome. In *Travelling Companions*, he had invented a marriage for her, dramatizing the Italian circumstances of her meeting with her consort. He did not follow her into the daily domestic routines managed in the shadow of a dull man.

It was when he read *Daniel Deronda* that something came into his mind which had not occurred to him before – the dramatic possibilities of a spirited woman being destroyed by a stifling marriage. By coincidence, at this time he happened also to read *Phineas Finn* by Trollope, mainly as a way of getting to sleep, and was struck too by the marriage of Lady Laura Kennedy and the sheer interest such an alliance had for the reader whose sympathies had been drawn to the brave, bright heroine confronting her destiny with the illusion of freedom.

He set to work. By then he had lived some years in England, he felt that he could see America more clearly, and he wanted more than anything to bring to life an American spirit who was fresh and free, ready for life and certain only of her own great openness to others and to experience. It was not hard to place his young lady in his grandmother's house in Albany, the strange, cramped, old-fashioned rooms from which Mrs Touchett, bossy and rich, could rescue Isabel Archer and take her to England where so many of his heroines had longed to go. In England, he could easily surround her with his old and carefully wrought trio of suitors, the straight-talking serious one; the gentler, patrician one; and the one who would be her friend and the fascinated student of her destiny, being too unfit or ill or steeped in irony to be her lover.

He worked on the book in Florence and felt, as he woke each morning in his hotel on the river or later in rooms on Bellosguardo, that he had a great mission now to make Minny walk these streets, to allow the soft Tuscan sunlight to shine on her soft face. But more than that, he sought to re-create her moral presence more finely and more dramatically than he had ever done before. He wanted to take this penniless American girl and offer her a solid, old universe in which to breathe. He gave her money, suitors, villas and palaces, new friends and new sensations. He had never felt as powerful and as dutiful; he walked the streets of Florence and the quays and the steep, winding hill to Bellosguardo with a new lightness, and this lightness made its way into the book. It moved elegantly, easily and freely as though Minny herself were protecting him, presiding over him. There were scenes he wrote in which, having imagined everything and set it down, he was, at moments, unsure whether it had genuinely happened or whether his imagined world had finally come to replace the real.

Yet Minny was real for him throughout the years, more real than any of the new people he met and associated with. She belonged to the part of him he guarded most fiercely, his hidden self, which no one in England knew about or understood. It was easier to preserve her under English skies, in a land where no one cared to remember the dead as he remembered his cousin, where the flat present with its attendant order ruled. It was here he let her walk with the power and haunting resonance of an old song echoing through the years, sounding its sad notes to him wherever he went.

HE HAD FORGOTTEN, until he saw Holmes, how much his old friend loved the English; as soon as Holmes alighted from the train at Rye, he filled the air with stories of whom he had seen and how they were, how deaf Leslie Stephen had become since Julia had died, how Margot Tennant was not the same since her marriage, how charming his new friend Lady Castletown was and how grand. Henry did not even consider speaking, and he knew that if he had, he would have been interrupted immediately. Holmes was bright-eyed, almost fervid, and managed, despite the years, to look even more handsome than ever before, more gallant. Perhaps his time with Lady Castletown, Henry thought, had made him so.

'I'm afraid,' he said when he finally found a gap in Holmes's narrative, 'I'm afraid there are no lords and ladies at all in Rye. It will be very quiet. Indeed, it *is* very quiet.'

Holmes clapped him on the back and smiled as if he had just now noticed him. His elevation to the bench seemed to have made him less reserved, if anything. Maybe this was the way, Henry mused, eminent men in their fifties were behaving in America now, but then he pictured William Dean Howells and his brother William and understood that it was merely Holmes who was behaving like this. He tried to explain to Holmes that he had been working on not one but two novels and had not had much company over the previous months other than his servants. Holmes was extolling the landscape and too busy to listen and Henry was suddenly glad that he was staying at Point Hill for only one night. He knew from William and from Howells and others that Holmes had become a famous judge whose theories were discussed in the higher circles of law and politics as the theories of Darwin were discussed by scientists and the clergy. Henry remembered that he had asked William what these theories were and William had put it bluntly that Holmes did not believe in anything and had managed to make this view seem both reasonable and popular. His position was, William said, that he had no position. Howells, on the other hand, was not given to bluntness; he explained merely that Holmes had sought rather forcefully to apply the human and practical element rather than the historical or the theoretical or indeed the moral elements to law. Like Darwin, Howells said, Holmes had developed a theory of winners, but it was his pointed and plain rhetoric that won the day as much as anything else.

He had often wondered, Holmes now said as they made their way through Rye, if he should have come to England to live. He did not suppose, he added, that they would take him to their bosom if he planned to stay. Henry nodded in assent, but soon his mind was elsewhere.

They dined on the terrace, and having eaten they sat in repose watching the great plain below in the fading evening light. Holmes groaned and stretched his legs as though settling down for a long and relaxed evening while Henry wished it were an hour later and he could excuse himself. The talk between them was desultory as they carefully avoided the subjects which would divide them, such as William, with whom Holmes seemed to have quarrelled, and Mrs Holmes, who languished in Boston, and Henry's novels, on which he knew that Holmes had views. The subjects which they could discuss, the gossip about private and public America, the law and politics, soon petered out. Henry found that he had asked too many questions about too many old friends and Holmes had replied too many times that he hardly saw them and knew very little about them. He suspected, he said several times, that Henry knew more about them than he did.

The twilight lingered and the two men grew silent until Henry felt that they would never think of anything to say again. He moved his chair so that he could study Holmes and saw him now in the gloaming as a deeply contented fellow, at home with himself, and he felt a mild distaste for the aura of good-humoured complacency which Holmes gathered around him.

'It is strange how time goes,' Holmes said.

'Yes,' Henry replied, stretching. 'I used to think it went more slowly in England, but having lived here for so long I know that to be an illusion. I depend now on Italy as the place where time goes most slowly.'

'I was thinking of that summer when we were all together,' Holmes said.

'Yes,' Henry said. 'That glorious, heroic summer.'

Henry now expected Holmes to say that time had flown since then or that it seemed like yesterday and he wondered how he would respond to Holmes's banalities. He was already preparing a missive to William, telling him that Holmes as a conversationalist had been laid low.

'I can remember every moment of that month. Better than I can remember yesterday,' Holmes said.

They both were silent then; Henry did not know how soon he could take his leave without being rude. Holmes cleared his throat as though to speak and then stopped again. He sighed.

'It is as though time has moved backwards for me,' Holmes said, turning towards Henry to make sure he was paying attention. 'Once that summer was over, I could, as I said, remember it perfectly, but during those long days, with all that talk and all that company, it was as though there existed a great curtain around everything. I felt sometimes as if I were under water, seeing things only in vague outline and desperately trying to come up for air. I do not know what the war did to me, save that I survived. But I know now that fear and shock and bravery are merely words and they do not tell us – nothing does – that when you experience them day in day out, you lose part of yourself and you can never get it back. After the war I was diminished and I knew this; part of my soul, my way of living and feeling, was paralysed but I could not tell what part. Nobody recognized what was wrong, not even myself most of the time. All that summer I wanted to change, to cease watching and standing back. I wanted to join and become involved, drink up the life that was offered to us then as those wonderful sisters did. I longed to be alive, just as I long for it now, and the time passing has helped me, helped me to live. When I was twenty-one and twenty-two normal feelings dried up in me and since then I have been trying to make up for that, as well as live, live like others live.'

Holmes's voice was almost angry now, but oddly distant and low. Henry knew how much it had taken for him to speak like this, and he knew also that what he said was true. Once more they remained silent, but the silence was filled with regret and recognition.

Henry did not think he could say anything. He did not have a confession of his own. His war had been private, within his family and deep within himself. It could not be mentioned or explained, but it had left him too as Holmes described. He lived, at times, he felt, as if his life belonged to someone else, a story that had not yet been written, a character who had not been fully imagined.

He thought that Holmes had said all that he wanted to say, and he was ready to remain a while as a tribute to his candour and let Holmes's confession settle. But slowly he realized, by the way Holmes faced him, and by Holmes's filling his glass with brandy as though the night were long, that his guest had something else to say. He waited, and finally when Holmes spoke again his tone had changed. He was back to his role as judge, public figure, man of the world.

'You know, finally,' Holmes said, '*The Portrait of a Lady* is a great monument to her, although the ending, I have to say that I did not care for the ending.'

Henry stared at the encroaching night and did not reply. He did not wish to discuss the ending of his novel, but nonetheless he was pleased and satisfied that Holmes had finally mentioned the book, having never referred to it before.

'Yes,' Holmes said, 'she was very noble and I think you caught that.'

'I think we all adored her,' Henry said.

'She remains for me a touchstone,' Holmes said, 'and I wish she were alive now so that I could find out what she thought of me.'

'Yes, indeed,' Henry said.

Holmes took a sip of his drink.

'Do you ever regret not taking her to Italy when she was ill?' he asked. 'Gray says she asked you several times.'

'I don't think ask is the word,' Henry said. 'She was very ill then. Gray is misinformed.'

'Gray says that she asked you and you did not offer to help her and that a winter in Rome might have saved her.'

'Nothing could have saved her,' Henry said.

Henry felt the sharp deliberation of Holmes's tone, the slow cruelty of it; he was, he thought, being questioned and judged by his old friend without any sympathy or affection.

'When she did not hear from you she turned her face to the wall.' Holmes spoke as though it were a line he had been planning to say for some time. He cleared his throat and continued.

'When finally she knew no one would help her she turned her face to the wall. She was very much alone then and she fixed on the idea. You were her cousin and could have travelled with her. You were free, in fact you were already in Rome. It would have cost you nothing.'

By the time either of them spoke again it was night, and the darkness seemed strangely grim and complete. Henry told the servant that they would not need a lamp as they were ready to retire. Holmes sipped his drink, crossing and recrossing his legs. Henry could hardly remember how he got to bed.

IN THE MORNING Henry was still considering at what point he should have spoken to defend himself, or when he should have ended the discussion. Clearly, the matter had been festering in Holmes's mind throughout the years and clearly he had discussed it with Gray and the two lawyers were at one on the subject and at home accusing people of things. Now Holmes would be able to tell Gray what had been said.

At breakfast, Holmes was calm and steadfast as though the night before he had delivered a difficult but considered judgement and now thought better of himself for having done so. He arranged that he would return the following weekend, and, as he did so, Henry worked out how he would cancel these arrangements. He did not wish to see Holmes for a long time.

IN THE WEEK that followed he worked hard, even though the pain in his hand had become at times excruciating. He avoided the terrace and left the desk only to eat and sleep. He wrote to Holmes after a few days to say that in order to meet a deadline he was hard at work on a story and could not, unfortunately, entertain him for a weekend. He hoped, he said, to see him in London before Holmes departed for the United States.

For some days then he basked in the solitude his letter had won him, but he could not stop going over the conversation with Holmes in his mind; he began to compose letters to Holmes, but did not even get as far as writing them down. He believed that the accusation was unfair and unfounded and Holmes's discussing the matter so coldly and finally was outrageous.

He could not be sure what his cousin in her final months had written to Gray. He was aware that Gray had kept her letters, and he too in his apartment in London had stored away those letters which Minny had written to him in the last year of her life. He knew that she had accused him of nothing, but he now wished to know what terms she had used all those years before in her expressed desire to go to Rome. Slowly, he stopped working. His waking hours were consumed with memories of his early days in London and Italy and his receipt of these letters. He imagined finding them again – he knew perfectly where they were stored – and unfolding and rereading them, and he thought about this so incessantly that he knew he would have to travel to London. Like a ghost, he would enter his apartment in Kensington, flit through the rooms until he came to the cupboard where the letters were, and he would read them, and then he would return to Rye.

As he waited for the train, he dreaded meeting anyone he knew and having to pretend that he had business in London.

He dreaded speaking at all, so that even telling the servants that he would be leaving, and speaking with the cab driver and the purchasing of his ticket, had an enervating effect on him. He wished he could be invisible now for a day or two. He recognized, and this pressed down on him most as he travelled towards London, that the letters might yield nothing, might fill him with further uncertainty. He might not know, having read them again, any more than he knew now.

It struck him forcefully as he made his way from the station how calm his life had become once more after the disaster of his play. This was the first time since then that the equilibrium he had worked so intensely to achieve had disappeared. He began to feel that when he opened the cupboard in the apartment in which he kept his cousin's letters something palpable would emerge, and he tried to tell himself that this imagining was too much, too feverish, but it was no use.

He found the letters easily, and was surprised at how flimsy and brief they were, how the folds of the paper seemed to have corroded the ink on both sides and made some of her writing illegible. Nonetheless, they were from her and they were dated. He allowed his lips to move as he read:

> I shall miss you, my dear, but I am most happy to know that you are well and enjoying yourself. If you were not my cousin I would write to ask you to marry me and take me with you, but as it is, it wouldn't do so I will have to console myself, however, with the thought that in that case you might not accept my offer.

He read on: 'If I were, by hook or by crook, to spend next winter with friends in Rome, should I see you at all?' And then, in one of the last letters he received from her: 'Think, my dear, of the pleasure we would have together in Rome. I am crazy at the mere thought. I would give anything to have a winter in Italy.'

He put the letters aside and sat with his head in his hands. He did not help her or encourage her, and she was careful never to ask outright. If she had insisted on coming, he forced himself to complete this thought now, he would have stood aside or kept his distance or actively prevented her coming, whatever was necessary. He had himself, in that year, escaped into the bright old world he had longed for. He was writing stories and taking in sensations and slowly plotting his first novels. He was no longer a native of the James family, but alone in a warm climate with a clear ambition and a free imagination. His mother had written to say that he must spend what money he needed in feasting at the table of freedom. He did not want his invalid cousin. Even had she been well, he was not sure that her company, so full of wilful charm and curiosity, would have been entirely welcome. He needed then to watch life, or imagine the world, through his own eyes. Had she been there, he would have seen through hers.

He went to the window and looked down at the street. Even now, he felt that he had every right to leave her behind, to follow the path of his own talent, his own nature. Nonetheless, her letters filled him with sorrow and guilt, and added to these a sort of shame when he realized that she must have spoken to others, to Gray at least, about his refusal to entertain her. Holmes's phrase 'she turned her face to the wall' echoed in his mind now and did battle with his sense of his own ruthlessness, his own will to survive. And finally, as he turned back into the room, he felt a sharp and unbearable idea staring at him, like something alive and fierce and predatory in the air, whispering to him that he had preferred her dead rather than alive, that he had known what to do with her once life was taken from her, but he had denied her when she asked him gently for help.

He sat on a chair in his living room for most of the afternoon, letting his thoughts sink and glide and come to the surface again. He wondered if he might burn these letters, if nothing good could come of them in the future. He put them aside for the moment and returned to the cupboard where he had found them and rummaged there until he discovered the red notebook he had been looking for. He knew what he was seeking, it lay in the opening pages, written a few years earlier; its outline was fresh in his mind but its details were not. He carried the notebook into the better light of the living room.

During the time since Holmes's visit and in the midst of all his worry and suffering, his interest in the picture of a young American woman slowly dying, which he had noted down, had intensified. It was the story of a young woman with a large fortune on the threshold of a life that seemed boundless in its possibilities. She would come to Europe so that she could live, live passionately and intensely if only for a short time.

He read through his notes about a young Englishman, penniless, clever, handsome, who is in love with someone else, but whose task becomes to save the American girl, love her, help her to live, despite the fact that he is hopelessly compromised, a matter of which the dying girl knows nothing. His intended, penniless as well, also befriends the girl.

As he read his notes, he was horrified by the sheer callousness of the story. The young man pretending to love the girl, and perhaps get her money, his love a sort of treachery, and his real love watching over this, knowing that she could marry if they could get the money. The story, he thought, was vulgar and ugly, and yet it came to him powerfully now.

He took the letters in his hand again, looked at Minny's trusting, clean handwriting, the hand of someone who expected only good from the world. He saw her clearly coming to Europe for her last look at life. He gave her money, he imagined her as having inherited a fortune, and saw too his hero, one part of him full of love and pity for her, and the other part hardened and needy and ready to betray. The story was vulgar and ugly only if the motives were so, but what if the motives were mixed and ambiguous? Suddenly, he sat up straight and then stood and walked to the window. He had, in that second, seen the other woman, had caught a sharp view of her strange moral neutrality, how much she was sacrificing in letting the dying girl know love, how much she was gaining also and how careful she was, in her practical way, never to allow the two to appear on opposite sides of the weighing scales.

He had them now, all three of them, and he would embrace them, hold on to them and let them improve with time, become more complex and less vulgar, less ugly, more rich, more resonant, more true not to what life was, but to what it might be. He crossed the room again and gathered up the letters and the notebooks and brought them to the cupboard and put them brusquely on a shelf and closed the cupboard doors. He would not need them again. He would need to work now, apply his mind. He would, he determined, travel back to Rye and be ready again, when the call came, to explore one more time the life and death of his cousin Minny Temple.

CHAPTER SIX

February 1897

HIS HAND DID NOT IMPROVE. He held it now as though it were a foreign object placed in his care, unpleasant and unwelcome and, at times, venomous. He could write in the mornings, but by noon the pain was too intense along the bone running from his wrist to his little finger and the muscles and nerves and tendons around it. If he did not move his hand he felt no pain, but writing now, especially if he stopped to think and then resumed the work, caused him unbearable agony and he would have to put the pen down.

In pure frustration, then, he would read over the last few pages and make mental notes for emendations. He would discover that his mind had raced forwards, and he had continued his narrative effortlessly in his own head, constructing whole sentences, word for word. He found that he could put in an imaginary full stop and then finish another sentence. He did not speak them aloud, nor did he even whisper them, but they came to him complete and he did not have any difficulty remembering what the previous sentences had contained, or how each had begun. Now as he sat at his desk he wanted to write to William about this phenomenon but realized sharply that he could not write a letter, indeed had not written any serious letters for some time, so carefully was he preserving the energies of his right hand for the novel then being serialized each month, whose chapters, pain or no pain, he could not fail to deliver. In the few hours of the morning when he could work painlessly, he devoted himself to his fiction, but as time went on even these few hours were proving difficult.

William, who delighted in modern inventions, had written to him of the advantages of the stenograph, insisting that dictating was faster and easier, and if he concentrated sufficiently hard, produced seamlessly better results. Henry was sceptical about this and uneasy about the costs. Also, he was content with his own solitude, his own tight control over the words on the page. But when the pain extended to his entire arm and when, morning after morning, he had to bear the torture in order to keep the series running and the printers supplied with fresh pages, he knew that he could not go on. He was exhausted.

He would use a stenographer for his correspondence, he thought, and there was a good deal pending. He worried about his privacy, but assured himself that there was nothing in his correspondence which was entirely private. If he found such matter, he would instantly erase it. The stenographer recommended to him was a Scot called William McAlpine, who seemed efficient and trustworthy and competent as he arrived at the flat each morning, but these were minor characteristics beside his silence, his dourness and his lack of apparent interest in anything other than the task in hand.

Thus as Henry dictated his letters, McAlpine sullenly and dutifully took down his words in shorthand and presented him later with a clean typed copy. Soon, Henry began to dictate directly to the stenograph and he wondered sometimes whether McAlpine or his brand-new machine took the greater interest in the words he spoke.

His hand, he informed his friends, had been relegated to permanent and incompetent obscurity. Gradually, his stenographer became as omnipresent and strangely transparent as the very air itself, especially once Henry discovered that the practice of dictation could fit the company of fiction as much as, if not more than, the art of letter writing. As his hand healed, he began to write some of his own letters at night when his typist had retired, and used the new machine and its silent master during the day for the creation of serious narrative.

At the beginning he was careful not to broadcast his new method too freely, but soon he regretted telling anyone at all, as those who learned that he was now talking his words into a machine, that the art of fiction had become industrialized, took a dim view of his decision and, indeed, of his future. He assured them that he could be trusted not to be simplified by any short-cut, or falsified by any facility, that, in short, his commerce with the muse had been in fact assisted by the arrival of the machine and the Scot.

He loved walking up and down the room, beginning a new sentence, letting it snake ahead, stopping it for a moment, adding a phrase, a brief pause, and then allowing the sentence to gallop to an elegant and fitting conclusion. He looked forward to starting in the morning, his typist punctual, uncomplaining, seemingly indifferent as though the words uttered by the novelist equalled in interest and importance his previous work in the commercial sector.

He felt now that all of his working life had been leading up to this loud freedom, and after a few months he knew that he would not be able to return to pen and paper, to unmechanical solitude. Wherever he would go the Scot would have to come too, with the large, unwieldy typewriter, which soon replaced the stenograph, in tow. The typewriter would have to be carried and the Scot would have to be fed. Thus moving would require trouble and expense. His days of channel-crossing and railways and hotel life had come to an end. The call of other climates and glamorous cities was drowned somewhat by the dutiful click of the typewriter and the sound of his own voice.

*

IN THESE YEARS he had written so much, and in so much dramatic detail, about houses, that his friend the architect Edward Warren offered to make him drawings of Gardencourt or Poynton, Easthead or Bounds, houses he had described room by room, full of carefully created atmosphere, treasured ornament and faded tapestry. They could, Warren said, make special architectural editions of his books. Henry, each time he visited Warren's house, studied a drawing he had made of the garden room at Lamb House in Rye, viewed from the street, admiring the English essences, old brick and the sense of weathered comfort.

Henry dreamed of having a house of his own outside London; he imagined himself each evening seated in the rich glow of a lamp in an old panelled room, the floorboards darkly varnished and covered in rugs, the fire alight, the burning wood oozing and crackling, the heavy curtains drawn, a long day's work completed and no social duties looming.

When summer came, he spent time wandering in the villages of the Suffolk coast, delighting in the names – Great Yarmouth, Blundeston, Saxmundham, Dunwich – which suggested a gnarled legacy, an ancient history. He thought that a stone cottage on this coast, something simple and closely connected with the surrounding sea-faring culture, would be ideal for him. As he moved from place to place, his typist and his Remington in tow, oscillating between bad lodgings and expensive hotels, he hoped that this would be his last incoherent summer, but he knew that this patched-up, hand-to-mouth, unhoused way of life would continue, intolerably, to be his lot until he could put a hand on a lovely refuge of his own, for which, as time went by, he thirsted more and more.

In the Suffolk villages he asked anyone he had occasion to meet, explaining his needs and desires, proffering his address in London as a sign of his seriousness. A few times he was encouraged to look at a property, but nothing he saw came close to his dream; they were, in their own innocent way, all of them hideous, available to him merely because no one else wanted them.

Similarly in Rye he made clear his desire to find permanent lodgings. He had made friends with the local blacksmith who had partly graduated to the title of ironmonger and was much at his entrance on the lookout for fresh faces for idle chatter. On one of his strolls in Rye, Henry stopped at the door of Mr Milson, who after the first meeting greeted him instantly as Mr James, and knew him as the American writer, having his walk in a Rye he was slowly growing to admire and love. Upon his second or third conversation with Mr Milson, during his time as a resident of Point Hill, he observed that he longed for a permanent spot in the area, in the countryside, or indeed in the town itself. Since Mr Milson enjoyed talking, and since he was not interested in literary matters, and since he had not been to America and knew no other Americans, and since Henry's knowledge of ironmongery was rudimentary, the two men discussed houses, ones which had been for rent in the past, others which had been put on the market or sold or withdrawn, and others, much coveted, which had never been bought or sold or rented in living memory. Each time he visited, once they had initiated their subject, Mr Milson showed him the card on which Henry's London address was inscribed. He had not mislaid it, he had not forgotten, he insisted, and then enticingly would mention some great old house, perfect for a bachelor's needs, but sorrowfully would have to admit that the house remained firmly in its owner's hands and seemed unlikely to leave them in the foreseeable future.

Henry viewed his conversations with Mr Milson as a form of play, just as his conversations with fishermen about the sea, or the farmers about the harvest, were forms of polite relaxation, a way of drinking in England, allowing its flavours to come to him in phrases, turns of speech and local references. Thus even when he opened the letter which arrived at his London address, having noticed that the handwriting on the envelope was not that of someone accustomed to writing letters, and even when he saw the name Milson as the sender, he was still puzzled by its provenance. Only when he read it a second time did he realize who it was from and then, as though he had received a blow in the stomach, he understood what the letter said. Lamb House in Rye had fallen vacant, Milson told him, and could be had. His first thought was that he would lose it, the house at the quiet corner at the top of a cobbled hill whose garden room Edward Warren had drawn so lovingly, the establishment he had glanced at so achingly and covetously on his many tours of Rye, a house both modest and grand, both central and secluded, the sort of house which seemed to belong so comfortably and naturally to others and to be inhabited so warmly and fruitfully by them. He checked the postmark. He wondered if his ironmonger was freely broadcasting the news of this vacancy to all comers. This was, more than any other, the house he loved and longed for. Nothing had ever come easily, magically like this. He could do what he liked, he could send a cable, he could take the next train, but he remained sure that he would lose it. There was no purchase, however, in thinking, or regretting or worrying; there was only one solution and that was to rush to Rye, thus ensuring that no omission on his part could cause him not to become the new inhabitant of Lamb House.

Before he left he wrote to Edward Warren, imploring him to come to Rye also as soon as he could to inspect the inside of the house whose exterior he had so admired. But he could not wait for Warren and he certainly could not work, and on the train he wondered if anyone watching him would know how momentous this journey was for him, how exciting and how potentially disappointing. He knew that it was merely a house; others bought and sold houses and moved their belongings with ease and nonchalance. It struck him as he travelled towards Rye that no one, save himself, understood the meaning of this. For so many years now he had had no country, no family, no establishment of his own, merely a flat in London where he worked. He did not have the necessary shell, and his exposure over the years had left him nervous and exhausted and fearful. It was as though he lived a life which lacked a façade, a stretch of frontage to protect him from the world. Lamb House would offer him beautiful old windows from which to view the outside; the outside, in turn, could peer in only at his invitation.

He dreamed now of being a host, having friends and family to stay; he dreamed of decorating an old house, buying his own furniture and having continuity and certainty in his days.

As soon as he went in through the door he sensed an air of sombre comfort. The downstairs rooms were small and cosy, and the rooms upstairs stately and filled with light. Some of the oak panelling had been covered with modern wallpaper, but could, he was assured, be easily restored. Two rooms opened onto the garden, which was well tended and decorously planted, if rather too large for his needs. The guest room had once housed George I and would, he knew, be suitable for family and friends. As he walked about the house, opening doors and having doors opened for him, he did not speak, remaining fearful that if he expressed too much enthusiasm someone else with a prior claim on the lease would appear at the front door and loudly insist that he leave.

Nonetheless, when he walked from the garden into the garden room, whose large bay window looked down the cobbled hill, and he caught a glimpse of how he would use this room, how he would work here every day in the summer, basking in its brave, airy properties, its great light, he was forced to let out a gasp. And he could not contain himself any further when he sought to leave the garden room and stood facing the walled garden, the walls full of ancient creepers and an old mulberry tree offering shade and the brick turned russet with age and weather. Walking around the house and garden was like filling in a form, the more ground he covered the closer he came, he was sure, to placing his signature at the end, staking his claim.

The owner was alerted to the name and nature of his prospective tenant and quickly assented to a twenty-one-year lease at favourable terms. Warren viewed the house with a professional eye and listed the improvements which could easily be made over the winter, making the house habitable by the spring. Henry sent several letters, courtesy of McAlpine, to friends and to his sister-in-law informing them of his new house. He added the terms of the lease – seventy pounds a year – in his own hand once McAlpine had left for the day.

STRANGELY, in the months which followed, he felt mainly fear, as though he had embarked unprepared on some vast and risk-filled financial speculation in which everything he owned could be lost. He had arrangements to make now, extra staff to engage, furniture and household goods to buy, an apartment in London to lease or keep. He also had to ensure his financial future now that he had made these steep commitments. But something other than mere arrangements filled him with a vague, unnameable foreboding. It took him weeks to understand what it was and then it came to him in a flash: when he walked into the upstairs rooms of Lamb House, and into the room where he himself would sleep, he believed that he had come into the room where he would die. As he studied the lease, he knew that its twenty-one years would take him to the tomb. The walls of the house had witnessed men and women come and go for almost three hundred years; now it had invited him to sample briefly its charm, it had enticed him there and offered him its unlasting hospitality. It would welcome him and then see him out, as it had seen others out. He would lie stricken in one of those rooms; he would lie cold in that house. The idea both froze his blood and comforted him at the same time. He had travelled without hesitation to meet his own place of death, to remove its mystery, one of its unknown dimensions. But he would also go there to live, to spend long days working and long evenings by the fire. He had found his home, he who had wandered so uneasily, and he longed for its engulfing presence, its familiarity, its containing beauty.

*

HE GAINED strength that winter and early spring in the determination of practical matters. When Howells came to London,
they spent a long morning together, the fog thick outside, discussing, among other matters, the American market for story and
serialization. Howells's visit and his calm advice, and his intervention on his return to the United States, which resulted in
commissions and approaches from editors there, were part of the
magic of the season.

Slowly, other things fell into place. Lady Wolseley discovered
his new acquisition, and insisted on visiting it and offering advice.
She was, he knew, a great and talented gatherer of objects; her taste
was practical and she did not baulk at furnishing small rooms and
intimate spaces. She knew the dealers and their shops, and over
years she had instilled respect and fear in the best of them, while
taking the measure of the worst. She had also read *The Spoils of
Poynton*, as it had appeared in serial form, having had it sent to
her from America, and she believed that the widowed Mrs Gareth,
prepared to lay down her life for the carefully collected treasures
of Poynton, was based on her.

'Not the greed,' she said, 'and not the foolishness and not the
widowhood. I have never gone in for widowhood. But the eye,
the eye that misses nothing, can see how a Queen Anne chair can
be restored, or a faded tapestry hung in the shadows, or a painting
bought for the frame.'

She presumed that he had no money to spend, and she presumed that his taste equalled hers, and she got to know each room
of his new house and its requirements in every detail. She thought
Lamb House a perfect piece. She had wished that she could carry
it home, but since she could not, then she would console herself
by taking him shopping in London, showing him corners and side
alleys of the antiques trade and the old furniture trade. He learned,
to his surprise, that the years when she collected most of her small
treasures were the years when she and her husband had almost no
money, had inherited nothing, and managed on his salary and her
slight private income. Her eye, she said, was sharpened by penury.

As the days grew shorter, he moved through London with her, pushing open the doors of dimly lit shops presided over by watchful dealers who knew Lady Wolseley of old, some of them remembering ancient purchases of hers, bargains she had procured and objects she had added to her collection which had seemed at the time eccentric and part of her general wilfulness. This London, its shops all lit and its streets busy and its social life at its most rich and pressing, was a world which he had already begun to miss as he prepared to retreat into the safety and solitude of provincial life. He loved the late afternoon light and the freshness of the cold and he also loved, despite all his protestations, the promise of the evening. As he walked the streets with his acquisitive companion, he studied London fondly, and then, as they stood in the old storerooms and show rooms, conducted here and there by dealers who seemed the essence of decorum and discretion as though they were selling privacy itself, he imagined his new life and his new furniture, his newly painted walls or stripped-down wood, and he felt oddly light, happy that he was merely halfway towards his goal, that Lamb House in Rye remained for the moment in the realms of imagination.

SINCE THE elevation of Lord Wolseley to his position as Commander of Her Majesty's Forces, and since their return from Ireland in triumph, Lady Wolseley had grown more imperious with Henry, but she seemed gentle now, quite polite with the dealers. He had never known her to keep her voice down, but in the dusty old shops, as she studied the new arrivals or asked for old maps, her new obsession, to be presented to her, she seemed demure, and indeed seemed more so as the winter progressed. Nevertheless, she was full of certainty about what was worth buying and what was not, and she had a firm picture in her mind of each portion of Lamb House. He had to battle with her constantly due to her enthusiasm and her lack of patience, and on a few occasions he had to be careful to keep secret his longing for an object which she had casually dismissed.

Lady Wolseley provided him with a secret guide to London, to the hidden places from which he could fill and furnish Lamb House; she offered him also a version of London at its most densely packed, most resonantly inhabited. Each object he fingered and handled possessed a wondrous history which would never be known, suggesting England to him in all its old wealth and purpose.

In these months he worked hard, writing articles and stories, but on days when he had fulfilled his contract with himself and written his allotted number of words, keeping his Scot busy all morning, he would decide suddenly to go to the dealers again, mingle once more with the dust and the left-over objects, the untidy sold-off heritage, move from one shop to another aimlessly selecting a frame or a chair or a set of cutlery, but not buying, waiting until he was in a more decisive mood, or in the company of Lady Wolseley.

One afternoon, in the hour between four and five when the light became ambiguous and faded, he found himself in an antique shop in a Bloomsbury street which he had visited only once with Lady Wolseley. He remembered the dealer vividly for his extraordinary pair of eyes. The dealer had managed then to exert a sort of coercion on Lady Wolseley and her friend without speaking; he had succeeded in putting subtle pressures on them, managing also to throw a shadow of solemnity over the occasion by a mere glance. Henry recalled his slim light fingers, with neat nails, touching objects on his counter at moments, briefly, nervously, tenderly. He had noted Lady Wolseley's huge resistance, silent also, to making any purchases, even though the owner had shown them some perfect pieces, including a French tapestry, small but splendid, and some old velvet brocade, with a texture which both the dealer and Lady Wolseley agreed was almost impossible to find nowadays. She bought nothing, but studied certain objects at such length that the dealer's wise, patient gaze took on a hint of irony. Outside, she said the prices were too high, even though money had been barely mentioned, and said she believed that the owner, many years in business, should no longer be encouraged.

Henry had been thinking for some time about purchasing one object, something useless and perhaps overpriced, and certainly expensive, something that would catch his eye, an object he would want to have with him, close to him, which would have a meaning beyond its value. The French tapestry was something he thought of, the scene it depicted took its bearings from one of the Italian masters, Fra Angelico or Masaccio, and the pink threads running through the cloth had held their tone. He thought he would examine it again now, discuss it further with the dealer and perhaps decide to buy it without consulting Lady Wolseley, who, he knew, never changed her mind.

He found the door of the shop open and went into the lamp-lit interior, closing the door noiselessly behind him. It was typical, he thought, of the dealer's strange tact to allow a customer to enter thus. The front part of the shop was narrow and cluttered, but he remembered that down some steps was a much longer room leading to a large storeroom with stairs to a loft. He idled for a while waiting for the owner to appear and then began to study a teacup which he thought might be Sèvres. Having casually examined several other objects, he walked to the back of the shop until he had a full view of the store below. There, huddled over a chaise longue, discussing its covering and testing its strength, were Lady Wolseley and the dealer. Feeling for a second like a trespasser, he moved back into the shadows and waited. He had not expected to find Lady Wolseley there and he thought it might be better if she were left in peace. This was her territory; he had not sought permission. He believed now that it would be wholly proper for him to remove himself silently and forthwith from the shop.

Just then, however, another customer opened the door and did so noisily. He was a well-dressed gentleman in early middle age who seemed to have as much trouble closing the door as he had

had opening it. The dealer, when he came up the stairs, seemed to ascertain immediately that the two gentlemen had come separately and were not connected. He appeared surprised by the two arrivals, but quickly covered this up with fond recognition for Henry and something less than that for the more recent arrival. This time he seemed more clever than before, more foreign, more deeply intelligent and fine-featured; his dark eyes shone with a clever penetrating warmth. It was clear that he did not know that Henry had already observed Lady Wolseley and Henry watched him as he calculated smilingly what he should do. The dealer asked Henry if he could possibly wait for one moment and then made his way back down the steps. Henry heard words murmured below as he saw his fellow shopper take hold of an old silver bell with a carved wooden handle. He waited then for Lady Wolseley to appear, wondering what he, the intruder, could possibly say to her.

As soon as the shop owner reappeared, Henry noticed a tinge of concern in his expression. He was soon followed by Lady Wolseley at her most regal, and, he could not help feeling, at her most loud.

'I was not aware that you ventured out alone,' she said. 'Are you lost?' She smiled a glittering smile and let out a short laugh.

He bowed to her and noticed as he lifted his head that she knew the other gentleman. Both she and the dealer seemed anxious about his presence. When Henry looked towards him, he saw that in those seconds between his bow and his turning of the head, something urgent and almost alarmed had passed in glances between Lady Wolseley and the gentleman.

'Most of the objects in here are beyond your means,' she said to Henry. Both of them knew instantly that the remark, although meant as a joke, was too brusque and too sharp.

'A poor man can always look,' he said, waiting for her to retrieve the situation and wondering how she would do so.

'Come then and I will show you,' she said. She led him down the stairs, calling for another lamp.

He knew that it was a signal for the gentleman to go and was not surprised to hear the front door of the antique shop being shut once more. As Lady Wolseley ordered the lamp to be placed on an Italian cabinet, he wondered who the gentleman was and why they had not been introduced, and why the strain in the room had been so palpable and the encounter, considering Lady Wolseley's great social experience, so badly managed. Could Lady Wolseley, he wondered, have come close to compromising herself in an antique shop in London on an ordinary winter's afternoon? And what form would such a compromise take? And in what way was the dealer implicated? Both Lady Wolseley and the dealer now began to extol the virtues and beauties of the cabinet, Lady Wolseley agreeing vehemently with each phrase the dealer uttered, repeating some of them for emphasis, both of them insisting that a price could not even be mentioned, it would cause shock or scandal, it had better remain unknown to the current visitor who loved beauty but had limited means.

As they both spoke, and then as the dealer fell silent and the conversation was carried by Lady Wolseley, Henry was sure that he had understood perfectly the outlines of the scene just witnessed but not its meaning. Lady Wolseley had arranged to meet a gentleman here, but that alone meant nothing, as she moved freely in London and had taken Henry shopping without the smallest hesitation. The strain had arisen from her unwillingness to greet the gentleman or introduce him. Henry could make no sense of this, could not fathom why she had not either ignored the man totally or made light of knowing him. The conversation which resumed between Lady Wolseley and the dealer seemed to gather up silences and fill them noisily. He realized that he had witnessed a strange London moment whose essences belonged to others and would be kept from him no matter how much he speculated and how long their awkward loitering in the antique shop went on.

While walking up the steps towards the front part of the shop, his eye was caught by the tapestry, which had been moved since his last visit. Now it seemed even more rich and more beautiful. His two companions stopped behind him. He presumed that they too would see the pure delicacy of the colouring, the bright threads working against the faded, the texture suggesting a vast realm long gone.

'Is it eighteenth century?' he asked.

'Look a little and perhaps you'll make out,' Lady Wolseley said.

He looked again as the dealer brought the lamp nearer.

'Do you like it?' he asked her, wondering if she remembered seeing it on their previous visit.

'I don't think "like" is quite the word,' she said. 'It's flawed. It's been restored, some of the work is recent. Can't you see?'

He studied it more carefully, following the pink and yellow threads which seemed to him faded too, even though they stood out against the rest of the work.

'It was made to fool us all,' Lady Wolseley said.

'It's quite striking, quite beautiful,' Henry said as though he were speaking to himself.

'Oh, if you don't see the restoration in all its vulgarity, then you need me even more than you know,' Lady Wolseley said. 'You must under no circumstances ever venture out alone again.'

He would, he thought, return to buy the tapestry once a suitable length of time had elapsed.

HE WAS LOSING London; he put himself down for the Reform Club, joining the long list, knowing it would take many years and much attrition before his name would be at the top. He loved imagining a London life in the comfort of the Reform Club, the care and attention of the staff, and the vast city at his disposal. He had, he mused to himself, been exposed to London all his life, having been taken here at the age of six months on one of his father's early quests for eternal wisdom, earthly satisfaction and something nameless and numinous which would always manage to evade him.

He knew, because his Aunt Kate had told him many times throughout his teenage years, that they had rented a cottage near the Great Park of Windsor and were the most fortunate of families, possessing two healthy boys whose daily antics held their parents and their aunt in thrall, and having enough money for Henry senior to pursue his private interests among the most famous minds of the age, to search for truth, and, if it could not be found, to make the journey towards it memorable and serious and worthwhile. Henry senior was interested in goodness, in the great good plan which God had set for man; each of us, he believed, must learn to decipher this plan, and live as though no one had ever lived before. His task, in reading and writing and talking and bringing up his children, was to reconcile the essential newness and goodness of each member of the human species with the darkness which lay all around and lurked within.

As Henry prepared to leave London, Edmund Gosse became a regular visitor, making sure as much as he could that he was not disturbing Henry, or outstaying the welcome which was generally extended to him. He had been reading one of the few copies of the writings of Henry James senior to have made its way across the Atlantic and he had also become interested, for reasons of his own, in childhood experience, especially experience in infancy, which he believed, as a result of a series of lectures he had attended, could affect behaviour more than was previously imagined. He became fascinated by the account he read by Henry's father about a central experience in his life which had occurred in the house he had rented in the Great Park of Windsor.

His father had written of what happened to him in that cottage near the Park as a moment of revelation and exhilaration; he mentioned it often and Henry remembered that his mother's face darkened each time the subject was rehearsed. Aunt Kate's face darkened too, but it was she who had several times recounted the story to Henry, and there was, he remembered, in her expression a sense of satisfaction that the story could be told again and to as concerned and attentive a listener as young Henry.

Gosse had not known that Henry was an infant in the house when it happened. He had raised the subject merely to ask if it had affected Henry's father's subsequent behaviour. When he discovered that Henry and William were present, then he asked Henry, in a hushed and urgent tone, to tell him everything he knew about it, promising that it was neither for publication nor for dissemination. Henry pointed out that he was an infant and had no memory of it, and that his father's account was in the book.

'But it must have been spoken about in the family?' Gosse asked.

'Yes, my Aunt Kate spoke of it to me, but my mother disliked the subject.'

'Your Aunt Kate was present when it occurred?' Gosse asked.

Henry nodded.

'How did she describe it?' Gosse asked.

'She was a great story-teller, so one cannot be sure of her veracity,' Henry said.

'But you must tell me what she said.'

He tried to recount to Gosse how his aunt had told him the story. It was an afternoon in late spring, she always began, warm for the time of year, and bright, and once they had eaten and retired from the table her brother-in-law had remained there alone, rapt in thought as was his habit. Often, she said, he would move blindly from the table to reach for pen and paper and write obsessively, discarding some of the pages he read over by making them into a ball and flinging them fiercely across the room. Often he would search for a book, standing up suddenly and walking too fast across the room dragging his wooden leg behind him as though it were a burden. He could be very excited by the book's meaning or message. There was a battle going on, Aunt Kate used the same words each time, between his own sweetness and the heavy puritan hand which his father, old William James of Albany, had placed on his shoulder. Everywhere he went, she said, Henry James senior saw love and the beauty of God's plan, but the old puritan teaching would not let him believe his eyes. Daily, within him, the battle went on. He was restless and impossible, but he was also, in his searching, innocent and easily enraptured. His first great crisis had come in his youth when his leg had had to be amputated after a fire; now in the late spring in London, he was awaiting his second visitation.

'My Aunt Kate,' Henry said, 'was very dramatic in her delivery. She told me that they had left him reading. The day was mild and they had taken us young boys for a walk. He was alone when the attack came; it appeared suddenly from nowhere, like a huge obscure shape in the night, an angry, broken, pecking bird of prey, squatting in the corner ready to take him, all black spirit, yet palpable, visibly there, hissing, come for him alone. He knew why it had appeared, she said; it had been sent to destroy him. From that moment, he was reduced to the state of an infant terrified and then terrified again until he believed that it would never go from him, whatever it was. When they found him, he was curled on the ground, his hands over his ears, whimpering, calling for them. William and I were two and a half and one, and were in turn terrified by the sight of his fear and the sound of his whimpering voice. Aunt Kate brought us instantly away. William, she said, was pale for days afterwards and would not sleep without his mother in the room. Neither of us, of course, has any memory of it.'

'There is no guarantee of that,' Gosse said. 'The memory may be locked within.'

'No,' Henry said sternly. 'Nothing is locked within. We have no memory of it. I am certain of that.'

'Go on, please continue,' Gosse said.

'My aunt told me that my mother had to lift him from the ground, believing at first that he had been attacked by felons, and then she had to listen to his description of what he saw, telling him all the while that there was no black shape, no strange figure squatting in the corner, that he was safe. She could not stop his tears, nor could she fully ascertain what had happened. Soon, she realized that he was not talking about an animal or a thief; what had happened had occurred in his mind, his imagination. It was a dark vision and she did now as she had done in the first year of their marriage when he had nightmares. She found a pair of scissors and slowly and gently began to cut his fingernails, talking to him softly and making him concentrate on the motions of the scissors. Then he became calm and she took him to their room and stayed with him.'

'But she left you alone?' Gosse asked.

'No, of course not,' Henry replied. 'My aunt looked after us. When we were in bed that night and my father had finally calmed down, she sat with my mother and they did not know whom to consult or what to do. My father, once she began to comfort him, became silent, his eyes vacant, his mouth open. He did not stop making low whimpering sounds or uttering phrases which sounded like gibberish. They were away from home and knew no one other than my father's distinguished friends, and they did not know if they could call on Carlyle or Thackeray and ask them how the patient, if that was the word, could be treated, or indeed if such dark and terrifying moments were common to men who teased out the meanings of things to the exclusion of professional or domestic duties.'

'So what did they do?' Gosse asked.

'My father slept that night, as did we, but the two women watched over us, aware that life would change now. My mother knew what it was, my aunt told me, and she always believed it no matter what else was said. She believed that the devil had visited a philosopher, but it was a devil my father had imagined, or come to see in his own dreamlife which merged oddly with his reading life in those months. My mother believed in the devil, but knew that only he could see it, and to him it was utterly real, a face that lurked on the other side of the glass of every window he approached. No one else could see it because no one else had been delving into thoughts and beliefs in which darkness itself, and devilry, would be banished from our concept of the world. That was my father.'

'But what did your mother and aunt finally do?' Gosse asked.

'They had, Aunt Kate said, two children and a house to take care of and they only saw what was there. The doctors insisted he be quiet, neither read nor write, and not think, if he could help it, nor make visits. What Aunt Kate remembered most from these months was that every time my mother came into the room, my father stretched out his arms as though he were an infant seeking to be lifted. He lived in fear that what he had seen would return; he scoured the corners of rooms and the window with his eyes. He lived in a world beyond them; even his speech seemed impaired.'

'Did your aunt say how this affected you and your brother?' Gosse asked.

Henry sighed. He did not know why he had agreed to tell his friend the story.

'On one of those days when he seemed most helpless, it seems I began to walk,' Henry said. 'It came suddenly and surprisingly, and soon, I was an eager and confident little walker. It was as though I had changed places with my father. Slowly they understood why I had been so quick to learn. I wished to follow William everywhere he went; I watched William with hungry eyes in case he moved, and now if William went outside, or crossed the room, I followed him and clung to him, much to his annoyance. I had not, apparently, smiled or laughed easily, but now that I could walk I laughed at anything William did which seemed to me even mildly funny. It was, Aunt Kate said, a difficult household as the English summer began.'

'I can imagine,' Gosse said. 'How extraordinary!'

'In the end, of course,' Henry went on, 'it was all forgotten, or placed in history, as you know, as an important moment in my father's climb towards the peaks of knowledge and wisdom.'

'But did it seem like that to them?' Gosse asked.

'No.' Henry smiled. 'No, Aunt Kate said it never seemed like that to herself or her sister. And to their horror, my father began to describe his dark ordeal to all visitors and then to strangers.

And thus, as you must have read, in a watering place, he met a lady, a certain Mrs Chichester, and he described to her his squatting, hissing beast. Mrs Chichester responded immediately: what had happened to him had happened to others and was a sign that he had come close to understanding the great plan, God's dream for man, she said, and he must read the Swedish philosopher Swedenborg who understood these things as no one else did. During that time, it seems, my father took any new suggestion as vastly superior to the previous suggestion. In London he read two books by Swedenborg, even though he had foresworn reading, and in one of these books he found that what had occurred to him that afternoon was called a vastation, and nothing he ever heard again convinced him that it was not so. This vastation, it seemed, was a step on the road to the full understanding that God made us in his likeness, and that our urges and appetites, our thoughts and feelings are profoundly sanctified. Thus my father became happy again, and, filled with Swedenborg, believed it his mission to spread the truth to all mankind, at least to the English-speaking variety, and indeed, mainly in America, not, I should add, that any of them paid much attention.'

'Perhaps it explains why you have come back here,' Gosse said.

'To England?' Henry asked.

'Close to the scene of where it happened. The lectures say that a child can take in everything, hold it but not absorb it in what they call the unconscious.'

'Why is not William here then?' Henry asked.

'I do not know,' Gosse said. 'It is a mystery.'

'Perhaps you will understand when I say that I do not wish to discuss it again,' Henry said.

For several days he could not work and found when he woke in the morning that he suffered from a great regret at having told Gosse the story, until he put the episode out of his mind so that he might continue making his plans in peace.

*

SOME DAYS, Henry believed, he wrote too much and too quickly, working his Scot too hard. Once the stories were published, he paid little attention to them, revising them once for book publication and then forgetting about them. However, when his new collection *Embarrassments* appeared and Gosse had much to say about one of the stories, he read it over so that he could discuss it further with his friend. It was one of his ghost stories, called 'The Way It Came', and it seemed to him now too thin to survive even as a potboiler. Gosse wanted to discuss the technique of the first-person voice, how very difficult it was to make it convincing. He was, Henry thought, too polite and tactful to allow himself to stray from the general point to the particular story. But, as the conversation between them about the story proceeded over a few meetings and began to irritate him, a second matter raised by Gosse began to interest him profoundly. Gosse insisted that, since most readers did not fully believe in ghosts, then most ghost stories could not fully be credible. They needed, he said, both to be ghost stories and to have a rational explanation at the same time; they needed to be both frightening and within the bounds of the possible, he insisted.

Henry disagreed. He believed that a story should be able to suggest anything at all, including the most outlandish matter, but he was, nonetheless, interested in Gosse's argument, although it was too vehement and too eager to impose rules on subjects which, in Henry's opinion, required great latitude. Privately, Henry was appalled by 'The Way It Came' and regretted collecting it in a volume, knowing that it might have been better to let it sink. He quite resented Gosse for noticing it.

During one of those evenings with Gosse, he told him in passing how he had acquired Lamb House, mentioning the iron-monger Mr Milson as a ferryman waiting to take him across the water to ideal seclusion, managed happiness. He then told Gosse of Howells's visit, and how his financial circumstances due to new possibilities for American publication had been transformed, as though he were being handed a coin by an old friend to put under his tongue and assist him on his journey to Hades.

'Rye,' Gosse laughed, 'is indeed a death, especially on weekdays in the winter, but I daresay at weekends as well.'

'If I were Poe,' Henry said, 'I could write about one of those characters who is travelling to an unknown house whose door is a door into the grave.'

'You will long for London, and that will settle it, and you will escape with the mere fright which rural life offers the unwary,' Gosse said.

HENRY HAD promised Collier's a new story as part of Howells's interceding on his behalf, and, having consulted his notebooks and spoken more to Gosse about the problem of credibility in the modern ghost story but without telling him what his plans were, he set to work. This time he would frame the story, use the first-person voice as a narrative left behind by the protagonist and now retrieved to be read to a weekend party at a country house. He longed, as he dictated, to frighten the Scot, and watched him carefully as he began his tale so that he could note thereafter any shift in his countenance, any paling of his skin.

His narrator's voice would be prim and factual; seeping gently from her tone would be a sort of goodness, a readiness to appreciate each new person and each new experience as a reward sent to her in exchange for her quick intelligence and sensitivity. He sought a tone of voice full of calm acceptance, resigned competence, mingling authority with a devotion to duty, an orderly attachment to making the best of things; someone who would not complain and for whom shrillness would be among the cardinal vices. He wanted a voice that every reader would automatically believe and trust, but also a literary style redolent of fifty years earlier – our heroine was an avid reader – broken intermittently by simple vivid sentences.

It was the story which had lain in his notebooks for more than two years, and had come to him over that time in flashes and moments, but nothing close to a form or a way to begin had inspired him until now, when he knew that he would need such a story, firm and frightening and dramatic, for his new editor at Collier's, something that would grip the readers and make them want more. This was the vague tale told to him by the Archbishop of Canterbury of two children in a large house left by their guardian in the care of a governess detailed not to contact the guardian under any circumstances.

It was easy to put flesh on these bare bones, have a hearty, trusty housekeeper, make the little girl gentle and beautiful, make the boy both charming and mysterious, and make the house itself, the strange old house, into a great adventure for our heroine, the governess. He wanted her to have no skills at reflection or self-examination, he wanted the reader to know her by what she noticed, and what sights, indeed, she used her narrative to gloss over. Thus the reader would see the world through her eyes, but somehow see her too, despite her efforts at self-concealment and self-suppression, in ways she could not see herself.

The house was all emptiness and echoing sounds. The governess's two charges made nothing of their abandonment, they paraded themselves to the governess and the kind housekeeper as brimming vessels in need of nothing more than what was provided for them. All sound, both within and without, was ominous sound matched by ominous echo. He set down as soon as he could the moment when, on retiring for the night, the governess heard the faint distant cry of a child and then in front of her door the sound of a light footstep. These, he determined as he moved up and down the room dictating the words, should seem like nothing at the time and would only become significant in the light, or in the gloom, of what was to come.

He had begun the story as a potboiler, a way of fulfilling a contract, a tale likely to appeal to a wide audience, and he worked accordingly to have it completed by the end of the year. He did not know why it disturbed his waking life in the months in which he prepared his move to Lamb House. He did not know why the voice he had so thoughtfully created, and so carefully controlled and manipulated, seemed to have worked on him so that he allowed his governess a power and a freedom which he had never intended for her. He allowed her to fool herself, something he had never allowed anyone before; he gave her permission to wallow in the danger, to want it to come towards her, to motion it close, signal to it. He relished frightening her. He made her loneliness and her isolation into a longing to meet someone, for a face at the window, a figure in the distance.

This longing, he knew, would in time come to him too as the garden door creaked, or the branches of the trees beat against the window as he read by lamplight, or lay awake in that old house, and in one of those seconds before worthier thoughts could surface, the first thought would be to welcome what was coming now to break the sad, helpless monotony of the self, to feel a moment of desperate hope that it was come at last, whatever it was. Even in its darkest shape, it would offer the same moment of pure, sharp release as a flash of lightning offers to the brittle air in a dried-up landscape.

He worked. He moved everything slowly and deliberately towards excitement. He began the sentences simply, declaratively, so that the fright of what she saw seemed to harden the governess's diction, forced her into bald, true statement. The person looking in through the window was the person who had appeared to her. He was the same. His face was close to the glass and his stare into her face was deep and menacing until she realized something that she would never cease to believe: the added shock of certitude went through her fiercely that it was not for her he had come. He had come for the children.

As he laboured on the story, he did not think in any detail about the children. He gave them names and allowed their governess superlatives with which to describe them. Slowly, however, it became apparent to him that he had imagined for them strange private selves, which, while giving nothing away, maintained a strong resistance to the governess. She did not recognize it, and yet, whatever he had done with her words, he had handed young Miles and little Flora minds of their own.

Each time he came to describe the appearance of the ghost, or the ethereal and menacing presence of Peter Quint, none of this mattered. The scene itself, the emptiness of the house, its newness for the governess, and then the invasive figure, utterly real to her, and seemingly real also to the children and the housekeeper Mrs Grose, made him shiver as he began to conjure it up. He watched McAlpine for signs of interest, but none came. He knew that asking McAlpine if he found these scenes in any way disturbing would be a breach of decorum. Most of the time, however, he did not think about McAlpine, and even the sound of the Remington made no difference. Most of the time he concentrated on the voice itself, the governess's vivid version of each thing witnessed. His main task was to prevent the reader from asking why the governess did not contact the children's guardian; he sought to offer enough detail and swift movement and further development to preserve the fiction that she was alone and must act alone. He set out to cajole the reader into becoming her eyes and ears and thus entering into her spirit, inhabiting unquestioningly her consciousness.

The story appeared in Collier's in twelve weekly instalments. He had no difficulty meeting the deadline. He knew what had to happen and sometimes he lingered softly over the fresh fright he was causing to the governess, enjoying the darting logic of her mind, making sure that he signalled again and again that the children knew everything and nothing. They were the least dependable pair, Miles and Flora, that he had ever invented; they had learned to withstand it all, save the obvious danger, and at times as he worked he was not sure himself what that was.

He knew that his working conditions were the most perfect he would ever have. The Scot was silent and dutiful and accurate. Speaking out the sentences gave them a greater force and stability than when he wrote them in longhand. Seeing them in a fair copy that evening gave them an immediate authority. He always knew what to do, what emendations to make, and what deletions. And this flat in Kensington would soon be lost to him; he would sublet it or allow the lease to go, but it would no longer be his, and every day he moved about the rooms, alert to their atmosphere as though he would have a vital need to remember them. He had no visitors during the day, no disturbers, merely his shopping expeditions alone or with Lady Wolseley and his consultations with Edward Warren, who was dealing with the work at Lamb House. He dined out with relish now, and accepted invitations with delight. Soon, it would all be over, a part of the past. He would be leaving London.

As he worked each morning, drawing out the scenes in their full drama and fright, scenes of his own came to him in sharply packed shocks and forced him to hesitate and finally stop. On one of these mornings, as he dictated the scene where Flora was discovered having left her bed, her governess believing that she had lied when she stated that she had seen nothing, he found that he was about to use the name Alice in place of Flora. He corrected himself before he spoke. His story, so real to him now and rich and urgent, had been interrupted not by something ghostly, but by a memory which came in all its ache and concrete detail. It did battle with his tale of horror and it won. It took him over; he had to stop and move into his bedroom and stand alone by the window. And then he had to go and tell McAlpine that he would not need him any more that day. This, he thought, was the only time he detected a note of surprise on the face of his amanuensis, but it disappeared quickly and McAlpine arranged his things and left without any questions or comments.

Alice must have been five or six in the scene which had come to him. They had returned to Newport, or perhaps gone there for the first time, and she had been for some days under the care of Aunt Kate while their parents were absent and Aunt Kate had, Alice felt, imposed too much restraint on her small self, far more than was normal. When this was pointed out to her by the child, Aunt Kate had refused to budge, had insisted that her instructions be followed until Alice had become annoyed. She began, Henry remembered, by calling on her brothers for support, but they did not heed her, and then she pouted and sulked. Then, having learned that she would have two more days of this new regime before the return of her parents, she set about obeying Aunt Kate in every possible way, becoming a shining example, if Newport needed one, of an obedient girl.

No one else, save her brothers and Aunt Kate, noticed what she did to her aunt in the months that followed. Aunt Kate could not complain because Alice's assault on her was too sporadic in its timing, and too comic in its tone, and it was, in any case, done behind her back much of the time. If Aunt Kate smiled or greeted a visitor warmly, her little niece stood by her skirts smiling grotesquely in imitation of her. All her particularities of speech, her 'Oh my gosh' and 'well, well, well', became natural parts of Alice's speech, but exaggerated. Alice would often be found staring at her aunt cheekily, but would never do so for long enough to cause her mother to notice. She often followed her aunt for no reason, tip-toeing behind her, trying to mimic the gait of a middle-aged spinster lady.

Aunt Kate herself did not see the extent of Alice's efforts to undermine her and exact revenge, and Alice's parents passed the summer in happy contemplation of their children's innocence and lack of any form of hiddenness and mendacity. William enjoyed it most, and encouraged it, but the impulse came from Alice alone. It must have come into her mind as soon as she woke, and it never seemed to leave her mind as long as she was awake. It ended merely because Alice grew tired of it.

This was the world he made for Miles and Flora, his two innocent and beautiful and abandoned children. Their private selves remained apart; they made sure that their ability to maintain a distance from sweet duty was not apparent. He gave his story everything he knew: his own life and that of Alice in the years when they were alone in England; the possibility which haunted his family all their lives that the threatening black shape would return to the window and make their father shudder and howl with fear; and the years he was now facing in an old house to which he would soon go, like his governess, full of hope, but full also of a foreboding which he could not erase.

Alice was dead now, Aunt Kate was in her grave, the parents who noticed nothing also lay inert under the ground, and William was miles away in his own world, where he would stay. And there was silence now in Kensington, not a sound in the house, except the sound, like a vague cry in the distance, of his own great solitude, and his memory working like grief, the past coming to him with its arm outstretched looking for comfort.

CHAPTER SEVEN

April 1898

THE PHOTOGRAPHS CAME AS he had asked for them; one was close-up and detailed, showing in relief the monument to the soldiers of the 54th Massachusetts Regiment being led by Colonel Shaw, and the other taken from a distance, showing the Boston Common and Saint Gaudens's monument in the corner. Henry carried the photographs to the window to study them in a better light and then went back to the table and found William's letter calling the new monument a glorious work of art, simple and realistic. He could hear the certainty in William's voice. William had given the official address on the unveiling of this memorial to the 54th Regiment, the first black regiment of the American army, in which their brother Wilky had served. He had spoken for three quarters of an hour, and then been, as he put it, toted around for two hours in a brake at the tail end of the procession. It was, he wrote to Henry, an extraordinary occasion for sentiment with everything softened and made poetic and unreal by the time which had passed.

It was easy for Henry to reply to him, to say that he would have given anything to have been there and to add, choosing his words carefully, that the spirit of their poor dead brother Wilky would have been very much present on Boston Common during the unveiling of the monument, and that the event would have been a poetic justice to him. Henry noticed that William had not enclosed a copy of his speech either with his letter or with the photographs and was glad now that he did not have to comment on it. William had become a public figure, full of manly expression and fearless opinions. Thus he could speak for forty-five minutes to a crowded hall about the nobility of the Yankee cause and the legacy of the Union dead, especially the dead of the 54th and 55th Regiments in which both Wilky and Bob had served.

Henry's own sentences in his first story about the Civil War had remained in his mind through all the years: 'The exploits of his campaign are recorded in the public journals of the day, where the curious may still pursue them. My own taste has always been for unwritten history and my present business is with the reverse of the picture.' And he wondered, as he studied the photographs on and off throughout the day, what his own speech, his own reversed picture, might say about the 54th Regiment and the Civil War. He wondered also about the power of one unasked and tactless question which could have punctured the power of William's speech at the unveiling. It concerned William personally and Henry too; and in soft whispers now it asked why neither of them had actually fought, along with their two brothers, for the cause of freedom.

THE STORY OF his father's wooden leg was one of the often-told delights of his childhood. If Henry showed signs of illness, or hurt himself in a fall, or if he agreed to complete an arduous task, then he would be promised the story by his mother, who told it as though she had witnessed it. His father was a boy who loved to play, she said, and was happiest away from his parents who were very strict with him. He was most content when playing with his friends. One of the games they played in the park was dangerous and involved hot-air balloons. They used spirit of turpentine to produce the flame to make the hot air rise. When the balloon caught fire you had to be careful because the burning balloon could land on you, land on your hair or on your clothes and you too could catch fire, his mother said, her face serious and her voice slow and grave, because the turpentine was highly combustible.

He loved the word 'combustible' and made her repeat it. From an early age, he knew what it meant. But that day, she went on, his father had accidentally spilled the turpentine on his pantaloons, and, without understanding the danger he was in, he stood with all the other boys watching the balloons rise and then catch fire, one by one falling down, and all the boys standing out of the way, and warning each other to avoid them. But your father, she told him, saw one burning balloon floating towards the stables just beside the park, and he liked the horses there and the stable boys let him feed them sometimes, so when he noticed the balloon land in the hayloft above the stables he realized the danger and he ran towards the loft, climbing the ladder to stamp out the fire. But – and now his mother held Henry's hand – as soon as he stood on the flame, and it wasn't even a strong flame and the hay hadn't even started to burn, as soon as the flame came in contact with the turpentine and his pantaloons, your father, just barely thirteen, went on fire and no one could help him. He ran from the hayloft screaming, but by the time they could put out the fire his two legs had been so badly burned that one of them had to be amputated.

It was cut from above the knee, and at this point of the story his mother put her hand around his knee, but he did not flinch, and she too remained calm, as she explained how painful it had been and how brave he was and how hard he tried not to scream. But, in the end, she said, it was impossible and they always recounted that his screams could be heard for miles around. For two years afterwards your father had to stay in bed, she told him, and he had to contemplate a future in which he would not be able to run, or play games. He would have to have a wooden leg, and that was a bigger test of his fortitude than the pain of the amputation.

What was strange – and here her voice grew tender as she spoke – was that only good came from this accident. Up to then, she said, your papa's father was very strict with him, and was also much preoccupied with his myriad businesses – she watched him now as he nodded to signal that he understood the word 'myriad' from his Bible – and his mother had a large household and her other children. But now, after the accident, they came to their son's aid, they showed him a new and deep tenderness and he felt enclosed and protected by their love. At the beginning, they never left his side and his father seemed to sense his pain and share his panic until many times his father had to be taken away in tears. Later, as he began to recover, they made sure he had everything he needed, and gradually then, your father replaced his dreams of races and games with the life of the mind, with books and speculation. He began, she said, to contemplate the fate of man in the world and the life of man in relation to God as no one else in America had ever done. He had all due grounding in the Bible and in youthful theology, but in his two years as an invalid he was allowed to read whatever he pleased and, of course, he had time to think. And thus commenced, his mother said, your father's noble quest. Later, when he became friends with Emerson, Emerson always said that Henry James had an advantage over him: he knew about suffering first hand and he had learned to think and read away from school masters and fellow scholars. Emerson always said, his mother told him, that your father had a truly original mind.

On Sundays and during their holidays, when they were travelling and on days when there was no school, Henry stayed close to his mother; as the others found fulfilment in playing or boyish escapades, he would wait until she was free, or he would join in the work, and then they would move silently towards some comfortable place, often leaving Aunt Kate to finish what his mother had been doing, and his mother would talk to him, or read to him, or they would go through some of her things, tidying and putting them all in order.

*

THE FAMILY was divided into three parts – William and Henry, whose education was supervised in elaborate detail by their father; Wilky and Bob, whose noise-making skills and lack of scholarly initiative made their father unhappy, thus causing him to feel that sending Wilky and Bob to school together was not only convenient, since they were both so close in age, but that it might also be effective. Wilky might develop some of Bob's caution; Bob might, under Wilky's influence, learn to make himself agreeable to visitors and smile warmly at familiar faces. Alice was an independent republic.

When people asked them, especially in Newport, what their father did, all five James children had difficulty replying. Their father lived on his inheritance, the revenue from rent and dividends, but this was hardly what he did. He was also a sort of philosopher and sometimes he gave lectures and wrote articles. But none of this added up to a simple phrase, an easy answer. And when their father suggested they tell their enquirers that he was a seeker after the truth, the matter became more perplexing. As they grew older a second question, commonly asked, began to puzzle them further. What were they themselves going to become? William, at the beginning, was going to become a painter, and Bob, to the great hilarity of the others, wanted to open a dry goods store. Alice, clearly, was going to become a wife. But what were Henry and Wilky going to do? This question did not interest their father and could not be discussed easily with their mother and thus was left in abeyance, another example, if one were needed, of the strangeness of their family, which both they and the world of Newport had come to accept.

Since he relished clashings and new beginnings, Henry senior was ready to discuss any matter with any man, and was even prepared to discuss politics should the need arise, although he viewed the political world as a great distraction from, and impediment to, the possibility of human progress under the great light which God had made for humankind. The Civil War, however, began to fascinate him, not only because he saw it, in its essence, as a war between progress and cruelty, but also because he saw the end of the war as a time when protean energies could come to the fore, when there would be neither victors nor vanquished, but a grand transition in his country from youth to manhood, from appearance to reality, from passing shadow to deathless substance.

Nonetheless, in the early days of the Civil War Henry senior told anyone who came within his range that he was holding firmly to the coat-tails of his sons who were, he insisted, desperately trying to enlist. Henry senior did not believe that his own sons should join, he said, because he did not believe that any existing government, or any future government, was worth an honest human life or a clean one like theirs.

As his father discovered the pleasure of mixing political transcendence and prudent care for his family, Henry discovered a large bundle under the stairs of the house in Newport which contained back numbers of the *Revue des Deux Mondes*, complete with its salmon-coloured wrapping, which sang to him in the privacy of his room like a choir of angels. Even the names opened for him a world of possibility beyond the surrounding dullness and domesticity and patriotism and religiosity: Sainte-Beuve, the Goncourts, Mérimée, Renan. Names which suggested not only the modern mind at its most enquiring but the idea of style itself, of thinking as a kind of style, and the writing of essays not as a conclusive call to duty or an earnest effort at self-location, but as play, as the wielding of tone.

The shut door of his room, and his being left alone there, became the governing comforts of his life. He would appear at meals and accept the mockery of the others at his silences, his seriousness, his pale face and gaunt presence. Nothing mattered now except the spellbound time alone, not only with the *Revue des Deux Mondes*, but with Balzac, who wrote of a France that Henry had merely glimpsed, but enough to know that he himself would never possess a subject as richly layered and suggestive, as sharply focussed and centred, as the France of Balzac's *Human Comedy*.

As William went to Harvard and Wilky made efforts to leave Sanborn, a boarding school that was 'an experiment in coeducation' supported by Emerson and Hawthorne, and Bob, having already left Sanborn, sailed his boat and made a nuisance of himself, Henry's mother began to watch her bookish second son as though he were a patient. His mother protected his privacy and made sure also that no criticism of him was uttered by anyone, especially not by his father. Since Henry senior tended to find out what he believed by listening to his own utterances, his non-criticism of Henry meant approval, since he felt only benevolence for that towards which he did not express anathema.

His mother began to appear silently in Henry's room two or three times a day with a mug of fresh milk, or a small jar of honey, or a jug of cool water. She entered the room without knocking, and usually did not speak, and suggested in her placid movements and her quietness an approval for the work being done. For the first time, Henry later thought, Mrs James was witnessing her husband's theories about the need to discover and explore the secret pleasures of the self through reading and thinking put into practice without any accompanying fervid hint of the unreliable to unsettle her.

On one of those calm summer evenings at Newport, his mother came into his room to find that he had fallen asleep in his chair, his book on his lap. He woke to discover her hand on his brow and a worried look on her face. She went downstairs immediately and returned briskly with the maid who prepared the bed for him, his mother brandishing a freshly wetted cloth to attempt, she said, to cool him down. If this did not work, his mother said, she would call the doctor forthwith, but now he must go to bed. He had been overtaxing himself and he must rest, she said. He knew that he had not been overtaxing himself, knew that he had merely fallen asleep on a hot summer's day, but by this time Aunt Kate had appeared and he was a patient, getting all the close attention that illness received in the family.

His mother began to carry his meals to his room and excuse him when company not to his taste was in the house, making sure also that he was not confined to bed during outings he would enjoy or when company that would interest him was present. She did not discuss his illness with him and when she asked him how he felt, it was to know if he were much the same or slightly better; she did not leave him free to reply that he was not ill at all.

There began then a conspiracy between them, a drama in which each knew the roles and the lines and the movements. Henry learned to walk slowly, never to run, to smile but never to laugh, to stand up hesitantly and awkwardly and to sit down with relief. He learned not to eat heartily or drink his fill.

Soon after this when gleeful and full-blooded talk of recruits and the need to serve his country filled the air, his mother watched over him daily with greater worry and indulgence. Often, when he woke in the morning he found her sitting by his bed, having stolen into his room, studying him gently and smiling soothingly when his eyes opened.

There were a few times he could not disguise his strength, or hide his readiness to take part. That October a high wind from the sea blew through Newport and a small conflagration at a stable on the corner of Beach and State quickly became a raging fire. Two whole streets, including shops and bars and stables and private residences, were in danger, and soon, as one stable was gutted, horses and carriages and valuable belongings were removed to safety. Every able-bodied person was needed to pump water from wells or carry water from cisterns. That night, as frenzied activity and fierce urgent shouting went on all around him, Henry worked without thinking. It was only when the fire had been extinguished and his arms and back ached that he thought of the probable extent of his mother's concern.

She and his aunt, who had been alerted to his activity by Bob, were waiting for him when he came home.

They made him retire to the sofa and then set about filling a hot bath for him. He closed his eyes and lay back as they bustled about him. His mother's mouth was shut tight. Later, when he had emerged from his hot bath, scrubbed and tired and ready for bed, she expressed the fear that he had injured his back. They would know by the morning, she said, if the injury was bad. Now it was late and he should sleep for as long as he could.

The next day, he did not rise until suppertime. His mother told him to move slowly. She helped him down the stairs. He entered the dining room leaning on her, as his father and his aunt moved the chairs out of the way so that he could pass easily. They helped him to sit down and watched him carefully, encouraging him to eat and drink to build up his strength. Later, his mother helped him back to bed and for a few days he took all his meals in his room and had the sympathy of the entire household.

Slowly, in the months that followed, as Henry started to work on translations from the French, Henry senior gradually changed his mind about the war. He began to see it not just as a cause worth supporting in theory but as a cause worth volunteering for. And as he propounded his opinions at the family table, much to the delight of Bob, too young to join but old enough to be fired with enthusiasm, his wife became increasingly solicitous of Henry.

Neither before the war broke out, nor during its early months, did Henry or his mother ever discuss his illness or its symptoms at any length, nor did Henry ever allow himself any clear reflection on whatever malady was affecting him. He began to live with it, managing his disability as neither a game nor an act but a strange, secret thing. By not insisting on its being defined, by allowing the conspiracy with his mother to run its guilty course, never having contemplated any other possibility, he lived his illness, even when he was alone, with sincerity.

As news came in, however, in this first year of the war, of cousins who had joined up, including Gus Barker and William Temple, Minny's brother, who had been, much to his pride, made a captain on his first day in honour of his dead father, the fact that the James boys were remaining civilians, and Henry in idleness, could not but be noted by all those who paid even scant attention to the matter.

Henry's mother understood that Henry's nameless abstract ailment, his obscure hurt, could not continue indefinitely without a name, that a professional diagnosis would have to be arrived at. His father therefore accompanied him to Boston to see Dr Richardson, an eminent surgeon made even more eminent, in Aunt Kate's opinion, by his dead wife's large fortune. He was a known expert on injuries to the back.

Much time had elapsed since Henry had been alone with his father. On the journey to Boston, Henry senior seemed deeply uneasy with him, unsure, it appeared, whether he could share with his second son his views on the change which would come to America as a result of the war, this currently being the only topic that interested him. He was mostly silent, but not withdrawn. He looked like someone whose mind was working, whose brain was on the point of reaching some grand conclusion. When they arrived, Henry senior seemed to have greater difficulty walking in Boston than he did in Newport, as though his confidence or the power of his wooden leg had diminished as they reached the metropolis.

Dr Richardson's face was illuminated with a sharp little smile, and with this smile playing in his clear eyes and on his neatly shaved lips he looked at his patient. He then became silent as Henry senior began to talk, explaining the length of their journey, the number of his offspring, their situation and his hopes for a new America. The doctor, as he contemplated Henry senior, replaced his smile with a scowl. His eyes became cold as he waited for him to finish. And when it was clear that his father had no real intention of finishing, the doctor simply sprang up and moved towards his patient. With his two hands he motioned him to remove the upper parts of his clothing. As Henry began to undress, his father faltered for a moment until the doctor fetched him a chair and motioned him to sit on it. By the time Henry had stripped to the waist, the doctor still had not spoken. He made Henry raise his arms above his head and then slowly, painstakingly, he began to study his frame, the bones in his arms, his shoulders, his rib cage. He then began meticulously to finger his spine. Eventually, he made him lie facedown on the couch as he repeated each exercise. Then, having indicated to Henry that he should remove all his clothing save his undershorts, he ran his hand clinically along his hip bones and pelvis, repeating the earlier exercise on his spine and arms and shoulders, pressing hard until Henry winced.

Henry had presumed that he would be asked where the pain centred and what sort of pain it was, and he was ready to answer this, but Dr Richardson asked him nothing, merely probed and studied, his hands hard, his examination slow and thorough and methodical, his silence dry. Finally, he went to the basin and poured some water over his hands and washed them with soap and then dried them with a towel. He handed Henry his clothes and nodded as Henry began to dress. He stood up to his full height and stretched.

'There's nothing the matter a good day's work wouldn't cure,' he said. 'Plenty of exercise. Up early, out early, that's not the best cure for most things but it's the best cure for this young man. He is in perfect condition, his whole life ahead of him. I'll have to charge you, sir, for telling you this good news. There's nothing at all wrong with your son. And I don't make up my mind easily. What I tell you is the result of thirty years of observation.'

As Henry leaned over to pick up his jacket, Dr Richardson gripped his neck with his thumb and forefinger, pressing hard until Henry, his face contorted with pain, tried to wrench his hand away, but the doctor merely tightened his grip. His hand was strong.

'Up early, out early,' he said. 'You won't get better advice in many a long day. Home with you now.'

Even still, all these years later, he thought, he hated doctors, and had drawn a portrait of a most unpleasant member of the profession with much relish in *Washington Square,* using some of Dr Richardson's more obnoxious mannerisms in his description of his Dr Sloper's professional habits. He wondered indeed if the visit itself, in all its humiliation and roughness, had not in fact caused a genuine, serious backache that was with him to this day. He had suffered a great deal from constipation as well, and often blamed it on Dr Richardson, and made sure to keep away from others of his profession lest they should cause some new malady.

SEVERAL TIMES a day Henry looked at the photographs which William had sent him, having left them on a table in one of the downstairs rooms at Lamb House, and noted with more and more interest the place of honour which the monument had on Boston Common. His own name could have easily been among the dead, or the maimed, and he would have been a proud memory now to his brother and those who had survived.

As he explored the area around Rye, delighting in his new life, working on a new novel, feeling at home as though for the first time, he wondered at how easily it could have been otherwise. He was not cut out to be a soldier, he thought, but neither were most of the young men of his class and acquaintance who went to fight. It was not wisdom which kept him away, he believed, but something closer to cowardice, and as he walked the cobbled streets of his new town, he almost thanked God for it. He wished this gladness had been simple, but it came back to him, as much else, with guilt at its core and regret and memories of what had happened to his brother Wilky which these photographs made sharp and clear.

He remembered that he put on his jacket that day in Boston, and having watched his father pay the doctor, accompanied him to the street. Their silence on the return journey had a different tone. Now his father was deep in melancholy contemplation. Neither of them, Henry thought, would know what to say to his mother.

When they met her at the door of their house in Newport, he recalled that they both remained so solemn and their expressions were so worried that she believed, she told them later, that the news could not be worse. She suspected, she said, that Henry had a terminal illness. And now she was relieved to hear that the prognosis had been good, the injury to his back was not dangerous, not part of some wider ailment.

'Rest,' she said. 'Rest will be enough. You'll need to rest for the next few days after your long journey.'

Henry remembered that he watched his father and wondered if he was going to tell her the true prognosis but his father just then seemed to be having difficulty taking off his coat and had to be assisted. As soon as his coat was hanging in the hallway, his father found a book and settled down to read it. Henry guessed that even in the privacy of the night his father would not reveal what the doctor had really said. Yet there was no conspiracy between Henry and his father to deceive his mother. Henry felt now that his father had never told her that her son was perfectly healthy because it would have involved such a clear rebuttal of her own judgement, and implied a criticism of her. It would also have forced her to face the possibility that Henry's weakness and disability had been a search for attention and sympathy. This would undermine Henry's moral character in a household where illness was too serious a matter for such games not to be a sort of sacrilege, and this would be too unsettling for everyone, including his father.

His father needed time, Henry thought, to mull over the great discrepancy between the words 'Up early, out early' and the treatment Henry was receiving. He was conscious that his father's propensity for change could make itself felt at any stage; he knew how much it tended towards the irrational, if it were not controlled and channelled. He knew that idling in his room all summer, being cosseted by his mother and his aunt, could cause his father suddenly to stand up, leave his book aside, and with fire in his eyes declare that something would have to be done about Henry.

He moved carefully, consulting William about the advisability of a course at Harvard and then his friend Sargy Perry who was about to enter the college. He did not allude directly to his father's unpredictability and the course it could take. He maintained a high tone, explaining that it was time he ceased to idle at the family's expense and considered a career. William nodded.

'Have you considered the ministry? There will never not be a need for you, especially if you study divinity at Harvard, where the bedside manner, with exhortation to repent, is taught with such emphasis and zeal.'

He allowed William to joke, but did not let him stray from the subject. He was young enough still to care more about his immediate circumstances than any long-term vision of his career. Thus being left alone all summer reigned supreme among his desires. And when William said 'law', he realized that it was the only plausible option. His family, he knew, could number among their familiars some whose sons had taken a similar route. But more than anything, the study of law sounded serious and decisive, and it was also a change of direction. It would offer their father a brief thrill, and this would prevent him from wanting another such thrill – at least as far as Henry was concerned – for some time.

His mother, perhaps as a result of a chance remark or merely because of his father's silence on the matter, began to ask him if his back was not, in fact, much improved. She wondered one day if more exercise rather than more rest might not be the solution. He thought from her uncertainty and her vague worried air that his father had said nothing directly, but he was also aware of how close the danger was now, that he could easily have a decision made for his future without his being consulted. It would take just one night, his parents beginning their discussions before they went to bed and continuing in muffled tones until they would have a decision and it would be announced at breakfast as a fact, something which had been decided and could not be amended.

Henry waited for the moment. He would need both of them together. He would begin by discussing his own unsettled state and his urge to make a decision about his future. He would suggest that he had no clear idea what to do; but he was alert to the danger here – if he left this door open for too long, his father would be capable of closing it and locking it very quickly by proposing he join the Union forces and, having made the proposal, allowing it to become more gravely and deeply the entire focus of the discussion to the exclusion of other possibilities. He would need to move the discussion forward quickly, to say perhaps that he had spoken to William, although that would also be a risk as William went in and out of favour depending on nothing more than the vagaries of his father's thinking. He could not say that he wished 'to be' a lawyer as his father would pounce on the words 'to be' and lecture him about his own being as a precious gift to be cultivated with energy but also with subtle wisdom and consideration. Thus, his father would say, you cannot 'be' a lawyer nor can you 'become' one. Such language, his father would insist, is a way of offering offence to the greatest gift of our Creator – life itself and the grace our Creator offers us to move on from our being and become.

No, he would have to discuss his urge to study law rather than become a lawyer, to attend lectures about law, to broaden his intellect by applying it directly to a discipline. Such words, if uttered with spontaneity and sincerity, if he could speak as though his high hopes had focussed on this solution only now, as a result of this discussion, he might fire his father with enthusiasm at this change, and his mother would nod in agreement, carefully weighing up the consequences.

He thought of going to his mother first and telling her of his plan, but he knew that things had gone too far for that. In any case, his father would suspect both of them of conspiring at his exclusion. Henry's injured back would also have to be mentioned, but it would have to be delicately brought into the conversation, as neither a deciding factor nor an impediment, but as something that might fade from the horizon, annihilated once and for all by the force of a new decision.

He found them as he dreamed of finding them, his father reading and his mother moving quietly about the room.

'I need to discuss with you my present circumstances,' he said.

'Sit down, Harry,' his mother said, moving to a tall chair by the table and sitting there with her hands joined in front of her.

'I know that it is time for me to make a choice, and I have given it much thought, but perhaps not enough thought, and I have come to you both to see, perhaps, if you could help me clarify how I must live my life, what I must do.'

'Each of us needs to clarify how he must live his life,' Henry senior said. 'It is a matter for all of us.'

'I am aware of that, Father,' Henry said and then left silence. He knew that his father could not now declare a career for him or suggest that he get up early and go out early. He had left things open for discussion rather than decision. He could see his father becoming bright-eyed and excited that an ordinary morning with his family in Newport had suddenly been transformed and was awash with possibility.

No one mentioned the army, but it hovered over the conversation, swooping to eye level now and then; nor did any of them mention his ailment, but it too lingered in the atmosphere. Henry was careful not to mention anything specific at first, merely his restlessness and his ambition and his need to clarify – he used the word several times – what he might do now.

'I have become interested in America itself, Father, its traditions and history and indeed its future.'

'Yes, but that is a subject for all Americans, we all must devote time and energy to the study of our heritage,' his father said.

'America is developing and changing,' Henry said, 'in ways which are unique and require a serious approach.'

He wondered if the word 'serious' had not been a mistake, if it had not suggested that his father's approach to his chosen subject had been less than serious. His father was easily wounded, but his mind was too busy now, and his bustling confidence too complete to take offence. Henry watched him pondering the full implications of the last remark and then noticed his eyes become steely, his expression hard. He loved how his father could change like this and regretted that it occurred so seldom. He did not look at his mother.

'What is it you wish to do then?' his father asked.

In that moment Henry senior appeared and sounded like someone powerful, a man with a large private income at his disposal and a high puritan sternness. This, he thought, was how his father's own father must have been when plans and money were being discussed.

'I do not wish to become an historian,' Henry said. 'I want to study something with a more specific application. In short, sir, I wanted to discuss with you whether I should study law.'

'And keep us all out of jail?' his father asked.

'Do you wish to join your brother at Harvard?' his mother asked.

'William said it is the best law school in America.'

'William would not even know how to break a law,' his father said.

The idea of a changing legal system as part of a changing America, however, began to interest his father the more he spoke on the subject. When he had expounded on it at some length, he seemed to abandon whatever worries he had about the narrowness of the subject and indeed the confining nature of decisions themselves. The fact that his two eldest sons would spend their time, at his expense, in libraries while a war for the very survival of American values of freedom and individual rights raged outside, may have occurred to him, but, in Henry's presence, he did not let it cloud his new enthusiasm, and his wife, with her mild silence and her smile, also indicated her approval that he should attend Harvard to study law.

*

Now Henry had the summer free from his father's nervous, watchful eyes and his mother's ministrations. His case had been put to rest. His parents could occupy themselves worrying about Wilky and Bob and Alice. Henry could savour the stifling heat of his bedroom; he could work with freedom; he could read whatever he liked without the foreboding that his father would at any moment and without warning appear at his bedroom door and tell him that there was a war on, his country needed him, it was time to submit to army discipline, to wear a uniform and sleep in barracks and march in file.

In the days after his father agreed that he could go to law school, Henry discovered Hawthorne. He knew his name, of course, as he knew Emerson and Thoreau, and he had glanced at some of his stories, paying him less attention than the two essayists because of a perceived level of dullness and bareness in the work he had read. They were simple moral tales about simple moral people, light and slight and tenderly trivial. Both Henry and Sargy Perry, with whom Henry discussed these matters, had agreed that literature at its most valuable and rich and intense was written in the countries which Napoleon had reigned over and attacked; literature lay in the places where Roman coins could be found in the soil. Hawthorne's *Twice Told Tales* reminded him and Perry of just that, tales which could have been told by their aunt about her aunt with all the social detail and sensuous landscape absent.

This would be the fate, they felt, of anyone who tried to write about New England lives, they would have to confront the thinness of the social air, the absence of a system of manners and the presence of a stultifying system of morals. All of this, he thought, would make any novelist miserable. There was no sovereign or court, no aristocracy, no diplomatic service, no country gentlemen, no palaces, nor castles, nor manors, nor old country houses, nor parsonages, nor thatched cottages, nor ivied ruins; no cathedrals, nor abbeys, nor little Norman churches; no literature, nor novels, no museums nor pictures, no political society, nor sporting class. If these things are left out, he thought, for the novelist every-thing is left out. There is no flavour, no life to dramatize, merely paucity of feeling represented in paucity of tradition. Trollope and Balzac, Zola and Dickens would, he felt, have become bitter old preachers, or mad hairy schoolmasters had they been born in New England and condemned to live amongst its people.

Henry was thus surprised when Perry spoke with awe of *The Scarlet Letter*, which he had just finished reading. Perry insisted that Henry must read it immediately, and seemed disappointed a few days later when Henry still had not begun the book. Henry had, in fact, tried the opening pages and found them almost laugh-ably ponderous, and then had been easily distracted by something else and left the novel aside. Now, trying once more, he believed that the semi-comic tone of the opening, with its talk of prisons and cemeteries and sweet moral blossoms, arose from the lack of a proper background, a varied social world. Hawthorne had replaced artistry with solemnity. This was, he thought, a puritan virtue, of which Henry's grandfather, he was told, had been in full posses-sion. He did not mind, he told Perry, reading about puritans, and he did not even mind having ancestors who embodied their virtues, but he did object somewhat to a book in which they and their virtues, if you could really call them that, had seeped into the tone, the very architecture of the work itself.

On Perry's insistence, he kept the book close to him for several days as he busied himself with Mérimée's stories, which he was attempting to translate, and a play by Alfred de Musset that had begun to fascinate him. Beside these, the lack of colour in Hawthorne's observations, the thinness of his characters and the slow, wooden tone in which he began did not entice Henry to spend more time with the book. He was thus thoroughly unpre-pared, when he embarked yet again upon its early pages, for what was to follow.

The book's assault on his senses did not occur immediately, and even as its spell began to work on him he was unaware that he was being pulled in and held. He could not tell at what moment *The Scarlet Letter* started to glow and take on the same power as one of the novels by Balzac which he had been reading. At intervals, once he had supped with his family and the night wore on, he put the book down, amazed at how Hawthorne had not bothered himself with the daily, petty meanness of New England, the comic idiosyncrasies of speech or deportment or behaviour. Hawthorne had avoided whimsy; he had eschewed pettiness. He had even kept choice and chance at arm's length and had gone instead for intensity, taking a single character, a single action, a single place, a single set of beliefs and a single development and surrounding them with a dark and symbolic forest, a great dense place of sin and temptation. Hawthorne had not observed life, Henry thought, as much as imagined it, found a set of symbols and images which would set life in motion. From the very sparseness of the material, from the narrowness and frigidity of the society itself, from the very sense of undeveloped relations and uniform, colourless belief, Hawthorne had taken advantage of what was missing in New England and pressed on with a gnarled and unrelenting vision to create a story that now gripped its reader all through that summer's night.

Most of the books he read could not be discussed with anyone save Perry, or perhaps William, but now at table the next day he could ask his family about Hawthorne. Suddenly, his father became animated. Why, only six months earlier, he had met the novelist in question. When he travelled up to Boston for a meeting of the Saturday Morning Club, to which he had been specially invited, he found Hawthorne among the company. Some of the meeting was unsatisfactory, his father said, because Frederic Hedge could not stop chattering, and chattering high nonsense most of the time, so that it was difficult to hear what Hawthorne had to say. Not that he said much, he was very shy, but more than that, he was rustic and mannerless; he might have been happier saving the hay or walking on forest tracks. The main thing about him, Henry's father remembered, was that, once the food came, he took no interest in anything else; he buried his eyes in the plate and ate with such voracity that no person dared to ask him a question.

Aunt Kate said that years before in Boston she had known one of Hawthorne's sisters, who was a pleasant lady, all the more pleasant for being extremely limited. The sister had told her that her brother's marriage had crowned him, that up to then he had been a recluse, forcing his family to leave his meals outside the locked door of his room. He did not go out during the day, Aunt Kate said, and did not see the sun save through the small window in his room. He seldom chose to walk in Salem, where he lived, except at night. In the dusky hours, she said, his sister had told her that the novelist took walks of many miles along the coast, or else wandered about the sleeping streets of Salem. These were his pastimes, she said, and these were apparently his most intimate occasions of contact with life. And, Aunt Kate added ominously, his sister told her that Nathaniel had never made a single penny from all his work as a writer.

Henry senior then asked Wilky and Bob for their view, since they had both studied at Sanborn with Julian, the novelist's son. Even Wilky, who was seldom at a loss, could think of nothing to say except that Julian was a very fine fellow. Bob told the table that he had believed until this moment that the elder Hawthorne was a minister. He thought only women wrote stories.

Henry's mother had not spoken until now. She interrupted the general laughter to say that she had known all of the Hawthorne sisters and that they had told her of an injury Nathaniel received while playing ball which had caused him much pain and difficulty over several years so that he was confined to bed. It was, apparently, this very confinement, she said drily, which led to his becoming a writer.

Having sought out Perry to discuss the book with him and to tell him what he had gathered about its author, Henry discovered that Perry knew more, that Nathaniel Hawthorne had recently travelled much in Europe, especially in England and Italy, that he was not, as Henry's father had supposed, a country bumpkin, but a serious artist, well read, well travelled, possibly one of the most sophisticated minds in America. Over the rest of the summer, as Henry and Perry prepared to enter Harvard, they read and re-read all of Hawthorne's books and met most days to share their impressions.

THE WAR, that first summer, seemed oddly distant. Even the proximity of a field hospital at Portsmouth Grove did not bring the conflict any closer. They could, they were told, visit the convalescing soldiers, the invalid troops lying under canvas or in roughly improvized shanties, as onlookers, tourists almost. With Perry, Henry went over in the steamboat, unsure what he would say, or how he would avert his eyes from wounds or missing limbs. On arrival at the camp he noticed the silence at first; he and Perry were unsure whom to approach or if they needed to ask permission to do so. As no one came towards them, they spoke briefly to an unshaven soldier sitting in his underwear on a log outside a tent. His voice was soft, but his tone quite indifferent, and his eyes were drained of all energy. He was content to offer no detailed information, merely that the two visitors were free to speak to anyone or to go anywhere they wished. At the end of the exchange, when they were at a loss to know how to take their leave, Perry gave the soldier a coin which the man hastily put away, looking around him to check if he had been observed.

The sick soldiers lay inert, half dead, watching the two young men from Newport from the sides of their eyes. What struck Henry first was how young most of them seemed, so soft and raw. As he and Perry separated and each moved alone among the soldiers, he felt a great tenderness for them and a desperate urge to console them. He had expected open wounds and blood and bandages, but what he found instead much of the time were fevers and infections. He went where he thought he could, where a pair of eyes had fixed on him and seemed receptive, where a figure seemed not too fevered to be unreachable and not too hostile. He was careful not to say too much at the beginning in case his voice or his tone, added to his general bearing and his clothes, might appear offensively opulent, but soon it became clear that this did not seem to matter, that, if anything, it added to the shy guarded welcome he received from each of the soldiers he visited.

One of these, he discovered, was younger than he was, a blond youth with clear blue eyes totally devoid of fear or fright. He asked the boy politely how he had been injured, then leaned in close to listen to his reply. The boy said nothing at first, shaking his head from side to side, but soon, as though he had been interrupted and was resuming a previous conversation, he began to speak about how he had not felt the bullet entering his leg, he had not felt it at all, he said, as though that alone were his problem. It was nothing more than a bite from a bug, he said, and it was only when he put his hand down and touched the place, that a terrible burning began.

He had hated the waiting, the boy said, the days sitting doing nothing, getting orders to march one way and then orders to march another way, with rumours all the time and nothing happening. And now, he said, the waiting was all over and he wished he were back waiting again.

Henry told the boy that he was sure he would get better, but the boy neither assented nor demurred. He had learned stoicism, Henry thought, which sat oddly with his youth. The agony had somehow entered into his spirit and rested there, unyielding. Henry wondered if the boy's parents had been told of his missing limb, or if they knew where their son was. He thought of asking if he wanted a letter written or word sent, but he did not feel he could ask. It was obvious that if the infection did not clear he would have further surgery or he would die, and what Henry could not fathom as he tried to speak naturally and gently to the boy was his calm bravery, his whispering readiness for what was coming.

In the end, when he could think of nothing else, he offered the boy money, which the injured soldier quietly accepted, and he wrote his address at Newport down for him in case he was in need once he had recovered. The boy studied the writing and nodded, unsmiling. Henry did not think he could ask him if he was able to read.

He sat on a deckchair on the steamboat back to Newport that evening, he and Perry keeping apart as the creaking vessel paddled slowly home. While he watched the dwindling light and wallowed in the fading heat, he felt involved for once in an America from which he had kept himself apart. He had listened carefully but he had not known how to respond. He tried to imagine that young man's life under the canvas, battling for survival, expecting the worst while hoping for home. He tried to conjure up the moment when the surgeon's knife was solemnly unsheathed and the leg held down, and whatever available morphine and whisky were taken, and the arms were pinned back and the gag put into the mouth. He wanted to hold his young friend, help him now that the worst was over, take him home to his family to be looked after. But he also knew that, as much as he wanted to aid and console the soldier, he wanted to be alone in his room with the night coming down and a book close by and pen and paper and the knowledge that the door would remain shut until the morning came and he would not be disturbed. The gap between these two desires filled him with sadness and awe at the mystery of the self, the mystery of having a single consciousness, knowing merely its own bare feelings and experiencing singly and alone its own pain or fear or pleasure or complacency.

And suddenly now, on this return journey by steamboat in the warm evening, with the view of the soft and settling horizon, the realization of how deeply real and apart this self was came fiercely home to him; how intact and separate this self was once the knife was cutting ruthlessly into the flesh of someone else, into the fat and muscles, the tendons and nerves and blood vessels, the hard bone of another self, the someone in agony who was not you, the someone injured far from home under the canvas. He realized that his own separateness was complete, inviolate, just as the soldier could never know the comfort and privilege which came from being the son of Henry James senior, who had been kept away from the war.

In September 1862 his father travelled to Boston with Wilky and there he helped him and his friend Cabot Russell to join the Northern Army. Soon, having lied about his age, Bob James also joined. Wilky and Bob became the focus of all attention. Their most casual observations were treasured and often repeated; any scrap of news about either of the younger brothers was passed on without delay to the older ones.

In Cambridge Henry, after lodging with William for a brief stretch, found himself a small, square, low-browed room with deep window benches where he set about arranging his books with a highly refined system of classification. He walked the country roads around Cambridge and he studied with relish the solitary dwellings on the long grassy slopes under the tall elms; he imagined not only the life within, but how that life could be rendered, how it would be shaped and moulded were a young Hawthorne to pass by.

He joined his brother for meals at Miss Upsham's at the corner of Kirkland and Oxford Streets, listening to every word uttered by the other diners, enjoying the protection of his voluble brother and not being called on to speak much himself. He loved the spare, dry, witty talk of the theology student; he listened with respect to old Professor Child, whose tone when the war was discussed was as sombre and darkly morbid as the many ballads he had collected.

During the lectures, Henry paid as much attention as he could to the subject in question, but mainly he examined his fellow students, studying the types, weighing the expressions from the dull and vaguely handsome to the memorable and remarkable. He sought to let his eyes do the thinking for him, deciphering the faces, the smiles and scowls, the ways of walking and moving, and transforming them into characters and temperaments. Most of his fellow students were New Englanders, and he could easily detect in their solemn faces during the lectures, in their lack of softness or easy humour, in the way they composed themselves and walked, that their ancestors had stood in pulpits and preached with fervour the difference between right and wrong, and that they had been brought up in homes where such principles were firmly established.

Now, as they sat through law lectures, a shadow hung over them, the shadow of the war for which they had not volunteered, a war never mentioned among them unless there was fresh and urgent news. They did not look like young men who would easily accept or give orders, or march in unison, or have their limbs amputated. They believed in the Union and the abolition of slavery as they believed in God, but they also believed in their own freedom and privilege. They knew that abolition was a noble cause, and they included it in their prayers; at the same time they took notes and read large tomes to prepare themselves for their future. Looking at them, Henry found, was easier than talking to them. In their physiognomies he saw a boyish rectitude guarding the rest of them like a great stone wall.

While Henry attended his lectures assiduously, he barely opened a book on the law. Instead, he read Sainte-Beuve, he wandered into Lowell's lectures on English and French literature, he listened to Emerson, when he came to Boston, attacking slavery. He went to the theatre. He steeped himself in whatever life Cambridge and Boston had to offer. The war was a faint sound which at intervals became louder and a few times piercingly close. One day in Harvard he had seen his cousin Gus Barker, clearly home on leave, in the distance but he had not run after him, believing that he would see him in the days that followed. But he did not see him and when Gus was shot dead in Virginia, he could not reconcile the memory of his cousin, his skin so white and his eyes so brimming with expectation, his body so full of coiled strength, with the idea that he had been broken and destroyed by a bullet, that he, so young and unready, had been wrenched asunder with pain, and left lying there as others passed by before he was buried in a distant place where no one knew him.

His mother, when she wrote telling him the news of Gus, said that she had also written to William. As Henry went to his next meal at Miss Upsham's he did not know what he might say to William about their cousin, and he noticed as William came into the dining room a look of dark embarrassment crossing his face. He found himself shaking William's hand, and this made the unease between them even worse. William nodded at him gravely. Neither of them could say anything. It was only when William told Professor Child that their cousin had been killed in Virginia by a sniper's bullet that the spell was broken and Gus Barker's death could be discussed.

'All the doomed young men,' Professor Child said, 'all of them healthy and brave, and leaving those who loved them far behind, lying dead on the battlefield while the war goes on.'

Henry wondered if Professor Child was quoting from a ballad or if he was attempting to speak naturally. He noticed that William had tears in his eyes.

'The best went to war,' Professor Child said, 'and the best were cut down.'

Sometimes, during these meals at Miss Upsham's, Professor Child seemed on the verge of stating that those who remained at home, including his fellow diners at Miss Upsham's, were cowards, but then he appeared to restrain himself.

In the months that followed neither William nor Henry ever mentioned the name of Gus Barker to each other. Each of them felt, Henry guessed, a guilt which they did not wish to admit to, or discuss.

WHEN HENRY went to visit Wilky at Readville he could not believe that this soft companion of his childhood should have mastered, by mere aid of his own gaiety and sociability, such mysteries and such hardships as the army offered. To become first a happy soldier and then an easy officer was, it seemed to Henry, for his younger brother an exercise in liking his fellow man. He later remembered his brother's companions as laughing, welcoming and sunburnt youth, who, like his companions in law school, seemed to bristle with Boston genealogies, but, despite this, had taken to army life, displaying an openness, a joy in the outdoors and even a jokiness that belied their upbringing and background. The hospital camp at Portsmouth seemed very far away and, as he left that day to return to Harvard, he felt that a long war, or even a bloody one, was a distant prospect from the picture of golden order and good feeling that he had just witnessed.

His mother transcribed the parts of Wilky's letters which she judged most informative or most edifying or most alarming and included them in her letters to Henry and William. In January Wilky wrote home about a malignant fever called malaria which was affecting both armies. 'Two weeks ago,' he wrote, 'we buried two of our company in three days, and a great many have been taken sick with it.' He managed to sound both impatient for action and impatient for home, but what Henry took from the letters more than anything was his brother's idealism and belief in the rightness of his cause and his readiness to fight for it. Wilky wrote and his mother transcribed,

> I am very well and in capital spirits, but now and then rather blue about home. If things don't look more promising than they do now by the end of next May, I fear very much we shall not see home, for the government will I expect make an appeal to the 300,000 nine-months men to stay three months longer, that their services are really needed. What could they say to an appeal emanating from such a high place and for such a high cause. For myself, I am content to stay if the country needs it, but it would come hard I assure you.

Henry imagined his mother writing this out, having carefully selected it. He knew that she would have been in two minds about sending it as it suggested clearly where duty lay. She added nothing and Henry contented himself with the idea that she, as much as he or William, had engineered this state of affairs in which Wilky and Bob represented the James family in the war.

William and he did not communicate much with each other during these months, even though they ate at the same table three times a day. If a letter came from his mother which Henry thought that William should see, he handed it to him without comment; and William did the same. Both brothers were enjoying their solitude, the pleasures of introspection and intermittent company and freedom from parental interference and the noise of domestic life, but more than anything they were both wrapped up in their reading.

This was, on the other hand, an heroic time in Wilky's life, which he would not experience again, and would not, indeed, recover from. He volunteered to serve under Colonel Shaw as an officer in the 54th Regiment. Its departure from Boston was a glorious occasion, which Henry James senior travelled specially to Boston to see, using the house of Oliver Wendell Holmes senior as a vantage point to view the parade, which would be for him a pivotal moment in the history of his family and the history of liberty in America.

William and Henry learned of the event from their mother. When her letter came informing them of their father's arrival, it was clear that she presumed both brothers would wish to view for themselves Wilky's brave triumph and personally to witness a singular conjoining of the family's history with that of the country's destiny. It seemed not to occur to her that they might not wish to attend.

William wrote, however, immediately to tell her that he had an important experiment to perform in the laboratory on that very day, that he would make every effort to be there, but should these efforts fail, then the event would have to take place without him.

Henry waited until the date came closer and then he wrote to his mother about his back, which was providing him with pain, and his need for rest and his hope that he would be much improved by 28 May, the date of the event, and, in fact, he promised to do his utmost to be there, but should his back continue to trouble him, or take a turn for the worse, then he would not be able to meet his father and accompany him to the house of Dr Holmes. He did not read it over before he sent it.

On the morning of 28 May Henry did not go to breakfast at Miss Upsham's and, on arriving for lunch, found that William had arranged to absent himself from all meals that day. Professor Child and two of the others, all fanatical abolitionists, were preparing to attend the parade and presumed that William's absence was due to his eagerness to see his brother, whose bravery in joining the 54th under Colonel Shaw they all admired. It struck Henry that they also presumed he had organized his own viewing of the regiment and, as he got ready to slip away, no one asked him where he was going.

As Henry lay on his bed, having returned quietly to his quarters, he felt that the stillness and the silence were more profound than usual, as if all noise had concentrated itself into the path of the parade and left him in this place on the undisturbed margins where there was no sound or action or movement. He stretched and walked over to the table and drummed his fingers lightly on its polished surface and relished the dullness, the faintness of the sound. He took down from his shelf a volume of Sainte-Beuve and flicked through it, but the feeling of being away from the heart of things was overwhelming now. He was suspended like a caught breath. It was almost exciting, but, more than that, as the afternoon wore on, he felt something approaching happiness, which did not resemble the happiness arising from work done, or from pure repose. Rather, he was in a room with a bed and books and a desk on a day when the outside air carried danger with it. When everyone else had fire in their blood, he was calm. So calm that he could neither read nor think, merely bask in the freedom that the afternoon offered, savour, as deeply as he could, this quiet and strange treachery, his own surreptitious withdrawal from the world.

THE HOUSEHOLD, when he returned to Newport, was in a constant state of expectation. The family barely noticed his arrival and did not pay any attention to his semi-exiled state. At meals nothing but Wilky and Bob and their comrades, many of whose names were known to the family, was discussed. Each letter was greeted with a fluttering cry from his mother and Aunt Kate and Alice but was preserved unopened to be handed first to Henry senior, who read it slowly and judiciously and quietly to himself before handing it over to his wife, who would read aloud the parts she deemed worthy of immediate release. Then it was given to Henry or William, if they were present, and then to Aunt Kate and Alice, who read it in unison. Henry senior would then peruse the letter again several times over, deeming some of Wilky's correspondence worthy of reproduction in the *Newport News*, and he would set out alone, as briskly as he could and with much purpose, to hand over the missive to the editor.

It was a letter they received dated 18 July 1863 that told them Wilky was now entering his most testing time and that every day he would be in the most serious danger. The *Newport News* proudly printed it in full:

> Dear Father, We are sailing down the Ediston River, on our way to the front. I have only time to say that we came out of the fight on the 16th with 47 killed and wounded. The regiment behaved nobly; and I would give my right arm to keep up the good name it has won. We are now on our way to Morris Island, the new attack on Fort Wagner commencing tomorrow at dawn. I hope and pray to God that the regiment will do as nobly there as it did at James Island.

All of them knew about Fort Wagner. It was, Henry senior told them gravely, the strongest single earthwork in the history of warfare. It would have to be taken, he said, but it could not be taken easily. Henry senior was greatly exercised at the wisdom of sending in the 54th, a regiment whose footsoldiers were mostly black, whose very appearance would provoke a fury among the

Confederate soldiers. In the days afterwards, when they heard no news, he discussed this with the many anxious visitors who called to the James's house and repeated everything he said to the next visitor and the next until he was sure that his attitude towards the battle was the correct one, indeed the only one worth having.

All they could do was wait. They knew that the battle had been a disaster and that Fort Wagner was still held by the confederate soldiers. They heard that the soldiers of the 54th had excelled themselves in bravery. And they heard that many of them were dead. But they knew nothing of Wilky. In the hot summer days and nights, so deeply associated with ease and happiness and pleasure, they did not sleep, their meals became enforced, awkward gatherings, and as time passed they understood that Wilky could not have walked away unscathed from the battle. He would have notified them by now. And so they waited in dread.

Henry thought of him buried with a pile of bodies, having no name to mark his resting place.

'That would be the worst for your mother,' Aunt Kate said to him, 'thinking that he might have survived and thinking that he might come into the hall at any moment to surprise her. Your mother would never stop hoping.'

No one at any stage mentioned the threat, or rumour of a threat, that Jeff Davis had issued in a manifesto ordering the white officers of the 54th Massachusetts hanged if captured alive. When Aunt Kate found it in a newspaper, where Henry had already seen it, he watched her taking the paper into the kitchen and burning it in the stove.

In time, of course, they would discover the full horror of what happened at Fort Wagner, the ranks mowed down at almost every step, the bodies heaped high, the death of Colonel Shaw personally witnessed by Wilky, the death of his friend Cabot Russell, Wilky's first wound in the side, and then the shock of a canister ball in the foot. As he lay injured he was noticed by two stretcher bearers who began to carry him to a temporary resting place for the wounded when a round shot blew off the head of the stretcher bearer to his rear. Wilky witnessed his instant and horrible death. The other stretcher bearer took to his heels. Wilky woke the morning of the following day inside the tents of the Sanitary Commission, nearly three miles away. After a while he was moved to Port Royal Hospital, which was not really a hospital, but a field full of the desperately injured and the dying, barely covered with a thin canvas, its patients offered only the slightest medical assistance. Wilky lay there half conscious, his wounds slowly becoming infected, with no way of contacting his family.

He was saved by a miracle. Cabot Russell's father had travelled to South Carolina in search of his son, believing that he had been taken prisoner. Although he had been assured that his son had not survived the battle, he made a desperate, grief-stricken search in the tents where the wounded lay, and this was how he found Wilky, spotting him quite by chance among the injured soldiers. Immediately, he notified the James family by telegram and let them know that, while he would continue to look for his own son, he would also ensure that Wilky James was transported home. By the beginning of August, Mr Russell gave up his vain search in the chaos of South Carolina and accepted what he had originally been told – that his son was dead. He travelled by boat with Wilky on a stretcher as far as New York, Wilky's infection worsening all the time, the canister ball which had lodged in his foot having to be removed on board. The other wound, close to Wilky's spine, was even more severely infected but could not be touched.

When Wilky arrived in Newport, Mr Russell having travelled with him all the way, he was close to death. The stretcher was carried into the hallway, but the doctor ordered that it should be taken no further. The family gathered around him, relieved that the moment had come and he had been returned to them alive, but aware also that his time could be short, all of them sure that his survival was more important now than any other matter on the earth. Then they noticed the grieving face of Mr Russell, and Henry watched each of them as they tried not to sound too openly jubilant or too concerned about Wilky to the exclusion of all else in front of this broken father fresh from the battlefield where his son lay dead. In those first hours, as William took instructions from the doctor so that he could minister personally to his brother, and his parents held Wilky's hand and kept visitors at bay, and his aunt and sister moved from the kitchen to the hallway with hot water and towels and fresh bandages, Henry studied Mr Russell, impressed by his grave and steady gentleness, and aware of the difference it would have made for him to be observing the patient with a still more intimate pity. Mr Russell remained quiet and tactful as he waited to depart; it was this very quietness and tact which eventually seeped into the atmosphere until the idea that this good, kind man was bereft of his only son and yet sat erect and dry-eyed at the guarded fact of the family's relief made each one of them, as Henry saw it, move carefully and watchfully around him.

Less than a year earlier, Wilky and Cabot had lived in a state of complacent expectation, as if the stretch of earth they inhabited had been created and cleared especially for their freedom and happiness. In Boston and Newport and in the villages of New England, they were everywhere welcomed, their accents understood, their manners appreciated. In time their boyish openness would be tempered by experience, just as their handsomeness would ripen and their beliefs solidify. No one told them and no one warned their parents that they would be shot down before they were twenty. The New England which their grandparents and great-grandparents had created was not a place of violent death or battle roar or infected wounds, but of settlement, propriety, peace, righteousness. Henry knew, as he sat on a bench in the hallway close to Mr Russell, that their visitor's shock came not only from the brutal disappearance from the earth of his golden son, but from the idea that a public pact, a version of the civic order as ordained by history, had been cruelly broken.

Wilky came home with no belongings. Even his uniform was rotting and had to be carefully removed. The blanket that covered him was thrown aside and left in a corner of the hallway. It was a few days before Henry, doing vigil over his brother, noticed it and carried it to the kitchen. As he unfolded it there, the smell was overwhelming, but so fiercely redolent of what Wilky's suffering in the battlefield must have been like that he could not easily cast it aside. It smelled of tobacco, and it smelled of the strange mixture of rot and human sweat which Wilky's uniform had reeked of. But more than anything, it smelled of the earth itself, the earth of mud and muck and of war, the earth which had been stormed by regiments and disturbed by grave diggers, the foetid earth. He found a place for the blanket in a shed behind the kitchen and went back to the hallway, but the smell remained with him. It was the most vivid testament to what his brother had been through.

THE HOUSE lived on the ebb and flow of Wilky's pain. Henry realized that he had paid such close attention to Mr Russell on that first day because he would have done anything to avoid having to look at his brother and contemplate his future. Once Mr Russell had left, he had no choice but to take in the scene in all its horror. Wilky's hair was matted and his body limp and sweaty. Wilky did not seem to sleep; he lay on his side, constantly moaning and as the pain intensified crying out suddenly. Sometimes the cries turned into shrieks and they filled the house. Henry believed that his brother was going to die.

Over breakfast on the third morning, his mother said that all of them, in whatever way they could, should try to share Wilky's pain, take some of it from him and live with it themselves. Everyone in this house, she said, as her husband nodded, should dedicate themselves to taking the pain from Wilky and suffering a small part of it in their own bodies. When Henry looked at William, he discovered that his brother was nodding too, as though something eminently wise and practical had been said. When Henry went back to his room, he lay on the bed and concentrated on the infected wound in Wilky's side which the doctors had cut open but which had not been cleared of infection. No amount of wishing, he thought, could do anything to alleviate his brother's suffering. He went down to the hallway and sat close to Wilky who was groaning softly. He moved closer to him – as his Aunt Kate, who was already there, smiled at him – and held Wilky's hand for a moment, but since this seemed to cause him pain he withdrew it. He wished that his brother could smile as he had always smiled, but his drawn face now appeared as though it would never smile again. It would wince and wrinkle up in distress rather than open in warm recognition. Henry and his Aunt Kate sat there with Wilky silently until his mother came and without speaking took her sister's place on the bench beside the stretcher.

The family kept the gravity of Wilky's state from Bob, and only when the patient began to improve did they tell Bob the truth about him. Bob managed to send them a private letter expressing his opinion and that of many others about the assault on Fort Wagner – that large matters of strategy were overlooked. The slain, he said, were monuments to folly. Bob's letter did not please his parents; it lacked idealism and optimism. Bob, it became clear from other letters, was bored. He had suffered from sunstroke and dysentery and lack of respect for his superiors. His letters were read only by the immediate family, his mother expressing her disapproval by leaving some of the letters unread, allowing her husband to read her the more uplifting extracts, if he could find them.

As Wilky's wounds began to heal, his nightmares started. He cried out as though the heat of battle or the mayhem of retreat were upon him. Each one of the family took turns to stay with him at night once he was well enough to be moved to his room, but no one knew how to restore order to his sleep, make him believe that he was not being attacked and shot at and his friends and comrades killed all around him. His nightmares stopped only when all the thrashing and frantic movement in the dreams caused him to wake. It was the pain that brought him back to his senses.

Often the day was no better as the memory of what he had seen and felt became a waking nightmare for Wilky. His father remained optimistic, certain of his recovery, and certain also that the dead of the war would now experience an eternal morning, an unimagined happiness. Even Wilky's pain, he said, had united the family and could only lead Wilky to great spiritual distinction in the future.

Henry sat in the bedroom one day as Wilky, now able haltingly to speak, asked their father to preach a sermon. Wilky's voice was weak, but his eyes were eager and he watched his father with an innocent hunger as Henry senior began, explaining that each mortal, the healthy and the rich, as much as the sick and the wounded, was equally dependent on the Divine hand, and our best interest lay in becoming as innocently ready to follow him as sheep. He continued until Wilky, at first falteringly, but then louder and with tears in his eyes, interrupted.

'Ah Father, it is easy preaching faith in God's care,' he said, 'but it was hard, where I have been, to practise it.'

Henry senior was silent. They watched Wilky gasping for breath, trying to speak more. His father turned to Henry as though to ask if his second son would know whether he should go on with the sermon or wait to see if Wilky had more to say. Henry did not respond, but soon Wilky's voice found the strength to continue and he left them in no doubt that he did not wish to be preached to any more, even if it was he who had originally requested it.

'I woke up lying in the sand under my tent, and slowly recalled much that had happened, my wounds, my fall, the two men that tried to drag me to the hospital tent, the fall of one of them, my feeble crawling to the ambulance. I woke up to find myself forgotten, and sick and faint for loss of blood. As I lay wondering whether I should ever see home again, I saw a poor Ohio man with his jaw shot away who found, I suppose, that I was near to him and unable to stand, he crept over and deluged me with his blood. At that I felt . . .'

Wilky covered his face with his hands and began to cry uncontrollably, but he could shape no more words. His crying grew louder, more hysterical, until he shook in the bed, his father and his brother watching him helplessly. Once his mother came, she held him and calmed him and spoke softly to all three of them.

'When Wilky was a baby,' she said when Wilky had finally fallen asleep, 'and in his crib, he always seemed to be smiling. I tried to find out if he was smiling all the time, or if he heard me coming and began to smile only then. But I never could find out. That's what I'd like now, that's what I'm waiting for – that he will start to smile again.'

WILLIAM RETURNED to Harvard that September to continue his studies, but Henry did not follow him. His parents remained pre-occupied with Wilky but were much relieved when, on a further assault on Fort Wagner which, fortunately, had been evacuated just before the attack, Bob survived unscathed.

Henry remained in his room as Wilky recovered and Bob stayed with his regiment. His mother's response to his seclusion and his silence became sweeter once Wilky began to declare that he wished to return to the army as soon as he himself rather than his doctors felt that he could. His mother at mealtimes talked a great deal about the sacrifice and bravery of her two younger sons, but her tone was bitter rather than proud.

'They have both seen things which no one of their age should see. They have both witnessed horrors and felt horrors, and I do not know now how they will ever settle down without being haunted by sights that none of us will ever be able to imagine. I wish they hadn't joined. That's all I can say. And I wish the war had never started.'

Aunt Kate nodded, but Henry senior stared passively and vaguely into the distance, as though his wife had made some mild observation. As soon as each meal was over, Henry returned to his room. His mother began, once more, to worry about his back, bringing him cushions and making him lie down rather than sit when he was reading.

He did not know what to tell them when his first story, written in the French style about an adulterous woman, was accepted by the *Continental Monthly* in New York. It would be published anonymously, so he knew that he could keep the news from them if he wished. He waited for a day or two, but then, on finding his father in the library alone, he decided to reveal his secret. Within an hour his father had read the story and expressed his disapproval of its contents, less than uplifting, he thought, and dramatizing the baser motives. Then his father wrote to William, who sent Henry a note mocking him and wondering how he came by his knowledge of adulterous French ladies. Finally, his father moved around Newport spreading the news of his son who was about to publish a story in the French style.

WILKY WENT back to his regiment, but was judged too unwell to continue, and so he returned home once more, determined on improving so that he could see the war out and be there for the victory. Nothing dimmed his enthusiasm. It became Henry's habit, in this interlude as Wilky waited to rejoin his regiment, to sit with him silently reading while Wilky dozed or lay still without speaking. One night as he quietly prepared to return to his own room, leaving Wilky peaceful, he was confronted in the corridor by his Aunt Kate. She whispered to Henry that she had left some sweet-cake and some milk for him in the kitchen. Just as he was about to tell her that he did not want any cake or milk, he noticed her face darkening and her brow furrowing, and he understood that she wanted him to follow her to the kitchen.

On tiptoe the two of them moved down through the house. In the kitchen, she began to whisper something about Wilky's recovery until she closed the door and then could talk out loud.

'He's mad to go back to the war,' she said. 'As though he didn't have enough injuries, enough suffering.'

'He remains idealistic about the cause,' Henry said.

Aunt Kate pursed her lips disapprovingly.

'He'll never settle now, once this war is over. He is like all of the Jameses, except for you,' she went on. 'Headstrong, full of foolish enthusiasm.'

She studied his face to see if she had gone too far, but he smiled at her, amused, signalling that she could say more if she wished.

'They were all the same, your father's family. If they had one drink, then they had thousands of drinks. One night's gambling led to them losing every penny. One page of theology and then . . .' She stopped and shook her head and sighed.

'And half of them died young, you know, leaving your cousins orphans, the Temple girls and poor Gus Barker. Of course, the old father, old William James of Albany, was as rich at that time as Mr Astor, but the Astors were all good at business, level-headed people, and the Jameses, once the father was dead, were good at gambling and drinking and dying young and running headlong towards foolish causes. Every time I listen to Wilky talking about going back to fight, I see the Jameses writ large, always ready to do something foolish. And William wanting to be a painter one day and a doctor the next. You're the only one who takes after our side of the family, you're the only solid one.'

'But I studied law last year and changed my mind,' Henry said.

'You had no enthusiasm for the law. You did it to get away from here and with all the war madness going on, you were right. If you had stayed, they'd have joined you up and you would be limping around here with half of you amputated.'

Her voice was harsh now, and her eyes sharp, almost wild. In the dim lamplight she resembled a drawing of an old woman, both wise and mad. She stopped speaking and let her mouth and jaw settle. She watched him, waiting for a response. When he did not speak, she began again.

'You're the consistent one, the one who'll know how to mind himself. At least we have you.'

*

BY THE TIME his son's first story had appeared in print, Henry senior had grown restless once more and decided, he said, to move his family definitively to Boston. Henry was happy to leave Newport. He kept his stories secret now, letting his family see only the reviews he was writing for the periodicals – the *Atlantic Monthly*, the *North American Review*, the *Nation*. Without any of them knowing, he worked slowly and carefully every day on the story of a boy who goes to war, leaving his mother and his sweetheart behind. When he began he was involved in a pure and artful invention, as though he were writing a ballad which Professor Child might collect. He established the difficult, proud and ambitious mother; John, her courageous and light-hearted son; and Lizzie, the sweetheart, innocent and pretty and flirtatious. He created each scene with deliberation, reading over each morning what he had written the previous day, constantly erasing and adding. He tried to work quickly so that there would be speed and flow to the narrative and, on one of these days, in the family's new rented quarters on Beacon Hill, something occurred to him which shocked him but did not cause him to stop.

'On the fourth evening, at twilight, John Ford,' he wrote, 'was borne up to the door on his stretcher, with his mother stalking beside him in rigid grief, and kind, silent friends pressing about with helping hands.'

John was too ill to be moved, and his injuries were too severe for him to be visited by his sweetheart Lizzie. As he wrote, Henry felt that he was closest to what concerned him in his waking life and most of his dreams: the fate of his injured brother. His father could not blame him for immorality nor William mock him for writing about a world he did not know. Suddenly an image came to him and he held his breath for worry that he might lose it: 'When Lizzie was turned from John's door, she took a covering from a heap of draperies that had been hurriedly tossed down in the hall: it was an old army blanket. She wrapped it round her and went out onto the veranda.'

He wanted to go into the shed behind the pantry and look for the blanket he had taken from Wilky, but then he remembered that they were in Boston now and not Newport and that the blanket would surely have been thrown out or left there in the move. He began to summon up the smell of the blanket, its aura of the battlefield and the army: 'A strange earthy smell lingered in that faded old rug, and with it a faint perfume of tobacco. Instantly, the young girl's senses were transported as they had never been before to those far-off Southern battlefields. She saw men lying in swamps and puffing their kindly pipes, drawing their blankets closer, canopied with the same luminous dusk that shone down upon her comfortable weakness. Her mind wandered amid these scenes . . .'

The feeling of power was new to him. This raid on his own memories, this parading of an object so close to him, so deeply part of his own personal store that no one might ever know where this moment in his story came from, made him believe that he had done something daring and original.

CHAPTER EIGHT

June 1898

HE WATCHED HIS FRIEND the novelist moving towards the window in the drawing room, but did not suggest to her that she might be more comfortable where he had originally placed her. She sought a position with her back to the light. He wondered if she remembered that two, or even three, of her heroines had entered rooms in this way and sat happily and deliberately with their backs to a large window so that the company might view them in the most flattering light.

Once seated, however, Mrs Florence Lett did not seem to care about her face as she wrinkled her brow and grimaced. She could not utter a sentence without making passionate changes to her expression, smiling and frowning, and puckering up her rather perfect nose. He wondered how her face had withstood so many changes in its weather. Soon, he thought, there would be a land-slide, something would have to give. In the meantime, he enjoyed her talk of her time in Italy, her next book, her charming daughter, the slowness of the train to Rye, her sorrow that she could stay only a short time, and back again to her beautiful daughter, aged six, who was being fêted in the kitchen by the staff, her daughter's education and inheritance, and then back to Italy and the death, by suicide, of Henry's great friend, the novelist Constance Fenimore Woolson.

'In Venice,' she said, 'they spoke of you and why you departed so abruptly and why you have not returned. He is an artist, I told them, a supreme artist, not a diplomat, but they long to see you. Venice is sad, it was always sad, but more so now, and people whom I don't think ever knew Constance claim to miss her. Poor Constance, you know I could not walk in those streets. I had to turn back, I don't know what you will do.'

Slowly, the door opened and Mrs Florence Lett's daughter came quietly into the room. Her mother was in mid-sentence and did not stop. The little girl studied the room, her expression placid. She was wearing a long blue dress. Henry noticed also the intensely soft blue of her eyes and her clear fair skin. In that moment, as she stood there, respectful of her mother's conversation, he thought her immensely beautiful. From the sofa, he put out his arms to her and, without any further consideration, she came stealthily towards him and embraced him, sitting herself on his lap and putting her arms around him.

'We've all gone to see her grave, of course,' his visitor continued. 'With some graves you know that the person is at rest, that their lying there is part of nature. But I did not feel that at all with poor Constance, although that graveyard is the most perfect place. She would have loved it. But I don't feel she is at rest. I don't feel that at all.'

Henry listened as Mrs Florence Lett held forth. He did not speak to the girl on his lap, and he presumed that she would, after a few moments, move across the room towards her mother. Clearly, however, she had found comfort as gradually her arms fell limp and she settled into sleep. He did not know if feeling at ease with strangers was an aspect of the child's charm, but he decided not to ask her mother.

By the time the child woke, the light in the room was fading, the maid had taken away the tea and Mrs Florence Lett had exhausted a large number of subjects. The girl smiled at him as she opened her eyes. He felt enormously touched by her as though her coming to him with all the confidence of a child to a parent brought with it a trust and a good luck. He smiled as she stood up.

When Mrs Florence Lett did not comment on what had just occurred, he said nothing either. He would have given anything to spare the little girl embarrassment. She had come to him so naturally. As they were leaving and the servants came to say goodbye to her, it was clear that she had made a great impression during her visit to the kitchen and the pantry. The child now became shy for the first time and clung to her mother who spoke to her carefully and firmly, encouraging her to offer a withdrawn, half-willing smile and a small wave before she left.

When he returned to the drawing room and the sofa where he had been, he felt a residue of the child's angelic presence in the atmosphere. Since his return from London a few days earlier he had been trying to work, forcing himself to remain in his study for the daylight hours, neglecting his correspondence, and inviting nobody to see him. Mrs Florence Lett had outwitted him, announcing by telegram that she was coming, making clear that she required no reply, and then arriving as she said she would.

Now, as the lamps were lit in Lamb House, he went back to his desk and began to think over what she had said about Venice. He had a letter in front of him from Mrs Curtis, the owner of Palazzo Barbaro, whose hospitality he had enjoyed so many times. She used the same words about the city. She wrote about its sadness, and about the streets close to the building from whose second-floor window Constance Fenimore Woolson had flung herself.

Her death, like that of his sister Alice, lived with Henry day after day. Images of her came and went, sometimes of her inert body lying broken on the street below her window, and sometimes a detail, the way her lips moved quietly as he spoke to her, how desperately, despite her bad hearing, she tried to follow what he was saying. He saw her in the sunlight of Bellosguardo, maybe her happiest time, under a parasol wearing white and smiling at him, as though she were sitting for a cleverly arranged portrait and offering him, as she did so much, her full, proprietorial approval before he even spoke. She had been, he supposed, his best friend, the person outside his own family who had been closest to him. He still could not believe she was dead.

AMONG THE objects which Lady Wolseley had encouraged him to purchase for Lamb House was an old map of Sussex that testified to the changes of relation between sea and land in his corner of the coast. It gave him pleasure to think that Rye and Winchelsea belonged to shifting ground, the endless mutation of the shore. The lines here were not ordained or set in stone, but open, he liked to think, to suggestion. Sometimes, when he walked slowly up and down the bright space of his garden room, or sat upstairs in the drawing room looking out at the light, he fancied that with one stroke of his pen, or the sound of his voice, the river could change its course, the sea come rushing in, or a new, small indentation appear on the coast.

Both Rye and Winchelsea seemed almost foolishly placed now. He loved telling his visitors how Winchelsea was practically destroyed in the thirteenth century by a huge storm which cast up masses of beach, until it was clear that the future of the town was precarious. And thus the town was moved, the old one left like a ghost, he liked to tell his guests, or like an old family down to its last member, holding only memories and fading treasure while a usurping family thrived. But the success of this new enterprise was to be short-lived also. When there is a battle between the sea and the land, he would continue, it is generally the sea which emerges victorious and the land which melts away. Rye and Winchelsea, the new Winchelsea that is, were ready to be great ports with great plans and dreams. But then, in the centuries that followed, the land won, and slowly and slyly a modest plain where sheep now grazed began to form between these towns and the sea, pushing the sea back gently but effectively.

If the first Winchelsea suffered death by drowning, the second was left high and dry. He would talk as though this were a hard fact to accept. This plain, this strange addition to the land, he would say, put there by a quirk of nature, gave him a satisfaction, as though he had been personally involved in helping things along. It added to the mystery of Rye, and to his engagement with it – the sea had once come right to its front door, and now it had withdrawn, leaving only sea light and sea gulls and a flat plain, an ambiguous loan which the water had made to Sussex and its inhabitants.

To this world, from which the ocean had so politely withdrawn, he had moved, in his own gentle and polite way, creating space for his work to flourish and his sleep to come easy. He now had a household, much larger than any his parents had ever dreamed of, and the smooth running of his small empire was a matter of care and pride and worry and high expense.

From London, where they had served him loyally, he had transported the Smiths, Mrs Smith to cook and her husband to function as butler. In Rye, he had employed Fanny the parlour-maid, pretty and quiet and careful, and in Rye too he had found a treasure called Burgess Noakes, gnome-sized and not pretty, but making up for it in punctuality and the desire to please. Burgess was young, and this was his first serious employment, which meant that he had developed no bad or slovenly habits. He could be trained as both houseboy and valet without being made to feel that the duties of the former might be less dignified or worthy of his attention than those of the latter.

Henry had spoken to the boy's mother, who went to great lengths to explain how willing he was and clean and well spoken and mature for fourteen and how sad she would be to part with him. When the boy was finally produced, the discrepancy between his scamp-like face and frame and the boundless eagerness of his gaze made Henry immediately warm to him. He gave no sign of this, however, merely explaining to the mother, as the boy listened, that Burgess Noakes would be employed for a brief period so that his suitability could be tested, and after that period they could discuss the terms of his employment, as appropriate.

Henry enjoyed being known in Rye. As he walked the streets, he took pleasure in greeting all whom he recognized with courtesy and courtliness. He was often accompanied by his dog Maximilian, or by the Scot, who had found lodgings in Rye and become an assiduous walker and cyclist, or by whatever guests were staying at Lamb House. The idea of residing in a small and traditional English community belonged to his dreams; he found himself, especially in the presence of American guests, deeply proud of his acceptance in Rye and his knowledge of its denizens, its topography and history.

When visitors came by train, as they generally did, Henry met them personally at the station. Burgess accompanied him, skilfully pushing a wheelbarrow which served to ferry the guest's luggage up the hill to Lamb House. Henry marvelled at some of Burgess's social instincts on these occasions. He stood apart with the wheelbarrow in readiness when the train stopped at Rye station. He did not intrude for one moment as Henry and his guest indulged in greetings and preliminary observations, but negotiated effectively with the train's porter, establishing which luggage belonged to Mr James's guest without having to consult its owner. He made sure, however, that the traveller saw the luggage as it rested on the wheelbarrow. Then he moved easily behind Henry and his visitor as they made their way up the hill.

The house was, in its own small way, perfect and beautiful, even to those who only knew it from the outside. Its secret, however, was its garden, which was private, secluded, rich with ancient plantings and cultivated with care and taste.

As soon as he leased the house, Henry had retained George Gammon, a local gardener, part-time. Every day he had some discussion with him about changes which might be made, new plantings and seasonal adjustments, but mainly they spoke about what was blooming now, or likely to bloom soon, how different this year was to last year, and how much work could be soon completed. Both of them then took in the walled space in its detail and its totality. He enjoyed how George Gammon let the silence linger, adding nothing further, and waited until Henry decided it was time to go back to his work before moving away himself.

The Smiths did not take to Rye. During the ten years they worked for him in Kensington, living in servants' quarters in his apartment, they dealt with the same merchants each day and frequented the same establishments. They knew many other servants in the immediate environs. For them, a few streets of Kensington represented a village in which they were fully at home. Each morning, Mrs Smith, her expression respectful, but trying also, in a pained and shy way, to be alert and intelligent, took her day's orders from the novelist. When he was working, these orders were for plain, well-cooked food served with silent discretion by Mr Smith. Sometimes, when there was company, he gave the Smiths several days' notice and discussed the dishes at some length with the wife. When he was away he did not know what the Smiths did, but he presumed that they took as full a possession of his apartment as they dared and developed many bad habits.

When he was in residence, however, they were quiet and careful and cautious, and pleased with their employer who was generally, he thought, undemanding. When they had been working with him for six years and knew that he was going abroad after the death of his sister, Mrs Smith had approached him about a personal matter. Later, he realized how much discussion must have taken place between them before they agreed on this course of action. She visibly shook as she spoke. The request was unusual, and most employers, however benign, would have instantly refused, would have been concerned indeed at its forward nature, but he was struck by the energy Mrs Smith put into her speech and her fearful sincerity. He also, of course, understood her great need.

Her sister was ill, she told him, and would undergo an operation. She needed a place to convalesce. The patient could not look after herself during this brief time, and she had no one else to care for her. Since Mr James would be in Italy for several months and the apartment would, they supposed, be empty, she wondered if there was any possibility that her sister could move into the guest room and be cared for there. She would be gone, of course, before Mr James returned.

He was glad that he did not ruminate on the matter or seek advice. He made up his mind in that second and told Mrs Smith that, provided she and her husband could meet all her sister's expenses, then her sister could stay, but the apartment must be empty and silent when he returned from Italy. Once he had spoken he watched his cook trying to contain herself, trying to say thank you, but trying also to go back to her husband with the news as quickly as possible. She walked nervously backwards, thanking him all the while, before turning and fleeing the room.

He did not mention her sister to Mrs Smith in the days before his departure. He had made the conditions clear and thought it would be indelicate to bring them up again. Nor did he care to see Mrs Smith again in her importuning role. During his time in Italy, therefore, he presumed that Mrs Smith's sister was causing him no personal expense and that all traces of her would be gone on his return.

As soon as he came through the door two months later, however, he knew that a sick person was being ministered to in his apartment. He was interested when Mr Smith, who met him in the hallway, made no reference to this fact. When he asked Mr Smith, barely disguising his impatience, kindly to tell his wife that Mr James wished to see her in his study, Mr Smith managed to suggest that this was a normal request which could be conveyed without much concern.

Mrs Smith seemed braver than at any other time he had seen her. She stood before him quite in possession of herself. Yes, she said, her sister was still here, and suffering from cancer and she, Mrs Smith, was awaiting Mr James's advice about what to do.

Had it been a novel, his character would have said something very dry indeed to Mrs Smith, but Henry was aware that her sister lay stricken in a nearby room and that Mrs Smith had a heavy responsibility which he now shared, since the sick woman was under his roof.

'Does the doctor come?' he asked.

'Sir, he has been here.'

'Could you make sure that he comes again and soon, and that I have a chance to speak to him?'

The doctor was gloomy and curious. When he wished to know the status of Mrs Smith's sister in the household, Henry insisted that they stick to medical matters. It was clear, the doctor said, that the lady would need a further operation, but after the operation she would need a great deal of care and he did not know if such care would be forthcoming.

'It costs money, this care. It all costs money.'

When Henry opened the door for him, Mr Smith was hovering in the hallway.

'Could you see to the operation and let me know what care will be needed subsequently?' he asked brusquely.

'It will all cost, you must know that, sir,' the doctor said before he departed.

Sometime over the next two weeks, as the patient underwent her operation, Henry realized that Mr Smith was drinking. He waited until both Smiths were absent and the housemaid out on a chore before he went into the kitchen and found an empty bottle of whisky and some empty bottles of sweet wine and sherry. Later, he checked through the household accounts but found no evidence that these bottles were acquired at his expense. He felt foolish for snooping in the kitchen and determined that he would not do so again. If the Smiths wished to purchase alcohol, they were free to do so as long as it did not interfere with their work. Mr Smith seemed glazed, so to speak, especially in the late afternoon and early evening, but perhaps this effect was caused as much by the pressures of his sister-in-law's illness as by the alcohol.

The news from the hospital once the operation had been declared successful was that the patient would require twenty-four-hour nursing care for at least one month. As far as he could ascertain, Mrs Smith's sister, until she was well, had nowhere else to go. Since no guests of his own were due to arrive, he would have difficulty, he thought, passing the guest room each day knowing that it was vacant while Mrs Smith's sister, already familiar with the room, was suffering neglect elsewhere. Mrs Smith's difficulty would be even greater. He knew that she must be preparing herself for a final onslaught on his pity and decided that he could not bear the aura of preparation in the household before she would approach him, her manner full of abject and grasping humility. He decided to inform her forthwith that he would take her sister into his guest room and pay for her nursing care on the proviso that his own quarters were not disturbed nor his routine affected. Her face, as she listened to the news, seemed to suggest that her fear of him was greater than ever.

The Smiths were grateful. Once her sister had recovered and returned to her employer Mrs Smith even made a brief, formal speech to tell him so. Perhaps more significant, however, was the fact that his involvement in the sister's welfare seemed to tie him into the fate of the Smiths. Clearly, should either of them need medical care, or any other sort of care, it would be their employer's responsibility. He paid them reasonably well, and they had no expenses, Mr Smith wearing his master's cast-offs and Mrs Smith having no interest in finery, and this led him to presume that they were, as good provident people, saving most of their income towards a happy and easy retirement.

His agreeing to help them in time of need did not result in better service; nor, on the other hand, did the Smiths' work worsen in any radical way. Mrs Smith still took her instructions every morning and obeyed them as best she could. Mr Smith still appeared to be drinking, but no dreadful loss of decorum was immediately apparent, and it was only when he was scrutinized that his speech and his gait in the latter half of the day seemed laboured. Nonetheless, a certain change took place. Mrs Smith was now capable of discussing with Mr Smith a matter which had nothing to do with the household in the presence of their employer. She knew that Henry treasured silence, and she must have known, too, that he expected her and her husband to discuss private matters only in their own quarters. Yet Henry could not correct her; she had, in the days when he had offered her sister charity, won some invisible battle with him which allowed her to make herself at home in such subtle ways in the household. Looking after her sister, exercising mercy and pity, had shortened the distance between him and Mrs Smith.

Because he was excited and preoccupied in the months before his move to Rye, he had no memory of the Smiths' response to the news. As they were growing older, he thought they might enjoy the peace of a small town and the larger facilities of Lamb House. In any case, they made no overt protest, and he made sure that they would not be overburdened by the move, that their main task in these months should be the moving of themselves and their possessions to their new quarters at Rye. One or two of his friends, he knew, had noticed Smith's efforts to disguise the fact that he was drunk as he served dinner, but he believed that once away from the noisy pressures of London, Smith could be spoken to and guided to sobriety.

He discovered, as soon as they were installed in the house, that there was a problem. The Smiths were sleeping in the servants' quarters in the attic. Because there was only one staircase, they had to pass through the first floor of the house, where his study and sleeping quarters were, to get to their room. The floorboards in their room squeaked; one of them especially, which lay directly over his bed, seemed to move in and out of place every time one of the Smiths stepped on it. At night, during those first weeks at Rye, the Smiths ascended to their room at a normal hour, but they did not settle; they moved up and down irregularly, pacing the floorboards, becoming briefly quiet, then agitated once more, indifferent to the repose of their employer who lay below them. Sometimes he could hear their voices, and a few times he heard the sound of a heavy solid object falling to the floor.

Warren the architect was consulted. The floor, he said, was in good condition; a new set of floorboards would make no difference. The Smiths should be told, he said, to move more quietly, or their sleeping quarters should be relocated to the ground floor. There was, he pointed out, a small room off the pantry which would have space for their bed and could be made suitable for them by creating a larger window and putting up some sensible wallpaper. Thus the Smiths took up residence in a room off the pantry.

The shopkeepers of Rye did not warm to the Smiths; the butcher did not understand her notes, and took no pleasure in her remonstrances when the cuts he sent were not the cuts she ordered. The baker did not bake the bread she required, and did not find it amusing when she had to return to him on discovering that his rival baker did not produce such bread either, nor any other bread which was to her taste. The grocer did not like her London manners, and soon the list of orders had to be delivered to the grocer by Mr Smith, his wife's presence being unwelcome.

The Smiths discovered that Lamb House stood alone in Rye. Around it were smaller and more modest houses which had a parlourmaid and perhaps a part-time cook, but not a couple who had the standing of the Smiths. The houses with like-minded servants were the manor houses and great houses in the countryside, but these servants did not wander in the town as their peers had wandered in Kensington. The Smiths quickly ascertained that there was no one else like them in Rye, that there were to be no casual daily greetings and exchanges of news. Soon, in the shops, they were met with coldness or mild hostility, unlike Burgess Noakes, who was received with warmth and affection everywhere he went.

Mr and Mrs Smith retreated into Lamb House, Mrs Smith priding herself on never leaving its precincts and never having visited most of Rye's best-known monuments. In the kitchen, the pantry and the pantry garden she reigned supreme. When she took her orders, she managed a new tone which emphasized her steely competence and willingness to carry out her duties, but did not spare her employer signs of resentment.

In Kensington Henry had often had guests, but, though he cared about the quality of his own hospitality, the evenings when he entertained were mild distractions. Now, in Rye, he cared a great deal more about his guests, wrote many letters inviting friends to see his new abode, and awaited their arrival and their response to the house with some excitement. Thus the decor and daily cleaning of the guest rooms were essential, as were the quality of the food and the service, which would now include breakfast and luncheon. Mrs Smith was unaccustomed to many guests. At first when it was a novelty he explained to her who was coming and what their needs would be, but soon it became clear to Mrs Smith that there would be a constant stream of guests at Lamb House, and it would be her job to cook for them and ensure their comfort.

The morning meetings during which he gave her instructions became tense. Nothing she actually said made the difference; merely the set of her face, the silences and the slow, soft sighs. He paid no attention to her new attitude, he told her who was coming and what should be done and did not wait for any response. But after a while she began to detain him with sour comments, alluding to the increased cost of caring for guests, or the dreadful butcher, or the nuisance that was Burgess Noakes. A note of belligerence crept into her voice when more visitors were due. He could not contain his own longing to see old friends and members of his family and found it shocking and irritating that Mrs Smith should express her ill feeling against his guests in such clear terms.

Her husband, in the meantime, had developed a controlled gait and wooden movements, which many guests mistook for an old-fashioned formality, but which Henry knew to be ordinary drunkenness. He wished he could mention the matter to the Smiths, that he could approach them as Mrs Smith had once approached him, asking for their help, insisting that Smith should cease his drinking. But he did not have the courage to make such demands. He knew, in any case, that in her denials of her husband's intoxication, Mrs Smith's vehemence would come to the fore and he did not wish to face that.

Burgess Noakes, on the other hand, grew more obliging and willing as time went on. He missed nothing and forgot nothing. He did not learn to smile, but he soon knew the names and habits and needs of every guest, and seemed also to know if a telegram warranted an interruption of his master when he had company or whether it should be deposited on the hall stand. He trod the floorboards of his attic room with the utmost discretion.

Burgess greeted Mrs Smith's regular banishing of him from the kitchen with indifference. When he was not attending to his duties, he wandered into the depths of Rye where he began to perfect the art of bantam-weight boxing, at which he soon became a champion. He returned home happily, however, and always at the appointed hour, exuding a pride at his position in Lamb House and seeming to know everything which occurred within its confines. As Henry began to suspect Mrs Smith of joining her husband in drink, he knew that if he should ever require an account of the Smiths' personal habits, he would merely have to consult Burgess Noakes.

That his guests should be content with their stay and wish to return to Lamb House meant much to him. He enjoyed letters that mentioned past and future visits. He had no close companions in the town or locality; there could be no easy outings for a few hours in the evenings. Thus his visitors were important. He found the waiting for them, the sense of expectation before a visit, the most blissful time of all. He alerted everyone that he spent the morning hours in his study. Having left his guest at breakfast, he loved going there, knowing that they would come together again in the afternoon. In the meantime he would have several hours of solitude or dictation with the Scot. He also relished the days after a guest had departed, he enjoyed the peace of the house, as though the visit had been nothing except a battle for solitude which he had finally won.

Soon, however, his contented solitude could turn to loneliness. On grey, blustery days in the first long winter, his study in Lamb House, and indeed the house itself, could seem like a cage. Both he and the Smiths had been removed from their natural hinterland. He had his work, but he knew that they became, by the end of each day, quietly and effectively intoxicated.

He was not sure of the extent of Mrs Smith's drinking. She ran her kitchen smoothly; her cooking, as it were, did not falter. Her appearance in the morning, however, grew more slovenly and her response to the news of more visitors increasingly bellicose. Her hair hung dangerously close to where the pots and pans might be. Nor did the state of her fingernails invite confidence. He wondered if she knew why he had suspended soup when there were visitors, and gravy too, as well as any of the more runny sauces. Mr Smith could not be counted on to serve them safely.

As he served dinner, Smith managed not to stagger on the way into the room with each dish, but once he turned to leave the room he could not exercise the same control. Henry formed the habit of placing his principal guest facing away from the door. He noticed that once guests at the table saw Smith stagger or falter then they could not stop watching him. His aim was to prevent the matter from becoming a subject for discussion at the dinner table, or among the guests later. He did not want it known in London nor among his small circle of American friends that he employed drunken servants.

Burgess Noakes began to assist Smith, opening doors for him, urging him silently towards stability. Henry hoped that the problem would right itself, or even remain as it was. He did not want to take action because he knew what the action would have to be. He tried not to think about the Smiths.

ONE AFTERNOON, from an upstairs window, he saw Mrs Smith's sister approach the house. He heard her being let in and supposed that she was in the kitchen with her sister. He had not met her since the time she had spent in his apartment and though he had seen little of her then he had formed an impression of a solid and sensible person. He decided he would speak to her, and, on descending the stairs, and finding Burgess Noakes in the hallway, he asked Burgess to inform Mrs Smith's sister that he wished to see her when she had a moment. He would wait in the front sitting room.

Mrs Smith's sister soon arrived accompanied by Mrs Smith. While the former was a picture of respectability and good grooming, the latter was even more slovenly than usual and wore the brazen expression to which he had become accustomed.

'I am glad to see you well, madam,' he said to Mrs Smith's sister.

'I am very well, sir, much recovered, and many thanks to you for all your kindness.'

Mrs Smith watched him and studied the back of her sister's head with the attitude of someone who had been much put out.

'Are you visiting the area?' he asked.

'No, sir, I am married to the gardener at the Poet Laureate's. We live in the gardener's cottage there.'

'The Poet Laureate?'

'Mr Austen, sir, at Ashford.'

'Of course, of course, Alfred Austen.' He had thought for a moment that she was working for Lord Tennyson.

He was about to ask if he could see her alone when he realized that he had clearly interrupted a difficult conversation between Mrs Smith and her sister, from which Mrs Smith was still smarting. While the sister was doing what she could to disguise this, Mrs Smith continued to glower at both of them.

'I expect we shall see more of you then?' he asked.

'Oh I don't wish to disturb you, sir.'

'Not at all,' he said. 'You find your sister well?'

He looked at her plainly and made no effort to assist her when she lowered her gaze and said nothing. She had taken in the meaning of his question; he now left time for the implications of her failure to respond to become clear to the three of them. When he felt that this had been achieved, he decided that he did not wish to see her alone, that enough had been said. He smiled warmly and bowed to her as she left the room, paying no attention to Mrs Smith. He now knew where to find Mrs Smith's sister should he need her.

ALICE, his sister, would have laughed uproariously at his predicament; she would have made him describe the Smiths in detail. But she would also, he thought, have become imperious and demand that he take action forthwith. Alice, his sister-in-law, was the most practical of the family. She would calmly and cleverly work out a way of getting rid of the Smiths. He could not tell her, however, because he could not bear a letter from William on the subject. Nor was there anyone in London to whom he could turn. All of his English friends would, he thought, have dismissed the Smiths at the first sign of inebriation and sullenness.

He began to have imaginary conversations with Constance Fenimore Woolson. She would have been fascinated by the scenes in the kitchen, and indeed in the room off the pantry. She also would have known what to do; she would have worked out some way to convince the Smiths to go without rancour, or to reform. He thought about her calm grace, her easy warmth, her mixture of curiosity and sympathy; and he thought about her last days in Venice, the days before she hurled herself from the window. He sighed and closed his eyes.

AMONG HIS family and most friends, his closeness to Constance was not generally known. Neither William nor his wife was part of the small group who had been in Florence in those months when he had shared a large house with Constance on Bellosguardo (and when, he presumed, their relationship had been much discussed).

But those who knew continued to mention Constance in their letters to him, their references to her vague and mysterious; they regularly voiced their wonder at her death. But only one friend had asked him directly if he knew why she had committed suicide. Lily Norton was the charming daughter of his friend Charles Eliot Norton and the niece of one of his favourite Bostonians, Grace Norton. Lily had known Constance in Italy and, though being more than twenty years younger, had admired her and formed a great attachment to her.

He wrote to Lily as frankly and directly as he could. He explained that, as she knew, he had not been in Venice at the time, and had merely gathered information from others. Constance was out of her mind with fever and illness, he wrote, but that was not all. There was as well something that Constance managed to keep hidden from the wider world, and that was, he told his young friend, a condition of chronic and absorbing melancholy which was much sharpened by loneliness. He left it at that; Lily had been brave enough to ask, and now she should be brave enough to read the stark truth.

Lily Norton had never returned to the subject, but her Aunt Grace had mentioned in passing that her niece had been upset by the coldness and certainty of the tone in his letter. When Lily Norton accepted his invitation to Rye, and he knew that they would be alone for the first day, he wondered whether she would raise the subject of Constance. They would have, after all, many other things to discuss. Lily had become Europeanized. She would have, in the European way, many subjects on which to muse while studiously avoiding the dangerous. Discussion of her relatives alone, and their associates, should provide her and her host with several delightful hours. His interest in the Nortons, the Sedgwicks, the Lowells, the Dixwells and the Darwins, he imagined, could occupy at least one long meal, and perhaps a walk with his young friend through the streets of the town.

When he met her at the station, he realized quickly how formidable and interesting she had become. On alighting from her carriage, she saw him but did not smile. Her eyes were alert, her expression serious and self-conscious and beautifully placid. She had the air of a young duchess, someone who managed to be obeyed without ever having the need to be imperious. As soon as she started to walk towards him, however, Lily began to beam, her face opened out, as if she had suddenly and impetuously decided she was an American, one who knew how to play her natural and her created selves against each other to her host's delight.

Lily briefly glanced at Burgess Noakes as he and the porter loaded her luggage onto his wheelbarrow; she took this in and suggested her approval for the enterprise without making a single gesture. Once in the house, she promised Henry that she would never say the word 'pretty' ever again, but she would have to point out that the house itself was very pretty and the gardens were immensely so, and even the little parlour he had offered her in case she wanted to write letters was pretty, and her room, well, that too. She smiled at him warmly and touched his shoulder, now she had stopped admiring everything. She was so glad to be here, she said.

As they sat in the garden taking tea, he studied her carefully. She exuded a mixture of a mobile mind and personal charm in a greater degree than the women of the earlier generations of her family on either side. She had inherited something of the horse-face of the Nortons, but in her it was improved and softened. She had her mother's eyes and her mother's way of smiling before she spoke and often smiling while she listened. But when she abandoned her smile, and allowed her face its full elegant gravity, he saw a young woman whose tone and manners, her way of being both formal and friendly, were new to him. He looked forward to spending time with her.

He accompanied her through the town, proud of her glamour and enjoying her conversation, which ranged from the playful to the sharply observant. She knew how much he was watching her and how closely, in turn, they were both being observed by the townspeople. He admired her all the more for how deeply thoughtful she became as they moved along, how happy she seemed after a time to let silence reign between them and how easily now she let her face seem shadowy and meditative, her expression almost dark and forbidding, as though the mark of her ancestors had not left her.

She was over thirty now and something in her personality, something distant and ironic, suggested what her Aunt Grace had already told him – that she would not marry. She had a private income, not very large, but enough to allow her to wander freely in Italy and England and venture back to her homeland when it suited her, much as Constance Fenimore Woolson had done. He wished she had a great house to tend to, or a great name, and he sensed in her a kind of sorrow that she had settled for less, or perhaps settled for more, her independence. A few times, as they walked back towards Lamb House, her tone, the largeness of her judgement, the strange freedom in her phrases, and certain inflections in her accent, reminded him of his sister Alice. Both came from similar households where ideas were sacred, second only to good manners, where there was a pull between an ordered community who knew God and an idealism, a readiness to trust the spirit in all its flickering. Whereas all the restlessness within the Jameses had further unmoored Alice, Lily had inherited the calmness of the Nortons without sacrificing her sharp judgement. He would have given anything for his sister to have had Lily's poise and equanimity.

Before dinner was served, he left Lily alone in the upstairs sitting room so that he might inspect the dining room. He found Burgess Noakes standing at an open dining-room door, his small face wrinkled in worry, his movements nervous. Burgess indicated to him that the cause of his concern lay in the dining room, and when Henry entered the room he found a large fresh purple stain on the tablecloth.

'This should be replaced at once,' he said.

'She says it will do fine,' Burgess said.

'Mrs Smith?' he asked.

Burgess nodded. 'She won't allow it be replaced, sir.'

When he opened the kitchen door, he saw Mr Smith at the large table resting his head on his arms. Mrs Smith was by the stove stirring a pot. When she saw him, she did not speak but shrugged to suggest her own powerlessness and indifference. He spoke as loudly as he could.

'The tablecloth must be replaced instantly and the butler must resume his duties.'

Mrs Smith put the spoon down and moved towards the table. She stood stoically behind her husband and manfully grabbed his shoulders from above; she lifted him firmly and when he was standing straight she let him go. He had his usual glazed look as he acknowledged his employer's presence in the kitchen, and then, in his stilted and forced way, he began to move towards the dresser in the corner.

'In fifteen minutes, we will dine,' Henry said. 'I expect everything to be in order, beginning with the tablecloth.'

When he accompanied Lily Norton to the dining room, he saw immediately that the tablecloth had been replaced and the table reset to perfection. He situated Lily with her back to the door. He did not know whether Smith would serve their meal, or if Burgess Noakes or indeed Mrs Smith herself would take his place. When eventually Smith came in with the first course and began to pour the wine, it struck Henry more forcefully than ever that he was barely able to remain on his feet and could hardly see in front of him. It was a strange kind of drunkenness. Smith did not sway or stagger; it was rather the opposite – he walked straight as though along an invisible line; otherwise, he remained rigid. He was utterly silent. The alcohol seemed to have turned him into a block of wood.

Henry was careful not to look at Smith for too long; he attempted to make ordinary conversation even as Smith was pouring the wine. As far as he could ascertain, Lily Norton noticed nothing, yet he knew now that he would have to make arrangements for the Smiths' departure. He had two further guests for luncheon the following day and Lily and one of the friends for dinner the next evening. Then he would take action, although he did not know how he would begin, or what form the action would take.

'You know,' Lily said, 'I have not been in Venice since Constance died, but I have met others who have been there, and all of them say that there is something in that street, the place she fell. They all have to avoid it. And nobody can quite believe that she killed herself. It seems so unlike her.'

Her eyes lit calmly on him and then she glanced at the plate in front of her, as though some fresh thought had occurred to her. She looked up at him again.

'I spoke at length to someone who knew her sister,' she said. 'The family are concerned that so many of her papers are lost, letters and diaries and other personal papers. And how she spent her last weeks is a mystery to everybody.'

'It was,' Henry said, 'a sad affair.'

Smith opened the door and stood silently, peering into the room as though it were in darkness. Lily turned around and saw him. He was still for half a minute, his presence in the doorway a cross between a ghost and someone who has seen a ghost. Then he moved slowly towards the table to collect the plates. He picked them up in a set of muted and stylized gestures and left the room again without incident.

'She was, of course, quite a sad person and very lonely,' Henry said.

He knew as soon as he finished that he had spoken too quickly and brusquely.

'She was a very talented novelist and a great lady,' Lily Norton said.

'Yes, quite,' Henry said.

They waited without speaking for Smith to return. Henry realized that he could not change the subject now, Lily Norton's tone somehow prevented that.

'I think she deserved a better life,' Lily said, 'but it was not to be.'

In her last phrase there was no air of resignation or acceptance, but rather one of blame and bitterness. It struck Henry that she had planned this conversation, that what was happening in his small dining room was being quietly and effectively manipulated by her. At each moment he watched for Smith, hoping that no matter how drunk he was he would come to interrupt this strained talk between them which led so inevitably to strained silence.

'All of us were there with her that summer,' Lily continued, 'she was so busy and so full of dreams and plans. All of us remember someone who was happy, despite her melancholy disposition. But it was shattered.'

'Yes,' Henry said.

Smith opened the door with Burgess Noakes in view behind him. Burgess was wearing a jacket which was much too large for him. He had the look of a tramp. Smith carried a plate of meat with the movements of someone who was about to expire. Burgess followed behind with other plates. Lily Norton turned and studied them, and in one second Henry watched her grasp what was happening at Lamb House. All her subtlety and self-control failed her. She seemed most sharply alarmed, and her smile when she turned away from the two servants was forced. Smith at that moment began to pour more wine into her glass but could not keep his hand steady. The other three watched him helplessly as he allowed some of the wine to spill and then, as he tried to correct himself, poured a quantity of wine directly onto the table-cloth. When he turned from the table, his movements became a set of doddering, staggering steps as he left the room, abandoning the serving of the meal to Burgess Noakes.

They ate in silence, the subject he wished to change now accompanied by another subject which could not be mentioned. He knew that if he asked Lily some particular question about her aunt or her plans, she would either laugh or become heated.

He resigned himself to saying nothing; she would decide the flow of conversation.

Eventually, she spoke.

'I do not think she would have come to Venice for solitude. It is not a place to be alone at any time, but certainly not in the winter.'

'Yes, she might have been wiser to have moved,' he said. 'It is hard to tell.'

'Of course Mrs Curtis and she both believed that you planned to take a pied-à-terre in Venice,' Lily said. 'I believe that they even searched for a while on your behalf.'

He saw where she was going and knew that it was essential to stop her.

'I'm afraid they misunderstood my enthusiasm for its beauties and its pleasures,' he said. 'Yes, whenever I was there, I longed to hold the grand watery city, as it were, by owning a view, however modest. But these fancies can be entertained but briefly, I'm afraid. The rest is dull. It is called work and it makes demands.'

Her look was darkly pointed, but with a tinge of sympathy. She smiled.

'Yes, I can imagine,' she said drily.

IN THE MORNING he told Mrs Smith that he wished her husband to remain in bed where he would in the course of the day be examined by a doctor. Luncheon would be served by the parlour-maid with assistance from Burgess Noakes, who should be found a jacket which fitted him. He asked her if she could come out to the garden with him, knowing that Lily Norton was writing a letter in a room not overlooking the garden, and would not witness this scene. He wished to study Mrs Smith in clear daylight, and when he did so he saw that she could not continue in his kitchen, that she did not seem to have washed or changed her clothes in a very long time.

'I trust your guest is enjoying her stay,' she said. 'I trust everything is in order for her and there are no complaints.'

Her tone was almost insolent. When he understood that she was about to say something else, he stopped her by raising his right hand, and then he bowed gently and returned to the house.

He found Burgess Noakes and asked him to enquire urgently among the shopkeepers of Rye to discover the name of Mrs Smith's sister who lived in the gardener's cottage at Ashford. Soon, Burgess returned with the news that her name was Mrs Ticknor. As he turned towards his study, Burgess touched him on the shoulder, put his finger to his lips and guided him to the garden.

Henry watched amazed as Burgess checked that no one else could see them, his expression cautious and watchful. As Burgess led him to the outbuildings behind the kitchen, Henry wondered what his diminutive houseboy could possibly want him to see. Checking to ensure that Henry was following, Burgess motioned to him to enter one of the sheds and pulled back a stretch of canvas to disclose an enormous cache of empty whisky, wine and sherry bottles, which gave off a foul, sour smell.

By luncheon, Henry had summoned the doctor to call in the afternoon and had sent an urgent telegram to Mrs Ticknor. He was thus able to greet Lily's friend Ida Higginson, who, he appreciated, had known all her life only the most orderly domestic rituals which Boston could provide, and a friend from Eastbourne who had come for the day, as though his household was in good health and perfect harmony. He knew that Lily Norton would not be indelicate enough to mention the matter to anyone save her Aunt Grace who would be too interested in the news to be fully deprived of it. He was glad he had not confided in her or in anyone else. He explained to the company that the butler was not well and hoped they would not be offended by the parlourmaid serving luncheon with the assistance of young Burgess Noakes.

As luncheon came to an end, Mrs Smith having once more miraculously cooked a meal, Burgess indicated to him that Mrs

Ticknor had arrived, and he asked that she wait for him in the front sitting room. He knew that this would prevent him from showing his guests around the garden, but he easily arranged that, since he had work that could not wait, in the shape of a novel appearing as a serial, Miss Norton should take her fellow guests on a walk through Rye, with which she had become thoroughly acquainted.

Once they had happily and innocently departed, he went to Mrs Ticknor and told her of his plight. He emphasized that it could not, would not, continue. He wished to dismiss both of them. He would settle generously with them, he said, but he could no longer employ them. Mrs Ticknor, he hoped, could make arrangements for them, but he would not help her in that, he said.

Mrs Ticknor said nothing, her face betrayed no emotion. She simply asked where her sister was and if she could speak to her. As they moved into the hallway, they saw the parlourmaid let the doctor into the house. Henry sent Mrs Ticknor to the kitchen, and, having briefed the doctor, dispatched him in the care of the parlourmaid to the room behind the pantry where, he understood from Burgess Noakes, Mr Smith lay.

That evening as he dined with Lily Norton and his friend from Eastbourne, the conversation ranged over political and literary matters. Lily was at her most persuasively charming and intelligent. Considering her insistence on raising the issue of Constance Fenimore Woolson the previous evening and her insinuation that he had abandoned her friend and left her to her fate in Venice, he wondered if she, too, Lily Norton, had been abandoned, or if she lived in fear of such an eventuality. Her not marrying, not being allied with someone who could offer her greater purpose and scope for all her flair and charm, was, in his view, a mistake and would likely seem more so as time passed. As he looked at her across the table, it occurred to him that the re-creation of herself, her deliberate broadening of her effect, could have atrophied other qualities more endearing to a potential suitor. Constance, he thought, might have written a very good novel about her.

The doctor returned in the morning and professed the case hopeless. Mr Smith, he said, remained drunk because the daily intake of alcohol over so many years had made him so. Once the supply was withdrawn, he would suffer enormously. Mrs Ticknor returned with her husband and told Henry that his generosity was appreciated and indeed would be needed as the Smiths did not have a penny. They had saved nothing. They had spent all their income on drink and in fact owed money to several suppliers in Rye. Mrs Ticknor was brisk in her tone and her husband stood beside her, clearly embarrassed, his cap in his hands.

The Smiths were, as their goods were gathered, he thought, simply two saturated and demoralized victims with not a word to say for themselves, even Mrs Smith moved in silence to her doom, avoiding his glance. He knew that they would not find work again, and that, when his payments had run out, and their close family could no longer manage them, they would face the abyss. The Smiths, he thought, who had come with him so faithfully through so many years, were lost. But he knew that he would have given anything to get them out of the house.

He wrote to his sister-in-law about the episode, but mentioned it to no one else. It was, he said, a perfect nightmare of distress, disgust and inconvenience. He realized that everyone in Rye would soon discover the fate of the Smiths. Even though they were disliked, the speed of their dismissal, he knew, would cause people to observe him closely as he walked through the town.

This episode and the enervating weeks that followed as he lived servantless and ate in a local hostelry filled him with an unhappiness that only work could cure. In the mornings he sat at the wide south window of the drawing room which caught all the early sunshine and he read over the previous day's work. The window overlooked the smooth green lawn and he loved to watch George Gammon at work under the shade of the old mulberry tree. Later, as he took his stroll in the garden, he would enjoy being protected from the world by the high garden walls of Lamb House.

CHAPTER NINE

March 1899

NOTHING CAME TO HIM simply now. Nothing he saw and heard in this, his first journey out of England in five years, came as new and fresh experience to be wondered at and treasured. In Paris he met Rosina and Bay Emmet, the daughters of Ellen Temple, Minny's sister. Both had been born after Minny's death and had known her merely from the few photographs which had been taken and as a shadowy absence. The girls were not alike. Rosina was prettier and more outspoken; Bay was small and somewhat stocky, more quietly confiding and trusting than her sister. Her ambition as a painter was already clear from her keen observation of the work in the galleries and the life in the street, the latter seeming to both girls to rival the former for its artfulness and beauty.

Sometimes when they spoke he heard Minny Temple's voice. He envied them their lack of self-consciousness, their unawareness that their American voices, so filled with enthusiasm, were not as original as they imagined, nor as uncomplicated by history as they supposed.

He was old enough at fifty-six to be able to deplore things with full conviction, and Bay Emmet playfully insisted that he was imitating Dr Sloper from *Washington Square* on his tour of Europe with his unfortunate and ill-educated daughter. He deplored the girls' accents and corrected them regularly as they moved from one museum to another. When Rosina, for example, admired the jewels in a Parisian shop window, Henry immediately corrected her.

'Jew-el, not jool.'

And when she agreed that American girls did not nowadays speak out their vowels distinctly, he replied:

'Vow-els, not vowls, Rosina.'

Soon, both sisters, obviously enjoying their cousin's reprimands, began to find new outrages to commit against his fastidious ear. They reminded him now, more than at any other time, of the dead aunt who loved such an encounter and would relish the response a new remark could cause. The girls managed to stand their ground not by arguing with him, but by mocking him gently, dropping any consonant which came their way and using a modern idiom certain to irritate him. When Bay announced one morning that she needed to go upstairs to fix her hair, Henry asked her, 'To fix it to what, or with what?'

Paris was more splendid than he had ever seen it, but he sensed something behind the splendour of which he disapproved. He was careful not to discuss this with the Emmet girls. He loved how innocently alert they were to colours and vistas and textures; he enjoyed how they pointed out details to him and to each other, and how happily they bathed in the city's grandeur. A few times, when Bay Emmet grew silent and took no further part in jokes, and seemed to be absorbing the scene in a sort of reverie, and could grow easily irritated at any interruption, he felt the ghost of Constance Fenimore Woolson tugging at the air around them, serene and inward-looking, as sensitive to suggestion and shadow as Minny Temple had been to flourish and light.

His cousins thus brought ancient memories to life. Sometimes, so fascinated were they by their surroundings, they did not notice his darkening memories. He found their indifference to him charming, a relief, and he wondered if some of his old friends, who demanded his attention too much and monitored too closely what he said and did, might be encouraged to follow the example of the Emmet sisters.

He realized, as he travelled south, having left the girls to their European tour, that he could live easily without many of his friends. He would enjoy irregular correspondence, and, indeed, would treasure hearing of their lives and activities. But as he spent a night in Marseilles, knowing that the next day he would be in their grasp, he recognized that he could quite blissfully have passed by the abode of Paul and Minnie Bourget and not have seen his friends at all. The height of fame and wealth had given Bourget a twenty-five-acre estate on the Riviera on a terraced mountainside with a park of dense pine and cedar, complete with magnificent views. It had also given him an inordinate interest in his own opinions which, exacerbated by anti-Semitism, had become unpleasantly rigid and authoritarian.

There was another guest on the estate, a minor French novelist. Henry did everything he could, in the early days of his stay, not to discuss Zola or the Dreyfus case with Paul or Minnie Bourget or their guest, feeling that his own views on the matter would diverge from those of his hosts. His support for Zola and, indeed, for Dreyfus, was sufficiently strong not to wish to hear the Bourgets' prejudices on the matter. He could sense that the Bourgets' luxury and exquisite taste and the superior nature of their daily routine were connected with the hardness and hatreds of their illiberal politics. The English, he thought, were softer in their views, more ambiguous in the connections between their personal circumstances and their political convictions.

He knew Bourget, he felt, as though he had made him. He knew his nature and his culture, his race and his type, his vanity and his snobbery, his interest in ideas and his ambition. But these were small matters compared with the overall effect of the man, and the core of selfhood which he so easily revealed. This was richer and more likeable and more complicated than anyone supposed.

In return for all Henry's attention, he knew, Bourget noticed nothing. His list of Henry's attributes, were he to make one, would be simple and clear and inaccurate. He did not observe the concealed self, nor, Henry imagined, did the idea interest him. And this, as his stay with the Bourgets came to an end, pleased him. Remaining invisible, becoming skilled in the art of self-effacement, even to someone whom he had known so long, gave him satisfaction. He was ready to listen, always ready to do that, but not prepared to reveal the mind at work, the imagination, or the depth of feeling. At times, he knew, the blankness was much more than a mask. It made its way inwards as well as outwards, so that, having left the Bourgets' estate, and travelling on towards Venice, the possibility of future meetings with his former hosts had quickly become a subject of indifference to him.

HE HAD NOT forgotten how much he loved Italy, but he feared that he had grown too old and stale to be captured once more by it, or that Italy, under pressure of time and tourism, had lost its golden charm. He sat still in the train carriage during the three-hour delay at Ventimiglia, watching the stuffy, scrambling, complaining crowd, led by a party of affluent Germans. He would have given a great deal to have stood up and walked sturdily over the border, his baggage coming behind him on a wheelbarrow pushed by Burgess Noakes. He felt an immense impatience to leave France behind him and be brushed now by the wings of Italy. The manners in Italy were open and fresh; all the refinement was hidden and taken for granted. When finally he found himself sitting in an armchair close to the window of his hotel in Genoa basking in the Italian air and the revival of Italian memories, he felt relieved and happy.

ONCE HE HAD arrived in Venice and night fell, he knew that neither tourism nor time had harmed the city's mixture of sadness and splendour. He made his way from the railway station to the Palazzo Barbaro along side-canals by gondola, swerving and twisting through the dimly recognized waterways. These journeys had a gravity attached to them, as though the passenger were being led theatrically to his doom. But then, as the vessel was let float softly and slacken in pace, and gently bumped against a mooring post, the other side of Venice appeared – the raw sumptuousness, the shameless glitter, the spaces so out of scale with actual need.

Venice was laden down with old voices, old echoes and images; it was the refuge of endless strange secrets, broken fortunes and wounded hearts. Five years earlier, having sorted out the affairs of his friend Constance Fenimore Woolson, he had left the city believing that he would not return. It was as if both he and Constance had risked too much in their gamble with Venice, and she had lost everything while he had lost her. Venice's reso-nance for him now was no longer vague and historical; the violence and cruelty which matched the beauty and grandeur were no longer abstract. They were represented by the violent death of his friend. As guest of his hosts the Curtises in Palazzo Barbaro, he worked on a new story in one of the rooms at the back, with a pompous painted ceiling and walls of ancient pale green damask slightly shredded and patched. He knew that just a few rooms away glowed the Grand Canal. If he stood on the bal-cony, as he had done so many times, he could study the domes and scrolls and scalloped buttresses and statues forming the crown of the Salute, the wide steps like the train of a robe. He could look up to the left and allow himself to be dazzled by Palazzo Dario covered with the loveliest marble plates and sculptured circles, exquisite and compact and delicate.

In that turning of his head from the Salute to Palazzo Dario, his eye was caught each time by the gloomy Gothic windows of Casa Semitecolo and this was when Venice ceased to be spectacle for him, when it abandoned its guise as vast pageant and became real and hard and filled with horror. It was from the second story of this building, five years earlier, that Constance Fenimore Woolson had flung herself onto the pavement.

HE HAD FIRST met her early in 1880 in Florence when he was writing *The Portrait of a Lady*. He was thirty-seven; she was forty. She had had a letter of introduction from Minny Temple's sister Henrietta. While she had read everything he had written, he had read nothing by her. He had met many American women travelling in Europe with letters of introduction to him. Such letters, if gathered together, he thought, would produce a hefty volume, but they would not be as tedious as many of their bearers, who included a number of lady novelists who wished that they had written *Daisy Miller* and were anxious to tell him that they were on the point of doing something quite as good.

Constance's deafness in one ear interested him as much as it seemed to irritate her. It pointed to something he might otherwise not have noticed so quickly. She possessed an extraordinary amount of reserve and self-sufficiency and seemed anxious neither to please him nor impress him. She lived, to a degree which he believed unusual, in her own mind. He was not surprised, as he showed her the sights, that she wished to avoid tourists, but he was fascinated by her lack of interest in Anglo-American society in Florence and her refusal to be introduced to his friends and associates in the higher echelons of Florentine society. She needed her evenings to herself, she said flatly; she could not happily absorb the company of so many people, no matter how rich and important they were.

He was unable to tell whether her responses to churches and frescoes and paintings were truly original. Nonetheless, the freshness of her intelligence, her likes and dislikes, and her ability to be puzzled and confused, made him interested in accompanying her through the city in the mornings. Two years later, when she read *The Portrait of a Lady*, she noticed, she intimated to him softly, his skill at displaying an American woman full of openness and curiosity and ideas of her own in Italy for the first time being quietly but firmly directed by a connoisseur, a man of slender means who had studied beauty. He had used that sense of her, attached it, as it were, to his other prior claimants, and written it sometimes on the very same day that he wandered in the city with his new American friend. So that Isabel Archer saw what Constance Fenimore Woolson saw and may indeed have felt what she felt, if only he could have fully divined what Constance felt.

She teased him about the tameness of his background; his being a native of the James family caused her much amusement, as did Newport and Boston and his European wanderings. She, the grand-niece of James Fenimore Cooper, had access to an America he would never know. Both in Ohio and Florida, she told him, she had been on familiar terms with the wilderness. And just in case, she smiled at him menacingly, he thought that she was a roughneck, she should point out that, while he was the first of his family to set foot in Italy, her great-uncle had lived in Florence and written a book about it.

Added to her background was her strange and busy independence. She saw him in the mornings, but in the afternoons she walked in the hills above Florence for hours, and at night she wrote and read. Each day, when they met, she had a new perspective on the city, a new experience to recount, and a fresh eye with which to view what he had arranged for her to see.

He did not mention her in letters to his parents or his sister Alice or brother William. In those years, they were all too ready to respond to the slightest hint of an amorous adventure which might lead him to marriage. He knew that every line of his letters was carefully analysed in case some clue might be offered about where his heart lay. For his relatives in Boston, hungry for news, his heart remained as hard as he could make it.

Constance and Henry met when their paths crossed in Rome and then in Paris. They corresponded over the next few years and read each other's work. Sometimes, he was preoccupied with his own writing or with other correspondents, but often when he had written her a letter he discovered that his old enjoyment of her company had been stirred again; he found himself writing another letter to her before he received a reply. He feared that she was confused by this sudden interest after a long silence and he knew that she was wary. She had become his most intelligent reader and, after he had extracted a promise that she would destroy his letters, a most trusted and sharp-witted confidante. And when she came to London, as she did when they had known one another for more than three years, she became his steadfast and self-contained and secret best friend.

Neither of them spoke about their private lives, their hidden selves. He spoke to her about his work and his family and she made observations which were personal in that they belonged to a very particular mind; they seemed like confidences no matter how general or vague the subject. She did not talk about her work to him, but he learned by implication and accident that the completion of each of her books brought with it a nervous collapse of which she lived in dread. The winters were not kind to her; dark days and low temperatures made her depressed so that there were times when she could not get out of bed, could not see him or anybody else, could not work, and could, as far as he could discover, see no hope, although she was desperate for him not to know the scale and depth of her suffering. She, who had been ready for his friendship and company, could be silent and withdrawn. He had never met anyone who shared to such a degree this readiness and its very opposite. He knew that he could trust her, that he could remain close to her while becoming distant, if he needed. She had a way of abruptly leaving his side as though she feared he was about to dismiss her and could not tolerate the pain and the humiliation of that. Nothing she did with him was simple; he was amazed and often concerned that he did not fully know her, could not fathom if these brisk gestures at parting were aspects of her vulnerability or her need to be alone, or her fear, or all of these things.

*

ONE EVENING in London in February 1884, Henry went with Mrs Kemble to see the Italian actor Salvini in *Othello*. It was a fashionable evening and a fashionable production and there were people there who were richer than Mrs Kemble and her escort, with titles and also beauty, neither of which Mrs Kemble nor her escort possessed, but there was no couple more fashionable in the audience, more noticed and observed, than the great actress accompanied by the author of *The Portrait of a Lady*.

Mrs Kemble was imperious with him, and he complimented her regularly on her wit, and listened to her with admiring attention, having seen her first on the stage when he was a mere youth. She knew that everyone around them wished to hear what she was saying and thus she alternated between a raised voice and a whisper. She nodded to some people and spoke briefly to others, but she stopped for nobody. Instead she proceeded through the throng to their box, making it clear from the manner of her gaze that no one was free to join them.

In the moments before the lights were dimmed, Henry saw Constance Fenimore Woolson take her seat. It was typical of her not to mention to him, although he had seen her a few days earlier, that she planned to come to the theatre. In the time that she had been in London, they had never once ventured into this world together. Her sortie into fashionable London life, when no one else was alone, took him aback. Constance looked worn and preoccupied, not like a distinguished bestselling novelist from an old American family who had travelled the world. Viewed from his box, she could have been a lady's companion or a governess. He did not know if she had seen him.

As he watched the tale of jealousy and treachery unfold on the stage, more intimate versions of the same matters came to him sharply. He could easily pretend that he had not seen her. But if she had seen him – and she generally, he felt, missed nothing – and if she had even the slightest intimation that he had sought to ignore her, he knew how deeply wounded she would be, and how private and hidden the hurt would remain, and how skilled she would be at silently nursing it over the London winter.

At the interval, he excused himself to Mrs Kemble and made his way through the crowd, finding Constance in her seat checking the text of *Othello*. In that one instant as he stood above her and she glanced up, he saw that she did not know what to do, and when he spoke, he realized that she could not hear him. He smiled and signalled to her to follow him. He knew, as they made their way towards the box, that Mrs Kemble was directing a hostile gaze at him and his companion.

As he introduced her, Constance seemed even more forlorn than when he had seen her taking her seat. What he caught now, as she tried to speak to Mrs Kemble, was what he caught before the play began – a loneliness and melancholy which seemed to outweigh the other qualities she was at pains to emphasize. Mrs Kemble, on the other hand, had never suffered from loneliness, and, as soon as she saw that Henry planned to invite his friend into their box, she turned rudely away from them, staring at a point in the far distance with the help of her glasses.

HE CONTINUED to meet Constance over the next two years as she lived outside London and to correspond with her. He watched her, especially after his sister Alice had arrived in England, going to great lengths not to be a burden, not to depend on him for anything, and to make regular mention of her plans for travel and work, her famous independence. He was not allowed to pity her, nor was he allowed to know her fully, except as a set of passionate contradictions underlined by two essential truths: she was immensely clever and she was lonely.

Her hearing deteriorated and when he spoke, she had to study his face and watch his lips so that she could follow what he was saying. Her face took on a worried gravity, and this became intense if he ever mentioned plans, where he might go soon, when he might travel. In these years, he most often planned to go to Italy.

He would look forward to the time when he had finished a book or a group of stories and he would be free. These plans were so much a part of his existence that he forgot them, changed them, remade them without consultation or hesitation. Slowly, he became aware that when he told her of his intentions, she went home and brooded about them. A few times, he noticed her surprise and mild irritation when she discovered that he had changed his mind and not discussed the change with her. He came to understand that his presence was powerful for her, and that everything he said and wrote was contemplated by her at length in private. To her he was a mystery, even more so than she was to him, but she put more thought and energy, he believed, into solving the mystery, or at least attempting to divine its properties, than he ever did.

When she began to arrange to leave England and return to Florence, he convinced her that she should know some people there, friends of his, and enter into society, however limited, in the city. She smiled and shook her head.

'I have seen enough Americans in America,' she said, 'and enough English in England, and I do not believe that the Italians will take much interest in me. No, I would rather work than take tea, would rather walk in the hills than dress in the evening.'

'There are two charming and very serious people I should like you to meet,' he said, 'people who do not themselves enter very freely into society. I do not wish you to live at the mercy of the entire Anglo-American colony.'

'In that case,' she said, 'I long for nothing more than to meet your friends.'

In writing to ask his friends to administer some social comfort to Miss Woolson on her return to Florence, Henry was taking a risk he had not taken before, having introduced her to no one in England. He understood that his old friend Francis Boott and his daughter Lizzie had brought a private income and the best of Boston reserve and refinement to Bellosguardo above Florence. In their tastes and habits they were simple people. Had they been less simple, he believed, the father's talent as a composer and the daughter's as a painter might have lifted them to great heights. They lacked the steel of ambition and dedication and they replaced it with exquisite taste and select hospitality. He knew that they would warm to an American novelist with the manners and pedigree Constance possessed.

The chance that they would not like each other was small. Lizzie, now aged forty, had recently married a bohemian painter, Frank Duveneck, and thus Francis Boott, who had been devoted to his daughter, would have time and energy to dedicate to a new friend. The real risk he incurred in introducing Constance to the Bootts was that they would like each other more than they liked him, that they would, as evening settled over Bellosguardo, discuss his case, and come to conclusions about him that would require further discussion, until he became one of the subjects which bound them together.

He did not flatter himself. He knew how careful Constance would be at first, how reticent and cautious, and he knew how much old Francis Boott would like conversation with a new friend to be general, confining himself if he could to rare old coins and old damask and long-forgotten Italian composers. Nonetheless, he knew that Lizzie Boott, whom he had first met in Newport twenty-five years earlier, had longed for him to marry and had conveyed her wishes to him and to his sister Alice, with whom she regularly corresponded, as her father corresponded with William. Once Constance had arrived in Florence, Henry realized, and been sent into their care, the Bootts would know what no one else knew: how much he had seen of Constance and how significant a presence she was for him; and they would wonder at how strange it was, considering their closeness to Henry and his family, that no one had mentioned this previously. It was not impossible that they might wish to discuss this with Constance.

*

WHEN SHE HAD settled in Florence and had, as he learned, seen a great deal of Francis Boott and his daughter Lizzie, he received a letter from Constance which surprised him in its frankness, its personal tone. Being with the Bootts, she said, in their quarters in Bellosguardo, was delightful yet, on the third or fourth visit something had struck her, however, and stayed with her; she had to wait until she had unpacked her books before she could finally be sure about it. The rooms in the house on Bellosguardo, she wrote, were precisely described in *The Portrait of a Lady*. The chamber in which she was regularly entertained was, indeed, brimming with arrangements subtly studied and refinements frankly proclaimed, and contained the hangings and tapestries, chests and cabinets and pictures, brass and pottery, not to speak of the deep and well-padded chairs, which filled the main reception room of Gilbert Osmond in that novel.

And not only that, she wrote half-accusingly, but the old man himself had been perfectly described in the book. He had, indeed, a fine, narrow and extremely modelled and composed face, and yes, its only fault was that it ran a trifle too much to points, which were emphasized by the shape of his beard. Sometimes, she said, when the father and daughter spoke it was as though Gilbert Osmond and his daughter Pansy were having a conversation. 'You have introduced me to two of the characters from your books,' she wrote, 'and I am grateful to you, but I wonder if you have plans to include me in the sequel.'

He did not reply for some weeks, and when he did, he failed to mention her observations about his novel and the Bootts. He ended his letter coldly, being certain that she would not fail to notice it, and believing that this, coupled with his delay in writing, might remove the discussion of sources for his novels to the realm of the unspoken, where he and she normally wandered freely as treasured citizens.

He remained deeply curious, however, about her relationship with the Bootts and Frank Duveneck. An idea came into his mind about an elderly American gentleman of private means and cultivated manners in Europe with his daughter. Both of them would, in his story, marry; the daughter first and the father some time later out of loneliness. Their partners, it came to him, could be two people who have secretly known each other, or have come to know each other now. He was doing, he understood, what Constance had suggested – placing her close to his other characters, the father and daughter from *The Portrait of a Lady*, to see what would happen. He put the idea for the story aside, not wishing to satisfy her speculation as to why he might have introduced her to the Bootts, and also believing that what he saw when he travelled to Florence might be more interesting than anything he might imagine.

Constance had rented her own house on Bellosguardo, Casa Brichieri-Colombi, which looked over the city and had ample space and beautiful gardens. But when Henry arrived in December, having extracted a promise from Constance and the Bootts that no one in Florence would be informed of his presence, Constance had not yet taken possession of it and was still staying in an apartment close to the Bootts, across a small square from Casa Brichieri-Colombi. She offered him the house, which lay empty, and he accepted.

Thus he found himself living in what was to be, in fact, her future home, seeing her almost every day, allowing her to direct his domestic arrangements, while none of his other friends in Florence was aware that he was in the city. The Bootts knew, but were preoccupied by the imminent birth of Lizzie's child. This did not, however, prevent Francis Boott from ascending Bellosguardo to visit him.

Francis Boott's exceptional cultivation was matched by his great mildness. He seemed incapable of giving or taking offence. When *The Portrait of a Lady* appeared and it was clear that he himself, his house and his daughter had been openly used in the book and that the cold villain of the novel had his very face, he made no protest to the author and seemed to be amused. He was an immensely proper resident of Florence, Henry knew, as he had been of Boston and Newport; as a host or guest, he was beyond reproach. He gave the impression, despite the mildness of his manners, that this extensive social propriety stood for other proprieties in which he also believed, but it appeared that he saw no reason to display his beliefs.

The old man was wrapped in a shawl as he sat on an easy chair in the main sitting room of Casa Brichieri-Colombi. Henry noticed his slow-moving feline shape, his fine long fingers and his face, which despite his interest in good food, had become oddly ascetic with the years.

'We have loved your friend, Miss Woolson,' he said. 'She has a rare charm and intelligence. Lizzie and I have become very fond of her.'

'And she has become fond of you, I believe,' Henry said.

'She has a gentle wit, you know, and a lovely way of leaving our company as if her life depended on it. We always want her to stay longer, but she has work, my, does she have work.'

Francis Boott's eyes sparkled with pleasure as he spoke.

'Of course we are fully conscious that she is merely our friend because of you. She admires you so very much. And trusts you.'

As his friend crossed his legs again, Henry noticed how beautiful his shoes were and how slender his feet. Henry wanted to bring the subject back to Lizzie and her confinement but he had already, on Francis's arrival, asked about her. Nonetheless, he tried again.

'You will give Lizzie my best regards,' he said.

'I tell her everything, as you know,' Francis said, smiling again. 'We both worry about Constance. There are depths which neither of us have fully explored, but we have gained a great idea of her.'

'Yes,' Henry said, 'Constance is deep.'

'And she suffers rather more perhaps than someone of her talent deserves to suffer,' Francis said, knitting his brows. 'But it is marvellous that she has met you and has known you. We both feel that too.'

Henry stared at him blankly.

'We both noticed the change in her over the past few weeks when your arrival was increasingly certain. You know, she grew much happier and wore lighter colours and smiled more. It was unmistakeable.'

Francis Boott stopped and coughed and found a handkerchief and sipped the tea which had been brought for him. He gave the impression that he had said all that he had to say, that he had made himself clear. And then he suddenly spoke again, loudly at the beginning as though he were interrupting someone.

'We wondered if you were happy here, in this house.'

'Oh yes, I adore the house.'

'With Constance so close and it being her house, or will be soon . . .' Francis Boott let his voice taper off, but made sure that he could be heard. 'No one knows that you are here, of course, so I don't suppose there could be any scandal. Bellosguardo, despite everything, is a sort of bastion.'

He tapped the edge of the chair with his finger.

'No, the problem is – what will she do when you go? This is what Lizzie and I worry about. Not about you being here and seeing so much of her, but about your not, if you get my meaning.'

'I will do my best,' Henry said. He knew the remark sounded weak, but as it made Francis Boott smile at him warmly, almost radiantly, he did not correct himself.

'I have no doubt you will. That is all we can do,' the old man said.

He finished his tea and stood up to take his leave.

IN JANUARY, once Constance took possession of Casa Brichieri-Colombi, Henry moved down to Florence. His days were idle, his afternoons and evenings taken up with the society Constance contemptuously avoided. He was bored and often irritated by the excesses of the colony, but he had learned to disguise any such feelings and eventually, in any case, one evening such feelings fled. Seeing the Countess Gamba, who, it was known, had possession of a cache of Byron letters, Eugene Lee-Hamilton, a great literary gossip, told Henry that her presence had reminded him of a story about another cache of letters. Claire Clairmont, Byron's mistress and Shelley's sister-in-law, had, Lee-Hamilton said, lived to be old. She had spent her declining years in seclusion in Florence with a great-niece. An American obsessed with Shelley, knowing that she had papers belonging to the two poets, laid siege to her, according to Lee-Hamilton. And on her death the man laid siege to her great-niece, a lady of fifty, until the great-niece invited the American to marry her if he wanted to see the papers.

Lee-Hamilton told the story briskly, as a well-known piece of gossip, not realizing how closely he was being attended to, how the drama of the tale affected his listener.

The implications and possibilities of this story filled Henry's mind for some time afterwards. He took note, as soon as he went back to his quarters, of the picture of the two fascinating, poor and discredited old English women living on into a strange generation, in their musty corner of a foreign city with the letters their prize possession. But as he considered the core of the drama, he saw that it lay in the hands of the American, who would come in the guise of both adventurer and scholar. The story of the three figures locked in a drama of faded memories and desperate need would take time and concentration. It could not be done in the mornings in Florence. Nor could he set his story in the city without everyone there believing that he was merely transcribing a story already known and often recounted. He would move the story to Venice, he thought, and, as more invitations came in, he decided he would move himself to Venice also, and work there on a story whose properties he came more and more to relish.

In Venice, he found rooms belonging to his friend Mrs Bronson in a dark, damp palazzo. The fact that Browning had once inhabited these rooms did not brighten them or rid them of cold, despite Mrs Bronson's certainty that their history made all the difference. He took to dining alone before taking a walk through the haunted streets of the city. Once night fell and the Venetians had returned home, they did not venture out again. Venice was misty and strange and, for the first time in his life, he wondered what he was doing in the city which he loved so much. He could easily have gone to England instead. The story was now clear in his mind and he had soaked up enough of the faded palaces where his heroines would live and the sense of old secrets and heroic attachments in these shadowy, bejewelled, inhospitable buildings, once full of sweet romance and high-toned gaiety, and now repositories of gloom and cobwebs, so many of them inhabited by the unsettled and the infirm.

One evening, having passed the Frari and crossed a bridge which led towards the Grand Canal, he caught a brief glimpse of a woman in an upstairs room with her back to a lighted window. She was in conversation; something about her hair and her neck made him stand his ground in the empty street. As the talk became more animated, he could see her shrugging and gesticulating. She was, as far as he could see, younger than Constance and much darker, and her shoulders much broader, so that it was not her physical presence which brought Constance into his mind. He found, as he moved away, that he hungered to be in that room where the woman was talking, he longed to hear her voice and follow whatever it was she was saying. And slowly, as he walked through the dark streets with lives hidden away in the buildings on either side, he realized that even though his time at Bellosguardo had lasted a mere three weeks, he missed the companionship, he missed his life with Constance Fenimore Woolson. He missed the mixture of sharpness and reticence in her manners, the American life she carried with her so abundantly, the aura which her hours alone gave her, her furious ambition, her admiration for him and belief in him. He missed the few hours every day they spent together, and he missed the lovely silence which followed it and came before. He decided that he would either return to England or go back to Florence. He wrote to Constance outlining his dilemma, half-realizing that she would read his letter as an appeal of sorts.

Constance replied immediately and briskly offered him his own quarters on a lower floor of Casa Brichieri-Colombi which looked through a single door and three arches to the Duomo and the city. He could work in peace there. While all of Florence was richly and intricately displayed for the pleasure of those residing at Bellosguardo, the opposite was not the case. Bellos-guardo remained apart from the city of palaces and churches and museums. Walking back there at night was, when he had moved a few streets away from the river, like walking towards any hill town in the Tuscan countryside. Constance inhabited the large apart-ment above him, and they shared domestic staff and the kitchen and garden. There was no one else living in the house. This time they did not even discuss the need for discretion about his pres-ence in the city. It was known to very few that he was living under the same roof as Miss Woolson and it was mentioned to no one. Henry wrote to William merely to say that he had taken rooms on Bellosguardo. He wrote to Gosse insisting that he was alone and working. He wrote to Mrs Curtis of the beauties of Bellosguardo and his happiness at the view. He did not state that this came courtesy of Constance.

Nor did he mention to anyone that in the time he had been away, much to the Bootts' alarm and the alarm of her doctor, Constance had entered into a deep melancholy and had taken to her bed where she had suffered, as Francis Boott told him, more than anyone could imagine. He could see signs of it when he arrived, despite her efforts to disguise it. She was happy for him to dine in Florence so that she could be alone in the evenings. Her deafness appeared to irritate her, and once they had been together a short time, she seemed compelled to withdraw.

But as the weather softened and spring came, Constance became happier. She loved her vast house and the garden that was now beginning to blossom, and she took daily pleasure in the old city beneath her without ever feeling tempted to walk much outside the confines of this small territory. Thus she guarded her privacy and respected his, and in the six weeks he stayed with her, they never appeared together in public.

He worked hard at his story of Shelley's papers and Claire Clairmont and the American visitor. He believed that returning to this beautiful house and idyllic setting had been slightly improper, that he had appealed to Constance's mercy when she had none left to give. She knew, as he did, that he would leave, that this would be a respite for him, from his full solitude, or his London life, or his other travels. But for her the season, the house and his steady presence would make this time the most gratified and beguiling of her life. Her happiness, such as it was, came, he believed, from the perfect balance between the distance they kept from each other and their need for no other company. She dressed carefully, mainly in white. She paid attention to the decor of the house and the state of the garden, and watched over the kitchen with a fastidious eye.

One afternoon as they met on the terrace for tea, Casa Brichieri-Colombi was visited unexpectedly by a lady novelist of the English persuasion, Miss Rhoda Broughton, whom he had known in London for many years. She had said, in a letter sent from London, that she would call, but had not specified a date. She expressed much wonder at meeting him and embraced him warmly.

'I knew that you were in Italy,' she said, 'I was told so by friends in Venice, but I did not know you were in Florence.'

Henry watched her as she settled herself into a wicker chair, having rearranged the cushions, talking all the while in her customary scatterbrained tone which could deceive the unwary into believing that she was foolish.

'And both of you here!' she said. 'How lovely! I could travel in Italy for years and see neither of you and now suddenly I have you both.'

Henry smiled and nodded as the servant served Miss Broughton more tea. That she never seemed to listen to others and appeared to notice nothing save her immediate comfort was, he knew, a high pretence. She tended, in fact, to miss nothing. He presumed that she knew all along that he was living under Miss Woolson's roof; he was determined that she should depart from Casa Brichieri-Colombi doubting the veracity of that knowledge.

They discussed various people in Venice whom Miss Broughton had seen, and then the conversation turned to the pleasure of leaving London.

'I always dreamed of living in Florence,' Constance said.

'And now you do,' Miss Broughton said. 'And now you do. How lucky you both are to have such a beautiful house.'

Miss Broughton sipped her tea as Constance stared sharply into the distance. Henry wished he were writing now, feeling that he would be able, in the privacy of his room, to come up with a proper reply. He needed to think quickly and did not know if he could manage a complete denial.

'Of course, Miss Broughton, I am merely visiting just as you are. Miss Woolson is the lucky one.'

When he looked at Constance, he saw that his remark did not seem to have interested her.

'Where are you staying?' Rhoda Broughton asked.

'Oh, I've been wandering a great deal,' he said. 'I've been in Venice, as you know, and may go on to Rome. Florence is marvellous, but there is too much society for a poor writer.'

'I was not even aware that you had come to Florence,' Rhoda Broughton said again.

Henry thought that she sounded even less convincing the second time and felt that they had discussed the topic of his whereabouts quite enough. Miss Broughton had now, fortunately, left him an opening. By bowing to her drily he was able to intimate that her not being aware may have, in fact, been part of his plan. As she was absorbing the implications of this, Constance changed the subject.

★

SINCE HE did not wish his new story to be read directly as the story of Claire Clairmont and her great-niece, and did not feel that moving the scene from Florence to Venice was sufficient, he made the dead writer American, one of the pioneers of American writing. He knew as he set this down that he could have been referring to James Fenimore Cooper, and as he concentrated on his American adventurer, he realized that he was using moments of his own return visit to Florence, his own intrusion, also. He began to understand, as he drafted the story, the irony of the case. If he were looking for an exiled spinster who kept papers and was related to a pioneer of American writing, then he had one upstairs, albeit one of great independence.

He wondered what would happen if he abandoned the spinster's offer of marriage, if he could make the story's denouement true to the strange, nuanced, open-ended and infinitely interesting life he was sharing now with Constance Fenimore Woolson, if he could make his adventurer begin to need, or half-need, the domestic life of a lodger with an intelligent and reserved woman who was lonely, but not willing to be preyed upon. She would ask him for nothing as obvious as marriage; what she wanted was a close and satisfying and, if necessary, unconventional attachment with loyalty and care and affection as well as solitude and distance.

ONE MORNING in Florence, when the maid had come, and he had opened a letter from Katherine Loring about the health and general welfare of his sister Alice, he began to discuss Alice with Constance.

'Life has been difficult for her,' he said. 'Life itself seems to be the root of her malady.'

'I think it's difficult for all of us. The gap is so wide,' Constance said.

'You mean between her imagination and her confines?' Henry asked.

'I mean between using our intelligence as women to the full and the social consequences of that,' Constance said. 'Alice has done what she had to do, and I admire her.'

'She really has done nothing except stay in bed,' Henry said.

'That's precisely what I mean,' Constance replied.

'I do not understand,' he said.

'I mean that the consequences get into the marrow of your soul.'

She smiled at him softly as though she had uttered a pleasantry.

'I'm sure she would agree with you,' he said. 'She is blessed in having Miss Loring.'

'She seems to be a ministering angel,' Constance said.

'Yes, we all need a Miss Loring,' Henry said.

As soon as he made the last remark, he regretted it. The very sound of the name Miss Loring suggested a spinster skilled only in the art of caring for others. He had meant it as a joke, or a sign of gratitude, or a way of reducing the intensity of their exchange, but he knew, as it hung in the air, that it had come out as a flippant expression of his own need, as though that was what he required from Constance. He turned to her now, preparing a statement which would take the harm out of what he had just said, but he observed that she did not seem to have noticed it, or taken it on board. He was sure, nonetheless, that she had heard him. She remained placid as she resumed the conversation.

BETWEEN HIS departure from Florence and her death, they continued to correspond and meet. Once when they were both staying in Geneva, living on opposite sides of the lake but meeting daily, Alice James began to detect their familiarity. Henry is somewhere on the continent, she wrote to William, flirting with Constance. When he returned, he found his sister more truculent than usual, difficult, almost angry, accusing him of neglecting her while he gallivanted with a she-novelist.

Constance left Florence, having found, or so she said, the interruptions and invasions of Florentine society too much for her. She moved to London once more where she established herself with her customary zeal, placing solitude and hard work high on her list of needs. She travelled in the east with spirit and independence and sent him regular accounts of herself, using a tone both playfully ironic and distant. When she returned to England to live in Cheltenham and subsequently in Oxford, her power of lonely industry, Henry wrote to Francis Boott, was as remarkable and admirable as ever.

They remained close, aware always of each other's whereabouts and preoccupations. When Alice James began to die and Constance was in Oxford, Henry kept her in touch with news of his sister's condition. Both ladies, in the early months of 1892, sent one another short, brittle, witty messages. Constance stayed in England for a year after Alice's death before finally deciding to return to Italy and live in Venice.

By that time, the two novelists had developed a strange, unstructured and contented way of remaining close. They became connoisseurs of the twenty-four-hour meeting in provincial English places, staying in separate small hotels, taking walks together and having supper with each other. She could, on these occasions, be brilliantly difficult and combative, begging to differ with him on books of the day or sights they had seen, and ready to tease him about his addiction to refinements. He wondered if they were to be studied by a disinterested spectator how they would emerge. They were both Americans who had been away from America for many years. Neither of them had known the compromises which marriage brought, or the cares of parenthood. Neither of them had attended to a child crying in the night. They might, he felt, be mistaken for a brother and sister. But then he watched her delighting herself with the workings of her own wit, the mistress of a hundred cases or categories into which she pigeon-holed her fellow mortals, and whole buildings and cities, and her memories and his observations.

And he knew, as she smiled at him, that nobody would imagine that his friend, so darkly ebullient now and funny and charming, was in the company of her brother. Just as they were a mystery to each other, he felt, they would remain a mystery to the thin slice of society that managed to notice them.

Henry met her in Paris as she moved with her belongings from Oxford to Venice. Packing and preparing to leave had taken her months. She was tired and bewildered, and a pain in her left ear was causing her immense misery. She made clear, on her arrival, that she would not be able to see a great deal of him. He could do the city alone, she said, and perhaps she could spend some time with him in the evening. But she was not sure, she added, that she would be able to see him at all.

Despite her warnings, on the second of these evenings Constance seemed well enough to dine with him. He noticed that her movements were slow. She was forced to incline her right ear towards him when he spoke so that she could hear him.

'I had a letter from Francis Boott,' she said, 'who knew you were coming to Paris, but was under the impression that you were coming alone and that we had not been in contact for some time.'

'Oh yes,' Henry said, 'I wrote to him about my plans which were vague at the time.'

'He was amused, I think,' Constance said, 'because I told him that we were going to meet here for a few days, and in the same group of letters came yours which stated that you were going to Paris alone. He asked me if you could be alone and in my company at the same time.'

'Dear Francis,' Henry said.

'I shall tell him that being partly invisible is merely a small aspect of my charm.'

She sounded slightly bitter, almost irritated.

'Venice, of course,' he said, 'will be beautiful. Once you are established there, it will be a dream.'

She sighed and then nodded.

'The hard part is the moving, but maybe staying can be harder,' she said.

'The great pity is that there are no hills above Venice,' he said. 'One has to be there, or not there. The advantage is that one can more easily find beautiful quarters than in Florence.'

'I dread going there now. I don't know why,' she said.

'I have always thought,' he said, 'that I would like to spend some of each winter there, the quiet times when none of our compatriots blocks one's path, and have my own haunts there, my own routines, and not be anyone's guest.'

'It's a dream,' Constance said, 'which everyone who goes to Venice has.'

'Since the death of my sister,' Henry said, 'my financial problems have greatly decreased. So it would not be impossible.'

'To lease a floor in Venice, a pied-à-terre?' she asked.

'Perhaps two pieds,' he said.

She smiled and for the first time seemed relaxed, almost animated.

'I don't imagine you on the Grand Canal,' she said.

'No. Somewhere hidden,' he said. 'It does not matter quite where, as long as it is difficult to find, with many blind alleys on the way.'

'Venice frightens me sometimes,' Constance said. 'The uncertainty of it, the possibility that I might lose my way every time I emerge.'

'We will all do what we can to guide you,' Henry said.

IN THE FEW years before he purchased the lease on Lamb House his London winters were easy; his routines when no one visited from the United States, when the Londoners whom he knew respected his habits, suited him and made him unwilling to travel. There was something in the distant, throbbing energy of the city which made him cling to London, even if it was a London whose news came to him second hand.

He loved the fixities of the morning, the familiar books, the hours alone fruitfully used, the afternoon slipping beautifully by. In London he dined out a few nights a week and spent the rest of his evenings alone, weary and oddly restless after a certain hour, but slowly learning to manage the quietness and the silence and his own company.

The letters from Constance, who was now established in Venice, suggested that she was changing her habits. She wrote about the Venetian lagoon and her exploration of the outer islands and small wayward places, hidden from the tourists, her journeys by gondola. But she also began to write about the people whom she was meeting, mentioning the names of friends of his in Venice – Mrs Curtis and Mrs Bronson, for example – and adding the names of others, such as Lady Layard, suggesting that she was part of their circle, or at least regularly invited to their houses and quite pleased to accept their hospitality.

Thus he began to believe that his old friend, whom he admired so much for her distance from things and her self-sufficiency, seemed to have entered willingly into the life of the Anglo-American colony in Venice, having allowed herself to be taken up by its richest and most socially ambitious hostesses. When she wrote to him to say that she and Mrs Curtis had been dutifully searching for a pied-à-terre for him, he became alarmed. He minded dreadfully that Constance was discussing his plans with people whom she did not know as well as he did. The tone of her letters and a letter he received from Mrs Curtis suggested that Constance had come close to making clear how well she knew him and how much she had seen of him in the past decade. He knew how easily and quickly this would be misconstrued.

As far as possible, he had lived an undisturbed life. He neither gave offence, he believed, nor took it easily. Publishers irritated him, and there was a theatre producer called Augustin Daly whose dealings had enraged him, and magazine editors required constant patience which often ran out; also, a payment not coming and being promised and still not arriving, or a book not printed in time, or a book not selling at all, or his work being maliciously handled in the newspapers, these could prey on his mind especially when night fell. But once a measure of time had passed, they became minor matters which took up very little time or energy. He forgot about them and did not harbour grudges.

Now, the idea of Constance in Venice, spending her evenings in the palazzi of the Grand Canal and discussing him freely, despite the stubborn reticence on which she prided herself, began to prey on his mind. A further letter from her describing her fellow lodgers at Casa Biondetti, including Lily Norton whose father and aunt were close friends of Henry and William, filled him with foreboding. He worked on his play and lived, he enjoyed telling Constance, the life of a hermit in London. He did not mention going to Venice or taking rooms there until he was pressed to confirm his interest by both Constance and Mrs Curtis, who now seemed to him to be working in tandem.

Twice, with the help of Constance, he had managed to inhabit the hill above Florence with almost no one knowing he was there. The road to Bellosguardo was steep and narrow and winding, and those who wished to visit would have to make an effort and have precise directions. It seemed that Constance had other ideas for him in Venice. It was not that he had ever imagined the possibility of living there in secret, but now that his association with Constance had been made public he foresaw a social round in which they would both be included. He imagined her listening with barely disguised impatience with her good ear to the oft-told tales of Daniel Curtis, or Mrs Bronson's accounts of her exploits with Browning. He imagined her turning to him and in a single, biting glance hinting at her contempt for the company. She would also, and this was what concerned him most, be ready to conspire on his behalf with his old friends now that she had joined their society. These conspiracies would be well intentioned, but they would interfere crucially with his inviolable need to make his own arrangements and do as he pleased. Slowly, in the weeks after he received the news that she and Mrs Curtis had been searching for an apartment on his behalf, he felt a powerlessness that he had not felt since he was a child.

In July he wrote to Mrs Curtis to correct Miss Woolson's misconception that he was looking for a flat in Venice. He realized, he said, that he had been toying with the affections of the watery city, but wondered if he had expressed himself clumsily to Miss Woolson in appearing to intimate that he might come to live in Venice. In fact, he had no plans to do so, he wrote, needing to live in London for all sorts of practical reasons. Every time he came to Venice, he said, and no doubt the next time would be the same, he cherished the dream of having a modest pied-á-terre, the dream being more vivid, he wrote, when he was on the spot, fading once he had returned home. He thanked Mrs Curtis for all her trouble, adding that while he had the fondest hope of going to Italy that winter, he had learned by stern experience not to make hard and fast plans.

He knew that his letter would be shown to Constance and he imagined her response. In England, they had come, in strange and subtle ways, to depend on each other. Even though there were matters which they never discussed, other things, including what they were writing and their relationships to editors and publishers, were shared. He knew how much she loved his confidences, such as they were, and later in solitude went over, he imagined, every detail he had told her. She would know now that he did not intend to take a place in Venice, but also that he seemed inclined not to visit in the coming winter, despite his promises to her that he would. She was to be left to her own devices in Venice among people, especially the idle rich, whom he knew she would come to despise.

Perhaps they could meet in the spring, he thought, in Geneva or Paris, but he did not think he would come to Venice. He had an image of her studying him critically as he arrived at the salon of Mrs Curtis and alluding sharply later to his charming behaviour as he enjoyed the hospitality of the Anglo-American society there, whose members viewed him as a valuable prize.

He did not hear from her as summer went into autumn. He presumed that she was offended and he imagined also that she was working, as he was. With all his correspondents, he allowed for large intervals in which he did not write to them. But the silence between Kensington and Venice was of a different order. Eventually in late September she wrote, but the tone was distant and chilly, the letter merely informing him that she had moved from Casa Biondetti, where she had been very well looked after, to more private quarters, where she could be alone, in Casa Semitecolo nearby. She mentioned almost in passing that she was exhausted, having written and re-written her latest novel, and hoped for nothing now except a bookless winter. Affectionately yours, she wrote, and then signed her name. He read the letter over, knowing that she would have chosen every word carefully. He looked at the mention of the bookless winter and considered it, but it was only later that he understood its ominous implications.

HE SPENT December in further dispute with the theatre producer Augustin Daly, who had behaved insolently and returned his play *Mrs Jaspar*. There was much correspondence about the matter, and for a number of weeks near Christmas the row with Daly filled a good deal of his waking life. His Christmas and New Year in London, however, were quiet and reflective as he rewrote his play.

One afternoon in January he was working quietly when Smith put a telegram on the mantelpiece. Henry must, he later thought, have left it there without looking at it for an hour or more, being engrossed in his writing. It was only when he broke for tea that he moved absent-mindedly to the fireplace and opened the envelope. The telegram informed him that Constance was dead. His first response was to go to Smith and ask him calmly for tea; he then returned to his study and, closing the door and sitting at his desk, he studied the telegram which had come from Constance's sister, Clara Benedict, in the United States. He knew that he would have to go to Venice and wondered now from whom he should enquire about the details of her death. He drank the tea when it was brought, and then he went to the window and frantically studied the street outside as though some distant detail there, some movement, a sound even, might help him to a full realization of what had happened or might erase such a realization as it slowly dawned.

How had she died? What occurred to him now and caused him suddenly to freeze was the suspicion that she had not died of any illness. She was strong, he thought, and perfectly healthy and he could not imagine her succumbing to an ailment. She had finished her book, and that would have left her, as it always did, forlorn. He knew that she hated the winter, and the winter in Venice could be especially dark and severe. He thought in cold fright about his own refusal to come to Venice and his not letting her know this directly. He was sure that his not having made arrangements to see her must have depressed her deeply. And thus, as he stood at the window, it struck him that she might have killed herself. And that was when he began to shake and had to move towards an armchair in his study, where he sat frozen, making himself go over and over the facts of her existence during the previous year.

Some time later he was interrupted by Smith with a second telegram. He opened it hastily. It was from Constance's niece, who, having been in Munich when she heard the news, had now arrived in Venice. She confirmed the news. As he put the telegram aside, he made the decision that he would not now go to Venice. He would be helpless there, and the idea of her inert body, the physical fact of her corpse, and her dead face masking and unmasking its own history as the light allowed, filled him with horror. He did not want to see her body, or to be close to her coffin, which was, the telegram told him, to be interred a week later in the Protestant cemetery in Rome.

He remained in his flat all day and told no one what had happened. He wrote to Constance's doctor, who was also a friend, in Italy, expressing his shock, still not sure how she had died. It was all, he said, ghastly amazement and distress. He had not even known she was sick, he said, and had a dismal, dreadful image of her being alone and unfriended at the last, someone who had had intrinsically one of the saddest and least happy natures he had ever met. As he finished the letter, an image of her face in all its complex life, her eyes shining, her expression brilliantly intelligent and receptive came to him. He allowed himself to cry before going to the window again and staring down at the scene below, at people who meant nothing to him moving on the street.

In the morning he knew that, although he had not dreamed about her, her spirit, the questing essence of who she was, had made itself known to him during the night, and he wanted, as soon as he woke, to close his eyes and go back to sleep to avoid the cold fact of her extinction. No one whom he knew had read his work as carefully, had tried to know him as clearly. No one had her mixture of ambition and sharpness, vulnerability and melancholy, unpredictability and bravery. No one had her great sympathy, and it became a heavy burden in the hollow of himself to imagine that sympathy coming to the end of its endurance.

He received no further news, and as every hour went by, he imagined a different scenario, following its path and working out its implications. He began to veer between definitely not going to Rome for the funeral and setting off immediately; several times he sent Smith to book and unbook a passage to Italy. And then, having prevaricated for several days, he opened *The Times* to find the news that Constance had jumped to her death from the window of the house where she lived in Venice. It was, the paper said, suicide. At once, he began to reassure himself that he was not at fault. He had owed her nothing, he thought, he had made her no promises that were binding. They had not been lovers; they were not related by blood. He owed her only his friendship, just as he owed it to many others, he told himself, and all of the others knew that when a book was being written, his blinds were down, he was not available. All of his friends knew not to make demands on him, and Constance knew that too.

Henry wrote to John Hay, a mutual friend who was already in Rome. He told Hay that he had, in fact, been ready to travel, to stand by her grave in the Protestant cemetery, but once the nature of her death had been confirmed, he had collapsed before the pity and the horror of it, he wrote, and he could not travel now. She had always been, he added, a woman so little formed for positive happiness that half one's affection for her was, in its essence, a kind of anxiety.

He resisted the thought that came to him when he had written the letter and was alone. It had a heavy crushing force, and he held it from him for as long as he could. He allowed himself to think that Constance had not lightly taken up his time, nor had she lightly allowed her own emotions to become so focussed. She had been subtle enough and nervous enough to make her demands silently, but they were all the clearer and more emphatic for that. He now had to face the idea that he, in turn, had sent her powerful and subtle signals of his need for her. And each time it became apparent to him what effect they were having, he retreated into the locked room of himself, a place whose safety he needed as desperately as he needed her involvement with him.

She had been caught, as it were, in a large misunderstanding, not only in the snare of his solitary, sedentary exile, but also in the idea that he was a man who did not, and would not ever, desire a wife. Her intelligence surely should have warned her that he would, under the slightest pressure, even out of fear, pull back; but her need and the quality of her sympathy came to outpace her intelligence, he thought. Nonetheless, she had been careful: she had acknowledged his needs and his reticence and was ready to make space for them, but when she moved too close, became too public, he rejected her.

He had his reasons for choosing to remain alone; his imagination, however, had stretched merely as far as his fears and not beyond. He had exerted control; what he had done made him shudder. Had he gone to Venice that winter, he knew, she would not have killed herself. If she had appealed to him to visit and he had refused, it might be easier for him now to feel simple guilt. But her appeals were all over and they would be for ever. He had let her down. He did not know if her friends in Venice, and friends of his, understood that this was the case and discussed it in the days after her death.

He could not face the idea that Constance's suicide had been planned for a long time. He wrote to others, to Rhoda Broughton, to Francis Boott, to William, saying to each in turn that Constance's last act had been rash, a form of madness, a demented moment. He did not fully believe what he wrote, although each time he set it down, it seemed to become more plausible and definitive. He did not express to anyone his reservations about this version of how she ended. However, as some part of her spirit brushed through his rooms in the weeks after her death, he had a sense of her as the only person he had ever known who was fully skilled at deciphering the unsaid and the unspoken. There was no need even to whisper the words, or let them form fully in his mind; her fresh ghost understood that he knew, he knew well that she was not given to moments of insanity or sudden abrupt gestures, no matter what the pressures. She was a woman of great determination who made decisions carefully and rationally. She had an abiding dislike for shrillness and theatricality.

Once night fell and the fire was blazing and the lamps glowing and he was alone, he came face to face with what had happened to his friend. She had planned her own death, he came to believe, having calculated for some time the possibilities. Her novel was finished and he knew that often, when she had completed a book, she did not think that she would write again. The winter was sad and damp in Venice where she moved between dark solitude and people she could easily begin to dislike.

And for the sake of something hidden within his own soul which resisted her, and because of his respect for convention and social decorum, he had abandoned her there. He was the person who could have rescued her, had he sent her a sign.

She planned her death, he thought, as she would plan a book, full of uncertainty and nerves, but also with ambition and a relentless physical courage. The influenza she suffered in those weeks, which he heard about from her doctor, would merely have added to her strength of will. She had decided, he knew, that she would be happier at rest, and she was prepared to do extreme violence to herself, to smash her bones and her head against the hard ground, to achieve her aim. Her restless curiosity, the pure honesty of her response, the practical nature of her imagination, all these came to him now, as what she had been powerfully visited him in the London winter, when her death had ceased to be news, until he knew that he would have to go to Venice where she died and from there travel to Rome where her broken body lay in the ground.

She came to him forcefully, palpably, in the days before he travelled. The woman he had kept at arm's length was replaced by a woman of possibilities, a phantom he dreamed about. His parents were dead, his sister had been dead two years; William was far away, and he cared very little about the London society to which he had once paid so much attention. He could do as he pleased; he could have lived at Bellosguardo sharing a household with Constance, or he could have encouraged her to find adjoining houses for them in some English coastal town.

Now he thought about her dead body, and the rooms she had filled with the passion of her aura, her books, her mementoes, her clothes, her papers. She preferred these rooms to most people; rooms were her sacred spaces. He began to imagine her rooms in Venice, at Casa Biondetti, and those at Casa Semitecolo, and her rooms at Oxford before she left England. He longed now for those spaces as though he had known them and had reason to miss them. He saw her figure, so tidy in its movements, flitting across these rooms, and as he did so, he came to understand something of his initial resistance to going to Venice when she died, or going to Rome for her funeral. He would have had to walk away from her, he would have had to enact their separation. From a relationship that had been so tentative and full of possibility, he would have had to face her absence in all its finality. She had no further use for him.

This feeling that he had been brusquely and violently rejected somehow brought him closer to her. Now the prospect of seeing her rooms in Venice, looking at her papers, staying in the atmosphere she had created, began to intrigue him. He longed for her company and wondered, as the day of his departure for Italy came near, if he had always longed for it, but if only now, when it had no implications, could he allow himself fully to indulge the idea.

In Genoa, as he waited for Constance's sister Clara Benedict, he wrote to Kay Bronson and asked her to secure for him the rooms which Constance had occupied the previous summer at Casa Biondetti at the same terms. He wished also that the padrone would cook for him as he had for Miss Woolson, remembering how happy his friend had been with the fare. He was not surprised when he received word that the rooms were free. Somehow, with Constance guiding him, he had been sure all along that they would be. She was now two months dead.

THE AMERICAN consul came with them to break the seal which the authorities had put on her apartment at the time of her death. Tito, who had been her gondolier, waited below for them. Mrs Benedict and her daughter stood in silence as the door into the house of death was unlocked. They seemed to Henry hesitant about stepping in. He stood behind them, trying to believe that her spirit was not in these abandoned rooms, merely her papers, her belongings, her left-overs, her gatherings, for she had been a collector of objects. He felt more sharply now that she had planned it all and foreseen it. In her love of detail, she would have been able to predict the arrival of the consul to break the seal, the boat waiting below, and she would have been able to imagine also the three others waiting to enter her room – her sister Clara Benedict, her niece Clare and her friend Henry James.

This, he thought, was her last novel. They all played their assigned roles. He watched as the American women stood in her bedroom afraid to approach the window to the small balcony from which she had jumped. Constance would have been able to conjure up their stricken faces and would have known, too, that Henry James would have studied the women, observing them with cold sympathy. She would have smiled to herself at his ability to keep his own feelings at a great distance from himself, careful to say nothing. Thus the scene taking place in this room, each breath they took, the very expression on their faces, each word they left said and unsaid, all of it belonged to Constance. It was pictured by her with wry interest during the time when she knew she would die, Henry believed. They were her characters; she had written the script for them. And she knew that Henry would recognize her art in these scenes. His very recognition was part of her dream. No matter where he looked or what he thought, he felt the sharpness of her plans and a sort of sad laughter at how easy it was to manipulate her sister and her niece and how delicious to direct the actions of her friend the novelist who, it seemed, had wished to be free of her.

The Benedicts did not know what to do; they employed Tito to ferry them from one part of the city to another; soon they spoke of him fondly. They sought comfort in Constance's friends; but when they heard that she had been found alive when she fell, that she had moaned as she lay dying, they were inconsolable. They cried each time they entered her rooms until Henry felt that if Constance could witness this, or if she had included it in her imagined vision, she would regret what she had done. She would never have been so hard.

Her sister and her niece remained helpless in the face of the practical. At first they did not wish to disturb Constance's papers and seemed happy to leave everything in situ. They appeared not to believe that she was dead; and touching her things, they thought, would be a way of consigning the woman who had possessed them to oblivion.

After several days, when all had been grief and confusion, softened by the ministering of Constance's circle of friends, with many lunches and dinners and gatherings to distract and console the sister and niece, Henry arranged to meet them at the apartment, to which he had now been given a key. Constance had kept a great deal of paper, half-finished and unpublished work, letters, fragments, notes. He had touched nothing on his early visits to the apartment, but he made a mental map of the terrain. He knew that should there be a battle between him and the Benedicts over what should be kept and what should be destroyed, he would lose the battle. As he waited for them, he determined to avoid even the slightest skirmish.

When he heard their key being turned, he shivered. Their voices seemed like interruptions. This was the first time he had heard an ordinary conversation between them which did not centre on Constance's suicide and their own shock and sadness. Once they entered the bedroom where they found him standing at the window they became silent and serious.

'I meant to ask you if your quarters are comfortable,' Mrs Benedict said.

'The apartment is pleasant,' he said, 'and its atmosphere is appropriately full of the presence of Miss Woolson.'

'I do not think that I could bear to sleep there,' Clare said. 'Nor here indeed.'

'This apartment is very cold,' Mrs Benedict said. 'It is the coldest place.'

She sighed and he felt that at any moment she was going to cry again. Both he and Clare watched her, however, as she seemed to gain strength. There was, he saw now, a toughness in her nature which matched that of her dead sister. In that moment, as she willed herself to speak, she could have been Constance.

'We must make arrangements,' she said. 'We have not been able to find a will, it may be buried among her papers. And we must begin to take care of practical matters.'

'Constance was a writer of significance,' Henry said, 'a very singular figure in American letters. Thus her papers must be treated with care. There may be unpublished manuscripts, a story or two that she did not finish or did not send to an editor. I believe these must be carefully preserved.'

'We should be so glad,' Mrs Benedict said, 'if you would look at her papers for us. Neither of us could bear it, I think, or have the concentration it would require. I think this room is the saddest place I have ever been.'

IT WAS ORDERED that fires be lit each morning in Constance's study and in her bedroom and that they should be maintained by a servant until the early evening. The Benedicts came and went in Tito's gondola, being kept busy by the American colony, and on each visit Henry had something to show them, an unpublished story, a number of poems, an interesting letter. They agreed that even fragments should be preserved, perhaps carried back to America and looked after in her memory.

He himself wanted merely one memento of her. Having viewed the general collection of her objects with sorrow and indecision, he eventually chose a small painting. It was a scene from the wild untamed American landscape she had loved. When he showed it to her sister and niece, they told him he must have it.

He remained at her desk from morning until darkness fell. Each time the Benedicts left the apartment he went to the window and watched them as they stepped into the gondola, observing their growing animation, and then he returned to her desk and found papers he had saved and brought some of them to the fire in the bedroom and others to the fire in the study. He consigned them to the flames and stood looking at them as they burned.

And when they were ash, he made sure that they could not be noticed among the embers.

He did not want the strange, cryptic and bitter notes from his sister Alice to Miss Woolson to be part of some cache of papers that would be open to others to read. He did not even wish to read them all himself. As he went through the papers and spotted his sister's handwriting, he put the letter aside, coldly and methodically, making sure that it lay under other papers and could not be seen by the Benedicts should they chance to arrive unexpectedly. He also found some letters of his own, and as soon as he saw the handwriting, he put them aside. He had no interest in rereading them. He wished them destroyed. He could find no diary and no will.

Among her papers, however, he found a recent letter from her doctor discussing her various illnesses and her melancholy. He read until he found his own name. He placed the letter carefully into the pile to be burned without reading any further. All of her literary manuscripts including drafts, he put aside for the Benedicts to take home.

MOST EVENINGS he dined with the Benedicts, making sure always that someone else was present so that the conversation could range over more general matters, not confined to the reason for their presence in Venice. He preferred the party to be large, thus making it more difficult for them to discuss with him once more the task he was performing and the arrangements they were making. Slowly, it became clear that they were tiring of Venice; the empty days, the rainy weather, the greyness of the light and the monotony of the company began to make them feel that they should prepare to depart. Also, he noted that their presence, as each day passed, was of less interest to Constance's friends and the wider colony whose sympathy had, at the beginning, been intense, but whose invitations grew less insistent now that the Benedicts had been a month in Venice.

On these evenings, he liked to rise early from the table, it being understood by all that he was involved in onerous work and thus was not confined by the normal rules. The Benedicts put Tito at his disposal if the distance to his lodgings was too great. Although the lower floors of Casa Biondetti contained some Americans, including Lily Norton, he was surprised at how easy it was to reach his quarters on the top floor without having to see them. Each evening, he found a fire lit and one lamp by his bed and another on a table close to an easy chair. The rooms were not opulent, but in this light they were rich in their colouring, and because the apartment was neither on the scale of a palace nor the quarters inhabited by servants, and because the landlord, who had been fond of Miss Woolson, made every effort, Henry found his room comforting and welcoming. The high soft bed offered him at first a deep and dreamless sleep from which he woke each morning refreshed and ready for the day's work.

He looked forward to the night. He longed to return to his quarters at Casa Biondetti not because he was tired, or bored by the company, but because the rooms themselves offered him a glow of warmth which lasted through the night.

Tito was always waiting. Like anyone who had worked for Constance, he loved her and wished to look after her sister and niece. He remained respectful and silent as he ferried Henry to his quarters, but he made clear, since he had not met him before, and since Henry was not a member of the family, that Henry's position was almost that of an outsider. Henry knew that should he want the most accurate account of Constance's state of mind during the last months of her life, Tito was most likely to possess such knowledge. As he became acquainted with Tito, however, he understood how unlikely he was ever to part with it.

Only once in Henry's presence did Tito speak of her. One night, as they waited for her daughter, Mrs Benedict asked Henry to compliment Tito on his dexterity, especially on corners and small canals. When Henry translated her remarks, Tito bowed solemnly to her and then said that Miss Woolson had sought him out not for the dexterity she had mentioned, which all the gondoliers had, but because he knew the lagoon, the open water, and could navigate safely there. Miss Woolson always preferred to move out from the city, out into the lagoon, he said. Many Americans, he said, love the Grand Canal and want to travel up and down it all day. But not Miss Woolson. She liked the Grand Canal because it led out to the lonely open water, where you would meet no one. Even in the winter, she had loved it, he said. Even in the bad weather. As far out as you could go. She had her favourite places there, he said.

Henry wanted to ask him if she had taken such journeys right until the end, but he knew from the way that Tito had finished his speech that no more information would be forthcoming unless Mrs Benedict were to ask a question. Once Henry had translated for her, however, she smiled at the gondolier distractedly, and asked Henry what he thought her daughter might be doing to keep them waiting so long.

AFTER A WHILE he began to wake in the night; the worried thoughts which came disturbed him, and in the morning there remained a residue of the night's unease. After a time, however, his waking was merely an interlude in his sleeping, another aspect of the night's deep rest rather than a disturbance; he felt no fear, and no worried thoughts came into his mind, but rather a sense of abiding warmth. In this period, he did not feel Constance's presence at all. He felt instead a nameless and numinous presence. As time passed, the glow on entering these rooms, and when he woke in the night, took on a more particular intensity. He found himself all day looking forward to this, and wondering if, when he left here and returned to London, such ease and sweet goodwill could follow him.

It was not a ghost, not anything unsettled and haunting, but rather it was a figure hovering gently, the shadow movements of his mother's protecting aura coming to him now in the night, pure and exquisite in its female tenderness, gentle and enclosing, cajoling him back to sleep in those rooms which had so recently been inhabited by his friend, whose death still filled him with guilt and whose sad, impassive spirit looked on at his determination each day, as he sat at her desk quietly setting aside letters from her doctor and from Alice's friend Miss Loring and, when the coast was clear, putting them into the fire.

AFTER MUCH negotiation with the American consul about their relative's estate, and much fussing and prevarication, the Benedicts oversaw the packing of her papers and the wrapping of her paintings and mementoes which they placed in the consul's care until legal matters were sorted out to his satisfaction. The month of April had been rainy and chilly and both of the women had caught colds and been confined to quarters. By the time they emerged again Venice had changed; the days were longer and the wind had died down and many of their acquaintances had also, for one reason or another, left the city. Thus their farewell dinner was desultory and badly attended with Henry eager to stand up from the table before nine, as usual, and shake their hands, and kiss them if they should need kissing, and look into their eyes, promising that, as he still had a key to her apartment at Casa Semitecolo, he would oversee the final clearing out of her effects and the return of the key to the landlord.

In the morning when the Benedicts had left the city Henry discovered that they had made no arrangements to dispose of Constance's clothes. They must have known, he realized, that her wardrobe and dressing tables were full because they had searched for her will there. He wondered if they had discussed the matter, or if it had evoked too much sadness for them to deal with, and then, at the end, they were too embarrassed to mention it. In any case, they had, it seemed, left him to deal with Constance's wardrobe and personal effects. He waited for several days in case one of their Venetian friends made contact to arrange the removal of the clothes. As no one did, he became certain that the Benedicts had taken advantage of his support and had fled leaving wardrobes full of dresses and cupboards full of shoes, underclothes and other items, that appeared not to have been disturbed.

He wanted no further discussions about Constance's estate, and therefore did not wish to contact any of her friends who would, he knew, quickly spread the news that her clothes had been left in the apartment, thus offering the freedom to visit and snoop as they pleased, asking for the key at will, and invading the privacy he had guarded for her in the time after her death. When he had pictured her planning each scene in which he and her relatives took part, this aspect of her demise was far from his mind. The throwing away, or giving away, of her clothes had not been, he was sure, part of her dream afterlife. While he had felt her deep displeasure as he burned the letters, now he felt a dull sadness and the grim weight of her absence as he contemplated the clearing-out of her wardrobe.

He confided in no one except Tito who, he felt, would be willing, under his supervision, to transport what was left of his friend's worldly goods. Tito, he believed, would know what to do with them. But when Henry showed him the mass of clothes in the wardrobe and the shoes and then the underclothes, Tito merely shrugged his shoulders and shook his head. He repeated these gestures when Henry suggested that perhaps one of the convents might be interested in old clothes. Not the clothes of the dead, Tito told him, no one will want the clothes of the dead.

For one moment, Henry wished he had handed the key to the landlord and left the city, but he knew that it would not have been long before he received letters about the clothes, asking what should be done with them, not only from the landlord himself, but from members of the colony.

Tito, in the meantime, stood in what had been Constance's bedroom watching him fiercely.

'What can we do with them?' Henry asked him.

His shrug this time was almost contemptuous. Henry held his gaze and sternly insisted that the clothes would have to be moved.

'We cannot leave them here,' he said.

Tito did not reply. Henry knew that his boat was waiting, he knew that together they would have to carry these clothes and place them in the gondola.

'Can you burn them?' Henry asked.

Tito shook his head. He was intensely studying the wardrobe, as though he were guarding its contents. Henry felt that if he made to empty the wardrobe, Tito would rush at him to prevent his interfering with his mistress's clothes. He sighed and kept his eyes down, hoping that the impasse at which they had arrived would cause Tito to speak or make a suggestion. As the silence between them lingered, Henry opened the windows and went to the balcony and looked at the building across the way and the ground onto which Constance had fallen.

On turning and catching Tito's eye, he saw that Tito wanted to say something. He gestured to him in encouragement. All of this, Tito said, should have been taken to America. Henry nodded in agreement and then said that it was too late now.

Tito shrugged again.

Henry opened one of the cupboard drawers and then another. Tito, when he turned, was watching him with an interest bordering on alarm. Henry stood and faced him.

Did he know, he asked him, the place in the lagoon to which he had ferried her regularly? The one he had told Henry about? Where there was nothing?

Tito nodded. He waited for Henry to speak again, but Henry merely gazed at him as he considered what had just been said. Tito seemed worried. Several times he made as though to speak, but sighed instead. Finally, as though someone were in the next room, he pointed surreptitiously to the clothes and then in the direction of the door and then in the direction of the far lagoon. They could, he silently asserted, take the clothes there and bury them in the water. Henry nodded in agreement, but still neither of them moved until Tito lifted his right hand and stretched out the fingers.

Five o'clock, he whispered. Here.

At five Tito was waiting at the door. Neither of them spoke as they entered the apartment. Henry had wondered if Tito would bring a companion and if they both could be trusted to take Constance's clothes and bury them in the lagoon without any further questions or hesitations. But Tito came alone. He managed to suggest that the work of moving the goods from the apartment to the gondola should be done now and quickly and by both of them.

Tito took the first bundle of dresses and coats and skirts and motioned to Henry to take the second bundle and follow him. As soon as he held the dresses in his arms, Henry caught a powerful smell, which sharply evoked the memory of his mother and his Aunt Kate. It was a smell so redolent of them, their busy lives around their dressing rooms and wardrobes, their preparations for travel, the folding and protecting and packing which they did themselves no matter where they were. And then as he crossed the room carrying the bundle he caught another smell which belonged to Constance only, some perfume of hers, something she had used in all the years when he knew her, which mixed in now with the other smell as he carried the dresses down the stairs and deposited them in the waiting gondola.

In their journeys from her bedroom to the boat, their movements fast and watchful as though they were doing something illegal, they slowly emptied the wardrobes. They carried her shoes and stockings and then, careful not even to glance at each other, her white underwear which they hid beneath the dresses and coats in the gondola so that it could not be seen. They were both out of breath as they went one last time to see if everything had been cleared. The smell had brought her so close to him that he would not have been surprised if, at that moment, he had found her standing in the bare room. He almost felt free to speak to her, and looking around the room one more time, after Tito had descended to the gondola, he sensed that she was there, an absolute presence, her old practical self glad that the task had been completed, that nothing of her remained; the room did not seem to him full of dust and air as much as filled with the sense that should he wish to linger she would be ready to outstare him.

As the light began to fade over the city, and a pink glow mixed with the pale and rich colours of the palazzi on the Grand Canal, and the water reflected the sky which was tinged with shades of red and pink, they set out towards the lagoon. They were relaxed now, although neither spoke nor acknowledged the other's existence. Henry took in the light and the buildings, glancing back at the Salute, feeling a strange contentment. He was tired, but he was also curious to know where exactly Tito would take him.

It was, he thought, like meeting her again, away from their friends and family and the social whirl, connecting in calm places. This was how they had known each other. No one would ever discover that he had come here; it was unlikely that Tito would ever volunteer this information to any of their friends. The only person watching them was Constance herself as Tito steered them out beyond the Lido into waters into which Henry had never before ventured. They moved out until soon they had merely the seabirds and the setting sun for company.

At first Henry believed that Tito was searching for a precise place, but he soon realized that, by moving at random back and forth, he was postponing the action they would now have to take. When they caught each other's eye and Tito intimated that Henry should begin their grim task, Henry shook his head. They might as well have been carrying her body, he thought, to lift her and drop her from the boat, let her sink into the water. Tito continued to circle a small area, and on seeing that Henry would not move, he smiled in mild rebuke and exasperation and laid down the pole until the gondola began to rock gently in the calm water. Before he reached for the first dress, Tito blessed himself and then he laid the garment flat on the water as though the water were a bed, as though the dress's owner were preparing for an outing and would shortly come into the room. Both men watched as the colour of the material darkened and then the dress began to sink. Tito placed a second and then a third, each time tenderly, on the water, and then continued working with a slow set of peaceful gestures, shaking his head as they floated away each time, and moving his lips at intervals in prayer. Henry watched but did not move.

The gondola swayed so gently that Henry was not aware of moving in any direction, merely staying still. As her underclothes sank, he imagined that the consignment lay directly beneath them, falling slowly to the ocean bed.

It was only when Tito reached to lift the pole that both of them at the same time caught sight of a black shape in the water less than ten yards away and Tito cried out.

In the gathering dusk it appeared as though a seal or some dark, rounded object from the deep had appeared on the surface of the water. Tito took the pole in both hands as if to defend himself. And then Henry saw what it was. Some of the dresses had floated to the surface again like black balloons, evidence of the strange sea burial they had just enacted, their arms and bellies bloated with water. As they turned the boat, Henry noticed that a greyness had set in over Venice. Soon a mist would settle over the lagoon. Tito had already moved the gondola towards the buoyant material; Henry watched as he worked at it with the pole, pushing the ballooning dress under the surface and holding it there and then moving his attention to another dress which had partially resurfaced, pushing that under again, working with ferocious strength and determination. He did not cease pushing, prodding, sinking each dress and then moving to another. Finally, he scanned the water to make certain that no more had reappeared, but all of them seemed to have remained under the surface of the dark water. Then one swelled up suddenly some feet from them.

'Leave it!' Henry shouted.

But Tito moved towards it, and blessing himself once more, he found its centre with the pole and pushed down, nodding to Henry as he held it there as if to say that their work was done;

it was hard, but it was done. And then he lifted the pole and took up his position at the prow of the gondola. It was time to go back. He began to move them slowly and skilfully across the lagoon to the city which lay almost in darkness.

CHAPTER TEN

May 1899

As Rome became more modern, he wrote to Paul Bourget, he himself became increasingly antique. He had fled from Venice, from the memories and echoes that had settled in its atmosphere, and had at first refused all Roman invitations and offers of shelter. He lodged instead in a hotel close to Piazza di Spagna and he found himself in his early days in the city walking slowly as though the heat of high summer had come in May. He did not at first climb the Spanish Steps, nor make a pilgrimage to any site further than a few streets from his hotel. He tried not to conjure up memories deliberately, nor to compare the city of almost thirty years earlier with the city of now. He did not allow any easy nostalgia to colour the dulled sweetness of these days. He was not disposed to meeting himself in a younger and more impressionable guise and thus feeling sadness at the knowledge that no new discoveries would be made, no new excitements felt, merely old ones revisited. He allowed himself to love these streets, as though they were a poem he had once memorized, and the years when he had first seen these colours and stones and studied these faces seemed a rich and valuable part of what he was now. His eye was no longer surprised and delighted, as it once had been, but neither was it jaded.

It was enough for him to sit at an outdoor cafe under a great awning and study the plasterwork on a wall as it moved out of shadow, the ochre colour suddenly becoming vivid and brilliant in sunlight, his own spirit seeming to brighten as well at the idea that something as simple as this could empty his mind of the shadow of Venice which continued to hover over him. It was easier to be old here, he thought; no colour was simple, nothing was fresh, even the sunlight itself seemed to fall and linger in ways which had been honoured by time.

In Venice, he had avoided the streets between the Frari and the Salute, keeping as much as he could to the other side of the Grand Canal, in case he should happen on the street where Constance had fallen to her death. On one of the nights before he fled the city, he had believed himself close to the Rialto Bridge as he made his way confidently back to Palazzo Barbaro without considering the danger he was in. He realized later that he should have simply turned back and retraced his steps and then found his way comfortably to the bridge. Instead, each turn he made led either to a blind alley or an opening onto the water or, more ominously, to a turning to the right which could only take him closer to that dreadful street which he had hoped that he would never again have to stand in. He felt that here in the silence of the night he was being led along, as though someone were guiding him and he was too weakened by guilt not to follow. He had loved this Venice which shut early and became still and empty; he had often enjoyed being the lone walker, the one who might easily take a wrong turning, allowing luck and instinct as much as skill or knowledge to guide him, but now he knew that not only was he lost but that he had come close to the site of her death. He stood still. Ahead was a blind alley which he had already tried, which seemed to lead to the water but did not. To his right was a long narrow street. He could only turn back, and as he did he felt an urge to speak to her out loud, with a sense that her spirit, so restless and independent and courageous, would inhabit these streets for as long as time lasted. She did not settle for an easy life, he thought, and now, whatever part of her remained was as yet uneasy and uprooted.

'Constance,' he whispered, 'I have come as close as I could, as near as I dared.'

He imagined the choppy sea out at the lagoon, and the nothingness that was there, wide water and the night. He imagined the wind howling out there in the void and the chaos of water, the place where there was no light, no love, and he saw her there, hovering over it, having become its equal. And he knew then to turn, to walk slowly back whence he came, step by guarded step, concentrating, making no mistakes until he reached a place that he could recognize, the palace where he was a guest, his books, his papers, his warm bed. That night he knew that he would leave Venice as soon as he could and go south and not return.

THE WEATHER in Rome was perfect; the very air glowed with lovely colour as his daily strolls began, daringly, to take in the Corso and stretch as far as Saint John Lateran and Villa Borghese where the new grass was knee-deep. Everything was radiant with light and warmth. The city smiled at him and he learned not to scowl in return as more tourists crossed his path and more insistent invitations arrived at his hotel. When he had visited Rome first, he thought, he was in his twenties and free to do as he pleased, make new friends, wander at will, ride out on the Campagna from Porta del Popolo along the old posting road to Florence in the mild midwinter, the country rolling away into slopes chequered with purple and blue and blooming brown. He had become like the eternal city itself: he was dented by history, he had responsibilities and layers of memory, he was watched and examined and in much demand. And now he would have to show himself in public. Just as the streets of the old city were cleaner and better lit, he, too, would put on a brave face, cover up old wounds and erase old scars and appear at the correct time, attempting neither to disappoint those who viewed him nor to give too much of his own secret history away.

The Waldo Storys and the Maud Howe Elliotts, each believing that he had spent his first days in Rome held in the other's captivity, now set about enticing him gently and firmly into their own particular Roman cage. The Waldo Storys inhabited the large apartment of William Wetmore Story at the Barberini and wished Henry to write a biography of the old half-talented but most serious-minded sculptor; Maud Howe Elliott and her artist husband required nothing more from him than that he would be a regular and unannounced visitor at Palazzo Accoramboni, mingle with their guests, and admire the view from their rooftop terrace as much as they admired it themselves.

Neither party lived in Rome for the pleasure it offered the solitary resident and, since neither party was skilled at imagining pleasure in which they themselves did not regularly indulge, his need for solitude seemed to both an almost scandalous excuse, not to be countenanced. After four or five days he gave in and found himself accepting their hospitality on alternate evenings. In England, he had watched with interest as the heir, on the death of his father, took over the great house, as though its comforts and contents were created for him alone. Now he watched the new generation as they adapted the city to their own uses, young Waldo Story putting in the same hours as his father at the chisel and hammer, meeting even less the public demand, sweetly spoiling even more blocks of pure white marble, and Maud Howe Elliott, the daughter of Julia Ward Howe, following in the steps of her aunt Mrs Luther Terry who had offered hospitality to artists and New Englanders alike two decades earlier at the Odescalchi Palace.

They were neither Romans nor Americans, but their manners were perfect and their habits well formed. They collected old friends and pleasing and distinguished visitors with skill and some kindness, having already collected as much antiquity as would tastefully fit into their palaces. Maud's husband, John Elliott, was a painter and, like his compatriots, was talented while lacking real ambition and fire. Both he and Waldo Story and their friends were bohemians in their studios, but in the company of their servants they knew how to give orders. In Rome, with a private income, it was more respectable to be a dilettante than in Boston where such things were frowned upon. For them, Henry was not only a fellow New Englander who also spoke Italian and had made his home in Europe, but an artist who had chronicled and given some significance to their peculiar aura, the strange dilemma and drama of their presence in Europe. They liked him too much, he felt, and were in any case not in the business of taking offence, to mind the tone of his novels, the sense of defeat and deceit which poisoned the lives of so many of his American characters in Europe. They had enough reverence for the past to include the 1870s in their area of interest, and since he had known Rome in those years, he could become part of the precious and thinly populated universe to which their parents had introduced them.

Thus he found himself on a warm May evening in the last year of the nineteenth century standing with a jolly group on a flowered terrace on the roof of Palazzo Accoramboni, overlooking St Peter's Square. They watched the dying rays of the sun and admired the Roman domes and rooftops, and beyond, the Campagna with its aqueducts encircled by the Albine and Sabine hills. He did not need to speak but merely nod in assent as his fellow guests pointed out Castel Sant'Angelo and the dark masses of trees marking the Pincio and Villa Borghese. They spoke in a sort of wonder and excitement. They were mainly young and their light summer clothes played beautifully against the early roses and pansies and lavender which their hosts had trained with such New World enthusiasm to grow in abundance on their terrace. The men could be easily distinguished as fellow Americans by the quality of their moustaches and the innocent and amicable expressions on their faces; the several women could only have come from New England, making this clear, he felt, by their willingness to allow their menfolk the right to speak at length while confining their own talk to short and brisk, intelligent interruptions or slightly disagreeable remarks once the men had finished. This was, he thought to himself, a group in which his sister Alice would have felt most uneasy and uncomfortable, but which all her friends would have adored.

The group in which he stood took in the scene, allowing themselves suddenly to become quiet if they so pleased and treating each other with familiarity. He knew that some of them bore proud American names and therefore had a deep sense of their own status which spread almost naturally to those with whom they were travelling. They did not need to establish their credentials by asking questions of the famous author; they managed to suggest that here on this rooftop in one of the grandest private apartments in the city, they were both modestly equal to anything which might come their way and strangely impervious to it. He was relieved that no one among the company saw fit to enquire if he were close to completing another novel, or if he were doing research for one, or what he thought about George Eliot. They listened to him briefly as he pointed out a local monument, in the same spirit as they listened to each other.

He noticed that his group was being observed by a young man who stood alone at a distance while ostensibly taking in the same scene. Soon, he observed that he himself was, from time to time, being watched by this figure who differed significantly from the young men who stood in the group. He had none of their easy-going manners, their mixture of confidence and tact. His gaze was too sharp, his pose too uncomfortable. He was, Henry noticed, remarkably good-looking, but it was as though his blond and big-boned handsomeness put him on guard and made him self-conscious. The tense aura he had created around himself meant that no one, among the growing numbers who had gathered to watch the sunset, came close to him or spoke to him. Henry concentrated on looking away and joined in the general marvelling over the glory of the dying light. Yet when he turned back the young man was staring at him openly in a way which made him determined to avoid him during the rest of the evening. He looked indeed like someone who would be quite prepared to ask about work in progress and future plans and have strong views on the question of George Eliot, but there was also something strangely soft about the man's face which worked against the intensity and tactlessness of the gaze and this made Henry feel further a need to keep away from him. The fact that he was an artist went without saying. As Henry descended the stairs from the rooftop to the apartment below, he wished to know nothing more and made sure that he kept his eyes averted from the young man for the rest of the evening. He was much relieved when he later found himself in the street, not having spoken to him.

A few days later, however, a more intimate gathering was held at the Elliotts' at which the young man was introduced to him as the sculptor Hendrik Andersen. Andersen had shed the posture and gaze of the earlier meeting and replaced them, as though with another work in hand, with an almost ironic politeness and then, as they sat down to eat, a concerned silence, listening to anyone who spoke, nodding gracefully but adding nothing. It was only when he stood up to take his leave that something of his former intensity appeared. As soon as he was on his feet, he studied each person, his expression almost hostile, and then turned briskly to go. At the doorway he lingered again, acknowledging Henry's glance with a short bow.

His Roman friends, he realized, did not tire of each other's company; they managed most evenings in the time before they would scatter for the summer to hold an event, however small, in which they could entertain each other. He was extended an open invitation, and he allowed such social occasions to become part of his routine in Rome. He was careful when he joined them not to dwell too much on his earlier life in the city, not to remark too often on how little or how much had changed or how things had been done in these streets, these very rooms, in the 1870s, even if he thought these matters might be of interest to the younger generation, resident and visitor alike. He did not wish to be regarded as a fossil, but he also wanted to keep the past to himself, a prized and private possession.

When Maud Elliott alerted him to a special dinner she was planning, however, he understood from her tone that she and her husband and the Waldo Storys cared a great deal for the past, for the city during the time when their parents were in their prime. She was giving a dinner in honour of her Aunt Annie, formerly Miss Annie Crawford, daughter of the sculptor Thomas Crawford, and for many years the Baroness von Rabe, and now a widow. Henry had not seen her for a very long time, but he knew from others that her flinty and formidable presence, her bad temper and her hard intelligence and flaring wit had lost nothing over time. He noticed that the Elliotts were expending a great deal of energy on the evening in question, the meal to be held on the terrace under the pergola; they were planning toasts and speeches and were behaving as though uniting their elderly aunt with her old friend would be one of the highlights of the Roman season.

THE BARONESS took in the company sharply, her thin hair elaborately combed and her skin like bottled fruit. When one of the young men asked her about the changes she had witnessed in Rome, she pursed her lips, as though she had been approached by a ticket collector, and spoke loudly.

'I don't go in for change. It is not one of my subjects. I have always taken the view that noticing change is a mistake. I notice what is directly in front of me.'

'And what do you notice?' one of the young men asked archly.

'I notice the sculptor Andersen,' the Baroness said, nodding in the direction of Henrik Andersen who was seated nervously on the edge of a chaise longue, 'and I should say that noticing him, despite my advanced years and my gentle upbringing, gives me nothing but satisfaction.'

Andersen sat watching her, like a rare, sleek animal, as all eyes turned on him.

'And I notice you too, Baroness, with equal pleasure,' he said.

'Don't be a fool,' she replied and stared at the sculptor until he blushed.

When Maud Elliott, once supper had ended, asked him to speak, Henry was tired of the brittle old lady who enjoyed the wine more than was entirely necessary and felt free to comment on many matters and several people with a frankness which gave way to a brusqueness as the evening wore on. He took pleasure as he began his speech in the idea that she could not interrupt him. He spoke, as he had not intended to, about the Rome he came to a quarter of a century earlier not because he wished, he said, to become nostalgic or mark the changes, but because on these occasions with old friends and some new faces, as the summer season was soon to begin, it was time to light a candle and go through the house and take stock, and this was what, in the Roman context, he proposed briefly to do. No one who had ever loved Rome as Rome could be loved in youth, he said, will want to stop loving her. It was not only the colours and the manners which were all new to him when he had sojourned in the city in his own twenties, but the shadows of certain former presences in the studios of the American artists, notably that of his compatriot Nathaniel Hawthorne who had a decade before that found so much inspiration in the city and offered so much in turn. It was in this city in the rival houses of the Terrys and the Storys that he had first met the actress Fanny Kemble, that he had encountered Matthew Arnold, that he had first imagined some of the characters who would people his own books, figures for whom Rome was the ground of their making and their undoing, a place of exile but also a place of refuge, a place of beauty and, in the small world of Anglo-American life, a place of immense intrigue. Even the names of the palaces would be enough, he said, to conjure up a sense of nobility, of dedication to art, and indeed to hospitality. For a young man from Newport, he said, the apartment of the Storys in Palazzo Barberini or the Terrys lodged in Palazzo Odescalchi, or even Caffé Spillmann on Via Condotti, were places of glory, long held and treasured in the memory, and he wished to raise a glass not only to the Baroness, whom he had first met in those years when American beauty flourished in Rome, but to the old city itself which he had never ceased to love and hoped that he would never cease to visit.

When he sat down, he noticed that the sculptor Andersen, who had been watching him, had tears in his eyes, and he noticed him further as he listened patiently to the Baroness von Rabe discuss the merits of her brother the novelist Marion Crawford and those of Mrs Humphrey Ward.

'They have, of course,' she said, 'a very great talent, and they are popular with the reading public on both sides of the Atlantic. And they treat Italian subjects very beautifully, perhaps because they understand Italy, and their characters are so refined. I and many others have enjoyed reading their work. They will endure, I think.'

The Baroness, in finishing, looked at Henry as though daring him to contradict her. Clearly, he had displeased her, and she seemed uncertain whether she had made herself disagreeable enough. He sat with her as she made up her mind that she had not.

'I read several articles by your brother William, and then a whole book of his,' she said. 'It was given to me by an old friend who knew all of you in Boston, and in a note he said to me that your brother's style was the very model of clarity, not a word wasted, and no nonsense, every sentence beginning and ending in exactly the right place.'

He listened as though the Baroness were describing a very large and delicious meal she had devoured, nodding regularly. No one else was paying any attention to them except Andersen who smiled at Henry when he glanced at him; his expression seemed to make clear that he understood what was taking place. Henry, Andersen's eyes said, had all his sympathy. The Baroness was not yet finished.

'I remember you when you were young and all the ladies followed you, nay fought with each other to go riding with you. That Mrs Sumner and young Miss Boott and young Miss Lowe.

All the young ladies, and others not so young. We all liked you, and I suppose you liked us as well, but you were too busy gathering material to like anyone too much. You were charming of course, but you were like a young banker collecting our savings. Or a priest listening to our sins. I remember my aunt warning us not to tell you anything.'

She leaned towards him conspiratorially.

'And I think that is what you are still doing. I don't think you have retired. I wish, however, that you would write more clearly and I'm sure the young sculptor, who is watching you, I'm sure he wishes the same.'

Henry smiled at her and bowed.

'As you know, I do my best to please you.'

As others began to distract the Baroness and absorb her attention, Henry moved towards Andersen.

'I thought that your speech was magnificent,' the sculptor said. Henry was surprised at how American his accent sounded.

'And I do not know what the old lady was saying to you, but I think that you are a very patient listener.'

'She spoke,' Henry said quietly, 'as she promised not to – of old times.'

'I loved what you said about Rome. It made us all wish we had been here then.'

Andersen had been leaning against the wall, but now he stood to his full height. The expression on his face was almost solemn and, although he commanded a view of the entire room, he directed his attention only to Henry. After a few moments, he moved his mouth as though he wished to speak but clearly thought better of it. In the shadowy light of the apartment, he veered between displaying a vulnerability, an extraordinary, half-blank handsomeness and a strangely thoughtful introspection. He swallowed nervously before he whispered.

'Obviously, you love Rome and you have been happy here.'

It was close to a question and he watched Henry, waiting for a response; Henry merely nodded, conscious of the mixture of strength in the frame and a kind of weakness, like sadness, in the eyes of the sculptor.

'Do you have a place you go to, I mean a monument or a painting in Rome that you love and visit regularly?' the sculptor asked him.

'I have been going almost daily to the Protestant cemetery which I suppose is in itself a work of art, an important monument, but perhaps you meant—'

'No,' Andersen interrupted him, 'that is what I meant. I asked you the question because whatever it is, I should like to accompany you there. Even if it is your habit to go alone, I would ask you to make an exception.'

Henry could see an earnestness breaking through the shyness with some resolve and determination. He had expected another tone altogether, intense perhaps, but ironic as well, and rather more easy and worldly. This moved him with its sincerity, its lack of any reserve.

'I should like to do this soon,' Andersen said.

'Tomorrow at eleven, then,' Henry said simply. 'We can meet at my hotel and set out together. Have you not been to the cemetery before?'

'I have been there, sir, but I should like to go again, and shall look forward to tomorrow.'

Andersen gazed at him for a moment, having noted the name of the hotel, and did not smile and then bowed and made his way artfully across the room.

IN THE MORNING Andersen, Henry saw, was nervous and shy. He did not speak when Henry appeared, merely offered his customary bow. Henry could not tell how alert he was to his own handsomeness, a handsomeness which, when he smiled, gave way to an astonishing clear-eyed beauty. As they made their way by cab to the old walled graveyard near the pyramid, Andersen's expression managed to be both searching and tenderly hesitant at the same time. Even though he spoke like an American, he did not have the calm and confident manners of one. Henry wondered if his seeming indifference to his own appeal, his lack of brashness and his intense presence arose simply from his Scandinavian origin. Yet when Andersen alighted from the cab and turned and waited for him at the gate, there was an aggression in his movements which belonged to someone more confident than he seemed when he smiled or spoke or allowed his face to rest.

For Henry the cemetery, more than any of the city's monuments or works of art or famous buildings and thoroughfares, was the place where art and nature had most sonorously and resonantly combined, and now, in the shade offered by the gnarled, thick-growing black cypresses and the well-worn paths and the carefully tended flowers and shrubs, it was a place of comfort, of great warm peace. As they walked directly towards the pyramid itself and the grave of the poet Keats it seemed to him that Andersen's shyness and reticence had cast a spell on them both which could not be easily broken in this most solemn of places.

He was not sure if Andersen was aware of the story of Keats's last days in the city, or even if he knew that the gravestone, which was not inscribed with the poet's name, marked his final resting place. Henry felt acutely the sculptor's presence; he liked being beside him, the silence broken by birdsong, with only cats for company; and the sense of the dead, including the tragic young poet, deeply at rest, protected in warm, rich earth. And the air all around, the clear sky and the secluded spaces of the cemetery, proclaiming that with rest came the end of sorrow; and this rest seemed to him now, on a May morning in Rome, suffused with love or something close to it.

They walked quietly and at random through the graveyard. Andersen held his hands behind his back, and read each inscription and then remained as though at prayer. Henry was his guide only in that he moved when Henry moved and stood still when Henry stopped.

'The names never cease to interest me,' Henry said. 'The sad names of the English who died in Rome.'

He sighed.

Andersen shook his head briefly and turned to study the skinny tan-coloured cat which hovered behind him, tail in the air. Henry looked around too, as the cat purred lazily and narrowed its eyes and then moved against the back of Henry's legs, pushing the full weight of its bony body against him, rubbing itself, and then moving nonchalantly away to find a spot in sunlight and settle there.

'The cat knows what it wants,' Andersen said. His laugh was loud and sudden, almost shrill, and it made Henry want to walk away. Instead, he turned and smiled and edged along the pathways until they reached Shelley's grave at the back wall of the cemetery where the birdsong was at its most vibrant.

Now that the silence between them had been restored, he felt that the sadness he had spoken about meant nothing against the act of completion which the spirits all around them had undergone. Here in this cemetery, which they began to stroll around once more, the state of not-knowing and not-feeling which belonged to the dead seemed to him closer to resolved happiness than he had ever imagined possible.

Andersen must have believed, Henry thought, that this lingering at certain graves and not at others was, with the exception of the graves of the poets, quite without a plan. He seemed puzzled as Henry made his way purposefully, there being no direct path, to the grave of Constance Fenimore Woolson whose name, Henry believed, could have meant nothing to him. This spot had been his final destination on each of his earlier visits; now he almost regretted having come here once more, knowing that he would have to say something about the grave and make sure that it was understood. He was relieved for a moment when Andersen's attention fell on the carved stone angel over the tomb of William Wetmore Story, which Story had carved himself, and went towards it to study it more closely. Andersen touched the white wings and the face, stood back to contemplate them, his face suddenly hardened in concentration. As his friend moved around the angel a second time, Henry saw to the right the grave of John Addington Symonds and thought, as he did on each visit to this hallowed ground, about how the Wetmore Storys and Symonds and Constance had loved Italy, they had that much in common, that they had lived in beautiful places believing that the light and the views and the grand rooms were worth all the years of exile, the loss of their native countries. Constance, he thought, would allow herself to meet the others irregularly; the wealth and social ambition and soft art of the Wetmore Storys would bore her as much as Symonds's sexual obsessions and purple prose. The tablet with her name engraved on it was a model of decorum compared with the elaborate tomb of the Storys. In the evenings, he smiled to himself, she would wish to be alone. Her America was not theirs, her Italy was more modest and her art more ambitious. But she would have known how to write about them.

He glanced up and saw that Andersen was watching him.

'Constance was a great friend,' he said. 'I knew the Storys of course and was in touch with poor Symonds, but Constance was a great friend.'

Andersen looked down at the tablet and must have seen, Henry thought, that Constance was one of the recent dead. He made to speak, but clearly thought better of it. Henry sighed and turned away, realizing that he should not have taken someone he knew so little to such an intimate place. But more important perhaps, he felt that he should not have spoken just now, as the saying of her name had brought tears to his eyes. He turned away and tried to regain control but found that he was being held by the sculptor, his shoulders cupped against Andersen's chest and Andersen's hands reaching around to grasp his hands and hold them as firmly as he could. He was surprised at Andersen's strength, the size of his hands. He immediately checked that there was nobody in view before allowing the embrace to continue, feeling the other man's warm, tough body briefly holding him, wanting desperately to allow himself to be held much longer, but knowing that this embrace was all the comfort he would receive. He held his breath for as long as he could and kept his eyes closed and then Andersen released him and they walked quietly back to the cemetery gate.

IN THE CAB as they travelled to Andersen's studio in Via Margutta, he wondered how he would tell Andersen about how he had lived. As an artist, he recognized, Andersen might know, or at least fathom the possibility, that each book he had written, each scene described or character created, had become an aspect of him, had entered into his driven spirit and lay there much as the years themselves had done. His relationship with Constance would be hard to explain; Andersen was perhaps too young to know how memory and regret can mingle, how much sorrow can be held within, and how nothing seems to have any shape or meaning until it is well past and lost and, even then, how much, under the weight of pure determination, can be forgotten and left aside only to return in the night as piercing pain.

Andersen suggested that before making a tour of where he worked they eat lunch in the small restaurant below his studio. Almost as soon as he entered the small and, for him, familiar space, being welcomed with friendly gestures by the proprietor and his wife, he became talkative and engaged. Henry was surprised not only by how much the sculptor knew about him, but by how freely now he relayed the information. He was also surprised at how unselfconsciously Andersen spoke to him about his own talent and how fluently he could quote those who had come to admire it.

He listened to Andersen as lunch was served; the sculptor's face seemed to change as much as his personality had changed. His eyes had lost their softness and sympathy and his expression became more focussed as he reacted to each thing he himself said, adding to it in a torrent of explanation and contestation. His earlier silences, Henry realized, had been part of a great withholding which was now being released. In the dim light of the restaurant, Henry relished the sight of him across the table, his young face moving in rapt animation, so restless and ambitious, so ready for life, so raw.

Henry had imagined that Andersen's art would be exquisite and finely wrought, made slowly and deliberately, but now, as the sculptor stood up from lunch, his cheeks flushed, it struck Henry that his work might just as easily be distinguished by its lack of discipline. He had no means by which to judge him. Although the Storys and the Elliotts included Andersen in their gatherings, they had not spoken of him privately. As he went up to Andersen's studio, Henry remembered when he came to this city first, when he visited the studios of so many artists who had failed or prospered as the years went by. Now all these years later he was here again, led by a young sculptor who was full of protean innocence, who was so tentative in some ways and so overbearing in others, so full of mixtures and so mysterious. He watched Andersen ascend the stairs ahead of him, studying his strong white hand holding the banisters, the wonderful open agility of his movements, and dreamed that he could stay in Rome for a while longer than he had planned and come here every day to the studio of his new young friend.

There was a sense of frantic work in the large studio, a great deal of it half-finished by an artist in love with the classical tradition, the classical body, a sense of work done for public and triumphant display. He wondered if this was merely how Andersen's work began, full of roaring and rhetorical disproportion, and then if the sculptor set out, with subtlety and an eye for telling detail, to refine it. As he moved from piece to piece, he expressed his opinion that his friend had a large talent and expressed also his awe at so many figures and torsos, asking himself if Andersen now planned to work on the faces, or if he would choose to leave them blank and anodyne. He was led to the work which seemed most in progress, a large statue of a naked man and woman holding hands. He marvelled out loud at its scale and ambition as Andersen stood proudly beside it as though he were going to be photographed.

As the day wore on, Henry learned much about Hendrik Andersen. Some of it astonished him, especially the news that the Andersen family had, on arriving in America, settled in Newport in a house a few streets away from where the Jameses had lived, and that the sculptor still viewed Newport as his American home. When Andersen began to speak of his older brother and the burden of being a second son, Henry informed him that he, too, had spent his youth in the shadow of his brother William. Andersen seemed to know this already and wondered aloud if this had brought him and Henry together, asking many questions about Henry and William and, often before Henry had finished responding, comparing the answers with his own experience with his brother Andreas. As the conversation went on, Henry discovered that Andersen knew a lot about Henry's family. He mentioned that his own father had the same love for alcohol that Henry's father had shown in his youth, a matter which was never discussed in the James family but which must have been trumpeted in Newport loudly enough for it to have reached the ears of Hendrik Andersen.

'We are brothers,' Hendrik laughed, 'because we have older brothers and drunken fathers.'

Henry watched him with interest, observing the livid colours of his cheeks, his nervous talking and the way he moved from one subject to another, paying no attention to the response or lack of one. Henry's suggestion that he should take leave of the sculptor was met with an insistence that he stay, making Henry agree that they stroll together through the old city and find a place where they could perhaps take some refreshment. Before they left, Andersen took him through the studio again. On seeing the figures once more, Henry wondered if Andersen was not interested in creating a single, individual likeness. The bodies done in marble and stone had a fleshy presence, the generic bottoms and bellies and haunches sculpted with enormous confidence and zeal. He expressed once more his admiration and his hope that he would return to the studio to see each piece completed.

HE SAW Hendrik Andersen almost daily, meeting him alone or in the company of others, and as he learned more about him, he was struck by how close the sculptor was, in his background and his temperament, to the eponymous hero of his own novel *Roderick Hudson*, which he had published more than twenty years earlier. While the American colony in Rome knew him as the author of *Daisy Miller*, the more serious among them, including Maud Elliott and her husband, had also read *The Portrait of a Lady*. They knew the difference between the former, a popular tale light in its tone and impact, and the latter, more subtle and daring in its construction and its texture. None of them, however, as far as he could make out, had ever read *Roderick Hudson*, even though it portrayed a young impoverished American sculptor in Rome, with all of Andersen's talents and indiscretions, with his passionate and impetuous nature. Both Hudson and Andersen made clear to anyone who knew them their ambitions and dreams. Both of them were doted on by a worried mother back at home, and both, once installed in Rome, were watched over by an older man, a lone visitor, who appreciated beauty and took an interest in human behaviour and kept passion firmly in check. As Henry saw Andersen and tried to make sense of him, it was as though one of his own characters had come alive, ready to intrigue him and puzzle him and hold his affections, forcing him to suspend judgement, subtly refusing to allow him to control what might now unfold. Andersen had been taken up, much as Roderick Hudson had, by people with money who believed in him, and thus he had never compromised his art or flirted with commerce. His work was a set of large, energetic gestures, commensurate with his dreams. The slow, sly systems used to write a novel, the building of character and plot through action and description and suggestion were of no interest to him, just as he did not seek, through careful observation and calm effort, to sculpt a living face. Had he been a poet, he would have written Homeric epics, and now, as a sculptor, he talked to Henry about his plans for large monuments.

Henry listened with interest most of the time, having prolonged his stay in the city, and managed to think about Andersen's charm and his shortcomings in equal measure when he was alone in a way which offered a golden tinge to those hours and that solitude. He wondered what would become of Andersen. In wanting, like his Mallet in *Roderick Hudson*, to help him and advise him, to take the measure of who he was and what he would amount to, he managed, he hoped, to disguise longings which he did not entertain with much ease or equanimity.

The idea that he had published certain books which no one had read now, and which no one saw reason to allude to, added to a feeling that he belonged somehow to history, just as Andersen and his associates gave their loyalty to the future. It was this feeling that, in the end, made him prepare with a heavy heart to go home, but he also felt, as soon as he made his plans, a tenderness for Andersen and a longing to see him in England. This tenderness arose also from an impression which grew in him the more he saw Andersen – and sometimes in these weeks he saw him twice a day – that the young sculptor's silences and his intense conversation both seemed to spring from a desperate need for approval and a loneliness which the creation of monumental sculpture could do nothing to assuage. He knew also that his own involvement with Andersen, the way he listened and studied the sculptor's words and movements, had interested Andersen enormously, but that Andersen, in turn, had watched Henry hardly at all, had chosen to believe him as not in need of close observation. He had never, for example, alluded to the scene in the Protestant cemetery and had seemed to presume that the novelist's solitude was an essential aspect of his art. What he had taken from Henry was Henry's interest in him; he had opened himself for regular scrutiny, as a church opens its doors for prayer. He was both puzzled and fascinated by himself. His prodigious talent and his grandiose ambitions, his origins, his fears and his daily tribulations emerged as subjects for conversation, innocent and unguarded and undisciplined and endearing. He talked but did not listen; he grew silent, Henry noticed, because he knew the effect his silences had on others. And he was deeply and instinctively alert, Henry saw, to how these changes in himself – how soft his eyes could become in their expression, for example, or how strong and imposing he could seem in other circumstances – drew people towards him as they drew Henry now. And then, when they were close, Andersen did not know what to do with people save that he did not want to lose them. He wanted their full attention, their reverence, and perhaps their love, and when he was sure he had these, he was gently indifferent to them.

Once winning fame as a sculptor came into question, however, he was like a wild animal searching for food; he was ruthless, and he cared more than anything for the chaotic hunting ground of his studio, working on his huge figures, showing them off, smoothing out their haunches and loins and torsos, but never allowing them a face, having no interest, none at all, in what a face might conceal or disclose, just as his own face managed most of the time a wonderful blankness, a pure, bland beauty which made Henry interested all the more in gazing at him and being in his company and made his efforts to picture the face, when he was away from him, all the more intriguing and time-consuming and exasperating.

He wondered, as he prepared to leave the city, if he had placed too much emphasis on the dullness and provinciality of his life at Lamb House. Andersen had nodded in approval when he explained his need for such a life and his wish to return to it, but Andersen, he knew, had not left Newport and come to Rome in search of dullness and provinciality. He was actively admired in their circle in a manner which would not be part of daily life in Newport or Rye. This, he felt, would be the challenge for the sculptor in the years ahead – the possibility of failure and neglect and solitude. The idea of how he might rise to this challenge charged Henry's imagination. He imagined Andersen's face become haunted by the slow concentration of work, his eyes more inward-looking, his conversation more hesitant and subtle, and his sculpture smaller in scale and more intricate and delicate, more worked on and worried over. And in the years when this transformation took place, he believed, it might not finally matter to Andersen who admired him or where he lived.

On one of the nights before Henry's departure there was a gathering at the Elliotts' of twenty or more people, all of whom were known to Henry. He was careful to arrive and depart on his own, and enter into general discussion with many of those present while keeping a distant eye on Andersen. He eventually found time alone with him but they were interrupted by the arrival of Maud Elliott who began to allude to the friendship between them. She came from a distinguished family of alluders, he thought; her mother and her aunt and her uncle the novelist usually succeeded in breaking silence on most matters and did not have many unspoken thoughts. The raised eyebrow and the pointed remark ran in their family, he thought, as Maud Elliott drove Andersen away by asking him if he had ever had a friend as attentive as Mr James. Now that she had Henry in a corner, she made clear that he was hers until she had finished.

'I'm sure his mother wants him back in Newport, in fact I know she does, but we intend to keep him here. Everybody wants him. That is what is so lovely about him. I believe you have been a daily visitor to his studio.'

'Yes,' Henry said, 'I rather admire his industry.'

'And what we might call his genius perhaps? You must have known about him before you came to Rome. I believe his fame has spread.'

'No, I met him in your house for the first time.'

'But you had heard about him? He certainly had heard about you.'

'No, I had not heard about him.'

'Oh I thought you would have heard about him from Lord Gower who so admired him when he visited Rome.'

'Lord Gower remains unknown to me to this day,' Henry said.

'Well, he is a writer on many subjects and an enthusiastic collector. So enthusiastic indeed that he adored our young sculptor, saw him every day and wished to keep him.'

Her voice became confiding and conspiratorial.

'I'm told he wished to adopt him and make him his heir. He is tremendously rich. But Andersen would not have him, or did not wish to be adopted, or both, so he will not be inheriting all Lord Gower's money. Perhaps he is waiting for a better offer, or a more interesting one. He has not a penny of his own. Like one of your heroines, he is more interesting, perhaps, because he has turned down a lord. But I think in the end, if he is not careful, we will have to compare him to Daisy Miller. He flirts, does he not? In any case I cannot see him returning to New England.'

'Perhaps a spell there would improve us all,' Henry said. He smiled.

'Mr Andersen says,' Maud Elliott went on, 'that you have invited him to Rye.'

'Perhaps, since you have been so kind,' Henry replied, 'I should extend the invitation to you as well.'

THE NEXT DAY he called at Andersen's studio to find that another large piece was in production, a set of naked garlanded figures, both male and female, to represent the spring. Andersen was at his happiest under such conditions, sure that the work would shortly find a sponsor, and fresh from the physical exertion of the morning. As Henry walked around, his eye was caught by a small bust which he had not noticed before, it was rather more placid and modest in its style than the surrounding work. It was, Andersen told him, a bust of the young Count Bevilacqua and had been much admired. There was, Henry saw, something raw and clumsy about the piece, but also, perhaps because of the quality of the stone and its size, it could easily have been a piece of archaeology, something buried under one of the streets on which they walked. Immediately, he wished to take it with him and pay handsomely for it as a token of these weeks with his new friend. Once Andersen understood that he not only admired it but planned to buy it, he noticed him quicken with pride and ambition. Selling his work, making his mark on the world, Henry understood, seemed to mean more to him than any number of friendships. He darted about the studio in excitement and embraced Henry warmly once a price had been agreed, holding him with strong affection. He promised that he would come to England as soon as he could. He discussed how the piece would be packaged and sent and how soon it might arrive. What Henry noticed more than anything was how unable he was to conceal his pure delight.

They had supper together that evening in Andersen's local restaurant to celebrate Henry's purchase. Andersen, he saw, had dressed almost formally for the occasion and as soon as they sat down and a candle was lit at their table he adopted a tone which was new. His expression became interested and deeply involved as he asked questions and listened with care to the answers about how Henry lived, why he was in England and why he travelled less as the years went on. Henry was almost amused at the seriousness of his manner as he put the same boyish energy into his interrogations as he had put into his previous silences and monologues. It was only when Andersen attempted to draw out from Henry things about his father and mother that Henry ceased to be amused and wished instead to turn the conversation back to less intimate matters. As the sculptor began to rail against his own father, after a slight provocation from Henry, Henry was almost pleased although he viewed the sculptor's tone as too personal now and too petulant and too ready to discuss freely what Henry believed were deeply private matters. When they left the restaurant he was happy that Andersen would accompany him as far as his hotel, the night being warm and the streets of old Rome at their most seductive. This would be their last evening alone with one another, as both had agreed to attend a large gathering at the Storys' apartment on Henry's last night, which would fall on the morrow.

It struck him that he had not himself changed in the twenty-five or thirty years since he had strolled like this in Rome at night. He had never discussed his parents or his ambitions with anyone; his talk in all the years had been finely balanced and controlled; he approached his work even then with consistency and care. Andersen was not like that, and now, it occurred to him that Andersen would not change either. He would remain all his life innocent and confusing, charming and open. As they grew silent, Henry wanted to turn to his friend to say that he should take as much from life as it would offer him, that he was young still and should want everything and live as much as he could. As they reached the foot of the Spanish Steps, he was inclined for a second to point out to him the window of the room where the poet Keats had died, but he knew that such an invocation of death and suffering would break the spell of now. When Andersen, at the door of the hotel, stood back having embraced him, he could not help watching his smile intensely, trying to hold it in his mind, knowing how much he would need to remember it when he returned to England.

WHEN HE ARRIVED at Rye, being met by a cheerful Burgess Noakes, complete with wheelbarrow, he saw the town as if through Andersen's eyes. He realized how very small it would seem and how drained the colours. The spaces in Lamb House seemed like hallways or ante-rooms compared with the living quarters in Roman apartments, and even the garden, which he had spoken of so proudly to his new friend, seemed reduced, confined. He watched Burgess unpack as he set about repossessing his own house, wondering what it would seem like to Hendrik Andersen.

He did not write to Andersen until the small bust arrived, although he composed many letters to him in his mind, telling him how fresh he remained in his thoughts, and how satisfying, now that both he and the weather had settled, the English afternoon could be, and how magnificent, now that he had become accustomed to its proportions, was his own private, walled garden. He knew that none of this would interest Andersen very much, but he had difficulty finding a tone and a subject matter both warm and restrained.

When the bust was unpacked, however, and a broad base for it was constructed in the corner of the room at the chimney piece, and it rested there happily and easily, he could write to Andersen expressing his delight with the piece and praising its charm, knowing that such praise would interest his friend, being able to picture Andersen as he hungrily took in the words. For his own part, speaking to Andersen from such a distance about his work being tenderly unpacked and lifted and laid bare and having it constantly before him as an admirable and much-loved companion and friend gave him pleasure. Telling Andersen that his piece of sculpture was so living and human, sympathetic and sociable, adding that it would be a lifelong attachment, was easier than telling Andersen that he himself was in Henry's thoughts all day, that sometimes when he worked he would pause, wondering what the cause was of a strange glow of happiness or warm expectation which came over him, and realizing it was the afterglow of his time in Rome and his hope that Andersen would come to visit him in Rye.

Soon, Andersen wrote back and in his awkward handwriting and with his bad spelling announced that he would, indeed, come to visit. Despite the brevity of the letter and the rudimentary epistolary style, his voice was there in the sentences, rushed, undisciplined, serious, nervous, sincere. Henry held the letter close to him, finding that he did not want to part with it, until he forced himself to leave it aside. But he could not stop himself studying his garden, placing Andersen's ample frame in a chair under the wide-spreading old mulberry tree, imagining both of them in the languid sunlight. In the dining room as he ate alone he placed

Andersen opposite him and allowed the two of them to linger over the wine before ascending to the drawing room. He did not mind if Andersen's talk would be scattered or boastful. He wished for him to come before the summer was over, to share the long bright evenings with him, to keep all other company at bay so that he could enjoy his friend and so that Andersen could see life on a smaller scale.

It would be simple, he decided, to renovate the small studio which formed part of his property and gave onto Watchbell Street. As he wrote to Andersen and arranged the date of his coming, he began to imagine his friend, having seen how splendidly Henry managed to work in the garden room in the summer months, realize that the studio could so easily become a place for his labours during a part of his year. He found a key for the studio and examined its contours and saw how with close consultation between Andersen and the architect Warren, work could begin on making it a modest and stylish place for a sculptor to spend his days. He imagined his own solitary happiness, as he set about creating new work, knowing that not far away the sculptor Andersen was working in stone. He knew that his mind was moving too quickly and that the picture he drew for himself of their joint industry belonged to the realms of the unlikely, but this vision also allowed him to live his days with a sweet edge to them and allowed him to make other plans with a happier grace.

As the time for Andersen's arrival approached, despite the fact that he had promised to stay merely three days while he was en route to New York from Rome, Henry constantly dreaded his departure and prepared for the moment when he would meet him from the train while working out how best to entertain him during his time in Rye. This must be, he thought, how others felt, how his father must have felt in the time after he met his mother, or how William felt waiting for Alice to become his wife. He wondered if this state of bewitched confusion came to him more deeply now because of his age, and because of Andersen's short stay, and because of the impossibility of his imaginings. As he walked through Rye, or took his bicycle through the summer countryside, he watched people at random, wondering if they had ever experienced such tender longing, such rapturous tightening of the self in anticipation of another's arrival.

Andersen's decision to stay a short time was, despite his dreaming, not only a sentence of disappointment but a way for him to experience again, but more sharply now, the sense of doom which came with longing and attachment. As if to ward off the ache which fresh disappointment might bring, he went over the time in Paris with Paul Joukowsky more than twenty years earlier. He had gone through that night so many times in his mind. It lived with him in its drama and its finality. He remembered circling and circling, presuming that he would move away soon, return in the misty night to the grim sanctuary of his Paris flat. Yet he had moved closer. He had stood on the pavement as night fell and the mist became rain, and even thinking about it now made him afraid but also excited at what might have been. He had waited there, staring up at Paul's window which was etched in lamplight, desperately holding himself back from crossing the street and making himself known. For hours he had stayed there, his long vigil ending in defeat. For years, it had come to haunt him at unlikely moments, as it haunted him now.

BURGESS NOAKES was, by this time, used to visitors, especially in the summer months, and the rest of the staff, since the departure of the Smiths, were in constant readiness to receive the small stream of old friends and family who came to stay at Lamb House. Burgess Noakes was not by nature curious; he took things as they came. Now, however, just before the arrival of Hendrik Andersen he began to appear in front of Henry, embarrassed and slightly stuck for words, to ask various questions about Mr Andersen's habits and preferences.

On the day when Andersen was to be met from the train, Henry noticed Burgess Noakes hovering about the breakfast room and later standing idly at the door of his study. He observed that Noakes was dressed more carefully than usual and had a new haircut and seemed more sprightly in his movements. He smiled at the idea that his own vague and uneasy hopes and dreams had become palpable in his household. At seven o'clock, Noakes was waiting for him at his front door in semi-military pose, his wheelbarrow at the ready like a cannon waiting to be fired.

ANDERSEN BEGAN talking as soon as he alighted from his carriage. He wished to point out several people with whom he had shared his compartment and, as the train departed, he saw them off with many waves. Burgess Noakes, having taken control of Andersen's baggage and placed it in his wheelbarrow, kept his eye firmly on Henry, placidly studying him, and never once, as far as Henry could ascertain, cast the smallest glance at their visitor, and avoided him when they arrived at Lamb House as though he might bite.

Andersen moved around the house offering casual glances as if what he saw were familiar to him. Even the bust of Count Bevilacqua in the corner of the dining room did not receive more than a cursory inspection. Travelling seemed to have unsettled him so that he did not, he insisted, wish to go to his room and change his clothes, nor did he wish for any refreshment, nor a seat in the garden, nor a seat anywhere else. It was as if he had recently been wired for electricity and all the switches had been turned on. He was all buzz and blazing lights as he told Henry of his work and who in New York he was to see about it and what they might say and what they had already said. The names of dealers and collectors and city planners mingled with those of millionaires and society ladies. Paris and New York and Rome and London were all mentioned as places where there was much admiration, he said, for him and hunger for his work.

Henry had, since he came back from Italy, been deep in daily contemplation of a number of projects, knowing that at least two of them would require an immense effort. The work would be at first like breathing on glass in its uncertainty and its delicacy; he would hope that he could see a pattern before the breath was cleared away. And then the labour involved would be rigorous beyond anything he had ever done. As he listened to Andersen he felt a wry sense of satisfaction that he knew about difficulty and the shame of failure. He would remain dumb now, hoping that his friend would grow calm, trying not to interrupt him or compete with him, but instead feeling happy that he had arrived even if Andersen did not appear to have yet realized that he had done so.

In the morning, when he found that Andersen had not risen, Henry went to the garden room after breakfast and began the day's work. The Scot did not seem to notice his hesitations, his need to have whole sentences repeated, nor did he show any sign or make any comment when Henry began to dictate fluently and fast, as fast as the machine could move, so that nothing would be allowed to distract Henry, not the possibility that his guest was still in bed, or at his ablutions, or having a very late breakfast, or ready to appear at any moment. He had found this before when he had guests, that it was easy to disappear into his workroom and discover a strange and powerful concentration, fierce in its attention to each sentence, as a way of shutting them out, or enjoying the idea that he would soon see them, or both. He worked with added vigour and seriousness as a way of showing himself that he could. Thus he worked all morning until he saw that he had tired the Scot out and until he knew that he would find Andersen somewhere in his house or garden waiting for him.

In Rome he had observed that Andersen's clothes fitted in perfectly there with that of his associates, seeming neither too casual nor too narcissistic. Now, however, when Andersen stood up to greet him from his seat in a corner of the drawing room upstairs, Henry noticed his black suit, his white shirt and his bow tie the same light blue colour as his eyes. Andersen looked like a man who had spent much of the morning preparing himself for this interview.

As they ate lunch it became obvious that the weather would not hold and thus any possible excursion on foot or by bicycle would have to be postponed. He wondered for a moment what Andersen did on rainy days in Rome until he recalled that rainy days there were few and, in any case, irrespective of the weather, Andersen went to his studio. When Henry mentioned rainy days in Newport, Andersen spoke of his dreadful memory of them, the sense of being trapped in a small house, watching all day to see if it might clear and knowing so often as evening settled in that it would remain wet and soon become dark as well. Even still, he said, the memory of it made him shiver. He laughed.

Before lunch was over, the rain had begun to wash against the windows of Lamb House in great sheets, making the dining room appear dark and the garden inhospitable. Henry watched Andersen's spirits visibly sink. Were Henry alone now, he would have a most profitable afternoon's reading and would allow a single volume to transport him to suppertime and beyond, but Andersen, as far as he could discover, did not read and it was, anyway, unimaginable that he had travelled all this distance to bury himself for an afternoon in a book.

The previous evening, Henry had mentioned the empty studio in Watchbell Street and found over lunch that Andersen was anxious to see it, if they could find an umbrella and brave the rain. Henry wished that it were some distance away so that an excursion there could be time-consuming and require preparation. Instead, it was merely a few steps beyond the front door, and once Burgess Noakes appeared with umbrellas, watching Andersen now as though he were about to make a sketch of him, all three made their way briskly to the abandoned building nearby, Henry carrying the key.

He did not know, but should, he realized, have guessed, that the roof of the old studio leaked in two or three places. Once he had opened the door, the three of them stood at the door as water dripped copiously onto the cement floor. The light in the studio was scarce and disheartening and there were gathered in the corner a good deal of scrap and a number of old bicycles, and these, with the sound of the rain, somehow added to the sheer dreariness of the space. None of them seemed inclined to venture too far inside and they remained at the entrance in silence. Henry had spoken about this as a possible studio for a sculptor which would be especially suitable in the summer months when the Roman heat made that city unbearable, and could be used in the winter to store works with a view to showing them to the London galleries. Now, it looked like a leaky shed used to store rusting bicycles and Henry knew that his friend, occupied with plans for his future success in the vast cities of the world, was in possession of a large and ambitious imagination which had no mercy on such dingy and shabby spaces. Even Burgess Noakes in the demented way in which his eyes darted from a drip to its final destination and then to his employer and then to his employer's guest, seemed part of a plot to ensure that Hendrik Andersen would never set foot in Rye again.

Henry and Andersen spent the afternoon in desultory conversation and, when the rain finally cleared, their walk through Rye and into the countryside also had a desultory air. Andersen's mind was on his journey and on his stay in New York and Henry sensed that if his friend could slip away to London without causing a major break in whatever decorum he felt existed between them, he would do so instantly.

As they sat in the drawing room before supper was served, Andersen began to speak about his ambitions. When he said that what he really had in mind was to design a world city, Henry found himself asking in mild exasperation if he was planning to do so in miniature. In the heat of his expoundings, Andersen did not appear to entertain the possibility that the question had been asked sarcastically or even maliciously. He explained that no, he had in mind a genuine world city, a place of great buildings and monuments, which would include the best architecture and statuary of each civilization. It would be an adventure in harmony and human understanding, a place where mankind could come together symbolically, where all the episodes of civilization were represented, where princes and potentates and artists and philosophers could gather, where the best of all human endeavour was on display.

As Andersen spoke, his voice full of excitement, the final rays of the sun hit against the old brick of the garden wall; Henry found their worn texture, the crumbling russet colour, and the clear bright green of the creepers after the day's rain enormously comforting. He nodded regularly at Andersen. When they moved to the dining room, he placed himself facing the French windows so that he could witness the dusky light giving way to shadows under the trees. Andersen was now talking about the support he would need for this project and the support he already had. It would be easy for him to continue all his life, he said, making single pieces of sculpture such as Henry and others had admired, but he wished now, before he was much older, to embark on an integrated project which would take years to complete and which would make a difference to mankind.

'Mankind,' Henry found himself saying, 'is a very large business.'

'Yes,' Andersen said, 'and mankind is made up of many false divisions and false conflicts. Mankind's achievements have never before been brought together in one place that is a living city and not a museum, a place where beauty and human understanding could thrive.'

Henry's mind was half filled with the work of the morning. He had found a fictional character who interested him, a serious-minded journalist, sensitive, intelligent and talented, being offered a project close to the project which the Storys had offered him in Rome – to write a biography of their father leaving at his disposal all available material. He had this morning described such a figure coming to Lamb House after the death of a writer very like himself, standing in the very study in which he was then dictating, and taking possession of the papers and letters there. But the journalist as he imagined him was also as close to himself as he could make him, and thus he set out to dramatize his own self haunting the space he would leave when he died. Just now for one second he had a view of that figure of the journalist walking the dimly lit narrow streets of Venice, avoiding something, but he put it aside, not knowing how he could use it. No one reading the story, he thought, would guess that he was playing with such vital elements, masking and unmasking himself.

It would read like a simple ghost story, but for him, as he had worked, conjured up his own death and made a character who seemed all the more real to him now as the day waned, the story had a strange power. It gave him an idea for further work, but some part of him was still shuddering in the wake of having created it in the first place. Compared with the city which Andersen was inventing, it was both nothing and everything. In its detail and its dialogue, its slow movement and its mystery, it stood against abstraction, against the greyness and foolishness of large concepts. But it stood singly and small and unprotected, barely present; it would take up a small space in a great and monumental library in a city where reading in solitude would not be part of his friend's magnificent dream.

'We need,' Andersen said, 'more than anything to spread word of this project.'

'Indeed,' Henry replied.

'I wondered, since you have become acquainted with my work, if you have thought of contributing an article about it to some journal?' Andersen asked.

'I am afraid I am a mere story-teller,' Henry said.

'You have written articles?'

'Yes, but now I labour at the humble business of fiction. It is all I know, I'm afraid.'

'But you are acquainted with influential editors?'

'Most of the editors I have worked with are well and truly dead or well and truly enjoying their retirement,' Henry said.

'But you would write about my works and my plans if the journal could be found which was interested?' Hendrik asked.

Henry hesitated.

'I could, I imagine,' Andersen continued, 'find someone in New York who might be interested.'

'Perhaps we should leave art criticism to the art critics,' Henry said.

'But if an editor could be found who would like a description of my work?'

'I will do what I can for you,' Henry said and smiled. He rose from the table. It was already dark outside.

THE FOLLOWING morning, when he had finished his breakfast, he sat in the garden for some moments waiting for the arrival of McAlpine. Already the sky was cloudless; he carried his chair to the corner of the garden which caught the sun at this time. Andersen was still asleep, as far as he knew, but had said, in any case, that he wished to breakfast in his room. When the Scot arrived, they moved into the garden room and set to work immediately. He had looked at the typed pages from yesterday before he went to bed and made his corrections to them; now, within an hour, he would complete a story, and, as the sun moved hauntingly across the garden, and the day became warm, he started on another story, the scale even smaller than the one before, the effect almost defiantly minuscule and unportentous. He dictated with his usual mixture of certainty and hesitation, stopping briefly and darting forward again, and then going to the window, as if to find the word or phrase he sought in the garden, among the shrubs or the creepers or the abundant growth of late summer, and turning back deliberately into the cool room with the right phrase in his head and the sentence which followed until the paragraph had been completed.

By the time they sat down for lunch the day was sweltering. Andersen was wearing a white suit and had a straw hat at the ready as if he were preparing to go boating. They discussed how the afternoon might be spent, and when Andersen learned how close they were to the sea and how easy it would be to go to the strand by bicycle, he insisted that he had no greater wish than to bathe in the salt water and walk in his bare feet on the sand. His enthusiasm was a lovely relief as he refrained from mentioning any of his plans to win fame as a sculptor throughout the meal. Once lunch was over, they changed into clothes more suitable for both cycling and lounging on the beach and then set out on the two well-oiled bicycles Burgess Noakes had fetched from the shed behind the kitchen. They rode slowly down the cobbled hill and then set out for Winchelsea, the breeze from the sea cool and salty in their faces. Andersen, with his bathing costume and towel tied to the carrier, was in high good humour as he pedalled hard along the flat road and down the hill at Udimore to the sea.

When they left their bicycles and walked along the sandy path through the dunes, Henry noticed the haze of heat which made everything vague and the horizon barely visible. The mild exertion and the closeness of the sea seemed to have changed Andersen's mood, had made him quiet. When finally they reached the water's edge, he stopped and looked out to sea, narrowing his eyes against the light, briefly and affectionately putting his arm around Henry.

'I had forgotten about this,' he said. 'I'm not sure where I am. I could swim to Bergen, I could swim to Newport. If my brother was here now . . .'

He stopped and shook his head in wonder.

'You know,' he said, 'if I close my eyes and open them, I can imagine a stretch of sand and the light like this and I'm in Norway and I must be five or six years old, but Newport can be like this too on a summer's day. It's the air, the sea breeze. I could be home now.'

They walked along by the line the water made against the sand. The waves were calm and the beach was almost deserted. Henry stood looking out to sea as Andersen changed into his bathing costume and, leaving Henry to guard his clothes, he became a moving version of one of his own sculptures, his torso richly smooth and white, his arms and legs muscular.

'It will be cold,' he said. 'I can tell by looking.'

Henry watched him as he waded into the water, jumping to avoid each wave before diving under the water and swimming out, the strokes strong and firm. At times he disappeared under the waves, allowing himself to float in towards the shore, waving at Henry who stood fully clothed, enjoying the heat of the sun.

When Andersen had dried himself and changed back into his clothes they walked for miles along the strand, meeting almost no one. Both of them stopped regularly for no reason to look out to sea, studying the far horizon or a boat in the distance. Andersen listened when Henry explained how the land had been reclaimed, thus making inland towns out of places which had once been harbours.

'If this was Newport,' Andersen said, 'we would be able to walk to the pier and watch them unloading the catch or preparing for a night's fishing.'

Andersen began to talk then about the Newport he had first seen as a child, arriving from Norway with his parents, his two brothers and his sister. That was when he had heard of the James family, he said. He knew where they had lived and that the son had become a writer because everyone told him so. The Andersens, he said, had everything except money; his brother was so clearly a talented painter when he was a mere child, just as he too was precociously talented, just as his younger brother was a promising musician. Old Newport, the old ladies and the half-Europeanized families, believed in talent, he said, more than they did in money, but that was because they had plenty of money, or had inherited enough never to think about it. The Andersens, he said, might have seemed like that too when they went visiting or went to church, but at home they had no money, so money was all they thought about.

'They bought us oil paint and easels,' he said, 'and pretended not to notice our patched clothes. They discussed great art with us in the late afternoon and we could smell their hot suppers being made knowing that we were going home to cold suppers or grim suppers.'

'Rome,' Henry said, 'must have been a relief.'

'If only Rome had beaches and salt water,' Andersen said.

'And if only Newport had the Colosseum,' Henry replied, 'and if only the Andersens had possessed a fortune.'

'And if only the James brothers had had patches in their trousers,' Andersen laughed and punched Henry freely and softly in the stomach before putting his arm around him.

They freewheeled homewards in the twilight, dismounting briefly when they came to Udimore and again as they approached close to Lamb House. They arranged to meet in the garden for drinks after dressing for the evening.

As Henry waited for Andersen to come down, the scale of the garden, its modest and guarded proportions, in the raw slanted light which came from the dying sun, appeared more natural, closer to the scale of the landscape they had been moving in, and strangely closer to their range of feeling, Henry thought, than the openness and grand vistas of Rome. It might be easier, he thought, now that the rain had lifted and now that Andersen had seemed to settle, for them to relax together, to enjoy one another.

When Andersen came down, his hair was freshly washed and still wet at the ends and his light skin had been reddened by the day's sun. He smiled and made himself comfortable and sipped a drink and slowly examined the garden as though he had not seen it before. Henry had previously indicated the garden room to him as the place where he worked in the summer, but had not as yet invited him into the room. When he did so now, they walked slowly, drinks in hand, across the lawn.

'This is where all your work is done,' Andersen said when Henry had closed the door behind them.

'This is where the tales are told,' Henry said.

To the left of the entrance there was a wall of books, and when Andersen had studied the view and marvelled at the light, he walked over to inspect the books, not appearing to realize at first that all of them bore his host's name. He took down one or two and then gradually it seemed to dawn on him that this large high bookcase contained the novels and stories of Henry James in all their editions from both sides of the Atlantic. He became agitated and excited as he took volumes down and looked at the spines and the title pages.

'You have written a whole library,' he said. 'I will have to read them all.'

He turned and looked at Henry.

'Did you always know that you would write all these books?'

'I know the next sentence,' Henry said, 'and often the next story and I take notes for novels.'

'But did you not once plan it all? Did you not say this is what I will do with my life?'

By the time he asked the second question, Henry had turned away from him and was facing towards the window with no idea why his eyes had filled with tears.

WHEN THEY HAD talked for a while after supper, Henry went to bed leaving Andersen downstairs reading one of his collections, insisting that he would finish at least a substantial number of the stories before he left Rye the next day. After a time he heard the stairs creak and he began to imagine Andersen's tall frame, book in hand, arriving on the landing; he pictured him opening his door and going into his bedroom. Soon, he heard him cross the landing to go to the bathroom and then return to the bedroom and close the door.

As the floorboards creaked under Andersen's feet, Henry imagined his friend undressing, removing his jacket and his tie. And then he heard only silence as perhaps Andersen sat on the bed to remove his shoes and his socks. Henry waited, listening. And now after an interval came further creaks as, Henry surmised, he must have been removing his shirt; he dreamed of him standing bare-chested in the room, and then reaching to find his night attire. Henry did not know what Andersen would do now. He wondered if he would not remove his trousers and his underwear and stand naked studying himself in the mirror, looking at how the sun had marked his neck, observing how strong he was, staring at the blue of his own eyes, not making a sound.

And then he heard another creak as though Andersen had briefly changed his position. Henry imagined the room, the dark green curtains and light green wallpaper, the rugs on the floor and the large old bed which Lady Wolseley had made him buy, and the lamps on small tables on each side of the bed which Burgess Noakes would have lit, having, as was his custom, turned the main light off in each bedroom. Henry, as he lay on his back with the book he was reading left to one side, his own lamp still switched on and shining, closed his eyes and envisioned his guest now, naked in lamplight, his body powerful and perfect, his skin smooth and soft to the touch, the floorboards creaking under him as, having inspected himself in the mirror one more time, he got into his night attire and crossed the room to fetch his book perhaps, and returned to the bed. Then there was silence. Henry could hear only his own breathing. He waited, not moving. Andersen, he thought, must be in bed. He wondered if he were lying in the dark, or if he had continued reading. He heard the sound of a cough or a clearing of his throat, but nothing else. He took up the book and found his place and resumed reading, concentrating as hard as he could on the words, turning the page in the silence which had now descended on Lamb House.

IN THE MORNING, under clear skies, they went for a stroll through the town as Burgess Noakes packed Andersen's baggage and the Scot made clean copies of a number of stories which were ready to be sent to magazines. After lunch, the cases lying waiting in the hall and the train for London due within an hour, Henry and Andersen busied themselves with keeping the wasps from feasting on the desserts which they had taken on a tray into the garden with them.

Henry did not know how Andersen would remember his visit to Rye, or how genuinely he meant it when he said that he regretted the shortness of his stay and intended to return and remain longer at Lamb House very soon. He noticed in him a great restlessness which interested him but which he did not envy. He knew that in New York and later in Rome Andersen would attract friends and admirers with his good looks and his unsettling charm. Henry felt strangely protective of him and possessive. He imagined Andersen's mother in Newport, the effort she had made to find a place for her children in the world, and how this one, this golden youth, guileless and mercurial and vulnerable and surely not a regular correspondent, might preoccupy her, how she might want him home, as Henry wanted him here. Andersen, Henry thought, was ready for everything, except homecoming in any form it might take. The idea of the clash between the son's golden manners and his ambitions, so carefully refined by his Roman sojourn, and his mother's needs and worries and longing fascinated Henry now as a possible drama.

Andersen, he saw, was not interested in drama; he was in love with the future. He was what he appeared to be – a young man happily waiting for a train. He was affectionate and grateful, but more than anything, he was looking forward to the journey.

Andersen held Henry by the hand and then embraced him as his luggage was hauled into the compartment.

'You've been so good for me,' he said. 'It's so important that you believe in me.'

He embraced Henry once more before turning and stepping into the train, awkwardly handing Burgess Noakes a small consideration as he edged past him. Henry and Noakes stood on the platform, Noakes remaining still while Henry waved as the train left Rye on its journey to London.

CHAPTER ELEVEN

October 1899

ANDERSEN, HIMSELF SO FULL of plans, had asked him casually on his last morning in Rye what his plans were – where, for example, he proposed to travel, or what he thought he might write, or, indeed, if he had any visitors coming to Lamb House who would occupy the space which Andersen was about to vacate. Henry had hesitated and then smiled and said that he believed that he would spend the coming months working on stories and perhaps be fortunate enough not to have the inspiration for a new novel until well into the new year.

Later, when Andersen had gone, Henry had regretted not telling him that he was, indeed, expecting visitors, his brother William, his sister-in-law Alice and his niece Peggy. He regretted also that he had not told Andersen about his appearance on the stage at the end of the opening performance of *Guy Domville*. It had been easier to present a self in full possession of pride and confidence. He wondered if this might have changed had his friend stayed for two or three more days, but he thought not. Past failure did not interest Andersen who remained fascinated by future triumph. He knew that the young man would be puzzled by his involvement in something as dire and disastrous as *Guy Domville* and he was glad that he had preserved his own thick shell during Andersen's stay in Rye.

He was taken aback at how ready Andersen was to attack his own father, or discuss, in casual terms, his close and difficult relationship with his older brother. Since Henry had not responded by discussing the many vagaries of Henry James senior, or his own brother's constant willingness to wound him, believing that his father and his brother had first call on his loyalty, then he could not blame Andersen for feeling that he had nothing to say on these matters.

Andersen had made several references, during their meetings in Rome, and again in Rye, to the wealth of the James family, having heard of it discussed in Newport. He was, Henry knew, surprised at the modesty of his hotel in Rome and at the relative smallness of Lamb House. He had presumed that Henry's industry arose from his desire for regular publication rather than an income. Before his arrival, the matter of money had been at the front of Henry's mind and had become entwined with William's proprietorial interest in the family's business, William's need to offer advice when none was sought.

Lamb House, whose owner had died, had been offered for sale some time earlier by the widow for two thousand pounds. The prospect of possessing the place filled Henry with an anxiety to move quickly in case it should be lost to him and a deep satisfaction at the idea that he could shut his door and turn the key without anyone having the right to enter his domain. The money would have to be raised quickly, however, and he did not have ready money. He covered his expenses by his writing and paid great attention to the money he received for stories and serializations. His inheritance, his capital and the dividends which came from them were controlled by William. They consisted mainly of the rents received from certain buildings in the town of Syracuse, which he had seen once and hoped never to have to view again, which William managed with, as far as he could make out, competence and prudence. But he did not think, even as he wrote to William, that he would need to take money from the capital, or borrow money using the Syracuse properties as the bond. The money, he believed, could be raised more simply from his own bank and paid back quickly by the fruits of his own industry.

Since William was coming to Europe, he had written to him to say that his apartment in Kensington, which had been briefly sublet, would now be free, and he hoped William and his family would install themselves there for a time before coming to Lamb House. He had meant the offer in all kindness, but William made clear that he wished to make his own arrangements. William James and Alice, Henry was told, would be travelling first to Germany where he would go to Nauheim to take the cure and then to England. He seemed to be declining the offer of the apartment.

Henry wrote to him at Nauheim about his interest in purchasing Lamb House. Later, he realized that he had explained far too much, as though he were an errant son writing to a parent, or indeed a profligate younger brother writing to his wiser, older sibling.

He had not asked William for advice, or for money. In retrospect, he wondered why he had written to him at all, why he had not gone ahead and purchased Lamb House without consulting a living soul other than his bank's manager. He had described his new opportunity unthinkingly, in great excitement, and then had suffered the consequences. William had written him two letters in quick succession; the tone of the first was hortatory and hectoring: William as expert on the purchasing and disposal of real estate, on interest rates, and on the need for toughness and cunning in negotiation. Then, having met someone in Nauheim who had once seen the house and having discussed the entire matter freely with him, William wrote a second time to say that he believed the asking price was very extravagant and advising Henry that he should consult some wary business friend before in any way committing himself.

On receipt of the latter missive, Henry intended to write to him tersely to say that he had the matter under control and was not in need of any further advice. In fact, he would be grateful if William would not discuss the purchase of Lamb House at the price mentioned, or at any other price, with anyone, or indeed with him when they met.

He began the letter a number of times and then found himself, despite his original intention to be brief and cold, making clear that he would buy Lamb House in any case simply because he wanted to, but going on to explain its value and the reasonable asking price. He insisted that he was not yet wholly senile. He added to this letter when a further message came from his sister-in-law offering, with William's approval, to lend him money from her own funds to buy Lamb House. He emphasized proudly to both William and Alice that he would not, in fact, need to borrow a penny, and wished to underline that, while he was grateful to Alice, William should understand that the decision to buy the house outright would not depend on his opinion or be influenced by it.

Henry pointed out that he had never lacked faith in his brother's purchases nor sent him advice not sought for. He added that his joy at the prospect of getting the house had shrivelled under his brother's warnings, but would, he was sure, rebloom. It was such a rare joy for him to want anything as he wanted Lamb House, he wrote, and he expected his brother to understand this.

He finished the letter late at night and, without reading it over, sealed the envelope and left it in the hall to be posted early in the morning. Alice, his sister-in-law, he was sure, had meant her offer kindly, and William's advice had not been ill-intentioned, but they both suffered from a need, he felt, so deep-seated as to be well beyond their understanding, to have him act on their advice. And they would find it easier to spend time under his roof, had it been purchased on terms suggested by them.

When William wrote again apologizing for rubbing his brother up the wrong way, as he himself put it, he offered money from the Syracuse sinking fund which could in case of need be taken out. This merely added to Henry's resentment which had also been smouldering over William's refusal to accept definitely the offer of the flat in Kensington, and further resentments at his decision to go to Germany before he came to England. William was so proud of himself as a practical man, a family man, a man who did not write fictions but gave lectures, an American man plain in his habits and his arguments, representing gruff masculinity against his brother's effete style; his refusal to take Henry's flat seemed lacking in all common sense.

What Henry did not consider during this correspondence was his brother's reason for being in Nauheim. Although William had written to say that he had a bad heart and Henry had made sympathetic references to this, it did not seem to him that his brother's health might be in any serious danger. When, however, he met his brother from the train in early October, not having seen him for seven years, he was shocked at how much William had been weakened, although he sought to give no sign that this had been his first impression.

William had descended from the train looking as though he had woken from a deep sleep. He did not see Henry and stood waiting for his wife to step onto the platform before searching for him among the small crowd. As Burgess Noakes rushed to procure his luggage, William saw Henry and moved towards him, discarding instantly the pose of an old man and becoming enthusiastic in his movements. His face was thinner, Henry saw. When they had embraced and been joined by Alice, they walked back to supervise the loading of the luggage onto the wheelbarrow. William insisted on carrying one of the cases while Alice argued that he should not, and Henry pointed out that there was more room on the wheelbarrow and that Burgess Noakes was a champion athlete, much stronger than he looked. Burgess took the case, put it on the wheelbarrow and moved ahead.

William then stood and looked at Henry and smiled again. He had, Henry saw as if for the first time, an extraordinary face. His expression was open and perceptive, his eyes roved about as though he needed to take in the many competing aspects of the scene in front of him before making up his mind. His considerable and sparkling intelligence was close to charm in the way it manifested itself. His gaze was both provocative and amused; in his eyes and in the lines of his face there were signs of compassionate judgements and complex distinctions that he was clearly in the habit of making with great confidence and wit and clarity of thought. He did not look like an American, nor indeed like a member of the James family. He had developed a physiognomy entirely his own. Alice, Henry felt, was easier to place, handsome and well-groomed, her kindness not masking her intelligence nor diminishing it, demonstrating only that her sympathy would always come first. Before they were halfway up the hill, he felt that they had come as parents might, the father slightly distracted and withdrawn and the mother all smiles. He was glad that he had written to them so sharply about his purchase of Lamb House so that it would now be beyond their criticism, as he hoped he himself might be, during their stay.

It was apparent that Alice had decided that she would like Rye from the start, and put care into her remarks so that they would not sound too gushingly enthusiastic and undiscriminating. She spoke about how beautifully old the town seemed, about how private Lamb House was, like a country house in the town, she said. William assented to this as they stood in front of it. The garden, Henry explained, was not at its best, they must come in the summer for that, and the recent weather had not helped. Immediately on entering the house he showed William the study he might use, then accompanied his guests to their bedroom, stopping at the room their daughter would sleep in when she arrived. Then he took them to view the dining room, the downstairs sitting room, the garden room, soon to enter its period of hibernation, and the kitchens. He introduced them to the staff and then led them upstairs once more to see his own room, saving the largest room, the drawing room, for last, presuming that William and Alice, so used to the proportions available in Cambridge and Boston, would perceive the other rooms as small.

He showed them the house as though they were prospective buyers; and they managed to make positive and supportive remarks. Over supper that evening, it struck him that were the Smiths to reappear, drunken and slatternly, Alice would have something cheerful to say about the quality of the service at Lamb House and William would nod in manly agreement.

AFTER LUNCH the next day, when the dishes had been cleared, Alice James closed the door of the dining room and asked Henry if she and William could speak to him, uninterrupted, on a matter of some importance. Henry found Burgess Noakes in the hallway and asked him if he could ensure that they were not disturbed in the dining room. When he came back into the room, Alice was sitting with her hands joined at the table and William was standing by the window. Their expressions were serious. Had a lawyer appeared at that moment to read a long and complicated will, Henry would not have been surprised.

'Harry,' Alice said, 'we have been to see another medium, a Mrs Fredericks. We have been a number of times. I went alone at first and I am absolutely certain that she did not know who I was or anything about me.'

'And then I accompanied her,' William said, 'and all in all we have had four sessions with her.'

'We thought to write to you,' Alice said, 'after the first session with her, but then as they went on we decided we would wait until we came to England. Harry, your mother has been in touch with us.'

'She spoke through Mrs Piper,' William interrupted, 'we know that, but there was something more personal in her message this time.'

'Is she at rest? Is my mother at rest?' Henry asked.

'Harry, she is at rest, she is simply watching over us all,' William said, 'through the mysterious gauze between her state and ours, in the vast white radiance that lies beyond.'

'She wishes you to know that she is at rest,' Alice said.

'Has she said anything about my sister?' Henry asked.

'No, nothing about Alice,' William replied.

'About Wilky or my father?' he asked.

'In none of the sessions did she allude to the dead,' William said.

'What did she say then? To whom did she allude?' Henry asked.

'She wishes you to know that you are not alone, Harry,' Alice said.

She looked at him gravely as he took this in without speaking.

'Her consciousness has not been extinguished, then,' he said.

'She is at rest, Harry,' Alice said. 'She wishes you to know that.'

William moved across the room and sat at the table. Henry could see more clearly now that he had lost flesh around his jaw; his eyes were sad but seemed to shine as he spoke.

'Our medium described this house. There were things she could not have known about. Yesterday when we walked through these rooms it was all confirmed for us.'

'Harry,' Alice said, 'she described that statue over the mantel-piece.'

All three of them examined Andersen's statue of the young count.

'And there is something even stranger in the front room,' Alice went on, 'it is a painting of a deserted landscape.'

Henry stood up suddenly and walked across the room.

'I don't know if you noticed me studying it yesterday,' Alice said. 'Harry, I did so because she described it in detail. She said that it meant something very special to you, but when I asked you about it yesterday, you said nothing.'

'It belonged,' Henry said, 'to Constance Fenimore Woolson. It is the only object of hers in this house. I brought it from Venice.'

'Mrs Fredericks described these rooms,' Alice said, 'the windows, the colours, but these two objects – the statue and the painting – she said were special. We have to believe her, Harry, we have to believe her.'

Henry moved towards the door and opened it. He stood in the hallway for a moment until the appearance of Burgess Noakes made him retreat once more into the dining room. William and Alice sat at the table watching him.

'I need some time alone,' he whispered.

They both stood up.

'We did not mean . . .' Alice began.

'Nothing,' Henry replied. 'Nothing. Give me a day or two to think. This is a great shock and I promise we will return to the matter when I am ready to accept the idea that my mother's voice is calling to us.'

IN THE AFTERNOON, he walked for miles and when he returned he made his way quickly and silently to the garden room but he could neither read nor write and he was cold. He wished above all that William and Alice might go now, having carried the message. At supper, however, as soon as he sat down, he felt an immense warmth towards them. He realized that his brother and sister-in-law, operating in unison, had saved many anecdotes about mutual friends until now. He watched William being funny and judicious and deeply informative on the rise of Oliver Wendell Holmes and the lives of John Gray and Sargy Perry, old before their time, he said, and William Dean Howells, whom he admired still. William told stories, moving towards pure malice before saving the moment with a remark which was so well phrased as to cause his brother a pure and self-forgetful delight.

That night when he had retired he wished his sister Alice were in the house with them too; he would have enjoyed her acid version of this formidable couple in their soft-spoken intimacy, a pair who were ostensibly offering an open smile while, in fact, operating like a great fortress built to repel all intruders. He wished he knew how to introduce the subject of his sister, and her contempt for mediums and her belief that seances were pure nonsense. Her diary, he was aware, had not spared her brother and sister-in-law.

Their dabblings in the occult were, for Alice, the grossest sort of idolatry. She had made this clear to them, but no one had ever told them that she had unmercifully mocked them by sending them, when they asked for a lock of her hair to use at a seance, hair belonging to a dead friend. She had cackled in glee at the solemnity of their reports from these sessions, but now, he recognized, despite the passing of the years, that William and his wife still could not be told of her trick, so elaborate and deeply serious was the system of protection they had wound round themselves and how firm their belief. He was still not sure what he himself believed. It was easier, he felt, to listen and make as little comment as possible.

WILLIAM FOUND his small downstairs study congenial and discovered a sheltered spot in the garden which caught the sun in the morning where he could sit reading. William and Alice went on walks in the vicinity, taking the dog Maximilian with them, and became known very quickly in several Rye establishments where they had coffee in the afternoon and bought cakes to take back to Lamb House. William walked slowly, but managed to suggest that it was deep thought that made him so deliberate in his movements. At first Henry attached no importance to the fact that Alice never let him out of her sight. If William were in the garden, she was at a window overlooking the garden; if he were in his makeshift study, she was across the hall with the door open. If he prepared to go for a walk, Alice immediately fetched her coat, even if Henry himself were to accompany him, or if he gently indicated that he wished to go alone. After a while, however, such watchfulness on her part, such attentive shadowing of her husband, seemed to Henry almost perverse and he noticed William being irritated by it. Since Alice was known for her tact, since she had a reputation for being neither perverse nor irritating, this display of solicitude, both obvious and without respite, was unlike her. Henry, once he began to notice it, longed for it to stop.

Suddenly, one afternoon, when they had been with him for ten or eleven days, he understood why his sister-in-law watched William with such care. He himself was in the drawing room upstairs after breakfast; he had been reading, when he chanced to go to the window, as he often did in the days when his brother was seated in the garden. William was obviously in pain and Alice was with him, standing over him, as he held his hands on his chest and closed his eyes in a sort of agony. Henry could not see her face, but could discern from her movements that she was unsure whether William should move or stay still. Henry stood back as his sister-in-law turned preparing to hold William in her arms. He then went downstairs as quickly as he could to the garden.

Henry learned in the days that followed that William's heart was damaged, that his reason for going to Nauheim was not to avoid his brother's hospitality. William was ill. Alice had been watching him in case he had a sudden heart attack, having been told that such an attack could be fatal. William was not yet sixty.

The next day on the train to London to see the best heart specialist in England, William insisted on reading and taking notes, refused to have a blanket placed over his knees and promised them both that if they should look at him one more time with pity or worry or the slightest interest beyond the normal, then he would expire on them immediately and leave his money to a dogs' and cats' home.

'And I should warn you both that the hauntings will not be normal. No medium will be required. I will pounce directly.'

Alice did not smile, but stared out the window, stony-faced. Henry wondered if the story of his sister and the lock of her hair might lighten their journey, but realized that it might have precisely the opposite effect. While William could joke about such matters, he did so from a serious perspective. The aura his brother and his sister-in-law created, in which such a story could not be told, seemed to have strengthened with William's illness.

Dr Bezly Thorne, the most recommended among Harley Street doctors who dealt with delicate hearts, was, William thought, far too young to know of such matters, but he was soon persuaded by Henry and Alice that this new doctor was unconta-minated by out-of-date remedies and was fully conversant with the new ones.

'I dislike young people, all of them,' William retorted, 'medical or non-medical, conversant or non-conversant, from the bottom of my heart.'

'Your heart indeed,' Alice said drily.

'Yes, I know, my dear, the part that is fully intact.'

Dr Thorne asked to see the patient alone, and when he emerged after a few minutes from the bedroom in which William lay resting in Henry's flat in Kensington, he remarked that Alice and Henry would now find Professor James much chastened, ready to rest, ready to maintain a strict diet with no starch, and ready, since the doctor had advised it, to be really ill, to be gravely and precariously ill, so that he should become better.

'My instructions are clear,' Dr Thorne said, 'he is to live. I have told him so. And in order to do that he must act precisely as he is told, and he must stay in London until I say he can move. He can read if he pleases, but he cannot write.'

They agreed to remain in Henry's flat in Kensington and in the days that followed, as William began his diet, and Alice awaited the arrival of their daughter Peggy, Henry and Alice had much time to converse.

William's ill health had not softened Henry's resolve that his own circumstances were closed to criticism. His sister-in-law, whose scent for what was suitable for discussion was, he thought, refined in the extreme, thus kept matters general, rarely even mentioning the attributes of her own children unless Henry specifically asked. One evening, however, when Peggy, who had arrived from France, had gone to bed and William was sleeping, Alice raised the matter of her own sister-in-law, now dead seven years. She did so carefully, her tone serious and considered. She spoke of Alice's dislike for her and reminded Henry that, at the time of her wedding, Alice had taken to her bed.

Henry became uncomfortable. His sister's memory was, as the years went by, increasingly tender for him; her suffering was something he was prepared to talk about only with sorrow and much sympathy. If there had been a battle between the two Alices, the one who was speaking now had plainly been the victor and he realized, as she spoke, that the spoils of victory included a right to discuss the vanquished one freely. His sister-in-law, he saw, mistook his relationship with his sister, thought that Alice James, on her arrival in England, had posed the same problem for Henry and that her peculiar nature could be spoken of between them as though Henry and his sister-in-law would take the same measure of it. Alice's tone was matter of fact.

'Alice James,' she said, 'might have found something more useful to do with her wit than direct it inwards at herself.'

Henry was tempted to stand up and excuse himself. He had presumed that his silence might have been enough to hush his sister-in-law on the subject.

'And,' Alice went on, 'she always managed to find some lucky person to take care of her and listen to her. Your poor Aunt Kate was not receptive enough, and that is why she came to England.'

It became apparent to Henry that his sister-in-law might be conscious of his discomfort, and that this was the thing that was encouraging her to go on. The idea was so unlikely that he watched her with interest, scarcely believing his own impression. Now, as if to confirm to his satisfaction the truth of his idea, instead of wishing to end the conversation or change the subject or leave the room, he wanted Alice to continue for as long as she pleased while he remained as coldly unreceptive as he could manage.

'I think Alice and Miss Loring were made for each other,' his sister-in-law went on. 'Miss Loring was a strong woman in search of a weak friend to care for. You know, any time I saw them together I thought that they were the happiest pair on God's earth.'

Alice's face had brightened and her eyes began to sparkle as she spoke. She was no longer the wise and sensible wife of William James, but someone with her own mind indulging her need to speak it. It appeared that if her views of the world should cause offence or verge on the scandalous, then so much the better. Henry had never before seen any sign of this in her. He wondered if she were like this when she was alone with William. He also wondered why he himself was so interested in it, why watching her speak gave him a strange pleasure.

'I've always said to William that Alice and Miss Loring might have had very good reasons for coming to England away from all their relatives and friends.'

Henry looked at her in disbelief.

'You know, Harry, the maid at home would talk, and, indeed, Aunt Kate might not always knock on the bedroom door before entering, and I think that in England Miss Loring and Alice could have found the sort of happiness together that is not mentioned in the Bible.'

As his sister-in-law glowed with satisfaction, Henry realized why he was listening so attentively. He calculated quickly that Alice could not have known Minny Temple, but she could have known about her. Her way of saying the unsayable in the company of a gentleman, without losing her poise and her wonderful and original curiosity at how the world was and how it might be, was what had distinguished Minny from her sisters and her friends. Minny's mind had the same capacity to run forward, and then hit home with a question or a remark which would make certain members of the company wish to leave the room, but, be prevented from doing so because of the charm of her delivery. Alice, thirty years after Minny's death, was performing with the same verve and courage.

'Women, you know, are not above suspicion in these matters, or in any others,' she concluded.

Henry now asked himself if she discussed his own private affairs in the same way. He thought back to the pointed questions she had asked about the visit of Hendrik Andersen, which she had heard about in Boston, and the presence of Burgess Noakes in Lamb House, which she had remarked upon. Indeed, he had noticed her observing Burgess, and now wondered if she were seeking material for further speculation about the personal lives of members of her husband's family and their servants. He found himself having to resist the temptation to smile at the image of his Aunt Kate opening a door on Miss Loring and Alice. Then his sister-in-law stood up and said that she would return the teapot to the kitchen and then see if William were still asleep. Henry announced that he would retire to bed. Calmly, they wished each other goodnight.

HENRY RETURNED to Lamb House while William, Alice and Peggy remained in London until Dr Thorne sent his patient to Malvern for treatment which quickly, according to William, made him worse. As London was cold and inhospitable and the Atlantic Ocean too tumultuous to cross for a man in his frail state of health, William and his wife and daughter came back to Rye as their surrogate home and seemed so happy and grateful when Henry met them at the station that he looked forward to having them at Lamb House for the festive season.

Despite his doctor's orders, William worked in the morning; then he rested in the afternoon and spent the evening making light of his ailments. He also made many jokes about his doctor and members of his family and remarks both pithy and interesting on the nature of the human dilemma. His daughter, Henry could see, adored him and, at times, to his delight, vied with him in his efforts to mock himself and his predicament.

When Lady Wolseley sent a note to say that she was in the vicinity, Henry thought a lunch for her at Lamb House with his family might interest William without overtiring him and allow Alice and Peggy to view an amusing and rare specimen of modern English womanhood. He was careful not to say too much about her in advance in case he intimidated Alice and Peggy, but once they realized that Lady Wolseley was married to the Commander-in-Chief of Her Majesty's forces and that she was a lady who had, as it were, earned her title, then Alice insisted on taking over the kitchen, doing so with efficiency and sweetness. Both she and her daughter tried on many dresses and costumes in preparation for the arrival of the Duchess, as Peggy constantly called Lady Wolseley in the days before her visit. Alice accompanied Burgess Noakes to the local tailor to have both a suit and a uniform made for him in double quick time so that he too would be suitably attired for the visit of her majesty, as William encouraged his daughter to call Lady Wolseley, but not, he warned, to her face.

When both Alice and Peggy noticed that Henry had removed a piece of faded tapestry from the wall at the top of the stairs on the day before the visit, and replaced it with a view of Rye, they teased him lightly about putting on his best show and taking down worn objects in readiness for the Duchess. He did not tell them that he had bought it in a London antique shop in Lady Wolseley's absence and against her wishes and was now afraid to face her with his wilful and perhaps foolish purchase.

LADY WOLSELEY was wearing scarlet silk which appeared immensely dramatic when her long black cloak had been removed. Her cheeks had been rouged, and even her hair, he felt, had received some reddening, thus making it brighter, indeed more brilliant, than he had ever seen it. Her manners too were brilliant and nothing that William or Alice or Peggy said did not meet with responses of great effusion. It was as though a thunder and lightning storm of the happiest kind had arrived by carriage at Lamb House in plenty of time for lunch and was playing itself out cheerfully in the drawing room.

'We all know, my dear,' she said directly to Peggy whose light blue dress and cardigan and light blue ribbons in her hair seemed almost colourless against the blazing fire of the speaker, 'that your country has the largest democracy in the known world and has bequeathed many gifts in its short history to civilization, but the most valuable gift of all, please be assured, is your uncle. He is the most wonderful flowering of your young country, and notice that he does not even deny it, for it is so generally agreed to be the truth.'

Henry was looking at William who was smiling warmly at Lady Wolseley, offering her all the soft weight of his irony.

Over lunch, their visitor asked many questions about Harvard and Cambridge and the difference between psychology and philosophy and what the lives of young girls were like in the wonderfully intellectual environment of the United States. She managed to listen to the answers very carefully so that her further questions displayed genuine interest in what was being said. William, Henry noticed, was almost flirting with her while his daughter stared at Lady Wolseley with her mouth open rather too wide. Alice fixed her eyes evenly on their guest in the calm and happy knowledge, Henry believed, that having listened to Lady Wolseley, she would now be able to write to her mother about the visit and discuss it with her husband over many days.

As the meal came to an end, William expressed much disapproval at the quantity of social life in London, insisting that, in comparison, their quiet life at Cambridge was bliss. He could hardly bear even the thought of so much activity, he said.

'Oh yes, it's true. You are quite right,' Lady Wolseley said. 'Cambridge must be bliss.'

Henry noticed his niece and thought that she was going to have to excuse herself from the room so close was she to a fit of nervous laughter.

'And the theatre in London is so ridiculous, so very vulgar,' Lady Wolseley continued. 'One cannot tolerate it. In fact, when poor Henry came to stay with us in Ireland, his wonderful play had just been insulted by the public. My husband, as you know, runs the army. I thought it was one night when there would have been a perfect excuse for his soldiers to shoot into the crowd. Perhaps it is fortunate that he has the command rather than I.'

Peggy excused herself from the table.

'Yes, England is ghastly. But of course Ireland, on the other hand, has changed so much,' Lady Wolseley went on, 'even since we left it. It is, I am told, the most peaceful part of the entire empire.'

'I wonder how long it will remain so?' William asked.

'Oh forever, I'm told,' Lady Wolseley replied.

William looked up quizzically as though one of his students had spoken out of turn.

'I met Lady Gregory, Henry, your old friend, in London,' Lady Wolseley said. 'Her estates are in the very interior. She says that there is no social outrage of any sort in Ireland. And more, she herself has begun to learn Celtic, and says it is full of many beautiful words and phrases. It is very old, she says, older than both Greek and Turkish.'

'I think the language is called Gaelic,' William said.

'No, Celtic,' Lady Wolseley replied. 'Lady Gregory assured me that it is called Celtic, and I do so wish I had known about it when I was in Ireland. I would have learned it myself and given parties in it.'

She smiled at Alice who smiled at her in return. William, Henry could see, was no longer prepared to flirt with Lady Wolseley.

'I travelled in Ireland a number of times,' he said. 'And I do believe that England has much to answer for in the way the country has been run.'

'Oh I quite agree,' Lady Wolseley said. 'And my husband spoke to the queen personally about the matter before he went there, and they both took the view that once Mr Parnell was removed and not replaced, then all the Fenianism would die down. And you should go there now, or speak to Lady Gregory. I believe that Ireland has been transformed.'

'Have you been to the United States?' Alice asked.

'No, dear, no. And I should love to go,' Lady Wolseley said. 'I long to see the Wild West. I should like to go there.'

She spoke sadly, as though her not having been there was the regret of her life, and then smiled warmly at Peggy as the young girl returned to the room.

'Henry, I am so glad we bought this dining-room table,' Lady Wolseley said.

'Lady Wolseley was of great assistance when I was furnishing Lamb House,' Henry said.

'My dear, we must get more rugs,' Lady Wolseley said. 'You cannot go into the new year without some extra rugs. I am told that a marvellous consignment has arrived in London and I must go upstairs again and look at the drawing room so that we can decide on the colours we need.'

'Yes,' Henry said. 'Let us repair to the drawing room.'

As they walked into the hallway, Henry came face to face with Hammond, whom he had last seen in Ireland when he was a guest of the Wolseley's. Hammond's face had changed, his eyes seemed larger and more gentle. He smiled shyly at Henry and stood aside to let him pass.

'Oh of course,' Lady Wolseley said, 'you know each other. I did remember that.'

Henry led them upstairs to the drawing room, leaving Hammond in the hallway.

'Yes,' Lady Wolseley said, 'Hammond remains with us. He is part of Lord Wolseley's guard.'

Lady Wolseley found herself a chair near the window while Alice and Peggy sat on the sofa. William stood at the mantelpiece, his face grave.

'We miss Ireland so much, Mr James,' Lady Wolseley addressed William directly. 'We brought Hammond back with us and two gardeners. And all our guests love them, Casey and Leary the gardeners, they delight everybody. I have to tell all of our guests "don't pay any attention to their charm, they don't mean it", but it's lovely how they talk.'

Henry left the room quietly before his brother had an opportunity to reply and made his way slowly down the stairs. Hammond was still standing in the hallway, as though he had been waiting for him.

'I did not know that you had come back to England,' Henry said.

'Yes, sir, I followed his lordship and I travel sometimes with her ladyship.'

His voice had lost none of its calmness which Henry felt as a warm relief.

'I am so glad that you have come to my house,' Henry said. 'I hope you have been looked after.'

'Your boy, sir,' Hammond said, 'made sure that I was well fed.'

When Henry continued to look at him, Hammond lifted his eyes. Hammond was beginning to blush. He seemed younger than when Henry had known him in Ireland almost five years earlier. His smile broadened but he did not move.

'I should like to show you the garden here and the garden room,' Henry said.

'Would you, sir?' Hammond's tone was gentle.

'It is better, of course, in the summer,' Henry said, walking into the dining room and opening the doors into the garden. The air was cold and dry. 'And your family in London, how are they?' Henry asked.

'Very well, sir.'

'And your sister is well?'

'It is strange that you remembered, sir. She is wonderful.'

They moved around the garden slowly, Hammond stopping for a second each time Henry spoke so that he could properly take in what was being said.

'You must come back in the summer when everything is in bloom,' Henry said.

'I should like to do that,' Hammond replied.

Henry turned the key to the garden room and they entered. He felt as though they had both walked into some half-forbidden territory, but when he turned and saw Hammond's face, he realized that Hammond did not share this perception. He was interested in the desk and the papers and the books. He went to the window and looked at the view.

'This is a most beautiful room, sir.'

'It is cold in the winter,' Henry said, 'too cold to use.'

'You must be a happy man here in the summer, sir,' Hammond said.

He moved over to the books on the wall.

'I have read some of your books, sir. One of them I have read three times.'

'One of my books?'

'*The Princess Casamassima*, sir. I felt that I was living in that book. All those streets of London are the streets I know. And the sister. It was much better than Dickens, sir.'

'You like Dickens?'

'Yes, sir. *Hard Times* and *Bleak House*.'

Hammond turned and began to inspect the books closely, kneeling to see the books on the bottom shelves. He turned and spoke softly.

'You must excuse me, sir, but some of these titles I have not seen before.'

He was loath to accept any books as gifts, and would only agree when Henry could demonstrate that he had a number of copies of the same edition on the shelves. Finally, after much discussion, he allowed three books to be set aside for him, Henry having become aware that his embarrassment and hesitation arose from the fact that he did not want Lady Wolseley to see him with the package and ask what it was. He wrote his address in London in clear letters on a sheet of paper and Henry promised that he would send these books by post.

'And I shall say nothing to her ladyship,' Henry said.

Hammond smiled gratefully.

'Nor shall I, sir.'

As they walked to the spot in the garden where Henry was proposing to build a new glasshouse, Henry could not help noticing that they were being watched with shameless interest by Lady Wolseley. She stood with William, Alice and Peggy at the drawing-room window. Lady Wolseley was pointing to something in the garden and, when Henry caught her gaze, she waved. As he bowed to her, he saw his brother observing him and Hammond with a sort of bemused intensity. He did not look directly at his sister-in-law or his niece.

IN THE DAYS that followed, he supposed that his brother and sister-in-law and niece discussed Lady Wolseley at length among themselves, but while Alice and Peggy seemed to have been much animated by her visit, William's mood had darkened. Henry did not know if something more had been said by Lady Wolseley after he left the room, believing that what he had heard might have been sufficient in itself. On her departure, as Hammond stood in the background, she had made clear, even more so than she had during her visit, her proprietorial interest in Henry and her admiration for him. He noted that she did not include his family in the invitation to see her both in the country and in London, which she had extended to Henry. She did not seem to think that William James and family merited any great attention, and Henry felt that this, as much as her views on the Irish question, might have irritated William profoundly.

As Christmas approached, Alice and Peggy, feeling snugly sentimental, began to plan a truly American festival, not understanding the extent to which the customs of their country coincided with those of England. William read and slept and spoke enough not to draw too much attention to his own deeply preoccupied state. After lunch one day when Alice and Peggy were making themselves busy in the kitchen, he asked Henry to wait in the dining room as he wished to speak to him. Henry politely closed the door behind him and sat at the table opposite William.

'Harry, I have, I know, offered before my doleful views on your not having stayed in America, and said how much we miss you as a chronicler of our society. I think America still awaits the novelist with eyes as sharp as yours and sympathy as wide ranging.'

'Indeed,' Henry said and smiled.

'But I do not think that you have found your subject in this country,' William said sternly. He stared towards the window as he spoke, as though he were rehearsing a speech or a sermon. 'I do not believe that *The Spoils of Poynton* or *The Awkward Age* or *The Other House* are worthy of your talent. The English have no spiritual life, only a material one. The only subject here is class and it is a subject of which you know nothing. The only striving is material striving and that you know nothing of either. You do not have in your possession the knowledge which Dickens or George Eliot or Trollope or Thackeray possessed of the mechanics of English greed. There is no yearning in England, no crying out for truth.'

'Thank goodness for that,' Henry said.

'In short,' William continued, as though Henry had not spoken, 'I believe that the English can never be your true subject. And I believe that your style has suffered from the strain of constantly dramatizing social insipidity. I think also that something cold and thin-blooded and oddly priggish has come to the fore in your content.'

'I am grateful to you for your opinion,' Henry said.

'Harry, I am an avid reader of you, and an admirer of your work.'

'You seem to feel that I should have remained at home,' Henry said and lifted his hand refusing to allow William to interrupt him, 'charting the lives of the pinched intellectuals of Boston. Yes, that would have been a supreme subject.'

'Harry, I find I have to read innumerable sentences you now write twice over to see what they could possibly mean. That is the long and the short of it. In this crowded and hurried reading age you will remain unread and neglected as long as you continue to indulge in this style and these subjects.'

'I shall,' Henry replied, 'as I work in the future then, strive to gratify you, but perhaps I should add that I might be even more humiliated if you should like what I do and thereby merge it in your affection with things for which I have heard you express admiration. Things which I would sooner descend to a dishonoured grave than have written.'

'No one is suggesting that you should lie in a dishonoured grave,' William said, 'but I did have a concrete proposal for you, a novel that is crying out to be written which would confound your critics, win you a large audience and give you immense satisfaction.'

'A novel I should write?'

'Yes, a novel with no grand English people, but dealing with the America you know.'

'You speak with great confidence.'

'Yes,' William said, 'I have put some thought into the matter. A novel which would deal with our American history rather than the small business of English manners, bad indeed as they are. A novel about the Puritan Fathers as told by you . . .'

Henry stood up and went to the window, forcing William to turn as he spoke. Henry felt that he had the advantage now by standing close to what light was left while his brother sat at the table in the deepening shadows.

'May I interrupt you?' Henry asked. 'Or is this a lecture whose finish will be marked by the ringing of a bell?'

William turned his chair around and seemed ready to continue what he had begun to say.

'May I put an end to this conversation,' Henry said, 'by stating clearly to you that I view the historical novel as tainted by a fatal cheapness and if you want a statement from me on the matter in clear American and since you wish me to pander to the crowded, hurried age as you call it, might I tell you my opinion of a novel to be written by me about the Puritan Fathers?'

He stopped, waiting for an answer.

'Yes, please,' William said. 'I cannot stop you.'

'It would be all one word,' Henry said. 'One simple word. It would be all humbug!' he said and smiled gently, almost patronizingly at his brother.

AT SUPPER it struck him that William had not confided in Alice that he had bravely attempted to lecture his brother on the failure of his fiction. William's eyes, he insisted, were sore and Alice tried to ensure that he slept more and did not read as much, while William, Henry saw, played the part of the unwilling and recalcitrant patient. William had begun to roam uneasily around Lamb House so that Henry was never sure in what room he would find him, or indeed at what time of the day or the night he would discover his brother restlessly creaking the floorboards in his bedroom or on the stairway.

He understood that William was attempting to fill Lamb House with his presence, using an invisible system, Henry believed, of imposing his authority, making subtle but insistent changes to meal times, for example, and how meals were served. William began to unnerve Burgess Noakes and the other household staff. At one point, until Alice forced him to desist, he even tried to alter the arrangement of the furniture in the drawing room and asked Burgess to remove certain ornaments from the mantelpiece which he did not like.

Henry avoided him; if he found him in the drawing room or one of the downstairs rooms, he quietly and diplomatically left him there. Alice still shadowed William. Although she seldom sat in the same room, she was always hovering close by, seeming to be busy. Peggy, on the other hand, buried herself in books, moving from classic novel to classic novel without lifting her head from them if she could help it. When she had finished with Jane Austen, she embarked on *The Portrait of a Lady*. Henry was surprised and amused to find that her parents felt free to express openly their disapproval of her latest choice, but was satisfied the next day that she had persisted with the book. She was, as she told them, too far involved in it now not to finish it. She would skip any passage which was too difficult or not suitable for her, she said. She was almost grown up, she added proudly. She looked at Henry calmly, without embarrassment, when he told her that, especially when compared with her Emmet cousins who spoke so badly, she was the most perfect young lady of his acquaintance.

WILLIAM, HENRY remembered, when he had come to London as part of a sabbatical in the year their mother died, had stayed with Henry also, and exuded the same strange resentment of his London life which extended to the very objects in the flat. And Henry had allowed William's disapproval to dictate where he went and where he did not go; he had allowed William to organize the household to William's satisfaction.

He recalled how it became apparent during that sojourn of William's that their father had not long to live. He remembered a telegram saying that their father's brain was softening and adding, as though with the same urgency, that William should not return. It was December in London. Alice, William's wife, was staying with her mother who was helping to care for her two young sons. Alice James, the other Alice, was looking after their father with Aunt Kate. Both Alices had, for once, concurred: neither of them wanted William to return. Both of them, on the other hand, wished Henry to be there. Their father, the telegram insisted, could possibly live for months, and thus it seemed easy to persuade William that, since he had given up his house in Cambridge, his return would involve inhabiting cramped quarters with no lectures to give at Harvard and no other duties there. Instead, he should continue his sabbatical in Europe, enjoy his leisure, make new contacts and write and read in freedom. The wording of the telegram had been, Henry realized, immensely clever. By stating that their father's brain was softening, both Alices had made clear to William that he would not be able, in his father's dying days, to discuss with him how their divergent ideas of the soul and the purpose of life might finally and beautifully be made to converge.

Henry had sailed alone for New York and when the boat docked he discovered that the funeral had taken place that very day. He was too late now to do anything other than listen to accounts of how his father had died peacefully and easily, inhabit the house so recently the house of the dead and read his father's will. In the years that followed, he never allowed himself to brood on the date of his father's burial and on their decision to consign Henry senior to the winter earth without Henry there to witness the burial or touch his father's dead face before the lid was placed on the coffin, though he was so close.

He came to understand that this decision had been firmly made by his sister Alice and he found himself too fascinated by her sudden brisk grasping of the reins of decision, in a family where she had never been allowed to decide anything, to be bruised by his strange exclusion. And in the weeks after the funeral he came to understand as well his sister's desperate need to keep William in England, to insist that Wilky, too ill to travel, stayed in Milwaukee and that Bob returned there. With William present, Alice James could not have been as deliberately rude to and impatient with Aunt Kate as she now was, since William would have stood between them, since his presence would have held everyone's attention, thus ensuring that Alice's efforts to belittle her aunt could not be as starkly successful. Nor would she have felt as free to cling so openly to Miss Loring, nor would Miss Loring, with the entire family present, have taken the same liberties in the James household before moving Alice into her own house.

Henry did nothing, once in Boston, to encourage William to return. William, without speaking or lifting a finger, would have replaced their father. Henry could not have had the silence of the house to himself, with only his Aunt Kate, whom he loved, for company. He could not have slept in his father's bed, feeling it his duty somehow to do so, nor come to possess the house in all its aura of absence waiting to be filled with as open a heart as he did now that William was so far away.

The fact that he, rather than William, had been made executor of his father's estate could not have pleased William. And that he could make the details of his father's last days known to William and the wishes and the kind condolences of old friends such as Francis Child and Oliver Wendell Holmes, and that he had placed himself in control without seeking advice, could not, he knew, have improved William's temper.

ABOUT A WEEK after his father was buried, a letter came in William's hand addressed to Henry James. Since Henry was awaiting news of William, it did not occur to him that the letter had been written to his father and that he should not open it. He had read the first paragraph before he realized his mistake, even though, as he subsequently noticed, the letter had begun 'Dear Father'. He held the letter for several days, telling no one about it, and then on a Sunday morning, the last day of the year, when it was quiet, the snow deep and the light scarce, he made his way to the cemetery where his parents lay close together. He was alone and he made sure as he approached the grave that no one was watching him. He hoped that his presence now might help his parents to feel the great ease he wished for them, to know how grateful he was to them and how raw with sadness he remained at their departure from the earth. He took William's letter out of his pocket and in a voice clear and audible he began to read it to the old ghost for whom it had been intended. But gradually, as the tears came, he reduced his voice to a whisper and several times he had to stop and put his hand over his face as these words, meant so tenderly, moved him more than any of his own words, or any words about his father he had heard since he arrived. He forced himself to continue:

'As for the other side, and Mother, and all our possible meeting
I can't say anything. More than ever at this moment do I feel

that if that were true, all would be solved and justified. And it comes strongly over me in bidding you good-bye how life is but a day and expresses mainly but a single note. It is so much like the art of bidding an ordinary good-night. Good night my sacred old Father! If I don't see you again – Farewell! A blessed farewell!'

Somewhere in the depths of the cold earth, Henry felt, his father's spirit lingered, enough for Henry to long for the letter to last, so that he would not have to walk away in silence, leaving his parents there in a place he now viewed as the most sacred and forgiving. He hated the barrenness of the winter season and the sounds of his own footsteps on the ice as he moved away.

He walked from the graveyard to the house where his sister-in-law was staying to find that William was, once more, threatening to come home. Alice showed him their sparse accommodation. In deep despair she explained that she was exhausted by caring for her father-in-law in his last days, when she had joined Alice and Aunt Kate beside his bed. Her children were also becoming a great toll on her energy, she said, and explained further that having a husband in a state of desolation in these few small rooms was something she desperately wished to avoid. Henry said that he would write once again to William. He almost told her that he understood what a burden William's idle and distressed presence could be in any household, but, since the intensity of her feeling on the matter struck him as somewhat odd, and so different from the way his own mother had dealt with his father, he did not speak.

That evening, Henry sat at his father's desk and told William what he had done in the cemetery, trying to bring to life for his brother how his final words to his father had been solemnly offered to the old man's spirit. He added his belief that William coming home would be an idle step and begged him to let the interest subside. But even as he did so, he knew that William, on hearing what Henry had done with his private and heartfelt letter, would resent such liberties being taken, no matter how solemnly.

He awaited his brother's reply and when it came it was full of hatred for the London he was being forced, almost against his will, to inhabit. William wrote of the filthy, smeary, smoky fog and the universal stupidity of the population whose like did not exist, he believed, anywhere else under the sun.

HENRY WAS BUSY. As the executor he had many meetings with the lawyers. He had been appalled by his father's decision to leave Wilky out of the will, his father having believed that Wilky had been given enough in his lifetime. Henry presumed that his siblings agreed that this was not to be tolerated and he set about correcting it by asking each of them to offer a portion of their legacy to Wilky, enough to make his legacy equal to theirs. He planned to travel to Milwaukee to see both Wilky and Bob and made further arrangements to go to Syracuse to see at first hand his father's properties there and consider whether it would be wiser to dispose of them or keep them and arrange for the dividends from the rents to be disbursed as the rents came in.

As he organized these matters, with much discussion of share value and income, percentages and bonds, William's regular missives from London, displaying self-pity and containing threats to return, made him impatient. His sister-in-law seemed increasingly agitated at the possibility of her husband's sudden and precipitous return. She showed him each letter William wrote, sighing at their tone.

Although he remained uneasy about having read these letters, and wondered about the state of his brother's marriage, Henry had no difficulty writing to William once more, demanding that he see reason. As he finished the letter late at night, adding many details arising from his role as executor, he felt a strange power which increased in the morning as he realized how hurt and infuriated William would be on reading it. He experienced a sense of lightness at that prospect coupled with a distinct feeling of being fully in the right and acting for the best.

William, in response to Henry's provocations, made clear his indignation at being treated like a small child who did not understand his own motives or interests. He made many insulting remarks about London and Henry's flat, and had attempted to break ranks on the plan to make up to Wilky for the injustice their father had done him. Then he had returned to Cambridge before his sabbatical in Europe was over, whereupon Henry had informed him that he would make his own share of the estate over to his sister Alice, and would allow William the control he desired by leaving the family finances in his hands. He was going to apply himself, he had told his brother, to his work in the very London which William so despised, from which work he, in any case, derived sufficient income not to have to bother with any further discussions about his father's estate and its management.

The death of Wilky the following year, followed by the death of Herman, William and Alice's baby boy, and then the death of their sister Alice, brought respite from their disputes, and the many sweet and healing letters, full of kindness and emotional generosity, written to Henry over the years by William's wife helped to restore tenderness to the relationship between Henry and William, as indeed the vast expanse of the Atlantic Ocean between them managed to pour calming waters on both sides.

NOW, HOWEVER, two decades later, it was as though an afterglow of the rancour of those months after their father's death continued to burn at Lamb House. Henry could continue his routine; he had his work, his servants, his books, and constant messages from friends and publishers. William was away from home. When William left his house in Cambridge to walk to Harvard Yard, he would be observed with a respect bordering on awe and greeted warmly, his fame gathering like a large protective shadow. This fame did not stretch to Rye; and its failure to do so, it seemed to

Henry, appeared to depress William even further so that eventually he did not wish to go out at all. Yet staying indoors day after day made him behave like an animal in a cage who had lost none of the ability to snarl.

One evening as he was preparing to go to his room for the night, and in search of the book he had been reading, Henry found his niece in one of the downstairs rooms. She seemed disturbed; he wondered if her father's mood had affected her and this made him concerned. As her warmth and delight at the Christmas season had managed to lift some of the gloom that hung over Lamb House, he had come to view her as a young figure of charm and intelligence, a source of much amusement for him as well as pride. When he asked her if anything was wrong she was at first unwilling to tell him why she appeared so listless and almost despondent. When he asked her if she were missing her brothers and her friends in Cambridge, she shook her head. When he was weighing in his mind whether he should allude to William's state of mind, his niece suddenly asked him if he intended to write a second volume, a sequel, to *The Portrait of a Lady*. She told him that she had, less than one hour before, finished the book. Henry told her that he had written the book twenty years earlier and had long forgotten it; he did not think he would write a sequel to it.

'Why did she go back?' Peggy asked.

'You mean, return to her husband?'

'Why did she do it?'

Peggy seemed almost angry. Henry sat down opposite her and tried to think, knowing that, above all, he must not say to her that when she was older she would come to realize how such decisions, matters of duty and resignation, were often more easily made than other decisions which might appear right to an imaginative young girl.

'It is very difficult for anyone in their lives,' Henry began, 'to make leaps into the dark. Isabel's going to Europe from Albany, leaving all her family behind, and then against everyone's advice and her own better judgement marrying Osmond, were leaps into the dark. Making such leaps requires us to be brave and determined, but doing so also may freeze any other possibilities. It is easier to renounce bravery rather than to be brave over and over. It could not, in her case, be done again. The will and the nerve needed for such actions do not come to us often, any of us, least of all Isabel Archer from Albany.'

As Peggy took her time to consider what he had said, a noise came from the room above them where William and Alice were sleeping. It sounded as though one of them had fallen out of the bed. Then they heard William's voice shouting and moaning and Alice's voice pleading with him and further sounds as though one of them were banging something against the floor. Peggy stood up and moved towards the door as Henry gestured to her to wait, to hesitate.

'No,' she said, brushing him aside. 'We must go upstairs now.'

She glanced back at him, her expression set and firm, her mouth and her chin an exact image of his mother's face. Her eyes were different, however, almost kindly, as she reached and caught his hand.

'We must go upstairs now,' she repeated.

Peggy led him upstairs to her parents' room and she opened the door without knocking. William lay on the floor in his nightshirt, his bare legs white in the lamplight. He was calling out and hammering the floor with his fists. Alice stood above him, fully dressed, motionless, her face like a mask.

'You have seen it and it is gone,' she said to William as though she desperately needed her words to be heeded and believed.

'It came to you and now it has left and we will all hold you, we will all stay with you. You will never be alone.'

She repeated these last words but nothing would calm William as his moaning went on.

Henry did not speak but when Burgess Noakes came down the stairs was brisk in directing him to return to his quarters. He was careful to remain in the doorway in case his presence distressed William further. Soon he stood back into the shadows as he saw

Alice helping William to his feet and leading him to the bed and pulling back the blankets.

'We will stay with you all night, William,' Alice said, 'and if you wake, no matter what time it is, you will find one of us here.'

William called out quietly and softly and curled up under the blankets.

'All of us are here, and all of us will stay here,' Alice said. 'Peggy will fetch a chair from her room and she will sit with us until you are soundly asleep. But I will not leave you. And Harry is watching you too.'

She moved to turn off the lamp on William's side of the bed.

'Sleep, now, sleep.'

She kept her hand on his head, exuding an unruffled kindness and a determination mixed with sadness. When Henry sought to capture her attention to ask if she wanted anything from the kitchen, she did not respond to him. Eventually, when William appeared to be asleep, she walked over to an armchair in the corner of the room and, once she sat down, did not take her eyes off her husband. Peggy had found a chair and was sitting close to her parents' bed. Henry withdrew, but did not close the door; he went noiselessly downstairs where he attempted to rekindle the fire. He found his book and kept it on his knee, but did not read, waiting instead for some sound to come from upstairs.

William had seemed to him in a state of rage as much as in a trance. He wondered, since William wrote of such matters, what name he would give this state and in what terms he might describe his wife and daughter's response to it. He wondered when William recovered whether he would remark on what happened.

Some time later, he heard footsteps on the stairs and he sat up, having fallen into a half-sleep. His sister-in-law came into the room.

'Peggy has fallen asleep and I have made her comfortable there. If he needs me, I will go to him quickly. But he will not need me, he will sleep now for hours and hours, nothing will wake him.'

She smiled at Henry.

'You are a very patient person,' she said.

'And you?' he asked. 'How will I describe you?'

'I am someone,' she said, 'who has learned a great deal, having known very little.'

'I wish I possessed some of your wisdom and your calm,' he said.

'You have much more. Your niece adores you, she thinks you are the finest gentleman. And so do I.'

'It is the season for such compliments,' he said.

'William suffers sometimes. His dark dreams overwhelm him, and when I first learned that about him I wanted him away from me. I wished to be elsewhere when he seemed ready to give into the darkness. There was nothing I could do for him, but I have learned, just as the boys and Peggy have learned, that it does not take much to comfort him.'

Henry attempted to convey by his silence that he would listen to her with sympathy for as long as she wished to speak.

'Peggy was a very difficult child,' Alice went on, 'and night after night she would scream when she was in bed as the light was turned off. And because we thought that she would have to learn to sleep in the dark we left her screaming. We thought that there was no earthly reason for it, but there was. A nun had assured her that her not being a Catholic would mean eternal damnation and she believed her. That was why she screamed. We realized that if we had asked her at the beginning why she was afraid, she might have told us.'

Henry moved to put more logs on the fire and they sat in a silence broken only by the mild sea wind and the crackling of the burning wood. Alice sighed. When Henry offered her a glass of port, she accepted. He poured one for her and one for himself, and, smiling gently, he handed her the drink.

'When I went to my first medium,' Alice said, 'when I first met Mrs Piper, neither of us could make sense of the messages that came. And then one day, perhaps the third time, we were alone with her and concentrating very hard, she asked me if my father had committed suicide and I said that he had, and then she asked if my mother and I and my sisters were far away from him then and I said that we were. And she said that someone was desperately urging me not to be afraid, that it would not happen again and I was to disregard my fear, which made me want William miles away from me when I felt his desolation. I would not let him near me when the night closed in on him. I wanted him in London when his father died and I did not want him to return. Mrs Piper could never say who it was, but they were telling me that I was to bring him close and be calm with him and that nothing would part us then, nothing terrible would happen to us then.'

She looked at Henry across the room and smiled.

'William will be fine now, he will be fine,' she said. 'In ways, it is easier for both of us when he is low, it is much more difficult when we are both in good sorts. We argue too much.'

They both looked into the fire. Henry guessed that it was after one o'clock in the morning.

'Harry,' Alice spoke very quietly, 'there was something we did not say to you about Mrs Fredericks.'

'You said that my mother is at rest.'

'Yes, she is, Harry, but there was something which concerned her.'

'About me?'

'Something, yes. She asked me to come to you if you should need me. She did not wish you to be alone if you should fall ill.'

'She watches over us, then?'

Alice swallowed as though she were holding back tears.

'You will be the last, Harry.'

'You mean that William will die before me.'

'Her message was clear.'

'And Bob?'

'You will be the last, Harry, and I will come to you when you call for me. You will not be alone when you are dying. And I must ask you for nothing in return except your trust.'

'You have that,' he said.

'Then I have given you her message. She wanted you to know that you would not be alone.'

When Alice returned to her bedroom to watch over William, Henry sat by the embers and pictured his mother as he had last seen her, the day after her death, her face in repose and lit by flickering candlelight, the idea of her love for him as an exquisite stillness as he sat in vigil; she was all noble and tender as his great protector and guardian. It did not surprise him in this dark house as the year came to a close that she would think of the end, as she had put such abundant energy into the beginning. The idea that she would not rest until he was at rest did not seem strange to him. He was humbled, and he felt afraid, but he was also grateful and ready for whatever might come now.

For New Year's Day, they invited Edmund Gosse to lunch. William had spent the previous few days in his study; his humour had returned and there was, Henry noted, a glitter in his remarks at the table. He discovered a short walk in Rye which he and Maximilian enjoyed and for several days in succession arrived back at Lamb House much refreshed, having spoken to several of the locals and having begun, he said, further to appreciate the topo-graphy of the place, the colour of the brick and the cobbles, and the manners of those he met. No mention was made of what Henry had witnessed in the bedroom.

Henry had not encouraged any visitors to Lamb House and had turned down all invitations, but when he said that he had received a letter from Edmund Gosse announcing that he would be in Hastings and could easily travel to Rye, William insisted that Gosse be invited and added several times how glad he would be to see him, not having done so for a very long time and being an admirer of his father's work.

Once more, Alice and Peggy moved into action, involving Henry in much discussion about Gosse's tastes and how they might pander to them. Alice had developed a set of jokes with Burgess Noakes which ranged from the quality of his footwear, of which she pretended to disapprove, to his haircuts, which she thought too severe. Burgess felt free now to inform her that Gosse had stayed at Lamb House many times and had had no reason to complain, but he enjoyed the fuss being made and entered into the spirit of the occasion, which Alice and Peggy tried to make as elaborate as possible while keeping everything simple, a formula of words which seemed to amuse them and which they rehearsed many times as they prepared the drawing room and the dining room and Burgess Noakes for the arrival of Gosse.

Henry explained to Peggy in the presence of her parents, much to their hilarity, that while Gosse himself was not great, he knew greatness when he saw it, and not only that but he knew the prime minister and the one before him as he would know the one after and the one after that. Peggy wrinkled up her nose and asked if he were old.

'He is not as old as I am, my dear,' Henry said, 'and I am old indeed. In fact, the word ancient comes to mind. So let me say that he is less than ancient. But the main fact about Gosse is that he loves London more than he loves life. So when your father mentions the quiet intellectual life in Boston, he will not understand. The man who is tired of London is tired of life, that is his motto. So you, my dear girl, had better find a subject on which your father and our guest can agree.'

In the days after William's recovery, Lamb House was turned into a club with many rules established by Peggy and Henry sometimes in consultation with Peggy's parents, sometimes in opposition to them. Rule number one concerned Peggy's bedtime which, Henry and she agreed, was extended to the same hour as the adults in the house, not only because of her semi-adult state, but because Peggy had discovered Charles Dickens, had devoured *Hard Times* in a matter of days and was now reading *Bleak House*. Rule number two governed Peggy's right to leave the table once she had eaten the main course and take her dessert with her to whatever room in which she wished to continue her reading. Rule number three gave William the right to snore unmolested in any part of the house. Other rules allowed Burgess Noakes to wear whatever he liked on his feet, and gave Alice the right to dip her morning biscuit into her cup of coffee as long as nothing dripped onto the Duchess's rugs, as Peggy called them. William insisted on a rule that would permit Henry to read a large two-volume biography of Napoleon without feeling guilty about wasting his time. All these rules were relayed to Alice's mother in Cambridge and read by Peggy's three brothers who were being looked after by her. Since they were all to sign the letter, Alice and Peggy had to adjudicate between William's desire for many exclamation marks and drawings and Henry's insistence that these be kept to a minimum.

Gosse arrived with small presents from London, and immediately declared that he was the happiest man in England now that he had quit the city, that it was a hateful place during the festive season with far too frivolous a social life and an unspeakable fog, some of which had entered into the crania of the very best minds of his generation.

William smiled in appreciation as Peggy glanced at Henry.

'I told my niece that you love London more than you love life,' Henry said.

'And so I do,' Gosse replied. 'But that does not say much for life.'

Gosse turned then to William who stood at the mantelpiece sipping his sherry. His tone was formal, having suddenly changed from being amused and charming, as he addressed William.

'May I say how much pleasure it gives me to meet you again? I have been reading you for many years. I share with Leslie Stephen the habit of reading you for pleasure, just as I read your brother for pleasure. I find very little nowadays which possesses such precision and such energy and such poetry, if I may say so, at the same time.'

William smiled and nodded and returned the compliment. Alice seemed to glow with happiness that someone had come to visit who would not annoy William. She smiled at Henry knowingly.

As the meal was served, Gosse informed them of the controversy over the day of prayer announced as a result of the defeat by the Boers. He did not, Henry noticed, make his own view clear on the matter but managed to let them know that he had listened to the Prince of Wales discuss the topic as well as Lord Randolph Churchill, Mr Asquith and Mr Alfred Austen. As he continued to outline the various positions of those he named, fixing each of them at the table with a significant stare as a new dignitary was mentioned, Henry noticed Alice becoming agitated and looking at William in a manner which he had not seen before, almost threateningly.

'Yes,' William said, when Gosse had left a gap in his narrative, 'I wrote a letter to *The Times* on the subject but they have failed to print it.'

'William!' Alice interjected.

'A letter to *The Times*?' Gosse asked. 'What line did you take?'

William hesitated and then stared into the middle distance.

'I said that I was an American travelling in this country and that I had noted the controversy over the proposed day of prayer and I would suggest that the principles established by one of the early Montana settlers might be the most useful and generally acceptable.'

'And what were they?' Gosse asked.

'Our settler was met by a very formidable and angry grizzly bear and he fell on his knees and his prayer was as follows: "O Lord, I hain't never asked you for help, and ain't agoin' to ask you for none now. But for pity's sake, O Lord, please don't help the bear." *The Times*, in its wisdom, did not print the letter.'

'I hope that you gave the outback as your address,' Henry said.

'I gave my address as care of Lamb House, Rye,' William replied.

'I think that is one of the main differences,' Gosse said, 'between the United States and our country. One can be sure about many things here and one is that *The Times* would not print that letter.'

'So much the better for *The Times*,' Henry said.

'So much the worse for my poor letter,' William replied.

'I'm sure there are a number of Irish periodicals that would print it,' Gosse said. 'You should not let it go to waste.'

'It has not gone to waste,' Alice said. 'He has just told us its contents, having made me a promise that he would never mention it again to a living soul.'

'Nor shall I,' William said.

'Perhaps you could convey the contents of the letter to the Prince of Wales,' Henry said to Gosse.

Gosse looked at him sharply.

'I wonder, since it is the beginning of the new year, if both of you, the writers here, might tell us what you have in store,' Gosse said.

'My brother,' Henry said, 'is to deliver the Gifford lectures at Edinburgh.'

'On the new science of psychology?' Gosse asked.

'On the old science of religion,' William replied.

'Have you written the lectures?' Gosse enquired.

'I have notes and ideas and some pages and a bad heart,' William said. 'So it takes time.'

'What position will you adopt?'

'I believe that religion, in its broadest sense, is indestructible,' William said. 'I believe the mystical experience of the individual, in any of its manifestations, to be a possession of an extended subliminal self.'

Henry made a sign to Peggy that if she wished to leave them now and return to her book, then she could do so. Her mother nodded in agreement. She excused herself and left the room.

'But what,' Gosse asked, 'if religion should be proved false?'

'I wish to argue,' William said, 'that religious feeling cannot be disproved since it belongs so fundamentally to the self. And if it is a belief that belongs so fundamentally to the self then it must be good, and, insofar as that goes, it must be true.'

'But if you look at what Darwin and his supporters can show, surely they can prove that certain beliefs are untrue?'

'I am interested in religious feeling or experience rather than religious argument,' William said. 'I wish to make clear that even the very words I use are open and evasive and sometimes useless, that there are no precise words because there are no precise feelings. We have mixed feelings and complex sensibilities and we must allow for that in our lives and in our law and in our politics, but most importantly, in the deepest core of ourselves.'

'In which the transcendental plays a part?' Gosse asked.

'Yes, but it may be more fundamental than that,' William said. 'The world beyond the sense, in which a sphere of life more powerful and larger than ourselves exists, may be continuous with our consciousness and we may know this and this may cause us to believe or have religious feeling, however vague, in a more satisfying way than we have religious argument.'

William spoke naturally and easily, his good humour adding to the almost conversational tone of his delivery, a tone Henry had never heard before.

'You sound as though you have written the lectures,' Gosse said.

'I have formulated them,' William said. 'Writing does not come naturally to me. I prefer talking but since in this case they want to publish them too, then I will have to write them out word for word.'

'Perhaps *The Times* will publish them when they are delivered,' Gosse said.

'*The Times* will receive no further communication from me. It had its opportunity.' William laughed and lifted his glass and drank.

'Henry,' Gosse said, 'it is your turn. You must tell us now what you will write so that we can look forward to it.'

'I am a poor story-teller,' Henry said, 'a romancer, interested in dramatic niceties. While my brother makes sense of the world, I can only briefly attempt to make it come alive, or become stranger. Once I wrote about youth and America and now I am left with exile and middle age and stories of disappointment which are unlikely to win me many readers on either side of the Atlantic.'

'Harry, you have many devoted readers,' Alice said.

'I have in mind a man who all his life believes that something dreadful will happen to him,' Henry said. 'He tells a woman of this unknown catastrophe and she becomes his greatest friend, but what he does not see is that his failure to believe in her, his own coldness, is the catastrophe, it has come already, it has lived within him all along.'

'Is that the end?' William asked.

'Yes, but there is also a man in a different story who goes to Paris from New England. He is an American of middle age, with much intelligence and a sensuous nature which has remained hidden throughout his life. He sees Paris and understands, like the man in the earlier story, that it is our duty to live all we can, but it is too late, or perhaps it is not.'

'And were a clergyman here,' William asked, smiling warmly, 'and were he to ask you what is the moral of these stories, what should he conclude from them?'

'The moral?' Henry thought for a moment. 'The moral is the most pragmatic we can imagine, that life is a mystery and that only sentences are beautiful, and that we must be ready for change, especially when we go to Paris, and that no one,' he said raising his glass, 'who has known the sweetness of Paris can properly return to the sweetness of the United States.'

'And which of these stories will you write first?' Gosse asked.

'I may already have embarked on both,' Henry said.

'And you, sir, what shall you write?' William asked Gosse.

'When I find the tone and the courage,' Gosse said, 'I shall write a book about my father.'

'But you have already written one and I very much admire it,' William said. 'The tension between the religious spirit and the quest for scientific truth is something which has mattered very much to me.'

'I shall write now,' Gosse replied, 'about the tension between my father and his son, and I shall spare neither of us. I must find a new style for it, however, and I must find time, but I do not think that this book will gain my father any new admirers.'

'That might be a great pity,' William said.

'And, no doubt, a great book,' Henry added.

WHEN WILLIAM returned from his walk, Gosse having left them an hour before darkness fell, he found the Lamb House Club in full swing. Alice and Peggy sat one on each side of the sofa, a lamp on the table, quietly reading. Burgess Noakes with his bad shoes came and went with logs and coal until a huge fire was blazing. The curtains were drawn. Henry sat with his biography of Napoleon in the armchair beside the fire.

'It was a winter's day,' William said, 'and now it is a winter's night.'

'In the morning,' Alice said, 'we must write another letter to the boys. I think they long for us to come home.'

'I don't want to write any more letters,' Peggy said.

'It is a new rule of our club that you are excused,' Henry replied.

William went out of the room and returned with a book.

'This was my mother's dream for us,' Henry said.

'That we would end up in England?' William asked.

'No,' Henry said, smiling. 'She always dreamed that we would, each of us, sit enjoying our books while she and Aunt Kate did their work, that there would not be a sound for hours but the turning of pages.'

'Was it never like that, Harry?' Alice asked.

'Never,' Henry said. 'My father would start an argument or your husband would kick something over or the younger ones would begin a quarrel.'

'And you, Uncle Harry,' Peggy looked up from her book. 'What would you do?'

'I would dream of an old English house and the fire blazing and nothing being kicked over.'

'I will refrain, if that is any comfort to you,' William said. 'My kicking days have passed in any case.'

As the night wore on, the wind blew up and the windows rattled. Peggy, concentrating fiercely on every word she read, had curled up against her mother who had left her book down and was staring into the fire. They had supper served on trays in the drawing room. When Burgess Noakes took the supper things away, Henry poured drinks for William and Alice and chocolate was found for Peggy. William returned to his book, taking notes. They could hear the scratching of his pen against the paper, and as time passed each of them became engrossed in their books again or in their thoughts so that no one noticed that William was sleeping until he began to snore.

'We will put more logs on the fire,' Henry whispered, 'but we will do it without waking him.'

Alice sighed.

'It is late,' she said.

'The rules say that I can stay up,' Peggy said.

'And allow William to snore,' Henry said gently, 'as much as he pleases.'

BY THE TIME they were ready to leave, having arranged to spend the rest of the winter in the gentler climate of the south of France, Peggy had finished several more novels by Dickens and was, Henry noticed on the morning of their departure, deeply engrossed in *David Copperfield*. She did not have to skip pages, Henry assured her, she could take the volume with her and any other books she cared to pack for her journey and her stay in France, except his two-volume biography of Napoleon, from which nothing would part him, he said, until he had read the final page.

After breakfast when William saw Peggy's book, he laughed.

'That's the one that got Henry caught,' he said.

Peggy looked up at Henry.

'He was sent to bed in our house on Fourteenth Street,' William said, 'because a cousin of ours had come from Albany with the first instalment of *David Copperfield*, which she was going to read aloud, and my mother did not think that it would be suitable for a small boy. Instead of doing what he was told, however, he hid.'

'What did you do, Papa?' Peggy asked.

'I was not such a small boy,' William said.

'He was a year older,' Henry said.

'And did she read it?'

'Yes, and there was much drama as she imitated all the voices. But suddenly sobs of sympathy rang from a corner of the room where Harry had been listening to the story and snapped under the strain of the Murdstones and had to be effectively banished. He was a great crybaby.'

'Did you not cry too, Papa?'

'I have a heart of stone,' William said and touched his chest and smiled.

Henry thought of the room in New York in which the chapter of *David Copperfield* had been read, all heavy furniture and screens and tasselled tablecloths, and his mother's voice rather than his cousin's, his mother cross at him when he was first discovered and then his mother taking him into her arms when she realized that he was crying. All this became vivid to him as though no barrier had been placed between that evening and now. He knew how far away it must seem to Peggy and he felt that for William, too, it belonged in the past. William had told the story as it had been told in the family for years, he had picked it up with the same good-humoured, businesslike air as he picked up his suitcases. Henry came out of the dining room and glanced at William as he prepared for departure. Henry shook his head and sighed.

Alice had left five pounds for Burgess Noakes who had appealed to Henry with a look as if to say that it was too much.

'Take it,' he said. 'My sister-in-law comes from the wealthy branch of the family.'

Burgess went ahead with the wheelbarrow, followed by Henry and William, Alice and Peggy, the three visitors having been long enough at Rye to be offered fond farewells by several of the locals. William, it struck Henry now, could not wait to get away, and it came to him that William had always been thus, impatient, ready for novelty, longing for new adventures, even if it were just leaving one room to go into another, or standing when he had just been sitting. When they were small, he would turn the page of the picture book before Henry had had time to absorb fully each illustration, and then refuse to turn back; eventually he would tire of even the picture book and want to go outdoors, leaving Henry free to start the book again alone and study it in peace before going to the window to see what William was doing now.

They were going to Dover and then to France. As the train came, Henry could sense that they did not know whether to smile or be sad. Peggy, he was aware, was desperate to return to her book. He accompanied her onto the train and found her a window seat, and then he stood back as their luggage was being loaded, while Alice urged William not to lift the cases. He embraced both William and Alice before descending to the platform once more. He watched with Burgess as the heavy door was closed.

Lamb House was his again. He moved around it relishing the silence and the emptiness. He welcomed the Scot who was waiting for him to begin a day's work, but he needed more time alone first. He walked up and down the stairs, going into the rooms as though they too, in how they yielded to him, belonged to an unrecoverable past, and would join the room with the tasselled tablecloths and the screens and the shadowed corners, and all the other rooms from whose windows he had observed the world, so that they could be remembered and captured and held.

Acknowledgements

I have found a number of books about Henry James and his family extremely useful while working on this novel. They include: Leon Edel's five-volume biography and Edel's editions of the letters and notebooks; *Henry James: The Imagination of Genius* by Fred Kaplan; *Henry James: The Young Master* by Sheldon M. Novick; *The Jameses: A Family Narrative* by R. W. B. Lewis; *Alice James: A Biography* by Jean Strouse; *Biography of Broken Fortunes: Wilky and Bob, Brothers of William, Henry and Alice James* by Jane Maher; *The Father: A Life of Henry James Senior* by Alfred Habegger; *A Private Life of Henry James: Two Women and his Art* by Lyndall Gordon; *The Metaphysical Club* by Louis Menand; *Alice James: Her Life in Letters*, edited by Linda Andersen; *Amato Ragazzo: Lettere a Hendrik C. Andersen*, edited by Rosella Mamoli Zorzi; *William and Henry James: Selected Letters*, edited by Ignas K. Skripskelis and Elizabeth M. Berkeley; *Dear Munificent Friends: Henry James's Letters to Four Women*, edited by Susan E. Gunter; *The Legend of the Master*, compiled by Simon Nowell-Smith.

I wish to acknowledge that I have peppered the text with phrases and sentences from the writings of Henry James and his family.

I am grateful to Peter Straus, Nan Graham, Andrew Kidd, Ellen Seligman, Catriona Crowe, Brendan Barrington and Angela Rohan for support and advice. Some of this book was written at the Santa Maddalena Foundation near Florence in Italy and I am grateful to Beatrice Monti for her kindness and hospitality.